A Simple Job

Kelly Kenyon

EBOUND BOOKS PUBLISHING

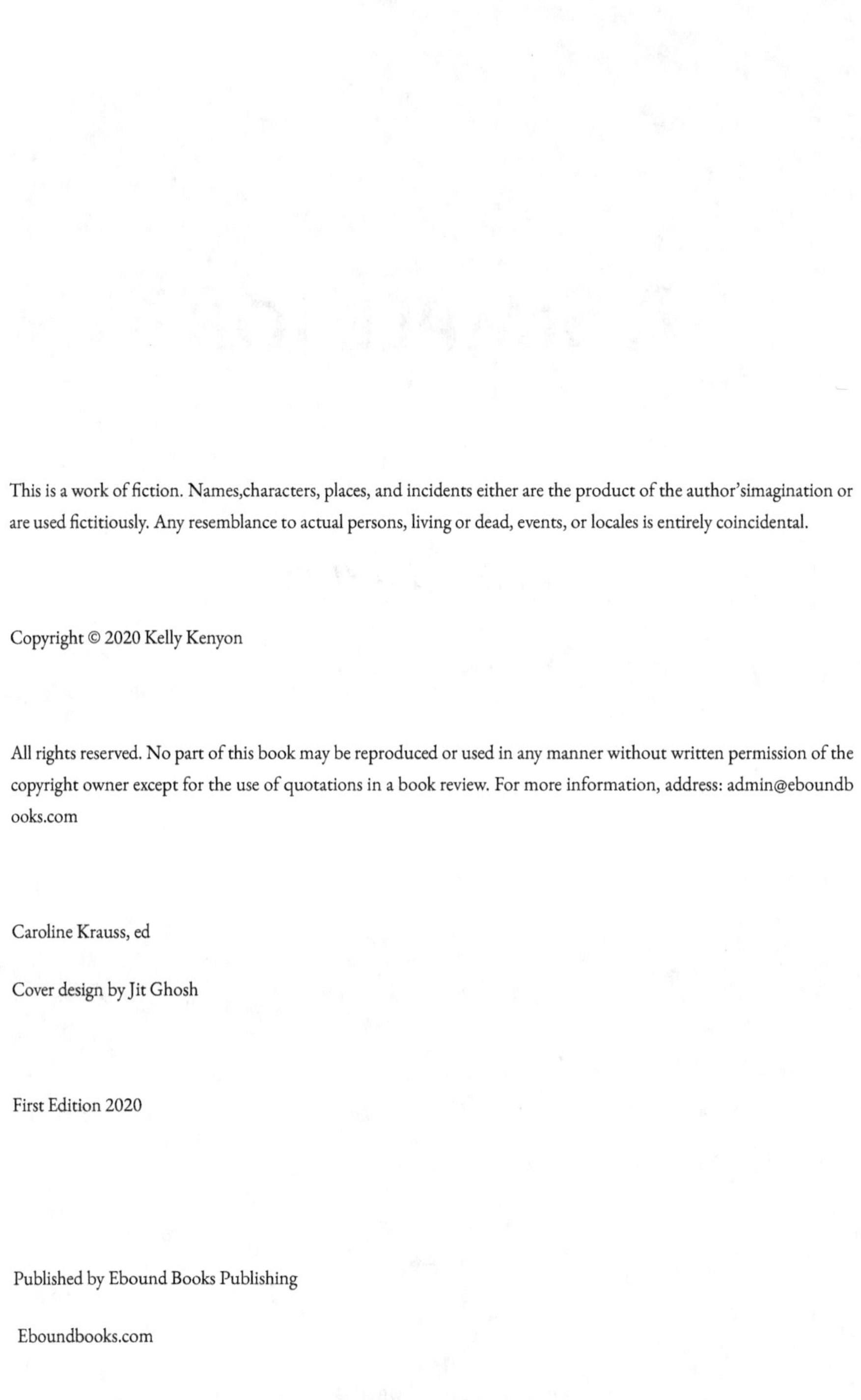

Caroline Krauss, ed

Cover design by Jit Ghosh

First Edition 2020

Published by Ebound Books Publishing

Eboundbooks.com

This is for you, my family of birth and my
family of the heart.
They say it takes a village. I had a great village growing
up, especially my parents.
With oceans of love and gratitude to you all.

CONTENTS

Chapter 1

A woman creeps down the hall with a cup of coffee in each hand. She steps on a toy car and bites her lip. *"How does one always escape detection until you are barefoot and trying to be quiet?"* she wonders to herself. When she reaches the door, she juggles both mugs and turns the knob. Quietly, she closes the door behind her and tiptoes across the floor. After slowly setting both mugs down on the bedside table, she leans over and gives her husband Eli's face a light kiss.

"Good morning, my love. Rise and shine. An amazing day is awaiting you. You are going to crush your interview today and no matter what happens, we love you so-so-so much!" she says punctuating every "so," with a kiss.

He opens his eyes reluctantly, but as soon as he sees the smile on her beautiful face, he smiles back. "Good morning," he says as he leans over and without looking picks up the mug that says Rachel in bold letters and takes a big gulp, which he immediately spits out, spraying her and the bedding - "Holy crap, hot!"

She is quick to recover from the shock of the coffee shower. "Poor baby, are you okay? You took mine. I set them both down to wake you up."

"I'll survive, he admits. I guess you're first in line for the shower now."

"Mm," she agrees as she lets her robe fall to the floor, "but since we are pressed for time, we'll have to shower together this morning."

He looks at the clock for the first time and sees it's 7 a.m.; a full half-hour before he needs to be up. Without a word, he follows her into the bathroom wearing nothing but a smile.

Fresh from the shower, Eli knocks on the door covered with dinosaur stickers, "Rise and shine, epic adventures await." He slowly opens the door and sticks his head in.

"Good morning, Mason." His son doesn't move except to squeeze his eyes shut tighter. "Okay, you don't have to shine yet, but you may want to rise. Mom made your favorite breakfast."

The boy burrows deeper into his comforter and secures the edge in his fist to prevent intrusion.

Eli knows his son isn't much of a morning person. He counts softly to himself to see how long it takes for what he said to penetrate the morning brain fog - "One, two, three, fou..."

Mason scurries out from under the covers wearing his favorite Batman pajamas that are well worn and a bit small. He doesn't spare a word for his dad as he sprints to the kitchen.

Elli follows him, stifling a laugh as the kid plows into his chair so hard it almost topples before he rights himself. He eyes the flapjacks which are on the table beside the eggs and bacon. His face erupts into an ear to ear grin.

"Why such a good breakfast? It's not my birthday, are we going..." he trails off as his fear teases him, "We aren't going back to regular school now, are we?"

Rachel kisses him on the top of the head. "No, my son, not now. Remember, your dad has an interview today for a new job."

"Oh!" Relieved, he digs in, shoveling syrup laden pancakes mixed with an occasional bite of bacon and eggs, like he hasn't eaten in days.

"Another growth spurt." Rachel announces. Used to the voracious appetite that precedes them. Eli winches unconsciously and heads back to the bedroom to finish getting dressed.

Eli emerges from the bedroom dressed to impress in shined shoes, nice slacks, a button-up shirt, and a stylish tie. Rachel whistles and makes cat-calls when she sees him. He blushes a little but makes a slow turn and pushes his tush out a little. "Jacket or no jacket," he asks, holding it in one hand draped over his shoulder like a model.

Mason gives him a thumbs down and Rachel gives her head a slight shake. "No jacket it is," he agrees.

"Unless it makes you feel more confident, then you should wear it," she adds.

His face tells her she was exactly right in her concern, but he says, "The jacket doesn't make this man," as he struts to the door with exaggerated bravado. "I'm off to conquer the world. I shall return with something hunted or gathered."

He gives a hardy wave and shuts the door as Rachel says, "If you bring home anything but good news, you will have to clean the house yourself."

Mason looks at his mom who makes a funny face meant to say, "Dad is crazy." They are both still laughing as they open the door to find Eli waiting on the porch, tapping his foot, making exaggerated gestures to look at a watch that isn't there.

"It took you guys long enough. I was afraid the two people I love most in all the world were going to let me forage the city without my safety love bubble."

"One good thing to come from Covid-19," Rachel mutters as the three mush together for a group hug. Mason kisses Eli's left cheek, Eli turns and kisses Rachel's left cheek, Rachel finishes the circuit with a kiss on Mason's cheek. He starts the next round with a kiss on Rachel's right cheek. When the kisses have gone full circle, the second time, they hug tightly for a moment and Mason declares, "The love bubble is in place."

"And it's strong," Eli agrees.

"Super strong," Rachel adds, "no germs are getting in here and nothing bad is happening in this love bubble."

Mason gives Rachel a side hug, and she puts her hand on his shoulder as they watch Eli walk towards the car. The mailman reaches their box just as Eli reaches the sidewalk.

"I'll take that Gene."

"Here you go. Have a good one." He hands him a small stack of envelopes, the window on the top one showing a bright pink notice.

"Thanks, you too." Eli says, quickly stuffing them in his pocket.

"Honey, I'll grab the mail," she says, starting toward the steps of the craftsman's porch.

"No, don't worry about it. I've got to run. Love you both." He gets in the car before she can get to the front walk and pulls away from the curb while still putting his seat belt on.

Standing on the steps watching him drive off, she says, "Cross your fingers your dad gets that job." She regrets the statement as soon as the words leave her lips. She sees the concern cross her son's face. He's been so stressed and scared of so many things since his accident. She hopes time will bring him to a happy medium between the fearless daredevil he was and the timid little guy he has become. "Don't worry my little lovey-dovey," she reassures him, plastering his face with kisses while tickling his side, "Everything will be okay either way, he just needs this."

Mason stops giggling; his face, earnest. "How come?"

With a deep sigh, "Because your dad can't see that who he is matters more than who he isn't and he's so focused on not being like his own dad."

"Why don't you tell him?" Rachel stifles a laugh. Oh, for life to be that simple again.

"Sometimes we need people to help us see the obvious stuff that we can't see and sometimes we need people to love us while we figure it out ourselves."

Confused but weary of the conversation, Mason drifts back inside. Rachel whispers a little prayer and follows him.

Eli sits in a crowded lobby wearing the handmade mask Rachel made and Mason decorated with a huge smile in fabric paint. He pulls out his phone to check the time. He scans his resume again, looking for errors or things he could improve, though he and Rachel had already put forth exhaustive efforts to perfect it in the previous months.

Finally, the door to the inner sanctum opens and a tall, imposing man approaches the assistant's desk just outside the door. Eli can't be sure but thinks he hears his name as the young man at the desk gestures in his general direction. Eli looks up and smiles as the man approaches.

Something out of the corner of his eye catches the man's attention. He stops in front of a guy sitting across and a few seats down from Eli.

"Hi, do you want the job?"

"Yes, I would love it."

"What is your name?"

"Abed Kader," comes the prompt reply.

"Well, Abed," the man says, smiling, "I'm Phil Townsend and you're hired."

Abed smiles back and stands to shake his hand. Phil leans in and whispers something to Abed.

Abed's smile grows, and he agrees, "Yes, it is."

"Can you start tomorrow?" Abed nods the affirmative.

"Be here at 9:30?"

Abed nods again and says, "thank you" and walks away with a smile.

Phil turns to face the rest of the room. "I'm sorry folks, the position has been filled. We are hiring as aggressively as we can and I promise your applications will remain on file and we will reach out to you before we place any future ads. Best of luck to you all, and thanks again."

Low groans and fake smiles fill the room. Some approach Phil to introduce themselves, hoping to stand out for a future position.

Eli shoots out the door and looks up and down the street. He sees Abed on the corner and charges towards him.

"What was that?" he demands.

Abed asks, "Excuse me?" when he realizes that the question is meant for him.

"What was that? What happened in there?" Eli repeats.

"A job interview," he answers with a question in his voice.

"That's not what it looked like to me." He notices a domed ring that looks like a bird on fire glowing in the sunlight. "That guy Phil, he had one of those too. What, did you go to the same college? Frat? What?"

"What exactly are you asking me?"

"I want to know how you did that. How you got the job I badly needed and thought I had a chance at by just sitting there, you didn't have to say a word. I want to know how you did it. I need to know, for my family's sake."

"Let me ask you this? Did you even want the job?"

"Of course, I'm here, aren't I?"

"I get it. You wanted the salary."

"And benefits," Eli cuts in.

"Right, and day one benefits. I understand that you and everyone else in that room wanted things the job offered. Did you want the job? Would you love it? Would you get out of bed excited to be doing it every day?"

"What? Are you kidding? No, it was just a job, but it was a great one. There are plenty of good jobs, but there is unbelievable competition for them right now. You know?"

"I get it, I do," he reassures, seeing the emotion on Eli's face.

"You are an honest man and I respect that."

Eli winces and he unconsciously taps his pocket containing the past due bills.

"Let me ask you one more thing; toilet paper?"

"Yeah?"

"Did you hoard it?"

Eli laughs out loud, enjoying the break from the tension.

He holds up his fingers in the Eagle Scout pledge position, "I do solemnly swear that I, nor anyone, living under my roof hoarded toilet paper."

Abed studies his face for a minute. "Okay, you seem like a nice guy who cares about doing right by his family, so I'll tell you what's up." He made air quotes for the what's up part.

"Members of a group wear this ring to identify each other. You're right, Phil has the ring, and he offered me the job because he saw mine."

"I want to join your club if wearing the ring will get me a job without even having to interview."

"I don't think you will want to join. There are costs. Yes, it opens doors that you can't even imagine, but it doesn't come free."

"Okay, what are the costs?"

"Well, for starters, it costs ten percent of your income for the rest of your life."

"So what? It's a religion or a cult or something?"

"No, not like that at all. Have you heard about the Skull and Bones?"

"That secret club at Harvard? That's not much of a secret since it's in a bunch of movies and it's known that some presidents were, or are, members?"

"Yale actually, but yes. Unlike that organization where you were born, your last name and your parents' net worth have nothing to do with acceptance. Like the Skull and Bones, it can open doors. The organization does many things to help people and the ten percent that members contribute help fund those acts."

"Okay, sure I'll give you ten percent of the nothing I've got, no problem. Where do I get my ring and job?"

"Don't agree to any of this lightly. The person you'll be by the end of your initiation will keep this agreement until your dying breath. You will find yourself willing to help with anything they ask for and hope you will be asked. Because you'll understand that it is an absolute honor."

"Okay, so you drank the Kool-Aid. I can see it's working for you." He casts a rueful look back towards the building Abed now works at. "If it isn't a cult, I shouldn't have to be all rah-rah, best-thing-ever to get more information. So, is it or isn't it?"

Abed pulls a card from his back pocket. "It is not, and I don't think it's for you. I might be wrong. Think about it, and if it is, call me."

"That's it? I can't come to a meeting or read some literature. I have to decide based on the scrap of info you gave me?"

Abed shrugs, "Pretty much. Oh, what is your name, just in case you call?"

"Eli Asher," he says, offering his hand.

"Abed Kader," he responds as they shake. Abed opens the door of the sports car they've been standing next to. "Good luck Eli Asher."

"I'd say the same to you, but you don't seem to need it." Eli says, motioning to the car and the office.

Abed gives him a small smile and gets in the car. Eli watches him pull away from the curb and drive off. He pulls hand sanitizer from his pocket and gives his hands a liberal squirt.

Eli mutters under his breath, "What a crock of sh... who the heck does this guy think he is?"

He crumples the card and shoots towards the garbage can in front of him. It hits the side and bounces back toward him. He is tempted to leave it but sees the disapproving look of a woman waiting at the crosswalk. With a sigh, he picks it up and stuffs it into his pocket.

Once he's back in the car, he pulls the stack of mail out of his pocket and flips through it. There are several medical bills, some are pink and there is a letter saying his appeal to get Cobra reinstated has been denied. He puts the normal colored mail on the dash and shoves everything pink back in the glove box under the registration and insurance information.

CHAPTER 2

Eli arrives back home as Rachel and Mason are coming down the walk. He pastes on a smile before he gets out of the car.

"Where are my favorite people on the entire planet off to?"

"We're going to take a quick trip to urgent care. He's got another headache and I just want to make sure everything is okay."

Eli takes a deep breath before addressing his son, "Look buddy, I know it was really scary hitting your head so hard and getting a concussion. I understand that it's hard to get over it when something that scary happens, but I don't think racing off to the doctor or urgent care or the ER all the time is going to help you. You are going to have to face those big kids again someday, and you are going to have to go back to regular school."

Mason turns and sprints back into the house. There is a loud bang when the front door closes behind him and a lighter one seconds later signals his arrival back in the safety of his room.

Rachel shoots him a death glare. "What the hell was that? You know it can take months or even a full year to recover fully from a concussion."

"I understand that. I just find it very interesting that every time the topic of school comes up his symptoms come back and we haul him off to a doctor's appointment that tells him what he wants to hear, not what he needs. For the record, most people are fine in a week or two."

"Hello, I'm a nurse. Do you think I don't know all of that? Why do you think I take him in? They remind him every time that he has to minimize screen time and not get too rambunctious when he plays. There is a cost along with the payoff that he gets. Eventually, it will tip the scale and he will be ready to face starting the fourth grade and being on the same playground and same recess schedule as the fifth and sixth graders. You trying to force him into it doesn't help."

"Those dang kids, I'd like to give them concussions. What were they thinking putting him on a ten-speed? He's never used hand brakes and could barely reach the pedals."

Rachel looks back at the house, torn between comforting her son and dealing with these concerning issues with her husband. She sighs and hugs Eli.

"What is going on with you? Wishing you could hurt kids isn't you. Taking this macho 'you've got to face things before you're ready' attitude with your son is not you. I'm guessing the interview didn't go well, but you've been off for a while. What is it? You know we can get through anything together."

He gives her a little squeeze in agreement. "There wasn't an interview. I drove down there for nothing."

"What happened? I thought it was a scheduled interview with the sales manager?"

"It was. They scheduled a ton of them. The waiting room was full of people. When it was finally my turn, the guy comes out and offers the job to a guy sitting by me. Of course, the guy takes it, so he turns around and sends everybody else home with the usual song and dance about keeping our information on hand for next time."

"That stinks! Why did he hire the other guy? Do you know?"

"I do. They know each other from some sort of secret club or something, so he got the job without even having to interview because they're in the same group."

Her eyes widened. "Really? How do you know that?"

"I followed the guy outside and asked him how he did it. How he snaked the job I needed right out from under me and that's what he said."

She tilted her head up to study his face for a minute, trying to see if he was serious.

"That's bizarre. It sounds like it's good you didn't get the job if weird stuff like that is going on. I mean, I know weird is what Portland is all about, but that's weird, even for Portland. I'm sorry, I know you must be disappointed; you've been trying to get an interview with them for months. What else is going on? I know that's not all that is on your mind."

"I feel so helpless," he admits. "Mason was such a cool kid, having the big kids invite him to play and hang out with them was a big deal. He was doing great in school and had tons of friends. Now this concussion and all the doctors and using that and COVID-19 to hide out from the world. I don't want that to be how he does life, because that will make it extra hard."

Rachel opens her mouth to speak. He continues before she can.

"Come on Rach, you know kids can be mean. I just don't want him to get left behind and suffer because he couldn't keep it together. I don't know how to help him."

"Love him, trust him, and trust us. He's got fantastic parents," she says smiling. "He'll get through this, but it's a lot. The timing was bad because he couldn't just go back to normal life after it happened and the longer it took, the worse it got, but he will get through it."

Eli runs his fingers through his hair and lets out a little groan, "You're right, who knew a concussion could be so expensive?"

"That's what insurance is for. I know there have been quite a few co-pays, but just imagine what this would be like if we didn't have insurance. I mean ten thousand dollars for a concussion, that's a decent used car. Imagine what something more serious would cost."

More like eighteen thousand dollars, he thinks, "Believe me, I can imagine."

"Are you worried about money? I know your unemployment has to be running out soon."

"Not soon, it's done. It stopped two weeks ago."

"Oh," she says, understanding, crossing her face. "That's what has been wrong. You're worried about money. Can't you get an extension?"

"I probably could have, but I turned down that commission-only job I applied for out of frustration and you can't turn down work on unemployment."

"I think you should reapply; now you know not to apply for any jobs you wouldn't accept. The worst they can do is say no."

He nods slowly, "You're right. I just haven't wanted to spend the time and energy on that instead of the job search, but I'll work on it this week."

"You know, I can always hit pause on school and work full time for a while. There are always jobs for nurses."

"No! You finish school and once you're a nurse practitioner, we won't ever have to worry about money again. I'll get a job soon, don't worry."

"I know you're joking about when I'm an NP, but I hope you know I wouldn't mind going back to work full time or for you to go back to school or be a stay at home dad when

I'm done with school. You're much more than a paycheck," she reaches behind him and gives his buns a little squeeze, "even more than your cute bod."

"Yes, I know you love me for relocating spiders and being the designated cleaner of throw up."

She grimaces while nodding. "And for your body heat."

"Honey, you know I would prefer that you say my hot body."

"Well, that too, but in this climate, the body heat is pretty great. You're my portable heater, even when the power goes out in a storm."

"I guess I'll take what I can get," he concedes.

She gets on her tiptoes to kiss him, "Don't worry, we'll be okay. I'm going to go get Mason and head out."

"No, wait. Let me take him. I want him to know I support him even if I am having a hard time believing some of this. I'll take him and we'll get some ice cream or something after."

"Are you sure? You've already had a stressful day."

"If I stay here, all I'm going to be doing is scanning the classifieds and pulling my hair out. You enjoy the quiet and get some studying done. I'll take him" "

"Okay, but remember, we already had pancakes for breakfast, maybe fro-yo instead of ice cream."

A few minutes later, Eli pulls away from the house again, this time with his son in the passenger seat. He goes around the corner and drives a couple more blocks before pulling over to the curb.

"This isn't the doctor's office. What are we doing here?" Mason asks, his voice laden with concern.

"I just need to make a quick call. Give me a sec, okay?" He assumes consent and pulls out his phone. Eli dials and holds the phone to his ear while it rings. "Hi Jen, it's Eli Asher, Rachel's husband. How are you?"

"I'm good, finally getting a few minutes to breathe." If the call surprises her, she doesn't show it.

"That's great. Glad to hear it. Listen, I was wondering if you could do me a favor. Mason is having another headache with the concussion and all I was wondering is if you could check him out. Just to make him feel better and us too, you know?"

"That's fine. I'm heading home now. I should be there in about five minutes."

"That's wonderful. We'll be there shortly after," he says, filled with relief.

"We're not going to a doctor?" Mason's eyes widen and his fists clench.

"No, we're going to see your mom's friend, Jen. She is a nurse practitioner, like Mom is going to be when she finishes school."

"Mom wanted to take me to a doctor."

"I understand, Mason, but do you know the difference between a nurse practitioner and a doctor?"

"No," he admits, shaking his head.

"Neither do I really, but your mom says the biggest difference is that somewhere during medical school and residency and all the stuff that doctors go through to become doctors their heads swell up so big it puts pressure on their ears and they can't listen anymore." He emphasizes the point with a small jab to the tickle point on the side of his son's ribs. "What do you think? Should we go to someone that can listen or to a doctor?"

Reassured, Mason agrees. "Someone who can listen."

"Good choice," Eli approves, checks his mirror, and pulls back out onto the street. They only drive about twenty blocks but cover a lot of ground in those couple of miles. The houses are twice the size of those in their neighborhood and there is more space between them, bigger yards, more gardens, and more trees.

Eli loves craftsman style homes but would give up their cozy little place for Jen's tri-colored Victorian on the corner lot in a heartbeat. He sees Jen's BMW SUV in the drive and likes his year-old Civic a little less. If the last one hadn't crapped out early on them, he would have gone for the BMW, but they had to pay off Rachel's car before they made the jump in payments. His old car blew the head gasket, and the repairs were more than the car was worth, so here he was again.

For the first time, he had a quick pang of gratitude for the whole situation. The one upside is that he doesn't have a bigger car payment to contend with. If the old one had held out until the COVID-19 lockdown, he wouldn't have a car payment at all. "You win some and you lose some," he thinks to himself and jumps when Jen knocks on Mason's window.

"Hi guys, how are you doing?"

Eli opens his door and gets out. Jen steps back so Mason can do the same.

"Hey, thanks for doing this. We appreciate it so much." Eli gives her a huge grin.

"My pleasure. I haven't seen you guys in ages." She holds out her arms to Mason, who gives her a quick hug. She gives Eli a brief hug as well. "Come on, let's go inside and make sure your big brain is all right, Mason."

He smiles up at his dad, making sure he heard the big brain part. Eli smiles back and gives his shoulder a little squeeze of reassurance. Jen leads the way into the house and Eli brings up the rear.

"Do you still like dogs?" Jen asks Mason. He gives her a nod.

She opens the door where the whining is coming from, and her two Rottweilers come rushing in like bulls out of the chute. They give both visitors a thorough sniffing and once convinced they pose no threat, nor possess any treats, one goes and lies down on the enormous bed in front of the bay window. The other gives Mason a rigorous face licking until Jen intervenes.

"Good boy, Shane. Axel, go lie down."

He sneaks in a last lick and Mason giggles, which makes the dog wag its nubby tail at high speeds. He looks at Jen to see if he's earned a stay from exile. "Now!" she points toward the bed in answer. Massive head hanging low, he reluctantly obeys.

"Come on guys," she motions for Eli and Mason to follow and holds up a halting hand to the hopeful Rottie on the bed. They follow her into the kitchen, where she has her medical bag on the table.

"Hopefully, you guys didn't wait out there for too long. I've been home for a few minutes, but I was bringing the garbage and recycling bins around to the back. I thought the dogs would bark when you rang the bell if you got here before I was done."

"We weren't out there long at all. We just pulled up when you came to get us."

She pats the chair across from her and pulls out a clipboard and a blood pressure cuff. She puts it on Mason and starts talking to him while she pumps it up.

"So, are you eleven or twelve now?"

He laughs and shakes his head. "I'm going to be nine in a couple of months. I think nine is a good age to get a dog, don't you?"

Jen misses Eli shaking his head and mouthing "no" behind Mason and says, "I think any age is a wonderful age for dogs. They're the best."

She notices the movement out of the corner of her eye and does her best to get her foot out of her mouth, "The best age is probably for a big birthday like when you turn double digits at ten or become a teenager at thirteen."

Eli beams at her, mouthing, "Thank you." Mason scrunches up his face in a scowl, trying to come up with a rebuttal.

"How tall are you, big guy?" she asks. He held up four fingers on one hand and two on the other. "Only little shrimps are forty-two inches. Do you mean forty-two feet?"

He shakes his head, smiling again.

"No, that can't be right," she agrees. "That's dinosaur big. I bet you know which dinosaur is that big."

"T-Rex is almost forty-two feet long," he exclaims with pride in his dinosaur knowledge.

"What do you weigh nowadays? Do you know?"

"Um, sixty?" he guesses.

Eli signals up with his thumb. "Hmm, maybe sixty-one?" she guesses.

Eli signals up again three times in rapid succession. "Let's see, is it sixty-four?" Jen asks.

Mason looks at his dad to see if that's right.

"Yep, he must be getting ready for another growth spurt. He does the same thing I did as a kid, gains a little weight, gains a little height."

"That's a relief. I thought you were going to say you've been stretching him on a rack."

"No," Mason declares, shaking his head like it's the most ridiculous thing he's ever heard.

"I'm going to shine this light in your eyes in a minute. You tell me if your headache feels worse, okay?"

He grips the edge of his chair and gives a brief nod.

She briefly shines the light in both eyes. "Now I want you to follow my finger with your eyes."

Very used to the drill, he starts out doing just that, but then adds his head, followed by his whole body until he is on the verge of falling out of his chair following the exaggerated moves Jen is now making.

"It looks like you have a headache, but maybe just a little one."

Being reminded that he is supposed to have a headache, he sits up and holds still.

"The good news is, I don't think your brain is broken. I think if you don't get too crazy bouncing off the walls and keep your screen time to what your mom and dad say without sneaking extra time, you are good to go."

She looks at Eli and gives a brief nod towards the backyard. He nods okay.

"It might help if you got some yard and dog time? It always makes me feel better."

Mason gets up and shoots out the door to the backyard without risking a look at his dad in case he might say no.

"Boys!" is all she needs to say.

Both dogs come trotting in knowing something good is about to happen, either treats, or play, or maybe both. When they see the back door open, they race into the backyard and jump around with glee when they find the boy there.

Jen gets a "chuck it," tennis ball thrower from the top of the fridge. "Come on, we can sit on the back porch while they play. Oh, I'm sorry, would you like something to drink?"

"No thanks, we are going to get some fro-yo after this."

"Gosh, it's so nice to have everything opening up again and more people willing to venture out in the world."

"Yeah," he agrees. "I bet you're happy to get a break. They were calling Rachel daily, trying to get her to work more days, longer shifts, or doubles, even though they knew she was in school. She said you were working non-stop for months."

She shrugs it off like nothing unusual has happened.

"Here you go, Mason." She shows him the chuck it and demonstrates it once, which is all it takes. She checks her watch. "That will give us twenty minutes if you have that long."

"Yes, that's great. He forgot his headache pretty quickly when he started playing with the dogs. I wish the doctors would be playful with him like you and not act like he is so fragile."

"I can't say for sure if he is faking or not, but I don't think you should be worried at this point. If there was something more serious, you would know by now. These things just take time."

"So, do you think we should take him to the doctor every time he says his head hurts?"

"I can't answer that for you, plus, I'm getting the idea that you and Rachel are on different sides of this one." She holds up her hand, halting him before he can speak, just like she had done to the dogs earlier. "This is what I will say. It won't hurt to keep taking him to the doctor. He keeps hearing the limits and that things aren't getting worse and, like I said, I'm not worried, so, if you two make a different decision in the future, I'm sure that will be fine too."

"Wow, great with kids... and a diplomat. If you ever tire of the medical field, you could have a career in politics."

She doubles over laughing. "Ha, with my wayward youth, I'd have a better shot as an evangelist. Of course, I'd have to give up my sinful ways and what fun would that be?"

He shakes his head, "I don't know".

He knew, but wasn't supposed to. One night when Rachel and Jen had gone out for a lady's night, Eli had to pick them up because they couldn't drive. On the way home, after dropping Jen off, Rachel had broken all the night's promises of secrecy and told Eli that despite being fantastic with kids, Jen didn't care for them and didn't want any of her own. That had caused the end of two of her relationships that probably would have led to marriage. After that, she dated two guys at the same time for a while, believing poly-amorous guys wouldn't be so gung-ho about having kids. She was wrong and ended up with two guys wanting her to have their kids. Then she just gave up, got the dogs, put on twenty pounds, and worked a ton.

Life was funny that way. Rachel had cousins that would probably commit a felony to get a man who wanted kids and marriage. Jen was attractive enough, he guessed. She was five or ten years older than Rachel and double that in pounds heavier. What made the difference for him between not noticing someone like Jen and not being able to keep his eyes off Rachel was that Jen was pale, blonde and sunny. Rachel is brunette, tan and smoldering.

While Jen struggled to find the right person, he was lucky enough to find and marry Rachel. He was glad she wasn't dating multiple people anymore, though. He didn't want that idea to catch on. It was impossible to imagine sharing Rachel, and Jen was one of her best friends; they introduced each other to new things frequently. It was unlikely Rachel would be interested, but it was still uncomfortable for him to think about.

After a slobbery visit to the huge water dish by the door, the dogs abandon the ball and collapse panting on the porch. Mason continues to chuck the ball, but after fetching it himself a couple of times, he understands he will not entice them into more play.

"Ready for some fro-yo?" Eli asks, hoping the promise of a treat would make leaving the dogs easier.

Mason looks at the dogs and considers his options. "I guess."

"Try to hide your enthusiasm. What do you say to Jen?"

"Thank you for letting me play with the dogs."

"And for making sure your brain isn't broken?"

"Yes, and that," he agrees.

"You're welcome. It was good to see you two and the dogs love the company." Jen leads them back through the house and stands on the front porch waiting to wave goodbye.

They get in the car and while Mason buckles his seat-belt. Eli asks, "TartBerry?"

Mason nods emphatically but then becomes side-tracked and still fails to buckle up.

"Finish buckling up." Eli encourages, "We'll go to TartBerry, but no candy toppings since we had pancakes and syrup this morning."

Eli hits the gas and waves to Jen, who waves back before walking inside.

CHAPTER 3

Ten minutes later, they find a parking spot and Eli steels himself, knowing that finding parking won't be the only thing that will require his patience in the next hour. They mask up and enter. Once inside the brightly painted shop, you must decide which of the many available flavors and toppings will make it into your self-service cup and which won't. A frequent tactic of Mason's was trying to get a bigger size by not making enough eliminations for it to fit into a small cup.

Trying to save both of them some frustration, and buy himself some goodwill for what was coming next, he looked at his watch and said, "If you can pick three flavors and three toppings in the next five minutes…" Mason gives a little hop and is ready to interject, Eli takes a page from Jen's book and holds up a halting hand, "Let me finish. If you can do that, you can get a medium."

"But Dad!"

"And one of those toppings can be candy."

Mason is off to the races, grabbing a medium cup and lining the bottom with malted milk balls. On his third lap around the store, he selects peanut butter and chocolate yogurt, adds pretzels and bananas, and makes another lap trying to decide on the final flavor. He lingers by the mint for a moment.

"Hey, buddy, I know you like mint with chocolate, but I don't think it would go very good with peanut butter. What do you think?"

That decides it, Mason goes directly to the maple bacon donut flavor and fills his cup to the absolute brim and a smidgen above, which is standard. Eli smiles at the cashier, though he isn't happy about a seven-dollar yogurt. It was hefty. He didn't doubt it weighed every bit what the scale said.

Mason stands there, waiting to see what his dad will say. Normally they would eat it outside unless it was raining, but for months, takeout was the only option. Eli grabs a stack of napkins and motions towards the door.

He covers the passenger seat and floor with most of the napkins and puts the seat-belt on his son while he holds the frozen yogurt in both hands as agreed. He closes the door and is walking to the driver's side.

"Eli, Eli Asher, is that you?"

He looks around to see who is asking and has a brief second of panic that maybe they were here to take his car. While he is reassuring himself that it is too soon, he isn't far enough behind for it to be repossessed; he spots Jim Cowan, a co-worker from the job he lost at the beginning of the pandemic.

"Hey Jim, what's up?"

The short squat man shrugs, not much, but says, "I got a new job and a new girl. How about you?"

"I'm still working on finding the right job, to match the right girl, which I still have."

Jim closes the distance between them and holds out his hand to shake. He always turns a shake into a one-armed hug. Eli takes a step back, motioning to the car. "I've got my son, and he has a lap full of ice cream...so that's kind of like a bomb timer ticking down. I've got to run, but call me and we'll have a beer or something."

"I'll hold you to that," he says in a way that is meant to be charming but falls short somehow.

"I know you will." Eli climbs in the car and pretends not to hear Jim say, "Good to see you."

He intended to go to the school around the corner and sit outside with Mason while he ate his treat. Not knowing where Jim is heading, he decides to go further just to be safe. He mentally debates between Sewallcrest and Laurelhurst. He decides and drives to Laurelhurst, figuring the duck pond will buy him even more goodwill.

Mason is more than halfway through with the yogurt when they arrive at the park with no major spills on the way. Eli helps his son out of the seat belt and out of the car rather than hold the gooey mess for him. Together, they drift towards the pond and sit on a bench.

"We've had so much fun today, huh?"

He gets a small nod. The malted milk ball trying to escape the spoon is more pressing at that moment. Eli watches and waits until he manages to corral it.

"I mean, I had a really fun time at Jen's and the park is great, especially with the pond and the ducks." He gets a bigger nod this time. "I bet your mom would have had fun too and she might feel bad that she didn't get to come. You know, Jen is one of her very best friends and she loves Shane and Axel. I don't want to make her feel bad, do you?"

Feeling apprehensive, Mason cocks his head, concentrating on what comes next.

"I think maybe we should let Mom think we went to the doctor and just sat in the waiting room for a while instead of having a super fun time talking to Jen and playing with the boys while she had to study. What do you think?"

"Lie?"

Eli knew he deserved the one-word answer he had gotten since both he and Rachel had drilled honesty into their son his whole life. He had to proceed with caution.

"No, not lie. Say someday in the future you find a pretty girl that you like and she asks you if her jeans make her look fat."

Mason scoffs out loud at the idea of liking a girl and sends a small spray of partially chewed pretzel at his dad. He is immediately ready for an irritable reminder to cover his mouth, but it doesn't come.

"I know it's hard to imagine at your age, but it will happen and when it does, it's okay to say you have beautiful eyes or a gorgeous smile or something like that if they make her look fat. Do you know why you do that? Why all smart men do that?"

Eli sees Mason is done and is trying to remove the napkins that dried sugar and cream have glued to his hands. Eli guides the boy to the restroom and opens the door. He turns on the water while Mason shakes the cup up and down over the garbage can until it breaks free and falls in. Mason washes his hands and accepts the paper towel that his dad hands him.

Back on the sidewalk, Eli kneels in front of him. "Do you understand why people say something nice about a lady instead of saying yes, something makes her look fat?"

Understanding this is important to his dad, he makes a guess. "So she won't get mad?"

Eli smiles, "That too, but they do it so that it doesn't make them feel bad. It's not lying because it's not saying anything that isn't true. That's what I'm talking about. Your mom will probably ask what the doctor said. We could say what Jen said because she is just like a doctor, but better, and if you tell her about playing with the dogs today, you could say it was at the park instead. That way we aren't lying, but we aren't making her feel bad."

Mason takes some time to contemplate what he is hearing. It seems to check out, so he slowly nods.

Relieved Eli says, "That's great, I don't like it when your mom feels bad. One more thing, we don't want to make her mad either, so if she asks about the frozen yogurt, we should probably let her think we got the usual size and skipped the candy topping. What do you think?" He senses his son's hesitation and feels like a first-class creep, but doesn't have any other choice. "Let's try it. What did you get at the fro-yo place?"

After a long pause, "The usual with chocolate, peanut butter and maple bacon doughnut with pretzels and bananas." Mason answers.

"Perfect! Great job, just for that you can get a candy topping next time we go; if you tell it just like that to your mom."

He swoops his son up into a big hug, which the boy returns fiercely, and though he doesn't fully understand what is happening, he somehow understands his dad needs the hug and maybe some help. Eli crosses his fingers for a moment, hoping he isn't damaging his son's moral character or their future relationship. Nothing is more important to him than Rachel and Mason.

Thursday evening finds Eli at the Bar of the Gods, or Bog as it's known by locals. The very fake Greek temple façade on the front of the building never impressed Eli, but the place always seems to do a steady business. It wasn't what he would have chosen; he knew Jim had suggested a place close to Eli's house to make it harder to say no to coming out. Jim also drove across town without complaint, so Eli was ready to pass the time for an hour or so.

Jim comes back from the bar with a Bog Mocha for himself, an iced coffee with vodka, cocoa liqueurs, and a splash of half and half. He sets a Bog Fire in front of Eli, who cocks an eyebrow and looks at him inquisitively.

"Try it. I bet you'll like it. If you don't, I'll get you something else."

Eli picks up the glass and takes a small sip. He tastes cinnamon and whiskey and wonders why he had never thought of pairing the two.

Unsure what to make of the look on Eli's face, he continues, "Don't worry, I'm only gonna have one. It's been a long week, still getting used to being back at work. That's why I got one with coffee, not so I could be a wide-awake drunk. I know how you are; nobody plans to drive drunk so don't start drinking without a better plan, which I have."

Eli's attention drifts in and out of Jim's monologue. That is a plus to hanging out with salespeople. If you're not in a talking mood, they will fill the gap for you. Eli tunes in to hear Jim say, "Without you there to be Mr. Moral Compass and still top dog sales-wise, I'm looking pretty good."

He reaches across the table and whops Eli on the arm while he laughs. Eli forces a smile and raises a glass to the good time he isn't having. The older man isn't a bad guy, not a great guy, but not a bad one, especially after so many years in sales. He still cares about what he sells and wants to believe in it. Eli had met some people that didn't care what they sold or what lies it took to sell it. He wasn't willing to work anywhere that hires people like that because, eventually, they bring down the reputation of the entire company. Trying to sell for a company with a bad reputation is about as much fun as beating your head against a brick wall.

"Seriously," Eli turns back in to find out what is serious now, "even though you'll make me look bad, if you want a job, I'll put in a word for you. I think they are hiring."

"Companies like that are always hiring because there is no base salary, no benefits and you work every evening and at least one day on the weekend, if not both, so no time with the family. Gee, what's not to love? I appreciate it, honestly, I do. But I just can't do it. I have a family; I have to get insurance for my kid and a job like that isn't worth a divorce. Not for me." Eli tries for a save and fails.

Jim, a trifecta divorcee, knows all too well the cost of the types of jobs that will hire him.

"Sorry, I didn't mean it like that. I'm just stressed right now. I need a job sincerely; but I need one that works for my family too. Besides, I wouldn't want to steal your thunder. You're a good guy. You deserve to be the big dog."

"I don't want to be pushy here," Jim's famous line before he got the sale or got kicked out of the house, "I mean you could come do this for the short term until you find the perfect job? Isn't an imperfect job better than no job?"

"No, you're right, it is, and you know how it goes. When you start out, you have that beginner's enthusiasm. You've had few, if any, rejections, no cancelations, and no unhappy customers calling you. You're making some money and suddenly the imperfect job doesn't look so bad. Sometimes those last sales calls of the night are an hour or two away, or you have a talker or one of those long battles where you know they will buy if you figure out what the real objection is and overcome it, and then you don't get home until eleven or twelve. You get home and you're still wound up from work, so you spend an hour or two in front of the TV, then climb in bed with your wife for a couple of hours before she is up and out the door."

Eli continues, "During the week, you're just a warm body in bed next to each other for a couple of hours and some notes back and forth on the kitchen table. You barely exist for your kid; you might as well be an absentee father. For enduring all that, on the weekend, they own you. You're up early for breakfast with the family, doing stuff with the kid, pitching in around the house or with errands and in the evening the wife wants to go out or maybe stay in and get some quality time so you're rolling out of bed a smidgen before noon Monday morning, unless, of course, you have an early sales call. Tell me, where in there I'm supposed to find the time to comb through classifieds and send out resumes; and let's not forget how much fun it is to schedule interviews when you have to tell them a week out that you can't run a particular slot?"

"Holy crap, I'm depressed now. Do you want another one? It's on me tonight," Jim offers.

"Sorry," Eli confirms, "this is why I hadn't called you back before we ran into each other. I know I'm a downer. I don't mean to be. I just need a job with a salary, plus commission, banker's hours, and benefits."

"A unicorn. Hold that thought," Jim says on his way to the bar.

"I don't want to hold the thought. I want to get the perfect job so I can quit thinking about it." Eli mutters, half under his breath.

Jim plops back down in his seat, spilling a little out of both drinks when he lands.

"Talk about your downward spiral. I'm sloppy drunk without being drunk." He slides another Bog Fire across the table to Eli, unsure of the reaction he will get.

Jim is always sloppy; it's kind of his signature look. He is always slightly disheveled and looks like he shops at the thrift store and dresses without a mirror. He is perpetually shaggy, like he is two weeks overdue for a haircut, always has scuffed shoes, and is almost always a little late. Eli assumes that's why the guy does pretty well in sales. No one sees him and puts up their defenses. Jim doesn't come across like a shark, or any predator for that matter. He is more of a deer in the headlights on the first day of hunting season. Eli has to admit, the guy is somehow likable even when you aren't really up to liking anyone.

Jim looks concerned, and he takes a small sip of his drink and sets it down carefully. Eli realizes he's let too much time pass without a response and doesn't want to share his thoughts, so instead he picks up the glass and downs half of the liquid in one long gulp, liking the way it burns. He holds his glass up to Jim.

"Thank you, Jim. Here's to good friends and jobs and the frigging economy recovering from the coronavirus. That little sucker is even more expensive than medical insurance or concussions."

Jim smiles, relieved, and starts in on his drink in earnest. After verifying that Jim has a way to get across town without driving, Eli just lets go. He feels all the stress that had been bottled up for months loosening and he is relaxing with the help of the drinks Jim keeps buying.

They pass the time telling tall tales, not unlike fishermen, about the best catches and the even bigger ones that got away. They are both shocked, and about halfway between buzzed and fall-down drunk, when the bartender shouts, "Last call!"

"What the?" Eli pulls out his phone, expecting to see the rescue call from Rachel that he asked for in case he needed help to extract himself from Jim's company. There isn't one. She can't be mad then, he reasons. He polishes off his drink while Jim closes out his tab. Jim comes back over to the table and waits for Eli to take his last swig so they can walk out the door together.

They are leaning against the fake Greek temple façade out front, waiting for Jim's Uber to arrive. Even in his current state, Eli knew it was going to be an expensive ride after a big tab. He felt bad that he couldn't offer to pitch in.

"Once I get that job, we'll do this again and it'll be on me."

"Sounds good, buddy," Jim agrees.

Something in his peripheral vision catches Eli's attention. He watches a guy stagger out of the bar and bounce off the side of parked cars for about half a block until he appears to find his car. His attempts at placing the key in the door are reminiscent of pin the tail on the donkey. Eli launches himself off the side of the building and locks on to his target.

"Hey, what the hell do you think you're doing?"

The offender steps back, gives his head a little shake and squints again, making sure he has the right car. He tries to merge the key with the lock again. A near miss leaves a small nick on the paint.

"Hey, I'm talking to you. There is no way you are driving. This is a family neighborhood. My family lives in this neighborhood. Give me your keys."

The guy takes two more quick stabs at the lock, trying to get away from the crazy guy yelling at him. Both fail, so flight is unavailable. He accepts the fight.

"Leave me alone, I'm getting in the not driver's side," he slurs, barely intelligible.

Eli holds out his hand, "Give 'em!" He demands and sways a little, his speech much clearer. Eli makes a grab for the keys. The drunk shifts them from right hand to left and instead of handing over the keys, he gives Eli a nice jab to the eye. Eli tackles him to the ground, and after a brief scuffle, comes away with the keys.

He rights himself with the help of a bike rack and storms back into the bar. He slams the keys down on the bar. "If you want to keep your liquor license and not get sued for everything you got or ever will get, I suggest you hold these until tomorrow."

He walks out again, feeling very proud. Back on the sidewalk, Jim and some stranger are helping the drunk into the back of a car. Once settled in, Jim walks over to Eli.

"Give me the keys," Jim holds out his hand, not bothering to hide his annoyance.

"What are you talking about? I'm not driving, I would never do that." This makes him superior.

"His keys," Jim jerks a thumb towards the car at the curb, "We're going to share my Uber; drunk dude needs his keys to get into his apartment. He'll walk over here tomorrow; he just lives over on Division."

Eli tilts his head towards the door. "Bartender has them."

The bartender follows Jim back to the door and hands over the keys when he sees the car with the Uber sticker on the windshield and the drunk in the back. He shoots a glare at Eli and locks the door behind him with a loud thud.

Eli turns to Jim to shake hands and is prepared for the one-armed hug.

Instead, Jim says, "You are one of the best people I know and you can be one of the biggest pricks, too. Whatever this is," he waves his arms to encompass the scene, "you've got to fix it; this just isn't good for anyone." With that, he walks to the car and slides into the back seat next to the drunk, who is asleep leaning against the other door.

Eli walks home in a huff; angry that Jim could take some stranger's side in a black-and-white issue. How dare he? Jim is the one that needs to fix something. There is nothing that a good job couldn't fix for him. Jim is the one that's a mess, almost twenty years older and he still doesn't have a successful marriage or a family or a single college credit. Between the alcohol, the late hour, all the energy he spent speed walking and being angry, he is exhausted by the time he reaches his front gate.

CHAPTER 4

A few hours later he is woken abruptly. "Oh my god, what happened to your face?" Rachel softly caresses his face, poking lightly to see if there is swelling around his black eye. He opens his eyes slowly, wincing at the light and the tenderness on the left side. "Are you okay?"

He holds his finger to his lips to shush her. She is about ten notches too loud this morning. She is silent and he turns his attention to his nightstand, looking for coffee that isn't there.

Losing patience, Rachel repeats quietly, "What happened?"

"Some drunk was trying to get into his car. He was a little reluctant to give up his keys."

"So, he hit you?"

"Yep, it was a lucky shot. He couldn't even get his keys in the door, but he managed to drill me one right in the eye." He demonstrates a fist to the eye and yelps at the light contact. Suddenly she is right in his face, looking in his eyes. She knocks the shade off the lamp, turns it on, and shines the light right in his eyes. He squints and tries to escape the light by turning his head. She stops him and moves the light around. He knows she is seeing how his pupils react to the light and watching how his eyes track the moving object.

"It smells like a distillery in here. I hope you had a good time."

He has a feeling she doesn't mean it, but he doesn't understand why because she usually encourages him to go out or do something fun.

"Mmm, yeah until that happened."

"Did you guys call the cops?"

"No, I took his keys, then Jim decided to be Mother Teresa and took the guy home in his Uber."

She knows there is more to the story. Giving someone a lift home isn't worthy of the anger and hurt she hears in his voice.

"Did you and Jim argue?"

"Argue, no. He was an ass and acted like I was the bad guy for keeping the guy from driving."

"I thought you said he couldn't get his key in the door."

"He couldn't. That didn't mean he wouldn't have. God, you sound like Jim. He could have killed somebody. I know I did the right thing." It felt a little hollow to him; he was less sure that it was true than he had been the night before.

"Hey, keep the gloves down, champ. I am team Eli all the way. I wasn't questioning you, I was just trying to understand," she reassures.

He squirms but doesn't say anything.

"Do you want coffee or sleep?"

"Sleep." The relief at the option is clear.

She walks out without another word. He is afraid she is mad and is trying to muster the energy to find her and try to smooth it over when something cold covers his injured eye.

"Do me a favor?" she phrases it as a question; her tone says it isn't.

"Yeah," he says, unsure what he is agreeing to, and too scared not to agree.

"If you ever get hit in the head while you've been drinking, will you wake me up when you get home and/or you will go to the ER and get checked out? That can be a really dangerous combination."

"Deal," he pauses, apologies always difficult for some reason. "I'm sorry I snapped earlier. I don't deserve you."

"That's not true. If it were, I would lord it over you for the rest of our lives. It's not; someday you will figure that out."

His only answer is his resumed snores.

The weekend flies by and Monday morning finds Eli rescanning the Sunday classifieds from the Oregonian, a welcome break from the online classifieds he combs the rest of the week. Rachel is making a half-hearted attempt at studying but spends more time looking at the weird cartoon Mason is watching than at her book. They hear the tell-tale buzz of a cell phone vibrating. They both check their phones; it's Eli's. He sees the restricted number on his phone and his stomach sinks. He smiles at his wife and points to his phone, "I'm going to take this outside, maybe it's a job? I'll be right back." She smiles at him and holds up crossed fingers.

He steps out onto the porch. He looks at the phone with trepidation and reluctantly answers, "Hello."

"Good afternoon, Mr. Asher. This is Donald with Premiere National Collections. I am calling you again about your past-due account. Last time we spoke, you said you would be making a partial payment and you have yet to do so."

"Yeah, I'm sorry about that. To be honest, I don't know when I am going to be able to. I lost my job at the very beginning of the pandemic and my unemployment ran out a few weeks ago. I will pay you, all of it, just as soon as I can." He hopes the man will hear his sincerity and that it will make a difference, though he doubts it will.

"Honesty, that is a good start. Let me be honest with you: I don't like having to explain to my boss why I haven't been more aggressive in my collection efforts for an account because I believed someone who said they would be making a payment. Since I don't enjoy that, I will be more aggressive. I believe this medical bill was for your son, Mason Asher?"

"Yes, I couldn't afford to keep my COBRA after the first month and I swear he got hurt just about the day after we lost coverage. I had no idea a kid hitting their head and getting a concussion could cost eighteen thousand dollars and counting. We had ten thousand saved up when it happened. I paid everything we had to keep it from going to collections."

"Very touching, and yet here we are. You would have been better off making a repayment plan and making the minimum monthly payment consistently," he said, hissing the last word.

"I found that out later when I couldn't make a payment the next month because I gave them everything I had the first month."

"Ah yes, companies that you owe money to frequently tell you not to make large payments, rather make small minimum payments over time so they never recoup their money. I could see how you would be disappointed in your expectation that they do this."

Eli flips off his phone so forcefully he knocks it out of his hand. He scrambles to pick it up.

"What was that, Mr. Asher?"

"I said I don't think this is very productive."

"Perhaps it would be more productive to talk about your son?"

"What makes you say that?"

"I wonder how he will feel when he turns eighteen and learns that his credit was ruined by his father."

"What are you talking about? His credit has nothing to do with this," he protests, moving down the stairs and towards the street so his family won't hear his raised voice.

"Ah, but it does. You see, when people with children destroy their own credit, they sometimes seek credit in their child's name and can rack up quite a bit of debt that the child is then saddled with. I liked you, Mr. Asher, and I believed you, but if I don't get a payment from you today, I will be adding your son's social security number to this collection account to prevent you from ignoring the situation and simply getting credit in his name."

"You can't do that."

"Let me assure you, Mr. Asher, I can and I will."

"Listen, the only money I have is for rent in a couple of days."

"It sounds like you'd better get a job, or some temp work, or sell something. My deadline isn't going to change. Are you going to protect your son's future or not?"

"AHH. What is the minimum payment I can make today?"

"Let's say the three hundred dollars you were going to send as soon as we hung up last time and, since we are already halfway to the next payment, let's round it out to a nice even four hundred fifty dollars."

"You're killing me!"

"I'm doing my job. Whatever is happening in your life is your responsibility."

"Yeah right. I created the coronavirus; I chose to be a nonessential worker."

"I'm not going to get into the ins and outs of personal responsibility with you today or any other day, Mr. Asher. Will you be making the payment or not?"

"You are literally taking rent money; do you understand that?"

"Yes or no?"

"Yes, yes I'm going to make the payment." He pulls his wallet out slowly and fishes out his debit card. "Are you ready? It's a Mastercard."

"Please proceed."

He slowly reads off the numbers.

"Thank you, Mr. Asher. Would you like the confirmation number now or shall I email you a receipt?"

"Email."

"As you wish. Good day, Mr. Asher."

"Yeah right, back at you." Eli hangs up. He grabs his hair with both hands and doubles over, choking back the bile and the string of profanities that threaten to escape.

When he goes back inside, Rachel looks up expectantly, "Good news?"

"What?" He is completely confused for a moment. "Oh, yeah, it might be. I'll have to follow up in a few days."

She changes the subject since he appears uncomfortable, "I'm going to go to the grocery store." She lowers her voice, "Do you want me to take Mason?"

He looks like he has just been handed a lifeline, "You are the best! That would be great! I could use an hour or so to return calls and figure some of this out."

She smiles and gives him a light kiss, "Mason, your show is over in five and you are out of screen time for the morning, so we are going to the grocery store in ten. Please be ready."

He waves a hand at her. She isn't sure if it is an acknowledgment or an attempt to wave her off.

"Mason?"

"Okay, Mom."

As soon as the door closes behind them, Eli starts looking up attorneys on his phone. He googles "what kind of attorney do I need for a debt collector." He is so glad he looked this up, he's feeling more confident and a few of the ads suggest you could sue a debt collector for damages. That would be amazing if he could get out of debt and protect his son's future credit at the same time. It would probably take a while; you never know though. He starts dialing.

He dials a handful of numbers and is frustrated by voicemails and an automated menu that he quickly loses patience with. He tries again and when a woman answers, he doesn't pay attention, not realizing there's a live human being on the other end.

"Hello?"

"Oh hi, yes, sorry. I was wondering about an experience I had with a collection agency," he starts to explain.

"Yes sir, there is a lot of that going around."

A lot of what going around, he wonders; she hadn't let him start, let alone finish. He realizes she is still talking.

"Did you want to schedule a free consultation, sir?"

"Yes, that would be great."

He starts to write down the date she is saying and stops when it dawns on him. "That is almost two months away."

"Yes, sir, as I mentioned, many people are having these issues right now. Did you want to make the appointment?"

"Yes," he agrees reluctantly, "Is this like an injury attorney where you only pay if you win?"

"No sir, the consultation is free and after that, if you should choose to proceed, payment is due as services are rendered."

That's what he was afraid of, "There is nothing sooner?"

"No sir, I can make a notation that you would like an earlier appointment, and should something become available, we'll let you know."

"Yes, please do that."

Her voice gets lower and difficult for Eli to hear, "If your situation is urgent, you may want to consult with a bankruptcy attorney."

"Why would I do that? There is no way I would ever do that. We want to buy a house; you can't do that if you have bankruptcy."

"You might be surprised about that; however, I was suggesting a meeting with one of them because you would be able to get some information about what creditors can and can't do in a timely fashion."

"I'll wait for the appointment, thanks anyway."

"Okay, we will see you then. If you do change your mind, please call us back to cancel your scheduled appointment. As you can see, we are quite backed up."

"Yep, that's my number one priority," he agrees in lieu of a goodbye and hangs up.

So much for that, he thinks with regret, then he remembers his conversation with Abed and that he hadn't thrown the card away after all. He starts searching for it, hoping to find it before his family gets home.

Eli opens the closet door and frisks his empty suit, feeling for the crumpled card he left in the pocket. When he doesn't find it, he yanks the pants off the hanger, breaking the small wooden dowel that used to suspend the pants beneath the jacket. He turns the pockets inside out, proving what he didn't want to be true. The card is not there. He drops everything to the floor, not bothering to find a new hanger or ever rehang what he can. Instead, he heads to the laundry nook by the back door. He opens the washer, then the dryer, and even checks the lint trap. He moves small piles of folded laundry around and checks the floor and pokes around in the trash.

Disheartened, he heaves a huge sigh and heads back to the living room just as Rachel and Mason enter, both carrying grocery bags.

"Oh, I'm so happy to see you," Eli greets them. Mason smiles, not caring why.

"Because you're hungry and we brought groceries?" Rachel guesses.

"Well, that too now that you mention it," he admits, "That wasn't it, I did it again. I misplaced something that I need now. I'm so happy to see you because it's time for a ten-dollar treasure hunt."

They both look at him, their interest piqued for different reasons.

"It's a business card, but it's probably a little crumpled up."

Rachel carries the groceries into the kitchen and starts putting them away. Mason follows and dumps his bag unceremoniously on the table. He grabs the car keys from the hook on the wall and heads back out the front door. Eli tries to follow.

"No fair!" Mason protests, "You can't watch all the spots I check or I won't ever get a ten-dollar treasure hunt again."

"Okay," Eli raises his hand in surrender.

Rachel laughs at the exchange and finishes putting away the groceries. Then quietly slips down the hall towards the bedroom.

Mason goes outside and looks back over his shoulder a couple of times.

Eli watches him through a slit between the curtain and TV. His son unlocks the passenger door, climbs in, and lowers both visors. He gets out and opens the back door and crawls in, his little hand exploring every opening. He climbs between the bucket seats back into the front and disappears down on the floor of the driver's side.

This is his father's dead zone. Almost everything he loses goes into the gap between the seat and center console and it comes to rest just out of sight when staring down into the gap. It's also just out of reach for his dad's much bigger hand and arm. Mason slips his arm under the seat, angling towards the gap and the rail the adjustable seat rests on. He pats the area with his fingertips, one, two, and three. He feels a ball of paper and pulls it out. He starts to smooth it flat but stops when he sees it is a very rumpled business card. Bingo, another ten-dollar treasure hunt won in the dead zone.

He carries the card out in front of him, raised and triumphant. Eli opens the door as Mason reaches for the handle and takes a big step towards him, backing his son out onto the porch.

He takes the card and looks at it for a brief second, "Nice job! Thanks, kiddo. You are pretty good at that." He pulls his wallet out of his pocket and fakes surprise to find only two singles in there.

"Oh, shoot, buddy, I'm sorry. Take this as your interest and I'll get you the ten next time I go to the bank, okay?"

"You won't forget?"

"I promise!" Mason nods agreement and Eli opens the door for them to go back inside. Rachel comes down the hall after hanging up the suit, annoyed by Eli's mess.

"I won, I won," Mason sings, kneeling on the couch taking a couple of little hops to show his enthusiasm. When he sees his mom's face, he turns around and sits on the couch reaching for the remote.

Eli gives his best I'm-a-little-rascal-type smile, "I'm sorry, sweetheart. I was just heading in to go clean that up. Looks like you beat me to it."

"Looks like," she agrees, annoyed but rapidly getting over it. "I'm glad you got what you needed both for you and the house."

"I'll be back," he darts out the door again. This time he bounds down the stairs, hits the walk, and when he reaches the fence, instead of taking time to open the gate, he puts a hand on top of it, swings his legs to the side and vaults over it. He walks to the street light at the end of the block before he pulls the card out of his pocket and smooths it out. He takes out his phone and dials the number, hoping he got all the numbers right.

"Hello."

"Hi, is this Abed?"

"This is he."

"Um, hi. You might not remember me. I met you a week or two ago when you got hired for your job."

"So, this would be Eli Asher?"

"Yes, that's me." He is relieved that Abed remembers him.

"How are you, Eli?"

"I'm not good, honestly, not good at all."

"I see, I'm sorry to hear that. How can I help?"

"Well, I was hoping to find out more about that group you're in."

"I believe I've told you what I can. If you have a specific question, you are free to ask it and I will answer if I'm able to do so."

That's just what he was hoping to hear. "I was wondering if there is some way that we could maybe take smaller steps with this whole thing. Like maybe I could get a job soon and gladly give you ten percent from that job for as long as I have it, and I could find out more about this whole deal before either side makes a lifetime commitment."

"Like a test drive?"

"Yes, something like that. You know, make sure it's a good fit?"

"I'm afraid not, Eli. This isn't a car dealership nor is it an employment agency. It can open doors, but there is no guarantee about what particular doors, and it does require a full commitment. Nothing less will suffice."

"I don't have a problem with commitment. I knew I wanted to marry my wife after I talked to her the first time. Someone that looks like she does, who is smart, and just a really good, kind person, it was a no-brainer. I still dated her for two years before I proposed."

"Eli," he starts to say more but stops himself. His voice softens for a second, "I remember what it felt like to take the leap. I don't regret it." He trails off again and when he resumes, the resolve has returned to his voice, "I am not allowed to cajole or encourage you in any way. This is a commitment that you must make of your own volition and as I said before, I don't think it's for you."

"Is that some sort of sales thing you're doing with that whole 'I don't think it's for you?' Some sort of take-away like the price is only good today, it will cost you way more if you want to think about it?"

"I assure you it's not. The offer is good indefinitely and the terms will not change. Now if there is nothing further."

"No, there is not. I was hoping you could help, but I guess you can't."

"Goodbye Eli, may you find what you need quickly."

"Bye Abed, thanks."

He hangs up, dejected and unsure of what he was thanking the man for, maybe for remembering him, or making this crazy offer, or just for that last thing he said, which was kind of nice. He doesn't know why, but a part of him likes Abed and he assumes they would have been friends, or at least friendly, if they had somehow both gotten the job.

Out of time and out of ideas, he whispers a plea, "Please show me the way." Then he goes back inside to be with his family.

CHAPTER 5

A few days later, Rachel and Mason are out for a walk when Eli's phone rings. As soon as he sees the caller, he is glad they are gone.

"Hi, Joe."

"Hi, I got your rent, well about half of it more like. You do remember it is twenty-two hundred, right?"

"I remember. I'm very sorry. I still haven't gotten a job yet and things are getting tight. I'll get the rest to you just as soon as I can."

"I know you have been struggling so I've let you slide a little here and there since you've been such good tenants for years before all this. I can't keep doing that, I'm going to have to charge you the late fee this time."

"I understand. You've been more than fair. Things seem to be picking up some more. I bet I'll have a job any day now and we'll be back to being great tenants again."

"I hope that's true. Listen Eli, if you are going to be short again, really short like this or late please let me know ahead of time. I count on rents to take care of my responsibilities and when they don't come, I have to do some juggling too."

"I understand. You're right. I don't think it will be an issue again, but if it is, I promise I will call you."

"All right then. I'll keep looking out for the rest of it and don't forget the late fee."

"Okay Joe, thanks, I appreciate it."

"All right," with that, he hangs up.

Eli beats his fist against his thighs in frustration. He would feel better if Joe yelled at him or was more cantankerous somehow. He can't help snickering at the thought of him,

Rachel thinks he is such a cute old man with his bald head, the baggy skin on his neck, and his rounded shoulders. Eli doesn't think he is cute, he thinks he looks like a turtle startled out of his shell. He gets mad at the collection agent all over again. He had the rent, barely, but he had it before that jerk extorted him. Then he has a little pang of gratitude for the collector and guilt about the rent.

Having the reminder that his situation would be much better if he hadn't handed over their entire savings to pay down Mason's medical bills, and knowing that he is going to be short on the rent no matter what he does, he had made a credit card payment and held back an additional three hundred in case of an absolute emergency.

Eli turns on his laptop and sits down at the table, preparing to look at the classifieds again. He is so tired of seeing the same crap job listings over and over while hunting for that needle in the haystack. Interviews were getting fewer and further in between, he wishes he had finished his degree, it would probably help in a job market like this.

He is just about to enter one of the sites he looks at daily when a news link catches his eye; "Hot dog, yay for big brother spying on us so they can get clicks and sell us things." The article is about legal aid and includes a phone number. He dials, what does he have to lose?

"Good afternoon, Legal Aid, how can I help you?"

"Hi, can I just ask you a quick question?"

"Very quick," Eli can hear the weariness and the phones ringing in the background.

"Can a collection company report on a minor's credit as well as the parents? Legally I mean, can they do it?"

"I'll be frank with you; this is not my area of expertise and this probably isn't a quick question. I'll tell you what I can and if you want to make an appointment, I can send you the forms to see if you qualify for services."

"Sounds reasonable."

"If your parents damaged your credit, you can declare bankruptcy to be excused of the debt, and depending on your financial circumstance you can pay the filing fee in installments or possibly even have it waived. You can try to work with the creditors directly to see if they will remove your name from the file since you were a minor when the debt was accrued. The challenge with that is they often want an official statement; a police report which may pose a risk of fraud or identity theft charges of some type to your parents."

"Neither of those sound too good. My question is are creditors able to do that? Legally?"

"To be honest I don't know, I know it happens because we get calls like these occasionally, I can send you the forms if you would like to make an appointment to talk to one of our attorneys."

"I bet I wouldn't qualify. I used to make pretty good money before. Thanks anyway."

"You're welcome." The end of the word is barely out before the call disconnected.

Everyone is so busy. He misses being busy, something he never thought he would. He enjoys his time with his family, but the days are so long without work or a purpose. He envies those that are homeowners and can do projects, and those that volunteer in different ways. They discussed it at the beginning of the pandemic and decided that Rachel's part-time work at the hospital was more than enough potential exposure for their family.

That night, he is restless and has a hard time falling asleep. When he does, he has a nightmare about a fire-breathing dragon chasing him through a post-apocalyptic downtown. The dragon transforms into a firebird and back several times, the one constant is being inches away from disaster. He is relieved when he races around a corner and looks back over his shoulder and doesn't see the monster. When he looks forward again, he is confronted by a Godzilla-sized version of his son. He points at him and says, "You ruined my life, you are a bad dad."

"I'm sorry, I'm sorry," he repeats. His son morphs into his father, all he sees is the back of him walking away. He thrashes around the bed as his arms go towards his dad, he isn't sure if it is to grab him to make him stay or shove him away faster.

"Eli, wake up. You're having a bad dream." Rachel gently strokes the side of his face before resting her hand on his shoulder. He rolls towards her, putting a knee between hers and a hand on her hip. He falls back asleep forehead to forehead with her, finally at peace.

The next day, Eli avoids Rachel as long as possible fearing that she will want to talk about his nightmare. They were rare for him, and he hadn't had one since her pregnancy when all of his fears and insecurities about parenthood wreaked havoc with his psyche. Once his son had been born healthy and he held him for the first time, the nightmares had gone away and had not returned.

Rachel sends Mason outside to play in the backyard and Eli prepares for what he thinks is coming. Instead, she throws him a curveball with, "I think I want to go back to work full time for a while."

"Why?"

"It would be nice to have a break from school; you're stressed out and I'm sure we could use the money. I don't like feeling like I'm not doing my share."

There it was right in front of him, a way out, a chance to unburden himself and tell his wife the truth about their current financial state. He could make her a true partner again as they had been before all this started with no secrets between them. He wills himself to say yes, to say something. Then he thinks of his father and how he walked out on him and his mom when he was younger than Mason is now. He remembers how hard his mom had worked and how they still struggled despite it all.

He promised himself before he even finished high school that when he got married and had a kid that his wife would work if she wanted to, and only if she wanted to. He would provide for his family. He wanted to be able to put her through school.

"You're crazy, it's a good thing you are so beautiful so you can get away with it. You always do your share and three other peoples' shares most of the time. I know it's been stressful, but I've got a really good line on a couple of things. One of them will pan out any second, so don't mess with my dreams of spending all that big money you will make once you graduate." He kisses her to emphasize the point.

"You would let me know if you needed help?"

"It's fine. In fact, I was thinking that you and Mason should go do something fun today. You've been studying and doing most of the home-schooling. He's been cooped up a lot. Go to a movie, grab some lunch somewhere, or something. Just getting out in the world a little in a non-threatening way will probably do him some good."

The idea is appealing. "You don't want to make it a family outing?" she asks.

"Of course, I do, but I really shouldn't. I am serious about having some solid leads. I bet I'll have a job by the end of the week, next week at the latest. I need to follow up on some things. Go have some fun. Next time, it will be a family outing to celebrate my first paycheck from my new job."

He gives her his most charming smile and is rewarded with a look of utter adoration from her. That look usually makes him feel ten feet tall and invincible. You would have to be to deserve a look like that from a woman like her. This time it makes him feel small, weak and completely unworthy.

He hides it all. "I'm going to look in the garage for some work clothes that will accommodate the dad bod," he says rubbing his belly where his pandemic lock-down weight accumulated. "Do you want me to send Mason in?"

"Yeah, we better get going. I want to have lunch first so I don't have a complete battle over the movie theater goodies."

"Have fun, I love you guys."

On the way to the garage, he gives his son the good news, a hug, and a kiss on the cheek.

Once he unlocks the door and turns on the light, he pokes around for a few minutes wanting to make sure they are gone before he gets what he came for. When he is sure enough time has passed, he goes for the treasure box his mom had given him right before he got married. He had been shocked; he had no idea she had anything that valuable or that she would give it to him after sacrificing so much already.

It had a variety of things in it, and she had told him would be worth three to five thousand dollars if he was ever in a pinch. He didn't remember everything in it, but knows there are a couple of men's rings, including his father's wedding ring, some coins, and currency. He opens it to find all that he remembered plus an old gun he should have gotten rid of before Mason could walk. There are also a couple of sports cards that look to be in rough condition.

He tucks the box under his arm and heads for his car. He puts the box in the trunk because of the gun. Once he is in the driver's seat, he looks at his phone to find a pawn shop. He passes them regularly but never pays much attention to them since he hasn't had a use for them until now. Jewelry and loan seems to be a popular word combo for pawn shops, so he sets out for the closest one with that in the name.

Once he arrives, he retrieves the box from the trunk and walks into the pawnshop. He isn't quite sure how things work in a place that both buys and sells stuff. Many stores didn't like you bringing in bags and backpacks, but you have to bring things in to be able to sell them. Annoyed with himself, he walks up to the counter with more confidence than he feels.

"How can I help you?" The man smiles and seems friendly enough, but Eli knows from working in sales that it is important not to appear desperate.

"I ran across this box in the garage the other day and I'm considering selling some of this stuff, depending on what you might offer for it."

"Let's take a look." He puts a towel over the glass countertop and gestures for Eli to put the box down.

"Oh, there is a gun in there, I don't know the etiquette on that stuff."

"Is it loaded?" Eli has to admit it's a great question and one that he hasn't even considered. Seeing he is stumped for an answer, the man handles it as though it is until he confirms it isn't.

"It isn't loaded. It is a Colt M1911 and it's suffering from some neglect, but it's not in bad condition overall."

The man turns it this way and that and pushes and pulls on things. Eli has seen the rotating barrel ones from Westerns and Russian roulette scenes in movies, and the ones with clips that slide in and out of the bottom in action movies. He can't see that this has either. It must store bullets somewhere. He knows next to nothing about guns but does understand having to reload between each shot would not be desirable. When the man is done inspecting the gun, he sets it down gingerly on the towel.

"I can give you twelve hundred for it." Eli bites the inside of his lip to keep from smiling.

"What about the rest of it?"

The man fishes around the boot box and pulls out the jewelry. He separates it into piles. He puts each on the scale, writing numbers down on the notepad. He attaches a little magnifier to the rim of his glasses and still squints while looking at the coins. He puts three back in the box.

"Canadians," he explains, "none of these are collectible but they are worth their silver weight."

Eli just looks at him, so he proceeds to weigh them and adds more numbers to the notepad.

"Between the jewelry and coins, you've got a couple of pounds of silver. I can offer you five hundred on that."

"Oh, I thought that would be more?"

"If it was gold it would be worth thousands more."

"Anything else in there interest you?"

"Oh wow, oh that's too bad."

"What?"

"You have a Joe Montana rookie card here. If it was a ten, I could offer you twelve thousand for it if it was a nine, maybe four hundred. In this condition, you might get ten or twenty bucks for it if you try to sell it online."

"Whoa, how do you go from twelve thousand to twenty bucks?"

"See this fold right through his face, the chipping on the edges, the stain on the back?"

"Does it hurt it that much?"

"It does. I told you the difference between a ten and nine is significant and this is nowhere close to a nine."

He puts the card back in the box and pokes around more. Eli pulls out his phone and enters Joe Montana's rookie card. The first thing that comes up values a PSA10 at fifteen thousand dollars. The man finds something else of interest and starts studying it.

Eli sees it is another sports card and this one is in a plastic holder of some sort. Maybe the value of the box's content was more than his mom had estimated.

First things first though, "It says here a PSA10 Joe Montana rookie card is worth fifteen thousand."

"Yes."

"Why did you tell me it was worth twelve?"

"I never said it was worth twelve I said if it was a 10, I could offer you twelve thousand. Don't forget this is a business I need to make some money. Things like that are slow movers in an economy like this."

Eli quickly pulls up the price of silver and sees there is a slim margin there.

"Listen, I'm offering the best I can on everything that comes through the door right now because I know a lot of people need it. You can look up my reviews while you are looking up the price on everything else, or you can run all over town to prove to yourself what I'm telling you. It doesn't matter to me either way."

He puts the other card back in the box waiting to see what Eli decides.

Working at being casual and largely failing he asks, "What about the one you just put back? What's that worth?"

"What's it worth or what can I offer?" he clarified.

"Both, if you don't mind."

"It's a Joe Namath rookie card and it's graded, see the PSA3 here. In this market eight or nine hundred. In a great economy maybe twelve hundred or more. I should offer five, I doubt anyone else will offer you more, but I will go six if you sell the rest of it."

"It's in much better condition than the other one and it's a three?"

"Entry-level collectors will buy a card like this. Heavy hitters want nine or above, if they can find one."

"What do those go for?"

"This one as a ten? Thirty, maybe up to forty thousand dollars. Condition is important."

"I guess," Eli agrees, hoping he will find something else of value in the box.

"You've got a couple of old fishing lures in here and a duck decoy. I know some of these things are worth nothing and some can be worth a lot. I don't know enough about them, so I won't offer you anything for it. You might be able to get fifty for your wind-up tin toy online. I'm not interested due to the condition it's in."

"Anything else?" he didn't walk in counting on five, but he hoped he could get close to four thousand. Now, he's desperately hoping for three.

"Not much. You've got some two-dollar bills that are worth two dollars. You have a stack of cards that might be worth a hundred if you sell them individually yourself. These are interesting. You've got some military payment certificates, one dollar and a five dollar."

"Did they shrink?" he asks.

"Nope, they are the right size. This stuff must have been your dad's," he guesses. "Was he in Vietnam?"

Rather than admit he doesn't know or care he lies, "Yeah, but he didn't like to talk about

The man behind the counter becomes suspicious. Working in a pawnshop for so long you get to be a pretty good lie detector or you go broke. Buying stolen goods is a costly mistake. He doesn't think the guy is a thief, but he is lying.

"This is your legal property, right? You have the right to sell it?"

"I do, my mom's the one that passed it on to me before I got married. I can call her if you want."

"That won't be necessary."

"What about those?" he gestures to the mini money.

"They have condition issues as well."

"My dad didn't take good care of stuff."

The man nods understanding the earlier deception, "Relationships can be challenging."

Getting frustrated Eli points again,

"With the condition issues, probably ten or fifteen."

"Hundred?" Eli hopes.

"Sorry no, ten or fifteen dollars each."

"Is that everything then?"

"Everything for me, you should get the decoy and lures checked out if you get a chance and you've probably got a couple hundred in online sales if you are patient."

"What's that add up to?"

"Let's see twelve for the colt, five for the coins and jewelry, six for the card. That's twenty-three hundred." He double-checks himself as he is talking.

Eli hates having to ask anyone for anything, but he has no choice. "Is there any way that you could do twenty-five?"

"I really couldn't. I'll meet you at twenty-four, if you promise me something."

"What's that?"

"When times are easier you come back and buy some sort of collectible to put in that box for your kids someday."

"How do you know I have kids?"

The man points at Eli's wedding band, "Most do, I'm sorry if I am off base."

"You're not and you've got a deal." Eli knows he doesn't have to keep the promise, but he does like the idea of giving his son a rainy-day box when he gets married someday.

"I need to see some ID and we need to do a little paperwork and then we'll get you paid." He carefully pulls what he is buying away from the box and spreads it out to show there is nothing hidden under something else before handing the box with its remaining contents to Eli.

While he waits for the man to finish reviewing the paperwork Eli does some math in his head. He could pay the rest of the current month's rent and pay half of the next month's rent a week early to hopefully soften the blow to Joe that the other half would probably be late again.

Rachel's paycheck should cover the car payment and insurance, and enough towards utilities to keep them all on. He still had two hundred in cash for groceries and they had a smidgen available on their only credit card. He wished he had gotten more cards or pushed for bigger limits before he had late payments on everything. No one wants to give you credit when you need it.

He accepts the money and the handshake, "Thank you."

"And to you, take care. I'll see you again."

He walks out defeated, pulling his mask off, stuffing it in his pocket and pulling out the hand sanitizer. He had done everything he could, given everything he had to give and they were barely treading water for two more weeks. He had two options, have Rachel quit school, which was a pill he just couldn't swallow, or make the call that was starting to feel inevitable. It started to rain, which wasn't surprising in the Northwest and somehow felt apropos, so he put the box back in his trunk and stood in the rain while he made his call.

"Hello, Eli." Abed must have added his number to his phone after the last call. Eli didn't bother with any small talk or niceties.

"I want to join the group. I'll do whatever I have to as long as it's ethical or at least legal and won't get me divorced. I need doors to open."

"You understand what you are asking?"

"I think so."

"This isn't an 'I think so' proposition, so let me clarify for you. You are pledging ten percent of your income for the rest of your life to this fraternal order. You will assist in any way possible if asked, you will keep it secret and only discuss its existence with seekers such as yourself. At some point, you will experience a rite of passage of some sort to verify that yours is a character worthy of membership. If you fail to gain entry, you will be released from your financial pledge, but must adhere to secrecy. Would you still like to join?"

"Yes. That rite of passage thing, does it take a long time? I know it's my fault I didn't say yes that day that I met you, but I'm really behind the eight ball right now. I need doors to open."

"The rite of passage is different for everyone and I am not the one who decides these things. I will pass along your immediate needs. It is probable that you may receive an offer of employment, possibly temporary, before you proceed with your initiation phase."

"That would help a bunch."

"Be open to possibilities in the next few days and Eli, good luck."

"Thanks." He shoves his phone back in his pocket, "I think," he mutters to the sky.

CHAPTER 6

The next morning, Eli wakes to his phone buzzing. He looks around confused, sees Rachel sleeping beside him. He eases out of bed, slips out of the room, waiting until he is in the hallway to answer.

He whispers, "Hello."

"Good morning, sir, I am attempting to reach Mr. Asher, Eli Asher."

"Yes," still whispering he steps out onto the porch.

"Are you Mr. Asher?"

"Yes, I am. Who is this?"

"I'm Danielle, but that's not the matter at hand. I've been instructed by my employer to call you. She heard that you were seeking an opportunity and wanted me to call you with one."

"Oh, great this is for a job? Where, what time do you want me there?"

"This is for temporary employment. It is out of the Portland metro area, out of Oregon entirely. You would be needed for four to six weeks and would be compensated ten to fifteen thousand dollars; your travel will be provided."

"Um wow, I didn't expect to travel, but that is pretty good compensation. Do you know what I'll be doing?"

"My employer is part of a network of individuals with varied interests. I can't say for sure what you would be doing or where. Are you interested?"

"Yeah, I guess. No, I am interested. You can't tell me any more?"

"I can tell you where you need to be and by what time."

"This is legal right? I mean I'm not going to get arrested or just plain disappear, I have a family."

"It's a simple job, sir. I can assure your safe return to Portland when you are through. There is nothing morally questionable about it."

"That's great. When and where?"

"Are you familiar with Atlantic Aviation PDX?"

"The airport? It's called Portland International, but yes I'm familiar".

"You aren't looking for the airport itself, you are looking for an FBO, fixed base operator," she clarifies. "I will send a text to this number with the address. Please be there by 7:30 a.m."

"Today?"

"Yes, that is correct."

"Wowzer, that's quick. My family is still asleep, I need to pack, and that only gives me about 10 minutes."

"Your plane leaves at 7:30 sir, I hope you will be on it." That's all he gets as a goodbye.

"Hello, hello?" He tries, not ready for the call to end even though he heard the click.

Eli glides through the house as quickly and quietly as possible. He grabs a big backpack out of the hall closet and shakes the contents to the closet floor. He shoves the heap back with his foot and pushes the door closed. In the bedroom, he grabs a couple of dress shirts, slacks, his favorite tie, and his best jacket. Next, he opens his dresser drawers one at a time and shoves things in by the handful. He is still pushing things deeper into the pack when he gets to the bathroom. He shoves a toothbrush into his mouth, grabs deodorant and cologne from the medicine cabinet and swipes a body wash from the side of the tub on his way by. He picks up the dress clothes on his way out of the room.

In the kitchen, he hunts around for a piece of paper. He sees a pen and shoves the toothbrush in the pack and the pen in his mouth. He finds a note from Rachel and turns it over. Luckily, it's blank and he scratches out "I got an opportunity to do a well-paying temp job. I'll be gone for a few weeks. I'll call you as soon as I can. I love you both all the way every day."

Before he can make it out the door Rachel and Mason both appear in the kitchen. Rachel radiant-looking like she's been up and ready to go, Mason sleepy-eyed and reluctant.

"What's going on?" Rachel asks, eyeing the backpack.

"Oh, I'm so glad you guys are up. I have to leave for a little bit. I left you a note, but now I get hugs." He squeezes Mason tight, then turns to Rachel and hugs more gently nuzzling her neck. He ends the embrace abruptly and races to the door.

"What about the love bubble?" Mason asks.

"I don't have time right now, I'm sure the last one is still strong." With that, he closes the door and dashes to the car.

Mason looks quizzically at his mom who sighs.

"Don't worry honey. He'll be back."

"Why did he leave?"

"I guess he got a job, let's go see what the note says, shall we?"

She picks up the note from the counter. "Here, this is what he wrote to us, why don't you hold onto it."

He reads it to himself until he reaches, "I love you all the way every day," which he reads out loud. He carefully folds the note and tucks it in the waistband of his pajamas.

"Well, we're up, what do you say to breakfast." Mason shakes his head no and inches towards the hall.

"Going back to bed?" He nods and goes back to his room.

Rachel sits down on the sofa and wraps her arms around herself.

Eli's driving is as erratic as his thoughts. He weaves in and out of the light traffic on the freeway. He is elated to be making some money, sad to be leaving his family, and intrigued about where he is going and what he is doing.

He is relieved when he gets to Atlantic air at 7:15. He pulls into the first parking space he sees that doesn't have a designation sign on it and heads into the building. When he sees the two massive fireplaces in the lobby, he lets out a low whistle. He pulls on his mask as he walks up the counter and a cute blonde immediately says, "Good morning sir, how can I help you?"

"Are you who I talked to on the phone?"

"I'm not sure sir, what is this about. I bet I can help you either way."

"My name is Eli Asher," he looks at her for a spark of recognition which he gets.

"Yes, Mr. Asher I didn't speak to you earlier but I understand you will be flying out shortly. Your pilot will be in to get you in a few minutes. He is very punctual, until then, please enjoy some coffee, pastries, or fruit."

"Shoot, I just thought of my car. I guess I'll be gone for a while, could I leave the keys with you and have my wife come get it?"

"If you'd prefer to garage your vehicle at home, I can arrange to have it delivered for you, otherwise you can leave it where it is. If you would like one of our mechanics to start it for you during your absence you can leave a key."

"Wow? How much does that cost?"

"Neither option would involve any cost to you, sir."

"This is the way to travel isn't it?"

"Certainly," she agrees before going back to what she was doing.

Eli slings the bag over his shoulder, lets his mask hang from his ear and sticks a fruit Danish in his mouth while he figures out how to get a vanilla latte out of the futuristic looking coffee machine. Coffee in one hand and pastry in the other he sits down and lets out a happy sigh as he feels the comfort and support of the leather chair.

He takes the last sip of his coffee and looks around for a trash can, not in a hurry to get up. He looks at the clock and sees it's seconds away from 7:30. He hears a sharp whistle and looks in the general direction of the sound. He sees an old man, possibly a mechanic near a different door than the one he came in. His attention drifts away. Suddenly the blonde from the desk is beside him.

"Sir, your pilot is ready." He looks around expecting to see somebody that looks like the "right stuff" in a sharp suit. The only person he sees in the direction she is leading him is the old man in the jumpsuit, "He isn't the pilot, is he?"

"Yes, sir, he is."

"Maybe in Vietnam back in the day, but not now, right? Isn't there an age limit on pilots?"

Her tone suddenly becomes very icy, "Korea and Vietnam and no sir, while commercial airlines have mandatory retirement at 65, there is no age limit in private aviation."

The closer they get the more the deep wrinkles on his shrunken face can be seen.

"Come on, Father Time over there? He isn't the pilot; he looks like one of those apple dolls my mom was into when I was a kid. He's got to be older than dirt."

She speeds up a little to reach the pilot ahead of Eli. She gives him a big hug, which he tolerates, "So good to see you, come visit me next time you're on the ground for a while, we've been missing you."

"I will, Kid," he agrees. "I've been busier than a one-legged man in a butt-kicking contest and it don't look like it's gonna ease up any time soon. I'll tell you what I've been telling everybody about everything lately; when I can I will." He gives her a paternal pat on the shoulder before he turns his attention to Eli.

"This him?"

"Yes, I'm sorry Zeke, this is Eli Asher. He is your lone passenger." Zeke sizes him up and doesn't look impressed at what he sees. The blonde enquired, "And your car, sir? What did you decide?"

"I guess I'll just leave it here, nobody needs to worry about starting it."

"Very well sir, good day," she says in a tone that means anything but. She flashes a bright smile at Zeke and turns walking briskly back down the hall toward the desk.

"Let's go, you're gonna make me late and I don't much care for being late."

"Okay."

Eli is surprised at how hard he has to work to keep up with Zeke. He marches up the steps of the Cessna Citation without pause. Eli follows and turns to the right as he has done every time he has ever boarded a plane in his life.

"Hold on there, Sonny. There ain't no service on this flight and I've got cargo in the seat belts. You're gonna be up here with me."

He not so gently nudges Eli toward the cockpit while he closes the door behind him. He almost knocks Eli over as he passes him to climb into the seat on the left. He puts on a head seat and motions to the seat next to him and another headset.

"I have to do a pre-flight check and get us in the air," he checks his watch, "almost three minutes ago."

Not knowing what else to do, Eli sits down and puts the headset on. He listens to Zeke talking himself through the pre-flight checklist that he must have done a million times.

Once they are in the air Zeke's demeanor changes and he physically relaxes. This is a man who is more at home in the cockpit than on the ground. He lets a deep exhale and turns to his passenger.

"We are going to head south until we get to California and then we'll hang a left and get you over to Mississippi. How'll that be?"

"Wouldn't it make more sense to just go diagonally? Isn't that the advantage of flying, you can just go the shortest distance?"

"A smartass, eh? The world's full of 'em, I reckon."

"No, I'm not trying to be a smart ass, I just don't understand."

"Well, that's because you're not in possession of all the info, now are ya?"

"I guess not. I don't have much info at all."

"Then it seems like you ought to listen more and talk less, don't it?"

Eli reluctantly nods in agreement.

"We are going south because I need to drop off and pick up a few items in Riverside. Then I'm taking you to Mississippi, where I understand you'll be helping rebuild some houses that were destroyed by a tornado in the middle of this pandemic business. Talk about a swift kick in the peaches while you're down huh?"

Eli squirms in his seat uncomfortably.

"What's got you in a twist?"

"That sounds like an amazing volunteer opportunity and I do love to volunteer when I can, but I was told this would be a paying job."

"Then it must be. These people I work for and with, you can take what they say to the bank. Hell, I've been doing just that for near thirty years now."

Eli starts laughing and is surprised when his eyes tear up a little. He swipes at them with the sleeve of his jacket hoping Zeke won't notice.

"What's got you cackling and twitching now?"

"I'm relieved. I'm very happy. I didn't know what I was going to be doing and I told them I didn't want to do anything illegal, but I just didn't know."

"And you got on a plane with a stranger to go who knows where on the word of a voice on the other end of the phone?" Zeke asks incredulously.

"Well yes and no. I was put in touch with that voice on the phone by someone I met in person who got a good job at a company with an outstanding reputation. That gave me a little hope, but bottom line; I need the money."

"Got debt?"

"Oh yeah."

"Gambling?"

"What? No nothing like that. I have a family. I lost my insurance when I got laid off and my son got a concussion that cost eighteen thousand dollars, if you can believe that! My unemployment ran out a bit ago and I haven't been able to get a new job yet. That's why I need the money, I need to take care of my family."

"You do that by leaving them?"

"I'm not leaving them! I would never do that!"

"They are in Portland, aren't they?"

"Yes," he agrees.

"And you aren't anymore because you left there, right?" Zeke continues.

"That is correct, I have temporarily left the area to make some money to pay rent. That is not the same as leaving my family which I would never do."

"You seem to feel pretty strong about that."

"Yeah, I do. My Dad was a piece of," he pauses, searching for an appropriate non-profane word, "work. He walked out on my mom when I was five, never paid a cent in child support, never called to say Happy Birthday. He never did anything for anybody but himself. I can't imagine walking out on my son. He is such a cool, weird little guy. I would miss him too much, plus I hate the thought of doing anything to hurt him period, but especially something that would hurt him that much."

"What about the missus?"

"I honestly don't know how I got so lucky. She would have an easier time than my mom did, she always worked two or three crummy jobs to make ends meet. Rachel can make good money as an RN and is in school now to become a nurse practitioner, plus she would have way more support from her family than mom had."

"If she can make good money, why are you heading into the wild blue yonder to pay the rent?"

"Because I provide for my family. I'm not like my dad, I'm not leaving my wife holding the bag, taking away all her choices and opportunities. I want her to be able to finish school and get a job she loves. Then maybe I can take a little time off to finish school myself. I mean, if I don't have a great paying job and we can afford it while still saving for Mason's college."

"What's a Masons College? I thought that was more apprentice or on the job training?"

"No Mason is my son's name. I want to make sure he can go to college."

Zeke shakes his head, "Used to be jobs were jobs and names were names, now it's all mixed up. Can't hardly figure out what people are talking about half the time."

Eli looks out the window, hoping Zeke will lose interest in the conversation.

"Sounds to me like you got lucky and married out of your weight class."

"Weird analogy, but yeah."

"Cept you aren't smart enough to take the win and move on. You still can't believe you got that lucky or that you deserve it and instead of enjoying life with her you make yourself crazy and I'm betting her too."

"There is nothing wrong with trying to be the best that you can, besides I know she loves me and I'm a good provider, well usually anyway."

"While you're all stressed and obsessed about being your best and being a good provider, have you ever considered, or even asked her, if what you're providing is what she wants."

Eli starts to respond and Zeke raises a hand to silence him. He starts speaking to a new voice on the headset saying things Eli doesn't understand, something like niner this. He looks out the window and is surprised to see how close they are to the ground.

They land without incident nor further conversation. As soon as the plane comes to a stop, Zeke starts another checklist which he flies through. When he's finished, he pops up, "Come on, you can help me unload."

He follows him to the passenger area of the jet. There are eight seats, and seven of them have a box on it buckled in.

A man is asleep and snoring loudly in the eighth seat. Eli shoots a quizzical look at Zeke who shrugs, "Co-pilot."

Zeke grabs a big box and stacks another on top of it. Eli goes to pick up a box and is shocked at how heavy it is.

"Not that one, that one." Zeke motions

Zeke motions to a very small box about the size of a ring box on the next seat. Eli casually picks it up, "What else?"

"Just that, but be careful with it. It's precious to the one it's being delivered to."

"Okay." Eli feels like an idiot following Zeke down the stairs with the tiny box in his hand while Zeke carries the big boxes like they weigh nothing. The looks he gets from others as they enter the terminal aren't lost on him either.

As they reach the counter, another cute blonde that could be a clone of the one from Portland rushes around the counter and waits impatiently for Zeke to set down the boxes so she can hug him. He tolerates it for a moment. "Alright, I'm happy to see you too, but we've got to get going. I need to get this yahoo to work. Do you have my boxes?"

"So soon?" she asks, dismayed. Zeke nods resolutely and she motions to two medium boxes sitting on the floor at the end of the counter. "Can't you at least have a cup of coffee?" she implores.

He looks at his watch for the third time since they entered the building and turns to Eli, "Think you can load those?"

"Of course."

"Alright, do that, hit the head, and do whatever else you might want to do in the next ten minutes." Eli bends over to pick up the boxes and finds they are deceptively heavy.

"You're going to want to use the hand truck for that, it's over there," Zeke says, motioning behind the counter. Some guy comes up and salutes Zeke before embracing him with a bear hug. An older woman joins him and hugs him too. Zeke squirms a little with the attention.

Miserable, Eli loads the boxes onto the hand truck, wondering why everybody treats that crusty old fart like he's a rock star or superhero. He easily rolls the boxes to the plane and carries them slowly up the steps one at a time. He sets each one gingerly on the towels that cover the rich, buttery leather seats. When he has buckled in the second box, he goes back downstairs to return the hand truck but sees someone else whisk it back into the building.

He considers going back inside until he sees through the windows that more people have gathered around Zeke the messiah. Annoyed, he shakes his head and goes back onto the plane to find the bathroom. Once he's finished, he sits down on the one open seat in the passenger area. "This is the way to travel," he thinks to himself. He buckles in and pretends to be asleep when he hears Zeke's approach, hoping he can avoid more conversation and maybe actually get some sleep back here.

"Scooch your boots," Zeke demands.

Eli tries to get up, forgetting he has the seat belt on. He struggles to free himself and stand up. As soon as he's clear, Zeke plops down another box.

"Let's go, time's a-wastin'."

Reluctantly, Eli follows him back to the cockpit and gets settled in the co-pilot seat. After they are back in the air, Eli gives a few yawns and leans his head against the side and pretends to be asleep. To his relief, Zeke doesn't say anything. After a while, he does drift off.

CHAPTER 7

When he awakes something is very wrong. The world is at the wrong angle, the seat belt is cutting into him, his arms are flailing and some sort of warning or alarm is blaring.

"Looks like we're going in," Zeke states like he is saying the sky is blue.

Eli looks in front of him through the cockpit window and suddenly understands what is wrong. The plane is in a dive straight towards the water. He has what feels like seconds, maybe a minute, to understand he is probably going to die and feels waves of regret more crushing than the waves they are screaming towards.

At the last possible second Zeke pulls back on the yoke and once he has the nose up, he flips them into a roll. He continues to climb as he pulls out of the roll and suddenly, they are over land with trees so close they must be tickling the bottom of the plane.

"Just kidding, not bad for somebody old as dirt huh?" Zeke laughs.

Eli, still stunned, sits there speechless. If this guy wasn't part of this organization, Eli would have read him the riot act. Finally, he gathers himself and his thoughts and instead says, "I'm sorry if you felt disrespected, I shouldn't have said it. I was uncomfortable and, as Rachel calls it, inappropriate humor is my go-to when I'm uncomfortable. That said, there is no excuse for what you did. I could have had a heart attack, you could have lost control and killed us both."

Zeke holds up his hand to shush him and he again hears the number and niners lingo from the tower that is meaningless to Eli.

Minutes later they are on the ground. Before he starts his checklist, Zeke says, "It's good to be uncomfortable sometimes, most people should do it more often."

Eli shakes off his seatbelt and gets up ready to stalk off the plane.

"Hold up there, Speedy," You need to take a few of those boxes with you and since you don't know where you are going you may want to follow instead of lead."

Eli, still angry, realizes Zeke is right. "Whatever. I'm never getting on a plane with you again. I guess that is what matters most."

Zeke either doesn't hear him or doesn't care to respond. He finishes his task, stands up, and heads to the back of the plane where he sorts a small stack of boxes by the door, which he opens and then drops the stairs down. Zeke climbs down the stairs and walks over to the biggest man Eli has ever seen, well other than Andre the Giant in wrestling and *The Princess Bride* when he was a kid.

The giant gave Zeke a casual two-finger salute or something, before engulfing the little old man in a hug. It looks more like a grizzly bear mauling someone than a hug. As usual, Zeke tolerates for a moment before pushing away. "Come on Terrance, you know I have stuff to do, places to be, people to see. I got a helper for you." He changes the tone of his voice when he says helper and makes it sound like a joke.

None of this is lost on Eli who starts bringing down boxes. Once they are on the ground he asks, "Where do you want these?"

"All business?" the man asks in his deep growl of a voice, "I'm Terrance Fishburn," he announces holding out his hand to Eli.

"I'm Eli Asher, nice to meet you." Eli offers his hand to shake and it disappears like a ball into a glove. He is more than a little relieved when he gets it back. Both men pull hand sanitizer out of their pockets.

"I don't have time for this lollygagging," Zeke says. "I have to fill up and get gone, you know."

"Okay, okay," the big man agrees. He walks up the steps, the plane sinking a little under his weight, bends deeply to get through the door. He appears a moment later with the large box that had been on the floor instead of a seat like the other boxes. He sets it in the bed of a truck with the other boxes and the whole truck sinks a little under the weight.

"See you next time," Zeke says already halfway up the stairs. What seems like a second later, the engine can be heard and he is taxiing over to get fuel.

"Do you mind if I take a quick minute and call my wife and maybe use the bathroom?" Eli asks, wanting to ask for lunch also, but not wanting to have things start poorly with Terrance.

Terrance rubs his fingertips through the short stubble he has on his chin. "I could use a bite, why don't you take care of your business and meet me in the cafe over there." Terrance gestures to the small building.

"That's perfect. Thank you. I'll see you in just a minute."

Acutely aware of the humidity pressing in on him he walks to the side of the squat building Terrance pointed to and calls his wife in the shade.

The call is answered on the second ring; "Hello, love."

"Hi, honey. I just have a quick minute, but I wanted to call you and let you know that I'm okay and that I love you and Mason so much. I know I say it all the time, but I still don't think I say it enough."

"We love you too. Where are you? What are you doing? How did all this happen?" Eli interrupts laughing, "I'm in Mississippi. I'm helping rebuild some houses that were destroyed in a tornado in the middle of coronavirus. How it happened is a longer story I'll tell you tonight."

"Tickets must have been a fortune for the same day, or did you have more notice?"

"I just found out this morning the same as you. We didn't pay for tickets, so don't worry and you'll never believe this, but I flew on a private jet, not a commercial airline."

"Honey this all seems a little strange, are you sure this is okay?"

"Well, I'm not a hundred percent positive, but I am ninety-five percent sure that this will be a good thing. Right now, I'm just happy I got here alive. My pilot was a jerk and had me follow him around with these tiny little boxes while he was carrying these great big ones and he is old as dirt so I looked like an ass. Everybody was giving me the stink eye and all I was doing was following his directions. And honestly, I wasn't enthused about getting on a plane with a pilot as old as Father Time."

Before Rachel can respond Eli notices Terrance through the window.

"I have to go. I'll call you this evening as soon as I can. I'll tell you everything I know and more about my flight and what I'm doing here. Don't worry I'll talk to you soon. Bye."

Eli pauses for a moment waiting for her to say goodbye back.

"Bye, I love you."

He hangs up and shoves his phone into his pocket and hustles into the building for the bathroom.

When he enters the café, the table is covered in plates. There are a couple of egg meat and potato breakfast options, a couple of burger and fry options, and some things he doesn't recognize at first glance.

Terrance smiles when he sees him and motions for him to join him at the table, "You're just in time. Hopefully one of these will appeal to you." He motions to the plates on the table. Eli's hand pauses above a plate filled with a burger and a huge pile of fries.

"Go ahead help yourself," Terrance encourages.

Eli sits down and pulls the plate in front of him getting ready to tuck in. He searches for something else to say and sees Terrance put half a hamburger in his mouth with one bite and decides he better get busy eating also. By the time Eli has finished his burger and most of the fries, the four plates in front of Terrance are also empty. He lets out a quiet burp, "Excuse me."

"I have to tell you, that was impressive. You've got to be the biggest guy I've ever seen."

"Probably the darkest too," Terrance says somewhere between a question and a statement. Eli nods suddenly uncomfortable. The big man laughs a deep hearty laugh.

"Tell you what, it takes a mighty awful lot to get me wound up, so you relax. I understand we're going to be working together for a while. I imagine the time will pass more comfortably if we're okay talking with each other."

"Sounds good, this is already off to a better start than my flight. I honestly don't know much about what work we'll be doing. I was told we're rebuilding some houses?"

"Let's get up and go visit someplace else. Once we get on the road, I'll tell you all about it," Terrance replies agreeably. He gets up and lumbers towards the cash register, Eli trails behind.

"I've got this."

"Thanks." Eli wanders towards the door to wait for Terrance to finish paying.

He follows Terrance out the door and back to the truck where they both climb in. Eli is amazed at how much the shocks compress when Terrance sits down. Terrance makes a few turns on what all looks like back roads until they are on a two-lane paved highway.

"So how was your flight?" Terrance asks to break the ice.

"That pilot is a piece of work; I can tell you that. I'm lucky to be alive. I can't believe that guy still has his license."

"Zeke? It sounds like he liked you. What happened?"

"Ha, liked me! I seriously doubt it. He almost killed me screwing around over the gulf. I'm telling you, we were this close from the water." He says, holding his thumb and forefinger a couple of inches apart to show what a close call it was.

Terrance nods, "I was right; he did like you if he helped you find your compass."

"Find my compass?" Eli asks, starting to have misgivings about Terrance thinking he may be crazy too.

"Oh, he does that now and again when he meets folks he likes." He pauses looking over Eli, "I'm guessing you've got kids?"

Eli nods in agreement, "Yes, a son."

"Yeah, he's got a soft spot for young parents. You should feel very flattered, he doesn't do that for everyone."

"Flattered is not what I was feeling," Eli says and tries to modulate his tone and be less sharp with the huge man sitting next to him, "I wouldn't imagine he does that for everyone, he probably wouldn't have his license anymore if he did."

"Zeke is one of the best pilots in the world. Most everybody I know would get in the plane with him before they would with one of them fancy Blue Angels. Between Korea and Vietnam, he saved an awful lot of lives and has been flying ever since, putting in more hours per year than hobbyists do in a lifetime. I'm sure it felt different and that's by design, but believe me, you were not in any danger for a second."

"Wow, I had no idea," Eli admits. "I'm still a little lost on the compass thing."

"Ah, that's Zeke's thing, that's what he calls it. It's about values clarification, I imagine. While he was serving, he had plenty of close calls with death and understands the clarity it can bring. Most people don't get that experience or if they do, they don't survive it. When people are facing their death, they don't usually wish they had worked more or bought a bigger car. Those seconds when you think your life is going to be over, it's the things you think about in those seconds that Zeke thinks are the most important. I know he isn't for everyone, but he was trying to give you a gift," Terrance insists.

"That is pretty out there but does make some sense. I still don't get the compass part." Now that he has a different perspective on the situation, he tries to fully understand.

"If you know what your values are you can figure out if you are going in the right direction or not depending on if a decision or action is in alignment with your values or not."

Eli is glad he is already sitting down. That would have knocked him on his butt. Wow, so simple, yet somehow elegant and it came from a most unexpected source. If these are the kind of people in this group, he is glad he made this crazy leap of faith. Still, there is one more thing that doesn't fit in this new wise man imparting gifts version of Zeke.

Eli, very careful to have his tone not sound confrontational asks, "Was he trying to give me a gift when he had me follow him through the FBO in Riverside with a tiny box while he had two great big ones stacked up over his head?"

Terrance burst out laughing his booming voice filling the small cab. He laughs so hard he swerves into the shoulder for a second before he quickly corrects, "He's still doing that?" he asks, still laughing. "He did that to me my first day in Vietnam. He wasn't as old then, but he was older than most of us. You have to understand Zeke, and I'll be the first to admit that's not an easy thing, but yes, he was trying to give you a gift there too. I'm guessing he liked what you had to say about being a father but thought your ego was puffed up or you were talking like a one-man show. Most of us could use a little more humility but not too many of us are open to the lesson."

Eli's mind is racing a mile a minute trying to recall his early-morning conversation with Zeke and wondering what he might've said that made the old man like him and worse, like him enough to want to give him gifts. As the silence lengthens, Eli gets uncomfortable and breaks it by asking, "What's his deal with young parents?"

Terrance starts squirming in his seat looking uncomfortable like a kid just caught with his hand in the cookie jar. "I don't carry tales about others generally and if I thought you'd ever get an answer I'd tell you to ask yourself." He looks around as if he is expecting Zeke to pop up out of the truck bed.

"Look I don't know too many people who like to talk about that stuff, especially with people that weren't over there. What I'll tell you is this, by the time Zeke got back from his third tour in Vietnam, his head was pretty messed up. He had a wife and a couple kids waiting for him, but the man that came back to them wasn't the one that left them. He was having a real hard time adapting and he was worried about how hard having him around was on them." His voice drops really low to signify he's getting to the deepest part of Zeke's secrets, "He was scared that he might hurt one of them, so he left to protect them. After he got himself straightened out, he worked things out pretty nice with his ex-wife and they were friends right up until she passed a couple years ago. I understand that he's got some contact with his daughter, but his son still doesn't have anything to do with him."

Eli flinches a little at the last line. He can't imagine Mason unwilling to be in his life, to talk to him, to spend time with him, just be in each other's presence. He is shocked to find his heart going out to the old cuss that had given him such a hard time this morning, but also to any father who walks out on his family. He hasn't had anything to do with his father in almost thirty years and his only regret is he hasn't had the opportunity to reject him should his father ever try to get in touch. Eli is all too aware of where that deep rut in his mind will take him if he follows it, he changes the subject, taking a page out of his wife's book.

"So, where are we going? What are we doing?"

"Reasonable questions." Terrance accepts the change of subject. "In case you don't know we were in Tishomingo, Mississippi and we're heading to Speck, Mississippi to rebuild a couple homes that were destroyed by a tornado during all this virus trouble. I reckon this would be a good time to ask if you got any construction experience?"

"Sort of," Eli responds wishing he could offer a better answer. "When I was a kid, I had a neighbor who was a handyman and he let me work with him sometimes on big projects or during the summer. I really enjoyed it. He taught me some things, but I've never worked construction..." his admission trails off.

"Don't you worry, I'm used to working with folks of all different kinds of backgrounds and experience levels. I'm sure we'll put you to good use." As if on cue, Terrance turns off the highway and two quick turns later, he pulls into a driveway. In the yard there is a foundation, the beginnings of a very small house.

A tiny elderly woman with white hair hobbles up to Terrance and gives him a hug as soon as he gets out of the truck. "I was just thankin' the Lord for you, you are certainly doing his work. I don't care what anyone else thinks, I know you're an angel. I am grateful for you." She waves both of her arms towards the newly poured foundation so enthusiastically that Eli is afraid she is going to tip over backwards.

"I see my house rising from the destruction and I am reminded that God is good all the time. Bless you." Before Terrance has a chance to respond, she shuffles off to the car waiting at the curb, the young woman in the driver seat looking impatient. The woman climbs in with an agility that belies her age and the car quickly speeds away.

"I take it she's the homeowner. How do you know her? Are you related?"

"Why, because we're black?"

Eli steps back shocked and miserable. It didn't occur to him that anything in his question could be seen as racist.

Terrance's deep booming laugh saves him from his misery, and he can't help joining in with the joyous sound.

"I'm sorry I just can't help messing with you. You make it too easy. I know Miss Hattie from church and no, we're not related."

"I have friends back home and we give each other a lot of sh..." he pauses trying to come up with a better option, "guff, but everything I've heard about the South? People say you need a passport to come down here and it just seems like the whole race issue is different here. Though I guess it's more complicated at home than I even realized."

"It is complicated here too, no denying that. I decided a long time ago to simplify it for myself. People that come at me with hate I avoid as much as humanly possible. People that come to me with kindness and love, that's what they get back from me. I don't care what flavor they are, all that other stuff's just details I don't fret about."

Eli looks more comfortable and confident with a big smile. He is quickly coming to like this mountain of a man. "Can I ask you something?"

"You can ask me anything you want. I'm not guaranteeing I'll answer." His smile implies he probably will answer.

"Why do you stay here, in the South I mean, Mississippi?" Eli trails off.

"You mean because I should take this handsomeness to Hollywood?" he asks, moving his hand over his face and body.

Eli knows someone his size could probably get some roles, but no one would mistake Terrance for handsome. His huge head matches his huge body, but his features are even more exaggerated, and they certainly aren't chiseled, more like they are partially melted.

"Well that too, of course."

"Why do you stay where you're from? Where are you from?"

"The Pacific Northwest. Portland, Oregon to be specific. I stay there because there's a lot of high-paying jobs, great schools, mild weather."

"Nope, that most certainly is not why I stay here." Terrance amuses himself with his answer and laughs again.

"Some years back when I was more involved with the church, I took a bunch of them Sunday school kids to one of them ropes course camp things. I watched those kids with the instructor whenever they let me. I thought it was pretty interesting. One thing that fella said stuck with me, he said that the course was challenge by choice."

Terrance walks over to the back of the truck, punches a box open, pulls the toolbelt out, gathers some things to fill it out and hands it to Eli who accepts it and puts it around his waist. Terrance goes to the cab of the truck, pushes the seat forward and pulls out the toolbelt of his own. "We better work while we jaw, I don't want to answer to Miss Hattie."

Terrance grabs a roll of papers from behind the seat also and walks to a stack of two by fours next to the foundation. He rolls out papers Eli can see they are plans; the top page has all the specs for framing.

"Do you know what this means?" Terrance gestures to the paper.

"Yes, sort of," Eli admits, "I'll certainly want someone double checking me at first at least. But yes, I understand what this is."

"Fair enough," Terrance takes out a carpenter's pencil and circles a section of wall and says, "Why don't we build this section together so we can see how it goes?"

The two men fall into rhythm working together very naturally. Eli notices that Terrance gives each nail a small tap to hold it in place and then sinks it entirely with one hit. He tries to mimic him a couple times, but the nails either go flying or end up bent so he goes back to his three or four taps to sink each nail. The only evidence that Terrance notices his failed attempts is the small smile at the corner of his mouth.

CHAPTER 8

As the day wears on, Terrance is working steadily when Eli interrupts, "How do you breathe here without scuba gear?"

Eli wipes the sweat from his face for the hundredth time in the last hour. Terrance carefully lifts the tarp, looks around the cooler and slowly pulls it out. He opens the lid and reveals it's full of partially melted ice, bottled water and Gatorade.

"I guess they make them fragile up there in the Northwest. Help yourself, if you need more, we can go get some later on." Eli grabs one of each, opens both, then alternates between the water and Gatorade taking deep gulps of both trying to quench his thirst and replace all the fluids he has lost.

"Talk about making them fragile. You look like a kid scared of a monster under their bed moving that tarp." Eli looks pretty pleased with himself, holding his own with the big man's ribbing.

"That's because you reach under things without looking and you're liable to get bit by a rattlesnake. I should've warned you of that from the start. We've got a couple different types, but the one you especially do not want to cuddle with is the Eastern Diamondback. They're much less common than they used to be, but they do enjoy a nice place to catch some shade, and since humanity hit pause for a while, they've been around more in areas that they normally wouldn't."

"I'd think a guy your size could just say boo and the snake would slither off crying," Eli replies, and Terrance smiles at him.

"I thought you said there were great schools out there in the Northwest." His smile turns into a cheshire grin.

"There are, I never said I went to one." Eli parlays back. "Can I ask you something?"

"We've been through this."

"Fine, fine. What did you mean when you said you think life is challenge by choice? It's been challenging for me lately and I sure don't feel like it was a choice."

"There are always going to be challenges. A lot of times you can choose your challenge."

"How so?" Eli interjects.

Terrance slowly ambles back over towards the work area, bringing a Gatorade that he sets by his feet. "Look at how most people eat these days; they eat a bunch of stuff that's easy. Fast food, processed food, a quick fix. Then they don't feel good or their kids get sick all the time. Or another example, school; it's not easy paying for college and doing all the work to graduate, but it's not easy to work low-paying jobs and struggle your whole life. It seems to me like a lot of folks would be better off choosing a little more challenge up front for a lot more easy down the road."

Eli sets an empty water bottle next to the cooler and reaches inside for another water and takes that and his half-full Gatorade back to the work area. Obviously deep in thought, he almost trips on his hammer he had left on the ground.

Terrance gestures to the loop on the toolbelt as if to say there's a spot for that.

"Never thought of it that way. That makes a lot of sense, and I can't say I disagree but how about the times that you can't choose your challenge? I don't think anybody would choose COVID-19. How does that fit into your challenge by choice theory of the world?"

"Like I said, a lot of times you get to choose your challenge, sometimes you don't. Those are the times you get to choose how you react to them. There are a lot of folks that did a lot of good for other folks during this hullabaloo. There's a lot of folks that used the time and all the free things available to learn new things and up their skills in some way or even just reconnect with family in a deeper way. Then there's a lot of folks that ran out and bought guns and hoarded things and became the worst as they prepared for the worst. All of those were choices and each of those choices has their own challenges. I believe you want to get paid in dollars not wisdom," he gives him a wink so Eli will know he is playing, mostly. "We better get back to it."

The two men fall back into their rhythm, working together and taking the occasional break to cool down and banter with each other. Eli is enjoying the exchanges with Terrance, humidity aside, he likes being outside after being cooped up so long and it feels good to be doing something to help someone else, even though he is getting paid. His body is starting to complain about the intensity and pace of the work, at the same time, it is the movement and exercise he has been craving and needing.

What he enjoys most of all is the time they work together without conversation. His mind is racing with this idea of life being "challenge by choice." Terrance made very good points about eating and health, as well as education and work.

Eli realizes Rachel is the one, more often than not, who is behind the food choices that keep them all relatively healthy. He can also see without her and without this realization, he would've gone far the other way with all the stress of the past few months.

He wishes that he'd had this conversation, before he lost his job or even shortly thereafter, about the family's medical coverage. With the Cobra payment being so large and his unemployment being a fraction of his wages, it was an easy choice at the time to let the insurance lapse.

As soon as Mason got his concussion and the medical bills from his ambulance ride and his night in the hospital, and the subsequent visits came rolling in, he knew he had made a huge mistake. That was only one of many that he could see now, and with money being tight, he wasn't able to put any of his unemployment aside for taxes either and as the year flies by, he becomes more haunted by the decision.

Rachel kept offering to hit pause on her nurse practitioner degree and work full time until he was able to get another job. That would be an easy choice and one he had been smart enough to see would be expensive on the backend. He wasn't able to start college until his mid-twenties because he didn't want to go into massive debt. His mom couldn't help significantly, but made a little too much to qualify for aid. He worked and saved and did a full year at the community college before he even started at the four-year school. When he dropped out of college with one year to go, they thought it would be a year at most before he was back in school.

Then they found out they were going to have Mason and the time flew by. You get a certain momentum when you're in a school that is hard to get back when you stop. He didn't want to take that chance with Rachel's education. He had wondered if he would ever make it back, after today he knew at some point, he would choose the challenge of going back over the challenge of continuing to do the types of jobs he had been doing.

The more he considers the challenges they have chosen consciously and unconsciously it becomes even more clear that Rachel instinctively understands the value of choosing the challenge that makes things harder today so that things can be easier in the future.

He wonders if she is aware of that or if it was unconscious for her. He doesn't like how the realization feels and he doesn't like the way he chose to react to some of the challenges he faced. He makes a vow to himself that once he gets home, he will choose his challenges and responses to challenges consciously and powerfully.

Terrance notices the difference in cadence with which Eli strikes the nails, it is faster with a more resolute smack. He looks over to see what is going on, Eli is deep in thought, about what, he can't guess. He turns back to work just as a horn honks and a car pulls quickly into the drive coming to a fast stop next to his truck stirring up a cloud of dust.

His lips crawl up into a smile when he hears a familiar voice barking orders. His mouth begins to water before the smell of the food reaches him.

"Young sir, you're going to want to get over here for this." He walks over to his truck and lowers the tailgate as a swarm of stairstep boys and girls bring dishes, food and silverware from the trunk to the makeshift table. The swarm quickly piles back into the car which is already moving before the last door is closed completely. "Thank you, Miss Ethel," Terrance calls out, waving the new cloud of dust from his face.

"Have you ever had real southern cooking?" Terrance asks Eli, licking his lips in anticipation.

Eli shrugs to say 'what's the big deal?' "I have had fried chicken before," he says nodding towards the heaping plate of it on the tailgate.

Terrance holds up a hand to halt him, "Before you try to defend what you had before as food, try some of this." He holds out his hand to get Eli to dish up first.

Eli does, suddenly starving, he piles his plate high with fried chicken, mashed potatoes, green bean casserole, and is quite disappointed to realize he doesn't have room on his plate for what looks like a big pumpkin pie.

Terrance also piles up his plate and Eli is impressed to see how high he can go vertically with food and not drop a crumb on his way to the now smaller pile of two by fours. He sits down and starts eating in the same instant. Eli is close on his heels and does the exact same thing. But he stops after his first bite, savoring the tenderness and all the new flavors in this fried chicken, completely unlike anything he's ever experienced before. He now knows in an irrevocable, experiential way that the fast-food chains that claim to have southern fried chicken are full of something that definitely isn't southern fried chicken.

They both focus on emptying their plates, loading them up, and doing it again. This time when they are finished, Terrance lets out a deep rumbling burp, "Excuse me." Eli waves him off does his very best to top Terrance's burp with one of his own but falls a little short. "Are you thinking what I'm thinking?" Terrance asks.

"If you're thinking about that pie then yes, I am." Eli agrees. Wordlessly they both make their third trip to the tailgate. Eli is startled to see how little of the massive spread remains.

"How big a piece do you want?" Terrance asks moving the knife around on the pie anywhere from a thin sliver to a half of the pie sized piece.

"There," Eli says when Terrance is at about a quarter of the pie. He scoops the piece out carefully and puts it on Eli's plate. He picks up the pie and his fork and goes back to the stack of wood. Eli takes his first bites, laughing a little about Terrance eating the other three-fourths of the pie straight out of the pan, "This isn't pumpkin but it's still delicious, what is this?"

"This here is southern sweet potato pie. I would've told you it's why I stay here, but it wouldn't have made any sense to you until now."

In between bites and "yums," Eli asks, "What is the deal with the food delivery service?"

"It's how folks are around here. If somebody dies, somebody's hurt, if somebody is sick or somebody's busy all day doing for somebody else, you're gonna get fed and fed right."

Eli surprises himself saying "Amen to that." They don't disrespect their pie with any more talking. When they are finished, they both rub their stomachs. Terrance looks at the sky and his watch. "I was hoping to get another hour or more in today." Eli tries to hide his disappointment and stifles a yawn as he stands up.

"I honestly don't think I have it in me after all this, if you don't either that's fine. If you want to work, you go on ahead, I'll be right here watching," Terrance says and Eli laughs and sits back down relieved.

His relief is quickly gone when he realizes he has no idea where he'll be staying the night. Just then a truck pulls up at the house. Two boys who look to be in their teens jump out and start waving their hands and pointing right and left to guide the driver so he can back the trailer up over the curb and park it in the center of the yard, where an orange extension cord and hose await a couple of feet away.

When they finish, one of the boys holds his hand up as high as he can over his head "What up, big T?" Terrance holds his hand easily two feet above the boys. The boy leaps straight up and catches the bottom of Terrance's palm for a high five. The second boy, a slightly shorter kid, comes to do the same thing, Terrance adjusting about 6 inches lower this time. "You guys staying out of trouble?" Terrance asks.

"Like we have any choice, Pop keeps us so busy we don't have time for nothing."

"Smart man your father. You tell him I said thank you." They nod in agreement and start walking towards the truck. The horn blares and the boys slow down almost imperceptibly. Terrance chuckles and shakes his head good-naturedly.

He turns his attention back to Eli, "I hope you don't mind the travel trailer. I'm in that one," he motions a few driveways down. "If you don't stay on-site, materials tend to walk away. If you're not okay staying here, I can run you over to my place and pick you up in the morning." Terrance offers.

Eli walks towards the extension cord and hose and says, "Honestly, wasn't expecting fancy things like electricity and running water down here in the South, so this'll do just fine."

"You're assuming that those connect and work." Terrance gets the last laugh seeing the dismay on Eli's face. "Luckily for you they do," he says with a satisfied grin as he quickly hooks up the trailer.

Terrance is busy leveling it, putting some blocks under the jack while Eli gets his bag out of the cab of the truck. Terrance is kicking some rocks under the back tires to prevent it from rolling. Eli pauses at the door to see if Terrance wants anything else.

"I usually like my breakfast first thing, but if you'd like to get some work done before it gets warm enough for you to start melting, we could have it a little later in the morning. What do you think?"

"I think as a comedian you better keep your day job. I'll eat breakfast whenever you want, especially if it's half as good as dinner was."

"I'll see you at six then. You know where I'm at if you need anything. 'Member to watch out for snakes if you go walking around." Seeing the skepticism on the younger man's face he continues, "I'm not trying to scare you, just make sure you pay attention. Most of the folks that get bit have it coming from trying to either catch or kill the snake. Can't blame any living thing for trying to defend itself when its life is threatened. The other reason people get bit is they aren't paying attention in areas snakes like to be."

"Okay, I'll pay attention. See you in the morning," Eli agrees. He enters the trailer, it's older but set up very efficiently and it's spotless. The double bed is fully made up for him, in the spot he assumes doubles as the kitchen table. He lies down prepared for misery and is pleasantly surprised when he finds the mattress to be incredibly comfortable. He is asleep seconds later.

Something is buzzing at him, his arm flails around trying to stop the sound that's disturbing his sleep. His hand makes contact with his phone and the rap to his knuckles wakes him up enough to realize someone's calling. He picks up the phone just in time to miss Rachel's call, as he goes to call her back, he can see that she's called several times over the last half hour.

"Hi honey," he says, his voice groggy.

"What are you doing? I was starting to get scared. I didn't hear from you and you weren't answering your phone."

"I'm sorry, I worked my tail off today, I laid down for a second to see if the bed was comfortable before I called you and I just woke up. You don't need to worry about me, Terrance is great. The only thing I don't like about him so far is that he doesn't live in the Northwest. I'd like to hang out with him if he did and I'd love for you and Mason to get a chance to meet him."

"That's great! I'm glad you like who you're working with and I know it can make work a lot more pleasant. Are you really rebuilding houses?"

"Yes, that's why I'm so tired. I haven't done work like this in a long time. It feels good though, maybe I'll come back without the dad bod," he yawns again, unable to stop.

"As long as you come back healthy and soon, I'll be happy. You sound really tired, you want me to call you in the morning?"

"I am really tired, but I don't think you're going to want to call me in the morning. Terrance is going to get me up at six, which is four o'clock your time. Hopefully, since we are starting so early, we'll stop earlier tomorrow and I'll be able to talk longer. There's so much I want to tell you about."

"Okay," she agrees.

"Let me say good night to Mason and then I'll say good night to you."

"It's 9:30 here. He's been in bed for almost 2 hours and I think he fell asleep as fast as you did tonight. I will wake him up if you want me to, but I think it might be better for both of you to talk tomorrow."

"Is he okay?" Eli runs his hand over the bedding seeking a tactile substitute for his wife and son.

"He is okay. I know he misses you and I think he's a little stressed. Change is hard for him. I will warn you now to be ready for the dog question when you do talk to him."

Eli groans "If our landlord would allow pets, he would have ten dogs by now just to be done with the conversation."

"Preaching to the choir on that one. I told him that we will get one someday. And reminded him again that we can't get one while we live here."

"And you still think he's going to ask me when we talk?" Eli is a little surprised. He and Rachel have always done a good job of presenting a united front on big issues. Mason gave up trying to divide and conquer, and other common kid workarounds, long ago.

"Turns out it was a poor choice of words, now he thinks we should move. You're fading fast and that's not good considering the state you were in when we started the call. We can talk about it more tomorrow, get some sleep. I love you."

"I love you too, good night." He disconnects the call, stumbles his way to the bathroom and is back in bed and asleep in two minutes flat.

CHAPTER 9

C hapter 9

Eli wakes up slowly, his whole body hurting. It takes him a minute to remember where he is and why he feels like he was run over by a truck. He sits up slowly and puts his legs over the edge of the bed debating the merits of getting up to relieve his bladder versus laying back down and not moving another inch until Terrance shows up. He can't get over how much he hurts. He takes walks with his son, picks up his son. He carries groceries, he helps clean the house. Sure, no gym for a long time and yeah, he gained a few pounds during the lockdown, but this is ridiculous.

Determined, he gets up and makes his way to the small bathroom with the plastic accordion door. He pees for what feels like an eternity and turns on the water in the shower to see if there is any hot water in the trailer. He gets his answer soon enough and quickly strips with his knees and elbows bumping into something with every movement.

He steps into the shower and savors the feel of the hot water cascading over his sore body. The shower pressure is moderate at best, and at that moment it's the second-best shower he can remember. He forgot to bring his own body wash or shampoo with him, so he is very grateful to whoever was kind enough to put a hotel-size bar of soap as well as a mini bottle of shampoo and conditioner on the shelf.

He lathers up and the hot water runs out. He jumps and stifles a yell. It isn't a polar bear swim, but it isn't warm either. He rinses off quickly and gets out. Cold showers aren't a favorite for him, but he has to admit they will wake you up. There is a towel on the hook on the bathroom door and since it is the only one in sight, he guesses it is meant for him and pats dry. He wraps the towel around his waist and goes to his bag. He pulls out a fresh pair of briefs, a comfortable pair of jeans, his lightest t-shirt, and fresh socks.

After he finishes getting dressed, he pokes around in the travel trailer some more towels. He finds a little closet with a broom and dustpan and three more towels folded on the shelf above the hanging rod. He gets all of the office-type work clothes he brought and hangs them up. "Better late than never," he thinks, noticing he will have to do some ironing.

He finds a twin pull-down bunk at the other end of the trailer and dumps the contents of his bag onto it. Once he has everything in the correct groupings, he pushes the bunk up. It hangs open an inch or two but is out of the way. He hopes it will go back to closing normally when he is gone. If it doesn't, he is sure Terrance will help him fix it.

He goes to the bathroom and empties the few toiletries he brought and finds homes for everything in the closet-sized bathroom's small medicine cabinet, on the sink, and the floor of the shower. He picks up his electric razor to shave and discovers the battery is dead. He plugs it in to be ready the next day. Terrance appears to be a fan of stubble anyway.

Finally, he rehangs the towel, gets his dirty clothes off the floor, and puts them in the now empty bag. He will use it as a hamper since there doesn't seem to be any other options. The clothes are pretty ripe with the sweat of labor and a body that hasn't learned that sweating does little to cool you in a humid climate. He closes the bag and tosses it on the floor of the closet. He goes back a second later and moves them so the office clothes won't be wrinkled and stinky.

He is moving better after the shower but is still feeling each movement in unpleasant ways. He lies back down on the bed and does some awkward approximations of some yoga stretches Rachel has shown him over the years for various aches and pains. When he finishes, he has to admit he feels better. That of course reminds him of the thousands of ways Rachel improves his life. He picks up his phone and glances at the time. He still has ten minutes before Terrance is due to arrive. It is too early to call Rachel, but he has enough time to send her a text she can see when she wakes up.

Good morning, my love. You wake me in such sweet ways. I know this isn't nearly as good, but I want you to know that I miss you and love you and after ten plus years I still really like you...a lot. I wish I could be with you this morning, but I will be again soon. Until then I'll be thinking of you both.

He fusses with the message and changes some words and pretty much ends up with what he started with. He hears a knock on the door, he hits send, relieved to be done with it. He doesn't understand for the life of him why that stuff is so hard sometimes. Rachel makes it look so easy too. She always knows the perfect thing to say and when the perfect thing is to say nothing.

He opens the door with a smile.

"Good to see you up. I was afraid you might still be in bed moaning and groaning about working half a day yesterday." The big man smiles to show his ribbing is good-natured.

"And miss a minute of quality time with you? No way." He jumps off the top of the two-step fold-under iron stairs Terrance must have pulled out this morning. He wishes he hadn't done it as soon as he hits the ground. It is only about a foot, maybe a foot and a half down, but his already protesting body reprimands him as though it had been ten feet.

He looks up and sees Terrance's neck. On the top step, he is close to eye level, on the ground he discovers he has to look up quite a bit more to see the man's face when they stand this close. "How tall are you anyway?"

"How tall do you think?"

Eli thinks for a minute; he is five-eleven, a little taller than average but not much. Terrance is much taller. Eli comes to his chest.

"Seven, seven-one?"

"Me? Naw." His voice is full of what turns out to be false modesty.

They both start towards the truck while they continue talking.

"That cute little fella, what's his name? Oh, right, Shaq. He is seven-one. I'm seven-four."

"What do you weigh?"

"Stop being ugly now, there is no cause for that."

Eli is unfamiliar with the phrase but understands he doesn't want to disclose his weight.

"Sorry I didn't realize you were sensitive about your girlish figure," he teases sliding into the passenger side.

"I was playing. I was about three-fifty in fighting shape, nowadays let's just say I'm around four."

Eli lets out a whistle. He's been one-seventy-five for years and was upset when the scale crept up almost ten pounds over the last six months. He can't imagine tipping the scales at four hundred. Of course, it would look much different on him than it does Terrance, who has a bit of a belly, but also has a lot of muscle and is far from obese.

"You're like a reverse Yoda."

"How do you figure, nerd boy?" he asks, pulling into the parking lot of a local favorite greasy spoon that is only open from six to eleven am.

"Yoda was little and green, you're big and black. You both have an interesting perspective and live in alien swamps."

"Ha, ha, you got jokes huh? Don't be having too much fun with the South if you're going to sit at my table."

"Will there be room for me?"

Terrance laughs and holds his thumb and finger together and looks at Eli between the two.

"That much huh? I'll make do."

They both pull on their masks and Terrance opens the door. Eli runs into him when he stops abruptly. Terrance takes a step back and pulls the mask down showing his face to the hostess at the counter.

"I'm just here to eat. I don't mean anybody any harm."

The hostess sits frozen.

"Just get in here and sit down. Stop making a spectacle of yourself."

A sassy little redhead barks. Terrance looks at the hostess, who looks at the redhead, who nods. The hostess gives him a little nod. He pulls his mask back on and walks to a table, Eli follows confused by the whole thing.

Once seated the redhead hands them menus. She is off before Eli can ask for the coffee he really wants. He moves to motion her back over.

"Hold up there," Terrance assures. Seconds later she sets down two cups, a glass pot, and a bowl of creamers so full they go everywhere when she slams them down. She whips a pen out of her pocket and looks at Terrance.

"The usual?" He nods.

"You?"

"Two eggs, over medium, hash browns, links, and wheat toast."

She walks off without another word. Eli can't quite discern if she is frosty toward Terrance and by extension him, or if she is just too busy to waste seconds or words on niceties. Eli adds some cream to his coffee, takes a sip and adds four times the cream and an ice cube. Terrance watches appreciating his treatment of the coffee.

"It could melt a spoon," he whispers, "now you understand." He points to the creamer and adds several to his cup.

"I notice you don't have the same ring that Zeke and some others I've seen had."

"Are you asking if I'm in his group?"

Eli nods.

"No. I am a Marine and always will be." Terrance lowers his voice and leans forward; Eli doesn't understand the need in the middle of the loud and busy restaurant. "And I'm a Christian, at least as much as I can stand to be. That's as much joining and belonging as I can tolerate. It's a good outfit best I can tell. They helped put Zeke back together when no one else seemed to know how and he got his jet shortly after he hooked up with them. He does better when he is flying. I don't know much more, he said he couldn't tell me, and I respected that. The only reason I know that much is I occasionally need help with projects and they occasionally have someone who needs something to do."

The waitress comes and drops Eli's order and a single plate in front of Terrance. She returns almost immediately with several more plates balanced on her arm. She fills in the empty spots on the table until it resembles a traffic jam.

Eli is still on his first bite when she returns with a new pot of coffee that she trades for the almost empty pot, she plops another bowl of creamers on top of the now empty one and sets the check on the corner by the big guy's elbow.

"She is efficient, but not the friendliest," Eli notes. Terrance shakes his head no.

Eli isn't sure what is going on, so he follows Terrance's lead and eats the rest of his breakfast in silence.

When Terrance finishes his food, he follows it with a final swig of coffee and says, "I'll meet you at the truck."

Eli notices some people giving Terrance sour looks as he walks to the cash register by the front door. He is bewildered now; he can't imagine anyone not liking his new friend. He walks outside and climbs in the truck that is unlocked. Moments later, Terrance climbs in and the truck tilts favoring the driver's side.

"So, there are some who are immune to your charm huh?"

"These days, quite a few."

"Mind if I ask why?"

"Would it matter?" comes the sharp reply.

Eli holds up his hands in surrender, "Yes, it does. You don't need to tell me anything you don't want to."

"I'm sorry, it just frustrates me so."

Eli sits silently waiting to see if he is going to say more. Once he pulls back out on the road he continues.

"Remember how I told you I used to work with the youth group and took them to that ropes course camp?" He continues without waiting for a response, "A few years back one of those kids came to me, she was barely over eighteen and in a bad way. She needed to get an abortion, and she didn't trust her momma or the local law not to force her to keep the baby, no matter how it got there.

I took her across the state line and on up to Nashville. She got what she wanted and if I had been a smarter man, I would have left it at that, like she wanted. I told them they needed to keep a sample from the..." he is at a loss for words for a minute, "sample for evidence since it was the result of incest and rape."

Terrance seems weary and Eli regrets asking. The situation must still be painful for him.

"We got work to do, so I'm going to give you the super-condensed version. By the time the smoke cleared, they ended up not bringing charges against the girl's father. The girl moved up North to live with an auntie so she could try to have a normal life. That man was roaming free and still had a son and another daughter living under his roof. I couldn't let it lie, people kept telling me, but I just couldn't let it lie. I went up there and I put the fear of God," his fist balls up as he says it and the anger is palpable, "in that vile wretch of a man."

Eli resists the urge to cheer.

"They started out trying to charge me for aggravated assault, not for laying hands on that filthy vermin, no matter what the official charges said, it was for helping that poor child get an abortion so she had some hope at a life. Thankfully, some other folks in the area agreed with what I had done, no matter what side they come down on the abortion issue. They made a big fuss and pulled strings and were going to get me a highfalutin lawyer when the DA decided it wasn't worth the hassle. He dropped it down to simple assault and I agreed so I could put it all in the rear-view. Thirty days in jail, a five hundred dollar fine, and I was quietly asked by the Reverend to stop attending church. Here we are, all this time later and you can tell what side someone is on by if they treat me like a saint or Satan himself."

He looks directly at Eli, the man's pain plain as day.

"I've read my bible cover to cover and I can't find a single verse that makes me believe any Heavenly Father would want that little girl to be forced to carry that burden. I used to follow along with the rest of them and think it was a black and white issue. Now, I think there is more gray than anything else in that can of worms."

Eli doesn't know what to say, he wants to applaud Terrance's actions, he wants to protest the way the man was treated. He wants to start a riot on courthouse steps. His mind can barely comprehend the injustice of having the girl's father skate completely and having Terrance spend time in jail and pay a fine. None of that seems like it will help his pain. Rachel occasionally gets annoyed when Eli wants to fix her problems instead of listening.

He tries to remember some of the things she's said to him over the years and finally says, "That was incredible, you are incredible, and I'm glad you were willing to tell me your story."

As they climbed out of the truck, they did what guys often do to ease tension and let off steam.

"You know you're not my type," Terrance says, smirking.

"Please there is no way you could get this. It's way out of your league. I might be an eight, but I'm married to a ten, there is no way I could fall that far."

"Who says you're an eight?" Terrance does an exaggerated belly laugh doubling over.

"She does," Eli says with pride holding up his phone to show a picture of Rachel and Mason.

Terrance nods his head in appreciation, "She is definitely a ten, but I'm not buying that you're an eight. That boy probably will be when he's grown. If he takes after his momma."

He pulls out his phone and kisses the screen before holding it up to show Eli. "This is my Willetta. We were married nearly forty years before cancer and the Lord took her."

"Wow talk about out of your league! How did you manage that one?" Eli responds.

He rests a hand on Eli's shoulder for a moment. "You're a good one Eli, I am glad you're here. What do you say we get some work done?"

Eli nods and no more is said until lunch which Terrance insists on calling dinner, saying, "Dinner is supper around here."

Eli interrupts their inhalation of dinner. "What was all that about the mask when we got to the restaurant? Other people were wearing them. It's a good thing, so what was that?"

"Self-preservation," Terrance quips.

Eli looks at him, waiting for more.

"Generally speaking, wearing a mask is good. When you are a black man in this country, especially one my size, it's complicated."

He looks at Eli to see if he understands. The perplexed expression is his answer.

"Self-preservation," he repeats. "When you look how I look, you want to make other people comfortable. You want to make sure they know they don't need to be nervous or scared."

Still, only confusion is present on the other man's face.

"If I walk in with a mask on and that girl gets scared, she calls the cops. They come and they get scared, I might get shot before they know they don't need to be scared. I make sure she isn't scared. We finish breakfast in peace and get to work."

"You shouldn't have to do that. What a ridiculous, frustrating waste of time," Eli argues.

"Pedestrians shouldn't have to pay attention at crosswalks. If you don't, you might still get killed. It's not about what you should or shouldn't have to do. Someday maybe it will change. Until then, it's about self-preservation." Satisfied, he finally gets his point across.

Eli hangs his head. "The world is way more screwed up than I ever knew."

He looks so sad. Terrance can't abide and does the only thing he can think of. Splat, a green bean hits Eli on his cheek.

He looks up bewildered. Slowly, understanding dawns, and he picks up a green bean from his plate and whips it at Terrance. He tries to duck to avoid it, but Eli had thrown short, so he moves lower just in time for it to bounce off of his forehead. Seconds later, both men are out of ammo and rolling with laughter.

They work the rest of the day with the same rhythm as the day before, periods of quiet while they work and breaks filled with conversation and teasing.

After they finish sharing the dinner or supper, depending on who you asked, that was delivered by another woman who wouldn't get out of the car and instead sent her kids, they both head off to their trailers.

CHAPTER 10

Having learned from his morning experiences, Eli takes a shower. He enjoys the hot water while it lasts and he hopes his aching muscles will be better for it in the morning. He stays in after the hot water is gone so there won't be any risk of falling asleep before he calls his wife. Once he is dry, or as dry as he can get in humidity and partially dressed, he climbs into bed and calls home. The call is answered on the first ring.

"Hi love, we are so glad you called, someone has been waiting very impatiently."

Before he can respond, his son's voice is on the line.

"Hi, Dad. I miss you. When you get home can we move and get a dog?"

Eli can't help but laugh. Subtlety is certainly not part of his son's repartee yet. He is glad Rachel gave him the heads up that the topic is alive and well so he is prepared.

"I need you to really listen. If the TV is on, I want you to turn it off. You need to hear everything I'm about to say, not just parts of it. Okay?"

He gets nothing but silence. Then an "okay." He can hear his son's exhales; he is listening closely no doubt.

"As soon as we can, and this is the most important part you need to hear, as soon as we can, once I have a new job and we have some money saved up, so not right away, but as soon as we can buy a house or find a rental that will let us have a dog, yes you can have any dog you want."

"I want a Rottweiler!"

Afraid Mason might mention their recent visit to Jen's, Eli moves on to distract the boy.

"Okay, you get a Rottweiler and I'll get a black and tan miniature wiener dog, do you know what that is?

"The hotdog shaped dog?"

"Yep, that's the one. We'll tell everyone they are brothers and your dog was the runt of the litter."

Mason erupts in laughter and Eli moves the phone away from his ear waiting for the fits of laughter to cease. It does after a moment.

"Thanks, Dad, I love you."

It sounds like the phone hits the table or some hard surface and the laughter moves farther away.

"Hello? Are you still there?"

"I'm here."

"What did you say to him?" She sounds tense.

"I told him that eventually when we can move after I have a new job and we can buy a house or move to another place where we can have dogs, he can have one."

"I can't wait for you to get home so I can kill you."

"What?"

"Why would you do that to me?"

"What do you mean? I didn't tell him anything you and I haven't talked about before."

"Except we didn't say yes, we said 'not now' before."

After such a good day and feeling pretty good about how he handled the situation with Mason, he is getting frustrated.

"I don't get what the problem is."

"You aren't here, you won't be the one that gets asked twenty-three times a day if we can move and get a dog now? How about now? You know how relentless he is."

"Put him back on the phone."

Exasperated she goes to get Mason whom she finds in his room working hard on a picture.

"Your dad wants to talk to you."

He takes the phone in his left hand not willing to let the call interrupt his artwork.

"What?"

"I want to make sure that you heard everything I said earlier."

"After you get a job and save money we get to move and have a big dog and little dog and we are going to say they are brothers."

Eli has to admit that is excellent recall for a subject that his son has very selective hearing on.

"So, you understand it will take a while and for sure not happen before I get home. Probably by the time you turn ten, but maybe not before then."

"That long?" His distress at the thought is clear.

"Maybe. I hope it happens sooner, but it could take that long. You need to understand that and not bother your mom about getting a dog or when anymore. Can you do that for me?"

"Yes, but we are for real going to get two dogs as soon as we can."

"Yes."

"Can I finish drawing now?"

"Yes. Give the phone back to your Mom."

As soon as he hears the passing of the phone, he starts talking, wanting to head her off at the pass.

"I don't think he'll drive you crazy about it. If he does, I will accept my strangling like a man when I get back."

Not totally convinced, and knowing it is too late to put the toothpaste back in the tube, she lets it go. For now.

"How are you? You sound much better today"

"I feel better. I am sore, but I've had a couple of hot showers and I even did some of those yoga things you showed me this morning."

"That's great. Speaking of morning, thank you for the sweet message. It made it a little easier to wake up without you."

"Good, as long as it doesn't get too easy."

"So, you do want me to suffer, just not too much."

"Yep."

"Be still my beating heart, you sir say the sweetest things. Stop romancing me and tell me more about what is going on."

He gets nervous.

"What do you mean?"

"Tell me about your flight and the guy you are working with, what you are doing, everything, catch me up."

He starts at the beginning. Almost the beginning, he leaves out his call to Abed and joining this order or group or whatever he has gotten himself into and starts at the FBO at the Portland airport.

He tells her about the luxury of the fixed base operator building and how nice it was to see how the other half live and how he thought he was going to get to sit in the spacious leather seats on the jet, but had been forced to sit up front with Zeke while the supposed co-pilot slept through the whole experience. He still wondered if the man was alive or if it was even a person and not a mannequin. He tells her about the scare Zeke gave him, but with the perspective Terrance added.

They laugh together about what a character he was. He tells her about the humidity, the work, and mostly about Terrance. The deep affection he already has for the man is clear to her. She is surprised and happy. Her husband usually isn't one to make fast friends, especially with older men. She had noticed Jim's fatherly affection for her husband right from the start. Eli still fought most of the man's attempts to bond and any offer of help that he ever made. This Terrance must be impressive in more ways than his giant size.

"Honey, you have a work wife. I'm so happy for you."

He is familiar with the term, she used it about Jen when they were working together so much before Rachel had gone back to school. He feels like he should resist the term, but he likes Terrance and certainly is spending more time with the man that he is his wife. Why not? He accepts it, smiling to himself imagining what Terrance's reaction to the title might be.

"I guess I do. Too bad this will be such a short marriage. You know I'm a long-haul kind of guy."

"I understand that, but I'm kind of relieved that I won't have to compete with that for long. Is he for real bigger than Shaq?"

"That's what he says."

"That's a big guy. Can you hold on for a minute, it's time to put Mason to bed."

Eli looks at his watch in disbelief, it has been an hour and a half since he made the call. "Sure."

He hears the tell-tale sound of fabric rubbing across the phone letting him know it is in a pocket. If he strains, he can hear what is being said. He puts the phone on speaker so he will know when she is back.

"If you go brush your teeth, I will take a photo of your picture and send it to your dad. You can say a quick good night while I get you a glass of water."

Eli smiles, the joy of bedtime, the routine and occasional negotiations that go with it. Luckily Mason likes his sleep and has since they brought him home from the hospital. When he did wake up after a quick change and feeding, he was out again, no heroics needed. He was sleeping five or six hours at once by the time he was just a few weeks old. Rachel had been worried about it, but he was gaining plenty of weight and was healthy, so they just enjoyed their good fortune. To this day they both hated it when new parents asked how long it took for him to sleep through the night because they either didn't believe the answer or resented them for their luck.

He googles Shaq while he is waiting for Rachel to come back, he's just finished when he gets a text from her. He opens it to see a picture of a black and tan dog-like creature that is as tall as the house he is next to, one side of him is another black and tan dog about as big as the monster's paw. On the other side of the house are three stick figures, "Dad, Me and Mom" spelled out in crayon above each one.

Suddenly he hears breathing through the phone.

"I like your picture."

"How did you know it was me?" Mason wonders aloud.

"Just a lucky guess," Eli says, breathing hard directly into the phone.

His son is still laughing when he says "Good night."

More sounds of fabric against the phone and what sounds like a hug and kiss before a second more distant good night. A few seconds later, she is back.

"What about me?"

"What?" He's confused.

"What about my dog?"

"You get any dog you want." If only it were all that easy.

"Darn right," she agrees. "Except I don't want three dogs."

He understands she doesn't want to be left out of something that is so important to their son.

"You can take him to the animal shelter or find the Rottie Rescue to get the dog," he offers as a consolation prize since he was the one to give the official yes.

"I can live with that. I never knew you wanted a miniature wiener dog."

"They are cool little freaks of nature you know, plus I thought it would be hilarious to have one that looked like a Rottie and say they are brothers."

"It's so sad Mason seems to have gotten your sense of humor."

"What's wrong with that? My sense of humor is great."

"It's something all right. Why brothers anyway?"

"Siblings," he corrects before changing the subject. "I looked it up while you were putting Mason to bed, Terrance is bigger than Shaq. He is three inches taller and apparently seventy-five pounds heavier."

"Apparently?"

"He is a little evasive about his exact weight. He told me to stop being ugly when I asked him."

"Good for him. Most women I know would love to use that response for those kinds of questions. He sounds like quite a character. Tell me more about him."

He tells her about his appreciation for Eli's work and work ethic and his frequent teasing about him being fragile because of how challenging the humidity is for him, and finally tells her about what Terrance has been through trying to do the right thing for the girl and challenges he was still having with some members of his community.

Rachel just about loses her mind. She is a big supporter of women's rights, civil rights, and justice in general. He has to keep reminding her to keep her voice down so she doesn't wake up Mason and reassures her that it isn't necessary for her to come down there and champion Terrance's cause. When he finally calms her down, they have been on the phone for almost three hours.

"I can't believe we talked this long."

"We can't do this every night. I feel kind of guilty about not spending more time with Mason this evening."

"I'm sure he didn't mind for a night, but I agree we can't do it every night. Besides that, it's two hours later here and I have to get up so early." He yawns at the thought..

"I can take the hint. Good night."

"Sweet dreams."

He hangs up smiling and replaying parts of the conversation in his head. He has always loved how passionate she is, but is very grateful she won't be unleashing her wrath on the unsuspecting community any time soon. He can't believe they can talk for three hours after only being apart for a couple of days. It reminds him of when they were first dating and had talked through the night on more than one occasion in their excitement to get to know each other. He falls asleep thinking of her.

CHAPTER 11

He wakes to his alarm the next morning. Getting up early isn't natural for him, and getting up early in a time zone two hours ahead of his is taking its toll this morning. He gets himself out of bed, relieves himself, and splashes cold water on his face. He decides the stubble will be okay for another day. He gets dressed, stumbles back into the bathroom for some deodorant, and gives his teeth a few swipes with his toothbrush. He opens the door to Terrance's knock with one word on his mind.

"Coffee." Neither a question nor a request, just a simple statement of fact.

"Come on, I've got you, buddy." Terrance pats him on the shoulder and steers him toward the truck.

"I'm not up for Little Miss Thing again this morning."

The big man is unsure what he is saying at first, then it dawns on him.

"Wanda Sue? The waitress?"

"I guess."

Still not clear what Eli is saying, he tries again. "Are you talking about the waitress where we had breakfast yesterday?"

"Yes," he says, acting like Terrance is the one not firing on all cylinders yet.

Terrance makes an abrupt U-turn and turns off the highway about a mile later at an unmarked road. They bounce along while climbing a steep hill. When they reach the top, there is a picturesque house framed by mature trees.

Terrance gets out and walks up onto the front porch. He turns back and sees that Eli has just opened the truck door and isn't even fully standing yet. He gives him a come-on wave and walks in the house, leaving the door open behind him.

Eli makes his way to the porch and notices the door is taller than normal. He finds the same inside. It's not a big house, but all the doorways and ceilings are high. Not completely on board with being fully awake, the strange dimensions have him feeling like he nibbled one of the cakes Alice sampled before she shrunk in her adventure. Once he is through the entry hall, the space opens up to a large kitchen, dining, and living room area. The back wall of the great room is a wall of windows showing a sloping backyard and many acres of trees beyond.

Terrance has just poured two cups of coffee and brings them both to the counter between him and Eli. He gets some flavored creamer from the fridge and a big jar of sugar from the pantry next to it. He sets them both down in front of Eli and fishes out a couple of spoons from a drawer on his side of the counter.

"Sit."

Eli pulls out one of the stools he notices under the overhang the butcher block countertop creates and complies.

Terrance flips the top of what appeared to be a kitchen island up and rummages around for a while, "Hash browns or grits?"

Eli cringes, "Hash browns, please." He's never actually tried grits and plans on keeping it that way. Uncooked, they look like maggots, and after they're cooked, they look like vomit. He doesn't have the imagination to see them tasting good. He adds some vanilla creamer to the coffee and takes a sip. He makes another face; it's very sweet. He overdid it on the creamer, expecting the coffee to be like it had been yesterday morning.

Terrance finds what he was looking for and lines up a few things next to the massive six-burner stove and flips the top of the island down.

He catches the look on Eli's face.

"Sorry, I should have told you my coffee won't burn a hole in your stomach."

Eli just shakes his head to say "no worries." He takes a big swig and adds more coffee to the cup and tries again. It is perfect.

Terrance has all six burners going and places a heavy cast-iron skillet on each burner. He has two burners cooking a heap of hash browns, two frying a dozen or more eggs, and one with bacon, and the last has sausage sizzling.

Eli is looking at the island, still trying to figure out what he had seen, when he can't, he asks, "What's with your island?"

"Freezer."

"What?"

"It's a chest freezer. Willetta was a bitty little thing, and as we got older, it got hard for her to haul in everything I can eat from out in the garage. I brought it in trying to make things easier for her, and we had us a doozy of a fight. I finally faced it with some old barn wood I sanded down and sealed, then I fixed this bit of quartz on top, and you'd have thought I gave her the Hope Diamond. Boy, did she carry on to anybody who would listen about how I had perfected the kitchen. She was like that, it would seem like there was no making her happy, then you'd get it just right and she'd act like you hung the moon."

On his third cup, Eli realizes Terrance hasn't had any. The other cup is still sitting empty. He fills both and adds a little creamer and takes one over to Terrance, looking at the freezer island as he goes.

"Here," he sets the coffee down by the stove. "Do you mind if I take a look?"

"Thanks, have at it."

Eli flips the top, expecting it to be heavy; he pushes a little too hard and it bangs on the backside. It's a big deep freezer full of what appears to be mostly meat. He closes it gently now knowing it's not hard to move.

"Here," Terrance hands him the empty cup and a plate full of potatoes, eggs, and links.

Terrance joins him after he empties the coffee pot into both of their cups so he can start another pot. He sets down two plates and takes the stool near Eli.

Eli notes the plates are very full, yet it's still less food than the multi-plate meals he's seen the big guy put away at restaurants.

"What's up? You watching your figure?"

"I may have been overdoing it as of late," he admits.

"I was just teasing, it seemed like a perfectly reasonable amount of food for someone your size."

"It is, it's just that my size should be about forty pounds less, give or take. Willie was none too subtle if she thought I was getting too big around the belly. 'Your guts getting as fat as your head,' she'd say."

"Ouch, sounds like she was a handful and an ornery one at that."

"That she was, that's why I married her. Nothing worse than a woman that doesn't keep you trying 'til her very last day. If it wasn't for her, we wouldn't have bought this land or had the money for this house, and I sure wouldn't have believed I could build it."

Eli is half done with his plate and notices Terrance is still early into his first one.

"I guess that explains the doors and high ceilings in here. Why didn't you think you could build it?"

"I had never even built a birdhouse. I think I owned a hammer and a hand saw for hanging pictures and trimming branches, and I did know which one was which. That was about the full extent of my knowledge. I had been doing manufacturing jobs and worked here and there as a farmhand when I could get the work. There are some decent jobs around here now, but then working in a mine or being a lineman were about the only two decent-paying jobs if you didn't have college. I was too big to go down in any mine, no matter what anybody else might have thought, and the same goes for climbing telephone poles."

"I understand the mine, but why not a lineman?" That was a job Eli had given serious consideration to before falling into sales.

"Have you never heard 'the bigger they are, the harder they fall?' People my size don't like being off the ground."

Eli finishes his last bite and stretches. He wants to know more of the story but understands he needs to let Terrance finish his breakfast.

"I hope you don't mind, but I shared with my wife what you have been through when we talked last night."

He swallows, "What did she make of it?" he asks, before he takes another big bite.

"I was up pretty late talking her down. She was ready to jump in the car and race down here to give everyone who gives you a sideways look holy hell. She'd probably go ballistic on the whole state. She thinks you should get an award of some sort, and if the right one doesn't exist, she will start the correct humanitarian organization to create and bestow it upon you. I had to agree to give you a hug for her and tell you that you have a huge fan in Oregon and would be most welcome if you would ever want to visit. Oh, and that if one of those folks that doesn't realize what a treasure you are gives you any more trouble, you let her know and she will call them right up."

Terrance throws his head back in laughter. "Sounds like I'm not the only one that married a handful."

Eli smiles, glad that he didn't offend the man by sharing his troubles with Rachel. Terrance stands up and Eli checks his plate to find it is still half full. He looks at him to see what is going on.

"Where is my hug?" He has a straight face, but Eli is sure he is setting him up for more ribbing.

"If I ever talk to her and you want me to vouch for you that you did what she asked, you better do it."

Eli willingly hugs him, surprised at how comfortable it is, and that the big guy seems to want it. As soon as it ends, they both sit back down and Terrance goes back to eating.

"Do you want me to start on the dishes?"

"Thanks, you better not. I have a gal that comes in once a week to clean up, and she's been scolding me, thinking I'm having her come because she needs the money when there is never a mess and I don't need anybody to come at all. This will make her happy."

Eli is more than willing to sit down for a few more minutes.

"Do you think the two of us can get that house framed up today or should we call some boys out to help?"

"I trust you and you know a whole lot more than I do about building houses, so I'll go with whatever you think."

"I think if we are smart and careful, we'll get it done just the two of us. Smart and careful don't often go with teenagers."

"True."

"Ready?" Terrance asks.

Eli nods and follows once Terrance heads out the door.

Once they are back in the truck, Eli asks, "So how did you go from never building a birdhouse to building a house?"

"Let's see, first Willetta found this property and told me we had to buy it. I told her she had lost her mind and she told me it was good I married such a smart woman. It turned out she had been pinching pennies and anything else she could out of the grocery budget for years. She scrimped and saved near enough to put half down. She said if she could carve that out of the grocery budget, imagine what we could do if we were both trying. I didn't understand the point of buying a piece of land anyway. It wasn't like we could afford to put a house on it. I went along with it, like I often did, because it was easier than arguing with her. Now that she is gone, I can safely admit she was right more often than not."

"Why did you have to wait for her to be gone to say it?" It seems pretty clear who the driver was between the two of them and she had to have known it.

"Oh my god, she was barely tolerable as she was, imagine if she ever heard me admitting she was right. She would have been impossible." Terrance shakes his head looking exhausted at the mere thought.

Eli laughs.

"Anyhow, we made the down payment and we both picked up extra shifts and if she saw some garbage furniture dumped on the side of the road, she'd make me drag it home. As she had time, she'd sand it and paint it or sew cushions for it or reupholster it, or whatever struck her fancy. After a while, it would be out on the front lawn for one of her yard sales. They got to be pretty well attended over the years and some folks started bringing her their discards to see what she might do with them. It saved me from having to haul it back here, so it was fine by me."

They pull up at the site.

"Ready?" Eli nods and follows Terrance to a small section. He picks it up by himself and carries it over to the foundation. He gently tips it over then pushes the bottom so the whole section is lying on the concrete. He climbs up onto the slab and Eli follows.

"I'm going to stand this up. Go ahead and climb back down, keep it from sliding off the edge. We'll put up guides when we do the big sections together. I just want to see how we do with this little one."

Eli gets back down and Terrance lifts the section up. It starts sliding before it is all the way upright, but Eli is able to stop it without much effort. Once it is upright, Terrance stabilizes it and tells Eli, "Push it back and make sure it is flush with the side of the foundation."

Once it is in place, he has Eli hold it while he nails in a couple of two-by-fours to act as temporary braces.

"Does that change your answer?"

Eli shakes his head. He wouldn't be comfortable doing this with anyone else he can think of, but he feels fine continuing.

"We'll do the next section together. We're going to do the same thing I did with this. We'll pick it up and get it over to the foundation." He pauses to double-check the number on the section.

"We'll tip it up there like I did before and we'll go around back and nail up some guides so it doesn't slide off the edge when we try to lift it. Then we'll get some braces on it."

Once they have the next section in, they both relax some, confident they can get it done safely together.

"Finish your story," Eli suggests now that they are comfortable.

"Let's see now, she was fixing up junk and selling it. I tell you she made over a thousand dollars some weekends with her yard sales. She worked her fingers to the bone doing it, but she loved it and we paid off the land in just over three years."

He pauses again while he gets the next piece set.

"After that, we kept working away and I guess she kept stashing away because about the time I thought she had got the fool notion of me building a house out of her head, I smacked my head on a door frame in the little house we'd been renting forever. It didn't happen often, but I about knocked myself out that time. I was looking back to make sure I turned off the lamp that was worrisome to me and hadn't paid attention to how close I was to the door frame and turned around just in time to take the top of my head off. I was sitting there seeing stars, blood running down my face and she brought me a cold cloth and went to find her sewing kit to stitch me up."

He catches Eli's cringe out of the corner of his eye.

"It's happened enough times in enough ways over my life, if Willie hadn't started sewing me up, we wouldn't have been able to keep food on the table. You get used to it after a while. Anyways, she was stitching me up and asked me if I was going to get smart and build a house with ceilings I could stand up in and door frames I could get through without knocking more sense out of me. I guess I said yes and that was all it took. She was on me day and night; we had a good chunk of change again and land already paid for, she wanted it and she wanted it yesterday.

I talked to some men I knew over at the church and spent many an hour hiding out from her at construction sites seeing how things were done and over at the hardware store talking to some guys that knew something besides how to talk. Finally, we hired somebody to draw it for us and I went and pulled paper on it. You could have knocked me over with a feather when it was all approved, we started on the foundation the next day. A few weeks later I had the sections framed out and had some of the fellas from church to come help get them set. Half the congregation showed, it was like an old-fashioned barn raising. We got it framed and had the roof trusses up by the end of the day and had one heck of a BBQ to celebrate.

The next day a few fellas showed up after work and we got the roof knocked out. The next Sunday a few more fellas showed up and we got the siding up. After that it was pretty much just me, I have nothing but gratitude for all the folks that helped out and the time they put in. In fact, Miss Hattie's husband was one of them that helped out on more than one occasion.

It took me almost another year to get the plumbing and electrical in properly. By then we had the money for insulation and drywall. The windows went in later as we could afford them especially the ones on the back. Willetta was the one that said just make a big room and spend less on wood making extra walls. After living in such a small place for so long, we both liked the space. Turns out she was ahead of her time, everybody wants open-concept now. We just called it elbow room."

The story continues in fits and spurts throughout the day. As soon as supper is delivered, they pile up their plates and dig in. After they finish, Terrance picks up the story.

"Over time we saved enough again to build the garage, by then I'd helped several folks that had helped us in the beginning with additions and remodels and was picking up work here and there as a contractor, so it was easy to get it done up and build the covered walk between the two. She thought it was stupid to connect the garage to the house and wouldn't hear of it, but she didn't want to walk in the rain to go back and forth. That covered walkway got me more favor with her than building the whole darn house did."

"Why didn't she want them connected?"

"I asked that same thing. She told me garages are for cars, that have exhaust and sanders that make dust and paints and chemicals that have fumes and all kinds of things, why on earth would you want it connected to your house and with a door that would let it all into your living space. I don't know if she was right about that one or not, but I still don't know that she was wrong."

"Why don't you park in the garage, or was that just this morning?"

"She liked fixing stuff that was garbage in others' eyes and turning it into something useful again. She kept doing it right up until she was too weak to get out of bed. The garage was her territory, plus she made me move the washer and dryer out there once it was built and turn her laundry room into a pantry. I was allowed in there if I needed to get tools, but that was about it. I got used to parking in the drive and haven't felt the need to change it just yet."

"I see," Eli looks at his watch. He needs to call his family, but is reluctant to say good night to Terrance.

Understanding it was time to part ways, Terrance spread his arms and let out an exaggerated yawn. "Time for me to get my beauty sleep. All this doesn't happen on its own."

"Far be it from me to interfere with all that. Good night."

CHAPTER 12

The closer to done the house becomes, the more the two men learn about each other. As the days go by and the completion of the project nears, both find themselves chatting a little longer on breaks and moving a little slower while they're working. Friday of the second week, Terrance takes Eli's phone and programs an address into the GPS.

"I called us in an order for some supper. Why don't you go get it for us while I finish cleaning up?"

Eli agrees without questioning, even though this is the first time supper hasn't been either delivered by a goodhearted community member or they have not gone together to get it. He easily follows directions to a place called the Rattlesnake Saloon. He is amazed when he gets there and sees the structure. The saloon is built under a large rock outcropping that has a waterfall cascading over the side. Eli has never seen anything like it and is grateful to Terrance for sending him here. It would be a shame to miss it while he is in the area.

He takes several photos on his phone of the saloon, the outdoor patio that is under the covered protection of the rock but still open air. He walks up one of the nearby hiking trails to get a couple shots from different angles, wanting to be able to share the unusual structure with Rachel on their nightly call. He smiles thinking about his son's amazement at the unlikely location of the restaurant, well, tavern, but when he shows his son, it will be a restaurant.

He walks in and gives his name; they hand him two bags and he is on his way. He is quickly back on the road, eager to get back and eat the delicious-smelling meal. When he gets back, Terrance is sitting in one of the chairs he brought over from his house early in the week. He has the two chairs and two small tables set up on the edge of the clearing and there is a cooler on the ground by his feet.

Eli sets the food down on the trays, the triumphant hunter returning, "Wow, thanks for sending me out there. That was breathtaking. I would've never guessed in a million years something like that was so close to here."

"I thought you might like it," Terrance says, obviously pleased with himself and the younger man's reaction.

They both open the to-go containers and dig in. A moment later Eli notices that Terrance is drinking a beer. He has never seen the other man drink and, not being much of a drinker himself, the subject has never come up. Between the good meal, good companionship, the pride in a job well done and the ever-present humidity, a beer has never looked so good to him.

Terrance opens the lid of the cooler and tips it towards him and he gladly fishes one out and pops the top. He takes a long pull on his cold beer and another bite from the best ribs he'd had and says, "It doesn't get much better than this, does it."

"No, sure doesn't," the big man agrees.

Eli texts Rachel letting her know that he and Terrance are having dinner and a couple well-earned beers and asks her to call when Mason is ready to go to bed.

Her response simply reads, "Have fun."

They work their way through a six-pack and are just starting in on a second. Still enjoying the company and now admiring the sunset, Eli knocks one of his empties over into the grass. He feels around blindly behind him watching Terrance, who is telling another Willetta story, when he suddenly feels a sharp pain in his hand.

"Ouch," he says abandoning the bottle and pulling his hand back.

Still relaxed, ready to pop the top off of his next beer, Terrance asks, "What happened?"

"I don't know," Eli says looking at his hand. He holds it up to the light and Terrance's demeanor instantly changes. He takes a close look and starts shaking his head, no, no.

"Where," he asks.

Eli points in the grass behind him. Terrance sees movement in the grass and a flash of scales as the snake heads away from the perceived threat. Terrance sets out after it while Eli sits down not feeling well.

A few minutes later Terrance comes back, breathing heavy from exertion.

"How are you feeling?"

Eli stands up and falls back down into his chair.

"I'm a little dizzy I guess, maybe those beers are hitting me harder than I thought."

"Don't worry about the beer. Can you do me a favor?"

"Anything," is Eli's immediate response.

"Take off your wedding ring and let me hang on to it for a little while we take a drive."

It seems an odd request, but he knows the big guy wouldn't do anything to cause him harm and he seems quite taken with Rachel between the stories Eli has shared and the few times the two of them have talked on the phone.

He hands the ring over and Terrance puts it in his pocket.

"I'm going to help you up by the back of your britches and we're going to walk over to the truck all nice and slow, okay?"

"Okay, my hand really hurts and those beers are kicking my butt all of a sudden."

"I know, it's all going to be okay. Just you relax and don't worry none." Terrance keeps talking in that soothing tone while they make their way to the truck. He loads Eli in the passenger seat and puts the seat belt on him. He keeps talking; soothing nonsense pouring out of him nonstop. He gets in, buckles up, pulls out onto the road and calmly makes his way to the highway where he puts the hammer down.

The old truck shudders a little but finds its get up and go, and they take off.

"Why are you going so fast?" Eli asks, his head moving around in odd patterns.

"Oh, don't you worry about that at all, just stay nice and calm. We'll be squared away in just a couple minutes."

A couple minutes later he passes a police officer on his way out of the hospital parking lot. Terrance races by and roars up to the emergency room door. He reassures Eli, "You just relax here for a second, I'll be right back."

Terrance rushes inside and comes back with attendants pushing a stretcher. The staff try to get Eli out of the truck, but he doesn't want to go, until Terrance is there telling him to. They get him situated on the stretcher and roll him inside. The cop he passed had made a U-turn and followed him up to the door. Once he is satisfied that there is an actual emergency, he tips his hat towards Terrance and saunters back to his cruiser. Terrance lets out a big sigh of relief.

Inside, the admitting nurse asks, "Is this the snake bite victim?"

One of the guys pushing the stretcher confirms it, "Yes."

Eli freaks out. He looks at his hand in the bright light and sees it's twice its normal size and already bruised. The puncture marks are clear, one side bigger than the other.

"Shi...shoot, I got bit by an Eastern Diamondback like you told me not to and I don't have insurance and if a concussion cost eighteen thousand dollars, I don't want to know what this costs. I ruined it all." He stops his flailing and puts a hand to his chest. "I, I can't breathe right."

The admitting nurse says, "Take him to three," and pages the doctor. She sets her sights on Terrance who is trying to follow Eli down the hall. "Hold on a minute there. Does he really not have insurance?"

"No, this will be workers comp. He's been working for me. He'll be covered under my policy."

He fishes some paperwork out of his wallet and sets it on the counter for her and again tries to go down the hall.

"Family only."

Eli's voice can be heard faintly from down the hall, "He's my brother."

"He was adopted," Terrance says to explain.

"Fine," she says, clearly not buying it but she has better things to do with her time.

He walks in the room in time to hear the doctor ask, "What type of snake?"

Eli again says, "Diamondback," but this time says, "Western."

"No sir, it was a pygmy, a ground rattler. I tracked it down so I could tell you. It was about sixteen inches." Terrance holds his fingers apart to show the length.

The doctor jumps at the unexpected voice behind him and steps back when he sees how big Terrance is. Terrance immediately holds up both hands in front of him.

"Thank you for that information. If you will please go back to the waiting room, we will update you after he receives treatment."

"He's my brother," Eli insists from his bed.

"How much has he had to drink?"

"Two, maybe three beers in," he looks at his watch, "about three hours. He got bit about twenty minutes ago, I made sure I could tell you the snake that bit him and we came straight here."

He nods to the nurse ready to inject something into Eli's IV line. She waits a minute watching him for any reaction, after another minute she adds something else to the line.

Satisfied, the doctor says, "Clean and dress the wound." He turns to Terrance, "You did a good job for your brother." He finally smiles at the big guy who immediately returns it. The doctor turns and walks out of the room shaking his head.

"Is that antivenin?" Terrance asked the nurse.

"Yes, and I gave him something for the pain."

Eli lets out a soft snore and they both chuckle.

"How long does that stuff take?" He motions towards the antivenin on the pole.

"Twenty minutes, two hours," she says casually. "It just depends. This looks like it might be a shallow bite, one side was barely punctured."

"That's good right?"

"As good as a snake bite gets. He's going to be sore and bruised, but the swelling doesn't seem to be getting much worse. I think he might get lucky."

Terrance looks ruefully at the chair in the corner of the room. She understands his challenge, not much is made for a man his size and there is no way he can fit in the chair.

"He is going to be asleep for a while. If it's your truck in the emergency entrance you should go move it unless you want it towed. While you're gone, I'll see if I can find a chair without arms or maybe an extra-large gurney so you can be more comfortable while you wait."

"Did you see where his cell phone went?"

She motions to the tray on the counter behind her. He picks it up and takes it with him. He walks out the door and climbs in the truck. He parks it in the visitors parking lot and pulls out Eli's phone. It's locked, he takes a guess and puts in Mason's birthday, day, month and last two digits of the year. He smiles briefly when it unlocks and he sees the home screen picture of Rachel and the boy. He takes a deep breath and calls Rachel.

"Hi, honey."

"You can call me honey if you like, but this isn't your husband."

"Oh, hi Terrance, how are you?"

"I'm just fine and yourself?"

"I'm good. What's up?"

"I know he calls you every night and he might still, but I didn't want you to worry just in case."

That was all it took to send her from zero to sixty on the worry meter.

"Oh no, what happened?"

"Now calm down. He's sleeping now."

Feeling bad about the whole situation and not wanting to make the worry he heard in her voice any worse, he chickens out.

"We had a couple of beers with supper tonight and I just wasn't thinking about how two weeks of getting after it hard on Miss Hattie's house and how the fragile little guy suffers in the humidity and how all that might affect him if we were to do a little drinking."

He smiles relieved when he hears her laughter.

"That's two benders in the same year. That's a first for him in the thirteen years I've known him. I'll have to tease him now."

"He got up a bit ago and went to the bathroom in the trailer and never came back. I was going to peek in on him but I could hear the snoring from out here. He left his phone, so I thought I better call you so you don't worry if he doesn't wake up."

"Thank you, Terrance, that was thoughtful. I appreciate it."

He could hear some noise in the background.

"Hold on a sec?"

"Go ahead."

"Do you have a second to say hi to Mason?"

"Sure, I do."

"Hi Terrance, it's Mason. Are you going to come visit us? Dad says he wants you to, or we will come visit you, but he is nervous about letting Mom east of the Mississippi. Do you know what that means? When I get to meet you will you give me a shoulder ride or am I too big? Mom says I'm too big."

"Well, I don't know, that depends on how much you weigh when I get to meet you."

"I'm sixty something now. Is that too big?"

"I expect I could manage for a short spell."

"Cool, then I'll be taller than Shaq and you!"

More noise in the background.

"Mom says I have to go. I have to settle down for bed and talking to you is too exciting."

"You better go then and Mason, I think talking to you is exciting too."

"Bye, I love you."

Before he can decide how to respond to that, Rachel is back.

"Sorry about that, we both just love your accent and Mason is crazy for the idea of meeting someone who is bigger than Shaq. Don't tell his dad I said this, but I don't think he minds not getting to talk to him tonight since he got to talk to you."

Anxious to get off the phone and make sure Eli is going to be all right and feeling worse with every exchange he clears his throat and says, "Your secret is safe with me, but I did a little drinking too tonight and I'm mighty tired so I better get going."

"Okay, goodnight. Thanks again for the call."

"No bother, good night."

Terrance enters the hospital through the emergency room again. The nurse flags him down as soon as she sees him and shoves a clipboard at him. He accepts it reluctantly and stands at the counter for five minutes filling out as much as he knows on the forms. When he's finished, he hands it over and starts off for the hall, but she waves him back. He is relieved it's only to give back his company insurance information.

When he gets back to the room Eli is still asleep, the nurse is putting something else into his line. Instead of a chair there is now a two-foot-high stack of folded mats in the corner.

"I'm sorry I couldn't do any better for you, a few mats from the PT room are it for now."

"Thank you, that was mighty kind of you."

She waves it away.

"How is he doing?"

She smiles wondering why the big ones are always such babies, she heard the quiver in his voice. They might not be brothers, but he obviously cares about the man asleep in bed.

"Actually, he is doing very well. Everything looks like it was a shallow bite and the reaction is pretty small, it looks like he got treated in less than twenty minutes."

"I kept him real calm. I don't know why he didn't put it together, but he didn't understand he was snake bit until we got into the ER. He knew he was dizzy and couldn't stand up too well on his own, but he assumed the beer was hitting him harder than expected."

"He might have had mild shock or just plain denial, whatever it was and whatever you did, worked. If it stays like this or improves in the next couple of hours, we'll probably discharge him."

"Really?" His face lights up at the news.

"Yes. It wasn't a dry bite, there was venom, but pygmies don't produce that much, and it looks like this one had bad aim. Maybe he was drinking with you guys?" she teases.

"He tipped a bottle over into the grass where the afternoon sun hits and it sounded funny to me when he did, like there was a delay with the sound or an echo. I wonder if that snake tried to bite the bottle before it got Eli?"

"Maybe," she sounds dubious, but admits, "I don't know much about snakes except to leave them alone and what I see here of people that didn't do that."

Terrance shakes his massive head. "I told him when he first got here to watch out and we've been working there for two weeks without any problems. We finally relax and what happens, poor guy knocks over a bottle, it rolls and he gets bit trying to pick it up. I should have known better than put the chairs over there."

"Don't worry, he is going to be fine. It looks like he is going to get off very lucky from this. Just relax he'll be awake in the next hour or two and we'll see how he's doing. He'll probably be discharged," she repeats herself, trying to comfort the big guy.

Terrance slowly lowers himself to the mats which then lower another five or six inches. He puts his back against the wall and lets his head tilt to the side so it rests in the corner. He is actually fairly comfortable and before he knows it, he is asleep too.

He wakes to Eli's voice, "Terrance?"

"Yeah, buddy, are you okay?"

"I think so, my hand hurts but it's not burning anymore."

"That's good, not burning is always good."

"Where are you? I can't see you."

"You're going to have to trust that I'm here, I'm on the floor and I only want to get myself up off of here once. The nurse thinks you had a shallow bite and maybe not a lot of venom. You should see if you have a call button and let them know you're awake."

There is some rustling and then a motorized sound as first the foot of the bed comes up a few inches, then lowers back down. Then the head slowly raises and once he can see Terrance wedged in the corner Eli smiles. He finds the call button and pushes it. He drops the control onto his lap and relaxes into the bed. They pass a few minutes in contented silence.

The nurse comes back into the room with some papers. She sets them on the tray and checks Eli's hand.

"Does the dressing feel tighter?"

He shakes his head.

"On a scale of one to ten with ten being the highest what number is your pain?"

He thinks a moment and moves his hand a little. "Probably a three."

"Do you remember what it was when you came in?"

"It hurt worse, a lot. It was burning, now it's not burning."

"Can you give me a number?"

"Seven?"

The doctor comes in. "How are we doing?" he asks.

Terrance begins the slow process of getting himself up from the floor, sensing the time has come.

Eli isn't sure who the question is directed at since he is the patient, but the man is looking at the nurse.

"The swelling has gone down since he arrived. His pain level is less than half of when he arrived. I haven't administered anything else for pain."

He holds out his hand to see the chart. He gives it a quick scan. "Are those his discharge orders?"

She nods in the affirmative. He gives them a quick scan and signs a few. He makes a couple of notes on one page and quickly jots out a prescription and adds it to the stack. He hands her a page and a prescription-sized piece of paper.

"Make the changes and I'll sign it." She scurries off to do what he instructed.

"You are a lucky man, it's a rare thing to have such a small reaction. Normally, unless it's a dry bite, folks are much worse off than you are. Even with a shallow bite such as yours. Your 'brother,'" he says with a dubious tone, but a nice smile, "did everything right and you are still very lucky. You may want to buy a lottery ticket in the morning."

The nurse returns with a single piece of paper, which the doctor reviews and signs.

"Be safe and stay away from snakes."

"Thank you," they both say.

The nurse reviews the paperwork with Eli. There are some aftercare instructions for changing the dressing. A prescription for ten Vicodin and a list of things that should they occur, he should seek immediate medical attention for. She has him sign each page then peels his copies off and stacks them up.

"Any questions?"

"When can I go home?"

"As soon as I rustle up a wheelchair."

"I can walk. I got bit in the hand not the foot."

Her shoulders fall. Like there is suddenly a large weight on them.

"I know. I understand and I'm sorry. The hospital's policy is that if you are wheeled in you are wheeled out. It used to be that everyone was wheeled out, so it's better than it was, but still frustrating for people like you. Please don't leave before I get back. I can get in big trouble."

"Don't worry, we'll be here. Thanks for taking good care of us." Eli assures her and Terrance nods along.

A few moments later she returns with a wheelchair large enough to fit Terrance.

"Sorry, this is the only one I could find."

"No problem, we're only going twenty feet." It is more like fifty, but neither Eli nor the nurse bother to correct him.

"This would fit you, too bad you couldn't have used this to sit in." The nurse smacks her forehead, she obviously hadn't thought of it.

"I'm sorry," she tells the big man.

"You did fine and you took good care of my bro. You got nothing to apologize for." He gives her a small pat on the shoulder as he walks by and leads the way into the hallway.

She follows behind pushing Eli in the wheelchair. When they are halfway through the waiting area Terrance turns to look back at Eli, "Do you have your papers?"

Before he can respond a woman comes in screaming, "Help her."

A man carrying a girl who is bleeding severely follows right behind.

Eli sees the blood and he leans forward in the chair and vomits on the floor. He stands up to get out of the way and immediately hits the floor.

"Oh dear," is all the nurse says.

CHAPTER 13

The admitting nurse pages everyone she needs with her "code this" and "stat that," seconds later the room is buzzing as they get the girl on a bed and wheel her to the back. They allow the man who carried her in to follow her, but wisely hold the woman who seems on the verge of hysteria at the desk asking her questions and reminding her to breathe while she calms down enough to be allowed back.

Once the trio in crisis have made it past, Eli squirms out of the vomit he has landed in and is trying to get purchase somewhere so he can stand up.

"Please wait. We need to assess you before you get up."

"Yuck," her requests are getting harder to comply with, but he lies there for an extra minute.

A different doctor kneels on the ground beside him.

"Sir, can you tell me your name?"

"Can I get out of the vomit first?"

"No, I am sorry, we need to do a quick assessment to make sure it's safe to move you first. Name?"

"Eli Asher." She looks up and gets a nod from the nurse and Terrance.

"Can you please look at this light." She abruptly shines the light in his eyes one at a time. Once she confirms his pupil response is normal, she continues.

"Please follow my finger with your eyes." He groans to himself but follows along. He could probably do the assessment himself by now. He tries to be as good a sport as anyone laying in their own vomit can be expected to be as she goes through the next few steps.

Then she takes off his shoes and pokes and tickles his feet. He tries not to laugh and appreciates that this part is new. She sits beside him again, "Sir, can you please squeeze my fingers with your hand."

He starts to and flinches immediately. He tries to hide it for the sake of getting out of the vomit, but he is too late.

"What hurts sir? Is it your wound?" She notices the gauze on his hand.

"That too."

"What else?"

"My shoulder," he sheepishly admits.

The doctor stands abruptly. "Was he in the wheelchair when he fell?" she asks the nurse.

"No, he was in the chair when he vomited, then he stood up and fell down."

"Had you instructed him to get up?"

"No, ma'am."

"Did he faint or slip?"

"I can't say ma'am."

She looks at the admitting nurse and then Terrance, both shrug, it all happened so fast no one knows exactly what happened. She walks over to the counter where they whisper intently back and forth. The admitting nurse keeps shaking her head no stubbornly. The doctor throws up her hands and seconds later, there is someone putting a cervical collar on Eli, then a couple of people roll him onto a backboard and lift him up to the waiting gurney. They take him back toward the exam rooms.

"I'll be right there, E," Terrance says walking to the admittance desk and fishing his paperwork back out.

The admitting nurse shakes her head and waves him off, "It's on us no matter how you slice it. If we could send discharges out the main entrance after hours something like that would never happen. If he hadn't waited for a wheelchair because of some one-size-fits-all rule to reduce liability, he would have been gone before those other folks came. They can be cheap or they can do things the right way. When it gets expensive enough, they'll figure it out."

"Are you sure?"

"More than."

"I have to admit I am relieved; I didn't know how to explain that one to my insurance company."

"That's one thing you don't need to worry about. He's back in three, they are going to test him six ways to Sunday to know and document the extent of their liability. I'm trying to get him a room so you'll be more comfortable. This isn't going to be fast, what with us being understaffed and an emergency surgery starting any minute."

"Okay, thanks." He heads back to the room they just left.

Shortly after, a young man comes in and with Terrance's help, they get Eli out of the dirty clothes and into a gown. He wipes off the worst of it with the paper towels Terrance hands him.

As the night wears on, they admit Eli and take him to a room. With some help from the nurse, he is finally able to have a shower. He is taken to X-ray. Eventually they are told it's not a break, but they can't rule out a fracture, because of a shadow on the X-ray.

Another hour passes and he is taken to another room to do an ultrasound while he moves his shoulder trying to ascertain if the pain is from a tear or fracture, or both. After he is returned to the room, both men get a couple hours of sleep; Terrance in a roomy armless chair someone found for him and Eli in the hospital bed. Eli encouraged Terrance to go to the site so materials didn't walk away or better yet, go home and get some sleep in his own bed. He declined to do either.

Eli wakes in a panic in the morning. "She is going to kill me."

Terrance slowly opens his eyes. "Who is killing you now?"

"Rachel, I didn't call her last night. She is going to be worried sick and I lost my wedding ring? Do you think the nurse has it?"

Terrance gets up stretching what needs to be as he unfolds. He reaches into his pocket and produces the ring with a flourish. Eli takes it and tries to put it on his finger with obvious relief, only to discover his ring finger is still too swollen.

Understanding dawns on his face, "That's right, you asked for my ring before we got in the truck. Man, that seems like days ago. Thank you. I don't suppose you know where my phone is?"

Terrance pulls the phone out of his other pocket. The sizable phone looks impossibly small in the big man's hand. Eli takes it and looks at the screen, puzzled that there are no missed calls.

"Ah, I called Rachel last night."

"You are the man," Eli says excited.

Terrance shuffles his feet a few times, uncomfortable with what he has to say next.

"I didn't tell her about the bite and I haven't talked to her since the fall. I just told her you were worn out from work and humidity and a couple beers hit you harder than expected and you fell asleep. I'm sorry, I was going to tell her about the bite, but she sounded so worried that I had called and I just plain chickened out."

Eli holds his hand out and Terrance takes it, not sure what is happening. Eli catches and holds his gaze. "Thank you, it is so...," he pauses searching for the correct word, "unbelievably cool to have a friend who does exactly what I would have wanted done when I can't say what that is."

Terrance is embarrassed and wants to look away, but Eli holds his gaze a moment longer to drive the point home. They let go of each other's hand just before someone else comes in.

"Good morning Mr. Asher, how are you feeling?" asks another new face.

"Honestly, I've been better."

For some reason that makes both men laugh and once they start, they can't stop. Terrance doubles over and Eli has his right hand on his stomach which hurts from laughing so hard while he tries to minimize the movement on his left arm.

Terrance raises his finger and points at Eli. "You're a mess," he manages to get out between fits of laughter.

Eli thinks they sound like teenage girls, which only makes him laugh harder. Slowly, it subsides to small chuckles and they both wipe at their eyes.

The man in the door is smiling, but asks, "Have you been drinking? Alcohol is absolutely prohibited on hospital grounds."

"No," Eli says. "It's just some much needed tension release." The man gives Terrance a stern glare.

"He's been here with me all night, ask anyone," Eli continues.

After a moment the man relents. "Okay. I'm here to take you for your CAT scan."

Eli groans inwardly about how much all this is going to cost, but doesn't want to complain in front of Terrance, who he worries might feel some guilt about the snake bite.

The man starts rolling him toward the door. Terrance gets up, pulls his chair across the room and picks up the TV remote. "I'll be here."

"Wait," Eli says. "You've got to be hungry. No need for both of us to suffer. Get some food and maybe bring me some clean clothes?"

"I'll be back," Terrance amends his previous statement.

Eli makes it back to the room first, he pokes at the food that is waiting for him. Hospitals don't make a lot of sense to him. He can't imagine too many people would disagree with the fact that getting enough sleep is important for health and well-being, yet they wake you up every five minutes in the hospital. He doesn't imagine too many people would disagree that fresh, real food is important to health and well-being, yet in the hospital when you're being charged more than he wants to think about for a meal, they give you processed everything that barely qualifies as food. For the price, you'd think they'd be serving filet mignon and asparagus, or maybe something a little easier on the cholesterol and fresh, delicious and recognizable as food.

After all the time he has spent outside the last two weeks, he is missing the green of the trees and the blue of the sky stuck in these stark white walls. He had himself worked up into a fairly foul mood when the day shift nurse came in.

"Oh good you're awake and eating your breakfast. How are you feeling?"

"I'd be a lot better if I could get released."

"I'm sure they'll get you out of here just as soon as they can." She is chipper and efficient as she takes his vitals and adds the information to his chart.

"You have any idea when they'll have the results from the CAT scan?"

"No, I don't, but I'll be happy to check on that for you. What's your hurry? Do you have a big date?"

"I wish. Actually, I'm married and my wife is at home in Portland."

"Which one?"

"Oregon. I came out here to do some temp work and everything was going great until I got bit by a rattlesnake and fell on my way-out last night. I don't know why this keeps happening to me."

"What's that?" She examines the bruising on his hand and double checks the chart, clearly having a hard time believing that bite was less than twenty-four hours old.

"Every time I get my feet under me and start to make some progress something happens, first the pandemic, then my son got hurt right after we lost our insurance and now this. I swear I'm not a bad guy. I don't know why this stuff keeps happening."

The nurse stops what she is doing and looks at him giving him her full attention. "You better be careful, sounds like you're at risk of turning into the victim or villain. I don't know you from Adam, but I get the feeling you'd rather be the hero."

He sits up and turns the TV off now, giving her his full attention. He is irritated but knows he was before she came and has to admit, he is curious. He also notices that she is an attractive woman, he can't tell her age for sure, but estimates it is probably within ten years of Terrance.

"What are you talking about?"

"Just something I've been doing probably twenty years now. As people come through and I listen to their stories, I try to figure out if they are the hero, the victim, or the villain of their stories."

"So, what makes you think I'm the victim?" he asks defensively.

"I didn't say you were, I said be careful or you could wind up one."

His frustration grows. "What makes you say that?"

"Heroes are responsible for everything in their life. Victims and villains aren't."

"I don't think I'm on painkillers anymore, but this conversation has me wondering. You're not making sense. None of that stuff is my fault, so how am I supposed to be responsible for it?"

"That's the rub, isn't it? Heroes are responsible for a hundred percent of their life, even when things happen that aren't their fault. Victims aren't responsible for what happens to them because it's not their fault. Villains aren't responsible for the wrong they do because the circumstances that lead them to do it aren't their fault. People try to spin that every which way you can imagine, to fit their needs or the circumstance. After all this time, it's pretty clear to me."

He is annoyed now. He doesn't like it, but has a funny feeling he wouldn't be annoyed if she wasn't right. It is similar to what Terrance said about life being challenge by choice. And yet different, there is more here, he is going to choose the challenge of having this conversation to see if he can learn something that will help him be a hero in his life and with his family.

"Okay, you've piqued my interest. Tell me more please." He hopes Terrance will get back before she leaves.

She looks at his eager face, checks her watch, and with a small nod looks back at him.

"There's not much more to it than that. If you're responsible for your life, you can change it; if you're not, you can't or you won't. Why would you if it's not your responsibility? Something like the pandemic happens, there's plenty of folks that are going to be victims. They're not going to try to do anything to change their circumstances or help themselves because it wasn't their fault and somebody else better fix it. There are going to be plenty of villains; they never would have price gouged on toilet paper or sold faulty masks, or the other rotten stuff people did, but the circumstances put them in a bad way. They had no choice but to get what they needed at the expense of others, or so they say.

Heroes, on the other hand, worked if they were essential and if not, stayed home when they needed to in order to save lives, and didn't worry about it not being their fault. They found ways to still be responsible for their lives, be it starting a new business online, continuing their education, or just being a point of positive contact for their friends and family."

"That makes sense. That's mostly what we did, we stayed home, and we stayed positive. I didn't think about starting a business or continuing my education because my wife's in school right now. I still don't get what's wrong with saying something isn't your fault when it isn't."

"There's nothing wrong with it. It's not about right or wrong, but it has an effect on your mindset."

He cocks his head to the side, waiting for her to continue.

"When you tell me something isn't your fault, how do you feel?"

He shrugs, "I guess I never really thought about it."

"Well, think about it, then tell me."

He does, his body slumps, causing a twinge from his shoulder, that elicits a wince. "I guess I feel kind of down, heavy, and maybe tired."

"Kind of sounds like depressed to me."

"Yeah, I guess so."

"So, do you feel empowered to go out and change what you don't like that isn't your fault?"

He shakes his head no.

"Now let's say you'd ordered something that was really important to you that didn't arrive by the time they said it would. Not only did it not arrive when it was supposed to, but on top of being late, it wasn't the right thing, so now you're stuck. You can't finish your job or do whatever it was you needed to do when you got what it was you ordered, and you have to wait a second time for them to ship it, fingers crossed that they get it right that time. You call the company and the person you talk to starts by saying "it's not my fault," but as soon as we get the wrong thing returned, we'll ship out what you ordered."

He is shaking his head and feeling the frustration just thinking about it.

"Now use that exact same scenario, but imagine when you call, the person on the other end says, 'I'm so sorry that happened, let me get that taken care of for you. I'll get that shipped express this afternoon; you should have it in a day, hopefully, two at the most. I'm going to send a return label for the mistake. I'd appreciate it if you could send it back to us, then we can figure out how the error happened so we can prevent it going forward.'"

He nods, smiling, feeling the difference.

"Which company would you want to do business with?"

"I get it."

"How do you think the public interacts with the two of them, and how do you suppose they feel about themselves and life at the end of the day?" she asks to make sure he gets the point.

That really drives it home. He knows the person in the first example would be miserable by the end of the day and probably hate life. The second would probably leave work with close to the same energy as when they arrived, plus they would have a happy, loyal customer base and probably a boss who loves them and gives them raises or promotions whenever they can.

"That could be life-changing."

She smiles, pleased. Another quick glance at her watch, "I have to get going. I'll be back to check on you after a while."

"Real quick," he wants to use her name and realizes he doesn't know it. "What's your name?"

"Pearl Pritchard," she answers halfway to the door.

"Pearl, I appreciate you sharing your observations with me, and I'd love to do something for you in return. I am only here for a short while, but if you would be willing, I have a friend who would be happy to take you out for coffee or lunch on my behalf. I'm sure he would enjoy hearing what you shared with me too."

She looks at him for an extra beat then shrugs, "You have to say yes sometimes." She fishes a piece of scratch paper out of her pocket and quickly writes her number down.

He beams at her, "Thanks, it might be a few weeks while he finishes up a pile of work, but I promise coffee or lunch for both of you, on me."

She gives him a smile and is off like a shot.

CHAPTER 14

Terrance returns after what feels like an eternity to Eli. He strolls in and doesn't have anything in his hands.

"Did you bring me clothes?"

"I couldn't find any except the dirty ones."

He had thrown those in the back of the truck and put them in the washer at his house on the way back.

"Oh, dang. I should have told you they were on the pull-down bunk." Terrance chimes in and says, "pull-down bunk," in unison with Eli. He pulls a small stack of clothes from under his arm and smiles.

"That's what took me so long. I had done everything but turn that trailer upside down and you were fixing to be stuck with church clothes, when I noticed the bunk wasn't closed all the way."

He goes to set the clothes on the edge of the bed, but drops them. The shirt and drawers land on the bed, the jeans unfold when he catches them.

"Hold those up to you."

"Are you sure your ego can handle it?" He teases even as he is doing it.

"I'll try to survive."

They both start laughing. "Those look like half a pair of basketball shorts for you."

"I was thinking doll clothes," Terrance teases.

There is a knock on the open door.

"Hi, sorry to interrupt the fun. I'm here to take you for your MRI."

Eli lets out an exasperated sigh and shakes his head.

"I'm going to go get brunch, since I looked for your clothes so long, I didn't have time to get breakfast."

"You're welcome to that," Eli pointed to his breakfast still sitting on the tray.

"I'm going to get some brunch." He pats his pocket for his keys and feels something odd. He fishes out a rolled pair of Eli's socks and adds them to the clothes on the bed.

"I'll be back quick this time." He raises an eyebrow, playfully letting Eli know he is the reason a second trip is needed.

"I'll be here," Eli replies.

Terrance hits the first fast food joint he passes. He rarely eats the stuff, but time is running short and he doesn't have time to sit down for a decent meal. He races back to his place and is happy to see his housekeeper transferred the laundry to the dryer. He checked it, close, but not dry yet. He restarts it and goes into the house where he paces while he eats some fruit to balance out the grease that is making his stomach unhappy already. A few minutes later, he folds the warm, dry clothes and adds them to the rest of Eli's belongings that are already in his bag. The church clothes are hanging in the truck. He isn't looking forward to saying goodbye to Eli, or telling him that their time together is up.

When he gets back to the hospital, Eli is back in his room, sitting on the side of the bed.

"I'll let you know just as soon as I hear anything," Pearl assures him before turning and running into Terrance.

Terrance lets out an "oomph" and puts his hands on Pearl's shoulders to steady her. She steps back shaken and slowly tilts her head up and up until her eyes reach his face. A slow smile spreads across both of their faces.

"That's a mighty fine drive you have. Sorry about that," Terrance says.

"The foul would have been on me; your feet were planted."

"Let's say no harm, no foul then," he croons.

She fans herself with her hand, still smiling. She nods agreement and slowly makes her way around him and down the hall, looking back over her shoulder before she turns the corner. Terrance follows her with his eyes until she is out of sight. By the time Terrance turns his attention back to Eli, he is standing and pulling his pants up. Once his pants are on, he yanks off the gown.

"Look at you being all charming," he teases while he gingerly pulls on his T-shirt.

"Are they releasing you?"

"Not yet, but hopefully soon. There can't be any more tests and my bite is great. Everybody that sees it double checks the chart, they can't believe it's not way worse. I bet I can put my wedding ring back on in another day or two."

Pearl comes back in as Eli is putting on his socks. "The doctor will be here soon to discuss the results with you."

"Are they going to discharge me?"

"You'll have to ask the doctor," she says in a loud voice while nodding yes. Eli gives a fist pump; Terrance gives her a wink and she fans herself as she walks past him again, smiling. Thirty minutes later, Eli is in a wheelchair with instructions for follow-up care for his bite and his bruised shoulder in his hand. When the aide starts pushing him out of the room, Terrance walks far ahead.

"Terrance, where are you going?"

Terrance doesn't even turn around, but replies, "I'm making sure nobody is bleeding on the way in the door."

"We are going out the main entrance," the young woman pushing Eli says. That doesn't slow down or stop Terrance's recon. Once he is sure it is clear, he comes halfway back to them with an eye to exit.

They'd almost made it to the door when Eli says, "Wait, I need to talk to somebody from billing."

"Why is that?"

"I'm going to have to make payment arrangements of some sort. It's going to take a while to pay all this off, I'm sure. I really don't even want to think about it."

She gives him a blank look, clearly not understanding. This is not normally something she knows anything about, but this situation is unique so she has been looped in.

"I know it's ridiculous not to have insurance. It was a bad and expensive decision."

"I can take you to billing, but my understanding is that you don't have a bill because you had Workman's Comp for your original injury and the hospital is responsible for the charges related to your second injury."

Eli is astonished.

"Did you still want to go to billing?" Eli sits there elated by the good news. He looks at Terrance, who looks away, embarrassed.

"No, thank you that won't be necessary."

She continues down the hall through the automatic doors into the sunlight and the weight of the humidity. He doesn't even mind the humidity to be back outside and seeing green trees and blue skies instead of white walls.

Once they reach the curb he gets up from the chair and says, "Thank you."

"You take care now." She quickly disappears back inside.

The two men walk the short distance to Terrance's truck in silence. They both climb in. Terrance drives out of the hospital parking lot.

"Thank you, Terrance. That was amazing. You didn't have to do that, but I really appreciate it."

"Don't think twice about it. That outfit that you're hooked up with is going to take care of it. Won't be a bother to you or me."

Eli doubts that is true but hopes it is. Either way, the weight of the world has just come off of his injured shoulder, knowing that he isn't going to be saddled with another huge hospital bill. He is lost in thought about it, so he doesn't notice at first that they aren't heading back to the worksite.

"Where are we going?"

Terrance pulls into a Walmart parking lot and drives to the far end, and stops near a semi-truck. "Eli, I'm sorry I didn't tell you before. I didn't want to stress you out while you were in the hospital. And honestly, I didn't want to tell you. I really enjoyed our time together and you're a helluva worker. But our time together is done. This outfit you're connected to is sending you off to a farm in Missouri to do some more work up there, I guess."

"Wow, this sucks." He is surprised by the intensity of his feelings. He is truly disappointed and not ready to be saying goodbye to Terrance.

"I know Eli, I knew it was coming and I should've told you sooner but I didn't know how. I thought we'd have our time together Friday night and I was going to take you out to the hot springs I've been telling you about this morning, while we were out there or on the drive back this afternoon, but you know what they say? We make plans and God laughs."

"What are we doing here then? Shouldn't we be heading to the airport?"

"No, you're heading to Missouri, little town outside of Saint Louis. I understand this fella in the truck is headed that way and you're going to be riding with him."

"I still need to go back to the trailer and pack my stuff." Eli is hoping for time, more than he is worried about the clothes and toiletries. Terrance is absolutely miserable now.

"I'm sorry Eli, I knew we were getting short on time so I did a little laundry for you. I packed up for you when I went to get breakfast this morning. Your bag is in the back and your church clothes are hanging behind you."

The guy from the semi-truck they are parked next to climbs down, walks over and knocks on Terrance's window. Terrance steps out for a moment and has a brief conversation with the man, who looks at his watch and walks away frustrated. Eli witnesses the exchange and slowly gets out of the truck. He walks around, next to Terrance.

"Here, I got something for you." He reaches into his pants pocket and pulls out the number the nurse gave him.

"What's this?" Terrance asked.

"It's the number of the nurse you were all gooey about earlier."

Terrance smiles for a second then the smile falls as he tucks the piece of paper into his pants pocket. "I don't expect she'd be interested in me anyhow."

Eli gives him a light slap on the shoulder, "You are the most beautiful man I've ever met and she would be a fool not to be interested. Either way, you're on the hook. You've got to take her out to coffee or lunch as my proxy because I told her that I wanted to, but I won't be here long enough to get it done. She is expecting your call in a few weeks because I thought we had more work to do."

"We did the last house that I was supposed to work on..." He trails off and lets out a deep sigh. "They decided they didn't want to have me do the work."

"That's why I'm going somewhere else? Because they're too foolish to know how blessed they would be to have your help?"

Terrance grins. "Tragically, few folks realize how lucky they are when they get to interact with me."

The truck driver approaches again in spite of the disapproving looks he receives. "Sorry fellas. I've got to get back on the road."

"Here," Terrance hands Eli his bag and hanging clothes. The driver goes back to the truck to store his stuff, saying over his shoulder, "Five minutes."

Terrance and Eli step toward one another at the same time and Terrance grabs him in a bear hug, careful to avoid his injured shoulder. Eli returns it wholeheartedly even though it doesn't have the same impact.

"You better come out and visit us. If you don't, I'll set my wife loose on Mississippi."

Terrance lets out a hearty laugh.

"Well, I don't travel too much, but if I get the itch to go somewhere, I imagine Portland's as good as anywhere. If you ever decide you want to build a house, you let me know and I'll be there start to finish."

"I never thought to build a house before, but now that I know you, it seems like an awful good idea. There is no one else I would ever consider doing it with."

"Come on now. Rachel would get jealous if she heard you gushing on like that."

Now it is Eli's turn to laugh. He reaches out a hand for a shake which turns into another hug, and he bites his lip to keep from tearing up at having to say goodbye to the best friend he's made in many years. He turns and climbs up into the passenger side of the truck and sinks down on the air ride seat. He gives Terrance a combination salute and wave as he is climbing back into his battered pickup truck. Both trucks start moving in opposite directions at the same time.

"Sorry to rush you. I've got some tight deadlines to meet. I'm Blaine by the way."

Eli is not ready to deal with new circumstances. He didn't expect to leave the hospital and leave Mississippi. He isn't ready to say goodbye to Terrance or start a new adventure and there is nowhere inside him that is open to a new friendship yet.

"No worries, Blaine. I just got out of the hospital and I was there all night, so I'm pretty tired. Do you mind if I take a nap?"

"No, I don't mind at all. I'm used to being on my own. There's a double bed in the back there if you want to lay down. It's probably more comfortable than bouncing your head against the window for the next five and a half hours."

Eli stands and turns to look in the sleeper. The space is a nice dark womb and compared to the stark whites of the hospital, it looks inviting.

"Great. Thank you." He escapes to the back and figures out how to close the curtain between the cab and sleeper before he lays down on the bed in almost total darkness and wills himself to sleep.

CHAPTER 15

Eli can feel the truck slowing down and is prepared to pretend to be asleep like he did the last time Blaine stopped for a bathroom break.

"Are you awake?" Blaine quietly asks as he opens the curtain, letting the light pour into the dark cube. Eli blinks his eyes, adjusting rapidly to the change in lights.

"We are here. This is where I'm supposed to drop you off." He reaches into one of two miniature matching closets in the sleeper and pulls out Eli's hanging clothes before exiting the truck. Eli picks up his bag and follows him with trepidation, wondering what's coming next. When he gets to the ground, he looks around and sees they are at the end of a very long driveway leading up to a farm. "You can't take me up there?" Eli asked.

"No, sorry," Blaine says. "I don't know what the ground is like and I can't afford to get stuck." He starts back towards the truck. "Catch you later," he adds as he disappears around the front of the big rig.

Eli picks up his stuff and hikes up the driveway. He's barely halfway when a pack of dogs charge towards him. After a brief, terrorizing moment of uncertainty, it's clear they are all friendly. He sets his stuff back down and quickly discovers even two hands are woefully inadequate to greet the pack of friendly animals.

Most are content with a quick pat on the head or scratch of the rump and after they've had their turn head back to the house to announce the visitor. The last one to approach is a scruffy little dog who is decidedly skittish, but eventually makes its way over to his foot. He slowly squats back down and reaches out a hand, allowing the dog to sniff it, before he reaches for the dog, who seems to accept him in its own good time. As he reaches out, it winces reflexively, but its tail starts to wag as soon as it feels the light stroke on its back. He pets the dog for a minute, reassuring it. Speaking nonsense softly, enjoying the moment.

He sees people coming out of the house at the end of the drive and after a last pet, he stands up, picks up his gear and resumes his trek up the driveway. When he reaches the open area in front of the house, there are two women waiting for him. He assumes they are related in some way as they look similar, but not identical. The younger of the two is taller, slimmer and reaches her hand out to shake his first.

"You must be Eli. I'm Harper Davis and this is my mother, Nora Davis." She motions to the older woman. Once Harper releases his hand, he offers it to Nora, who gives a brief limp shake.

He pulls his hand sanitizer out of his pocket and offers it to both of them after he uses it. They reluctantly accept.

"Social distancing is natural around here most of the time so we've been lucky to not have to think much about masks and hand sanitizer. We'll do better," Harper offers.

He takes his mask off, "If you've been distancing, I'm not worried about it. I've been following all the guidance since they figured out what it was." He holds his mask up, "Unless you'd prefer?"

"No, you're fine. About the only time we'll be closer than six feet is at the table, and you can't wear a mask while you eat," Nora responds.

"We need to figure out how we are going to handle all of this with the students," Harper adds. "You just got here and you're already helping out."

The small dog is back at his feet so he squats down and pets her again until he notices the astonished look on both women's faces. Suddenly uncomfortable, "Did I do something wrong?"

Again, the younger woman responds first.

"No, not at all. Her name is See-no. She is a little lady with a rough past; she was badly abused and barely alive when she turned up here. She's not a fan of men and doesn't take to most people. You must have a magic way with animals, or a really good heart for her to let you pet her so soon."

A storm of emotions crosses the older woman's face as her daughter is talking. He can't identify all of them, but he can see pain, frustration and some joy cross her face.

"We're going to put you in one of the student cabins over here," Nora says, regaining her composure and walking off to the left. Eli hadn't noticed any cabins, but he saw a huge building that he guessed is a barn. He smiles to himself wondering if he will be sleeping in a barn for the next however long. He realizes he doesn't know how long he'll be here and that he doesn't have much knowledge or choice in the matter.

He follows Nora to the barn. Once they're past it, she makes a left. When he catches up, Eli can see a small row of what looks like storage sheds from the big-box hardware stores. Nora opens the door for the first one, and shows him the interior, which is a basic but reasonable accommodation.

There's a bar in the corner for hanging clothes. There's a double bed, a small table that holds the coffee machine and a few plates and silverware pieces. There's a dorm-style fridge underneath and in the corner, and a door to a tiny bathroom. Nora turns and walks away, scooping up the little dog and carrying it with her into the house. Harper stands at the door looking at Eli. He's not sure what she's waiting for, so he takes a guess. "Thank you, this looks great. Should I unpack now or are we working today?"

Harper smiles at the question and thinks to herself, "That's a good sign, not everyone that shows up on the farm is as willing to work as Eli appears to be."

"No, we're done with work for the day. We start really early around here and we knock off by suppertime. Are you hungry?"

Eli is, but he is not interested in going inside and being forced to make conversation with these strangers, no matter how nice they appear. Harper turns and he notices a flash of light coming from her hand. He steps forward to get a closer look and sees the same ring that Abed, Phil and Zeke wear.

"So, you're one of them," Eli stumbles, not quite sure what to call the order or group or whatever he's got himself mixed up with yet.

Harper looks at the ring and smiles, "Yes, I'm happy to say I am."

Eli is impressed that someone so young, she looks to be in her early twenties at most, is connected with them. Next he asks, "And your mother?"

"No, just me. Momma wasn't particularly interested. She was supportive of my interest. She knows a little but not much. And that's the way it's going to stay. If you change your mind about supper, you're welcome to come on up to the house. Otherwise, I'll come collect you at sunup so we can get after it."

"Sunup?" Eli thinks to himself in distress. Six a.m. with Terrance was early. He has no idea what time sunup even is. On the plus side, the humidity is slightly better here than Mississippi, the weight of the moist air still presses in on him. No denying it makes sense to get an early start to try and beat the heat for as much of the workday as possible.

None of that particularly matters because no one is asking his opinion, he offers her a lame smile. She returns it with the same enthusiasm. "I'll let you get settled," she says and walks away, leaving the door open.

Eli quickly unpacks his bag, noticing the bathroom is very basic, only a toilet and a sink. He wonders where he is supposed to shower. He guesses he will find out eventually. He sits down on the mattress and discovers it doesn't have much give. He calls Rachel. He had thought about texting her on the ride over, but was afraid she would want to talk if he did. He didn't know how to explain the change in circumstances to her, nor did he want to tell her about his bite and fall because he didn't want her to worry when he was gone and would not be home for another two to four weeks.

He is glad he waited, but he can't wait anymore. She answers on the first ring, laughter in her voice, "Hello my party animal, how are you?"

He is taken aback, trying to understand why she would call him a party animal and then remembers Terrance had told her he'd fallen asleep from beer, heat and hard work.

"I'm just out of control. How are you guys?" Before she can answer, he hears his son's voice in the background wanting to get on the phone.

"Hold on," she says. The next thing he hears is his son's Darth Vader-like breath on the phone.

"Hi Mason."

"Hi Dad," his son says, his voice full of excitement. "Guess what?"

"What?" Eli says, trying to match the excitement.

"When I meet Terrance, he's going to give me a shoulder ride. It might not be a long one, depending on how much I weigh by the time I meet him. When I get a shoulder ride, I'll be taller than him and Shaq both. I'll probably be as tall as King Kong," Mason enthuses. Eli is glad his family is already smitten with Terrance.

"That's neat. I wish I could do that, but I think I'm a little too big now."

"Yeah," Mason agrees with no sympathy whatsoever.

"Are you being good for your mom?" Eli asks, changing the subject.

"Yeah," Mason admits, but with much less enthusiasm.

"Glad to hear it. Anything else exciting?"

"Not more exciting than that," the boy states. After a brief pause, "I love you dad, bye."

Eli knows the boy's phone etiquette needs some work, so he quickly blurts out. "Love you too," hoping his son hears it before he's gone.

He hears Rachel say, "Go work on your math." There's a pause then they both start speaking at the same time and they both laugh.

"You go ahead. I was just asking how you're feeling today and how Terrance is doing. He seemed pretty ready for bed himself when I spoke to him yesterday."

"Well," Eli stumbles. "We were both good. I assume we both still are. I'm not with Terrance now. We ran out of work there, we wouldn't have except the next house he was going to rebuild, the people decided they didn't want him to do the work. Now I am in Missouri where I guess I'm going to be farming."

Laughter erupts from the phone and continues for what Eli thinks is much longer than necessary.

"What's so funny about that?" He can hear Rachel take a couple deep breaths, trying to compose herself.

"I'm sorry my love. I can picture you as many things. I've never pictured you as a farmer. I can almost see you riding around on some tractor. I don't know, it just strikes me as funny."

"Well, being honest, it strikes me as funny too. It's not something I ever had occasion to consider before now."

"Where are you farming?" Rachel asks.

"I'm in Missouri, not exactly sure where, somewhere close to St. Louis. I don't know much yet. I arrived not ten minutes before I called you. I met a pack of dogs and a couple women. I don't know how many other folks are here or how big this place is or what I'm going to be doing or how long I will be doing it."

"Must be hard for you, Love."

Rachel's sudden sympathy feels nice but he's not quite sure what caused it.

"Why's that?"

"Because you don't like surprises. You like to have a plan, even if you don't get your way, you like to have a say." Eli can't argue with any of those. It's good to be known, it's great to be loved.

"True, fortunately so far anyone that has anything to do with this has been super, so I feel more okay about it than I normally would."

"I'm happy to hear it. At first, I wasn't sure about the whole thing and I wasn't very happy about you being gone. I'm still not happy about you being gone, but this has been good for you so far. You and Terrance hit it off. You need that, you don't let people in very often."

"Why would I?" he asks rather cavalierly. "When you have the best people in the world in your life already. Why keep looking?"

She smiles in spite of herself. "And there is the charm."

There's a knock at the door, irritated Eli asks, "Can you hold on for a second?"

"Sure," Rachel agrees. Eli sets the phone down and goes to the door. There's no one there. He looks around and doesn't see anything until he looks down. There is a plate, loaded with steak and mashed potatoes and a bunch of green beans.

He notices the little dog but can't remember her name. He quickly cuts off a couple fatty-looking bites from steak and tosses them on the ground outside the door for her.

Without waiting to see if she gets them, he turns around closing the door behind him and goes back to the bed.

"Sorry about that, I guess it was supper delivery. I don't know who brought it but there was a plate full of food at the door for me."

"That sounds nice, but don't get used to it." Rachel teases. She does more of the cooking, but they both are more than capable in the kitchen.

"Fair enough." He can't take his eyes off the plate.

"I guess I should let you go," she says ruefully, "so that you can eat."

"Do you want me to call you back when I'm finished?" He didn't intend to end the call to eat, but the smells are starting to get him and his stomach is growling in protest.

"That's up to you. What time is it?"

He looks at his phone. "It's six-thirty here."

"Oh, we're still two hours apart. I was hoping that you were closer to home. I know that you are closer and that's good, I just thought you might be a time zone closer."

He knows it is early, but his shoulder is sore and gives an occasional twinge, he had barely slept in the hospital and only had a little nap in the truck. Suddenly, it all catches up to him.

"I wish I was a time zone closer too. Do you mind if I don't call back and just talk to you tomorrow? I'm sorry, I really miss you. It feels like more than forty-eight hours since we talked, but all of a sudden I'm really beat and us farmers start at sunup."

Rachel lets out a little giggle, "Sunup? I wish I could be there to see that. That's fine. I'll just talk to you tomorrow night. Eli, if you can, get someone to take a picture of you farming for me. Please?"

Unenthusiastic, "If I can. Good night, I love you."

"Love you."

Eli digs into the plate of food, enjoying every bite. He's nearly finished when he hears a faint scratch at the door. He opens the door to find the little dog staring up at him expectantly. He opens the door and steps back from the door.

"I don't know if you're supposed to be in here, how about we find out? You might as well come in."

The small dog takes a couple tentative steps forward. Eli leaves the door open for a minute, not wanting to spook her. He returns to his plate of food, which is nearly empty and drops a green bean on the floor to see what she'll make of it and she gobbles it up. He gives her the last two from his plate, she scarfs them down. He's a little unsure about giving the dog table scraps. In the Northwest, most people are pretty serious about what their dog eats and not allowing strangers to feed them.

They seem pretty laid back here. The dogs have the run of the place, which means they can't fully control their diets. He shrugs and gives the dog a small bite of mashed potatoes. The dog eats it, her tail wagging. Eli eats the remaining bite of potato. He takes the final bite of steak, which he saved last, and cuts it in half. He pops one half in his mouth and offers the other half to the little dog, this time holding it instead of dropping it on the ground. She approaches tentatively and takes it gingerly from his fingers.

He wipes his hands on the front of his jeans and says, "That's it." He tilts the plate down a little to show the dog it's now empty before he sets it on the small table. He stands there, watching the little dog, waiting to see what she'll do and she sits there watching him, doing the same thing. To end the stalemate, Eli walks towards the door to see if she'll want to leave when he starts to close it. He closes it slowly, giving her every opportunity to leave. She doesn't, so he closes it.

"You're welcome to stay as long as you want. Scratch or bark and I'll let you out when you're ready," he says on his way to the bathroom. He relieves himself, brushes his teeth and shaves a couple days of stubble from his face. He knows he won't want to do it in the morning. He leaves his T-shirt and his Calvins on and folds his jeans, placing them at the bottom of the bed. He pulls out a fresh pair of socks and sets them next to his shoes to be able to get dressed quickly in the morning. He wishes he'd asked what time sunup is so he could set his alarm and be ready when the knock came, but he'll just have to live with it now.

He lies down on the bed and wishes for the bed in the trailer in Mississippi. He rolls and tosses a little trying to find a comfortable position, and about the time he does, the little dog starts whining. He looks over his shoulder towards the door, but she's nowhere near it. Instead, she jumps up on the side of the bed with her front feet and looks up at him. After a brief internal debate, he decides in for a penny, in for a pound.

He reaches over and gently pulls the little dog up. She walks over to him and lays down against his chest. She is a mix of soft and scruffy and it feels odd as he pets her. She presses harder against him and her warmth is comforting. Soon they both fall into a deep sleep.

CHAPTER 16

It feels like the knock on the door comes a mere five minutes later, rather than the nine hours it really is. He gets up. The little dog does not give any indication of wanting to join him. He lets her stay in bed, pulls on his pants and opens the door with one hand, still reaching for his socks with the other. Nora is awaiting him at the door. He notices she is shorter than him, by an easy six inches and is probably ten or twenty years older. He's guessing she's probably late forties, early fifties. She is certainly more well-rounded than her lanky daughter. Her face is contorted with concern.

"Have you seen See-no?" She wrings her hands anxiously.

Eli, suddenly guilty, backs up and motions to the bed with his arm, "I'm sorry ma'am, I hope I didn't do anything wrong. She came scratching on the door last night and I let her in. And then she jumped up to get on the bed and I let her on it. I didn't know what the rules were, and I didn't want to disturb you. I can see you were worried about her and I do apologize."

Nora's eyes widen as he explains. Instead of responding to him she yells, "Harper, she's in here."

Harper, in blue jeans, a tank top and cowboy boots, comes running over. She stands next to her mother and looks at Eli. Hearing the commotion, See-no sits up in the bed and is moving her head around trying to find an exit from under the covers. She pops her head out and the women reach for and squeeze each other's hand.

"Look at her," says Harper. Eli is not sure what's happening but the look that Harper gives him makes him confident his stock is on the rise. "That's amazing," she adds, "how on earth did she end up there?"

Nora answers first. "He said that she scratched at the door last night and that she tried to jump up on the bed." She tapers off somewhat disbelieving.

Harper looks to Eli for confirmation. He nods. Harper is not quite sold, asking, "Really?"

"Yeah, I hope it's okay. Like I was explaining to your mom here, I didn't know the rules. I hope I didn't do anything wrong. I'm sorry you two were worried about her."

Harper ignores him and plows into the room making a beeline for the little dog sitting on the bed looking very pleased with herself, tail wagging.

Harper smiles at her and strokes her head and back, "Look at you See-no. You're so brave," she says, kissing the dog all over on her face before she scoops her up in her arms.

"Oh my God, you made me so happy little momma. Such a sweet, brave girl."

She leaves the room as quickly as she entered carrying the little dog off to the house. Over her shoulder she says, "Come on and get some breakfast before we get started."

Nora smiles at him, still wringing her hands.

He says, "Let me get my socks and shoes on and I'll be right behind you."

Nora takes a step towards the house and turns back to Eli sitting on the edge of the bed pulling on a second sock.

"I don't know how you did it. She was obviously abused by a man and she does not like them. I can't believe she came to you or that she slept in your bed. I've been trying for two years, and she still won't sleep in mine. And she likes me better than anybody else. You're magic or a dog whisperer or something." With that she gives a pleasant smile and disappears around the corner.

Once fully dressed he follows, up the large steps to the wide front porch and after a moment's hesitation opens the front door.

"Come on in," Harper's voice greets him from deeper in the house. He follows it until he finds himself in a large eat-in kitchen. The table is set for three and Harper sets a plate down in front of an empty spot and places hers beside her momma, whom she joins.

"Dig in," she says as she starts eating.

Eli obeys, sits down and starts eating his farm fresh breakfast of eggs, bacon, hash browns and toast. What seems like a scant few minutes later, all three plates are mostly empty and the women deposit their dishes into the sink after scraping any leftover food into the bucket beside it.

He follows their example and they are out the door.

"I understand you have a hurt shoulder and that we've got to take it easy on it," Harper says on the way to the barn.

He is relieved she knows about his injury. "Yes, I have almost a full range of motion but not a lot of strength. I'm supposed to move it as much as I can, but not overdo it."

"We're going to stick you in the combine, so it'll be up to you how much you want to move it. This job won't require much."

She walks up to a massive machine, "Why don't you climb in on that side?" She motions to the passenger side. Nora walks to the other end of the massive structure and the massive doors slowly slide open. Harper fires up the machine and Eli sits on the small bench seat beside her.

Eli's nervous, assuming that they must believe he's got some experience if they expect him to drive something so big, expensive and complex.

"I don't know what they told you. But I don't have any experience with anything like this."

She laughs. "It's okay. It's not complicated, monotonous but not complicated. We're harvesting soybeans. We've already got the Draper head on; all you have to do is drive up and down in rows slowly so the machine has time to do its job. Once I show you the basics, it's simple. Here's your gas, here's your brake, it steers similar to a car but takes a little longer to start, stop and turn. I'm going to make a couple turns so you can see what it feels like, and then I'll switch spots with you."

Ready for the demo, Harper drives them out of the barn and across fields already harvested. Then they reach a field filled with brown plants, she does something that he isn't paying close enough attention to catch. The machine makes a noise and something on the front looks lower. She starts moving again, this time even slower. She was moving slower than a car in a school zone before, now she is moving at a snail's pace.

When she gets to the end of the field, she makes a long, looping left until she gets to the end in that direction. She makes another long, broad turn and continues.

"That's all you do. Don't worry about making tight turns, I'll take care of the center. If you get too hot, turn on the fan, sometimes the AC needs a boost in this old girl."

She fishes a tube out of her pocket and sets it on the dash.

"I recommend you apply some of this before it's too late in the morning."

He picks up the sunscreen and follows her advice, still sporting some pink on his face and neck from his time in the south.

She comes to a stop. Opens the door and climbs down saying, "Go ahead and scoot over."

He is appalled that a fifteen-minute tutorial is supposed to prepare him for driving this piece of machinery. She goes around the back and climbs up into the passenger side a minute later.

"Okay, go ahead and ease on the gas, nice and slow. You don't want to romp on it like you are racing a quarter-mile." He follows her instructions and the big machine slowly starts rolling forward. He gets up to about five miles and she cautions him, "Slow down, you want to keep it between three and four."

"Miles per hour?" He is amazed anything gets done at that speed. She just nods. He starts turning left. When she puts a hand on his forearm and says, "Hold on just a bit. I know it's deceptive with this big wall of glass you see everything, but being up this high, you are further off than it looks. Wait until you think you should turn and count to four."

He drives another ten feet, when he thinks he's going to overshoot the field and she says, "Now." He grabs the wheel, ready to use a lot of force to make a big turn. He quickly discovers it's not necessary. He loosens the grip on the wheel, corrects his line and follows the same pattern that she had.

"Why don't you go ahead and stop. You're welcome to listen to the radio if you want to, but keep your eyes open. If we need to talk to you, I'll get in front of you and flag you down. If you need to take a break, there's a porta potty on the back of the trailer on the other side of the field. I'll come back out to check on you in a little bit and I'll bring you some water and drinks to get you through the morning." She stops and thinks for a moment, "I think that's about it. You have any other questions?"

Eli is sure he does, but he can't think of any which is bizarre. How do you spend less than twenty minutes in a machine like this and be considered ready to drive it? Yet, that's what is happening. He shrugs, "I can't think of any," he says, disbelieving his own answer.

"All right then, see you in a while." Harper climbs back out and Eli slowly starts the machine moving. He can see Harper in the mirror, making her way across the field on foot, occasionally looking over her shoulder at his progress.

Eli keeps plugging along finding it easy to manage the machine, but still uneasy about being left alone so quickly with what must be an expensive piece of machinery. After about half an hour, as he is coming up a row heading back towards the farm, he notices Harper waving her arms at the edge of the field. He comes to a stop near her. She picks up the bag and a cooler and climbs up into the cab with him.

"Here is some water and drinks for you. There's a sandwich and some snacks in the bag. Mom's going to be over here in a little bit with the grain cart, when she pulls up beside you and honks push this button."

He nods when he is sure he knows what she is talking about.

"She's going to be driving alongside while you are working, to empty you, while you're rolling. I know this might not seem like a big deal to you, but I'm sure you can already tell it takes a while to get this done and you're a huge help."

Eli smiles, happy to know that he is making a difference. Remembering Rachel's request, embarrassed he pulls his phone out of his pocket.

"Is there any way you could snap a quick picture of me for my wife? She asked me last night to get a picture of me farming." Harper's answer is a smile, she takes the phone and disappears out of the combine. She reappears a minute later out of the driver side door where she takes a picture of Eli, snapping off a couple to make sure one turns out. She climbs up his side and he starts when she knocks on his door. He opens it and she hands back his phone.

"Just keep doing what you are doing. All day. I'll come get you when it's time to knock off. You can take bathroom breaks whenever you need of course and stop if you want or need to, but as much as you can, keep rolling along. Don't forget when Momma honks to push that button and then you don't have to do anything else, just keep driving along the same as you have been. She'll make sure that you guys don't run into each other. You just keep doing the same thing no matter what."

He nods in agreement, a little concerned about a new element being added, but realizing he had similiar concerns in the morning, and it turned out to be a very simple process. He keeps rolling along, as Harper put it. A short while later, he hears a honk and looks over to see Nora driving a tractor with something attached to the back of it that looks kind of like a semi-trailer without a top. He pushes the button Harper pointed out and is impressed to see stuff coming out of the chute and landing squarely in the bin that Nora is towing. He reminds himself to stay focused on his mostly straight lines and not stare too long in the side view mirror, which is a siren song for him.

It is so fascinating to be seeing all this first-hand and knowing that they could unload without stopping and let someone so inexperienced drive. Unfortunately, every time he looks that way, he tends to drift that way and Nora honks at him to show her displeasure. She stays with him for a few minutes and then makes the kill sign by running her hand across her throat.

He assumes she wants him to push the button again. He does, she gives him a thumbs up. Before she peels off and turns back toward the barn. He continues his slow laps of the field as the day crawls along, he eats the sandwich, fruit and chips and drinks all the water, most of the Gatorade and reapplies sunscreen several times.

About every hour, Nora or Harper come driving up with the grain cart and he pushes the button to open and close the chute as they direct him. When it is done, they peel away and he finds himself alone in the field again. There is something about the work that is starting to appeal to him. He can think about anything he wants. He certainly has plenty of time on his hands. However, something about it is mesmerizing and he is able to relax, which he finds he needs. He isn't trying to figure out how to fix anything. He isn't planning a next step; it is a rare moment if he is even thinking about Rachel and Mason.

He is just staring at the plants in front of him and the soil behind him once they are harvested and it is mulched with the excess plant material. He is starting to get sleepy and pulls out his phone, wanting to turn on some of his own music instead of what he is able to get on the radio. He finds the battery critically low, remembering that heat often drains it faster than constant use, he shoves it back in his pocket. He is glad to see Harper flagging him down from the end of the field again.

He brings the hulking machine to a stop near her and waits for her to climb up. Instead, she shows up at his door, which he opens, and she says, "Come on down. It's time to call it a day."

He gathers the cooler, his open Gatorade, and all his trash before he follows her down the steps to the ground. She takes all of it from his hands and leads the way back to the house.

"You got two choices on showers," she says over her shoulder. "There's an outdoor shower on the side of the house, you got privacy, it's fenced off, but no roof. There are towels out there if you choose that one, or you're welcome to come take a shower in the house."

"Thanks, I think I'll just use the outdoor shower. I feel like I'm wearing half your field, I'd hate to drag all this into the house."

She laughs, "You wouldn't be the first, nor would you be the last. Kind of hard to avoid around here, but that is why we put in the outdoor shower so that we can leave the worst of it behind."

As they get closer to the house, See-no comes to greet him, tail wagging. A couple of the larger dogs also come over to say hello. They crowd the little dog out, but as before, they're satisfied with a quick greeting before going off on their own again, leaving See-no to be his only fan.

"What is her name again?" Eli asked.

"See-no."

"Zeno?"

"Close, See-no. S-e-e-n-o," Harper says, spelling it out to clarify.

Eli is still unclear. "Is that a Native American word from the area?"

"No, when we were sure she was going to make it and decided to name her, momma said if she wanted to stay here, she would see no more abuse. And somehow it shortened to See-no and the name stuck."

"I like it. Can I ask you something else?" He squats down to pet the dog.

"Sure," Harper agrees.

"How'd you get so many dogs? Do you guys have a rescue or something?"

"You would think," Harper says. "No, people just dump them here. We keep what we get for the most part. We have a fair amount of people come and go. Sometimes a dog and a person that are supposed to be together find each other here, but for the most part, they come and stay."

"That's nice. Not that people dump them, but that you're able to keep them. They seem pretty happy here."

"They're treated right, well fed, and they just get to be dogs, so I imagine they are pretty happy. Unless they want to pester the livestock, that we don't tolerate, but pretty much anything else goes. This morning you said you weren't sure what the rules were and neither of us thought to fill you in. We were both a little thrown by See-no taking to you so quickly. The gist of it is if you want to let a dog inside, you're welcome to. If you want them on your bed, that's fine. You want to share a bite, that's fine. If you don't, don't feel like you have to. They'll take off if you shoo them away. We just don't raise a hand to anything here. That's it for rules when it comes to dogs or any of the animals around."

"More than reasonable," Eli agrees, squatting down again to give See-no the attention she'd been trying to garner from him, wagging her tail excitedly, waiting impatiently. Harper smiles at the two of them and walks up the stairs towards the front door, calling back, "We'll have supper in about half an hour. You're welcome to join us."

"Actually, I need to call home. It's about the time I need to say good night to my son before he goes to bed."

"Suit yourself," she says.

Twenty minutes later, Eli is freshly showered, sitting on the bed next to See-no. He snaps a quick picture of the little dog and texts it and a couple of the ones that Harper had taken of him driving the combine to Rachel. He strokes the little dog waiting for his phone to ring.

"Hi Dad, is that your dog now?" Mason is ecstatic.

"No, she is just a new friend. I can't have a dog either until we are ready to move."

"Why don't we move and you can have that dog and I can get a Rottweiler?"

"Remember what I told you last time we talked about this? It might take a while. I hope you haven't been driving your mom crazy over this."

"I haven't, I've been good. She is letting me stay up late so I can watch a movie since I've been so good."

"That's great. I'm glad to hear that. I miss you."

"I miss you too. The movie is starting. Bye."

Eli doesn't bother trying to get in a goodbye before his son is gone.

Rachel's voice comes on, "I love the dog. Now I'm getting a little dog crazy myself."

"She is a sweetie. They said she came from a pretty rough situation, abuse that almost killed her. I guess she doesn't ever like men, and she won't even sleep with the women that rescued her. She curled right up with me last night and she was waiting for me when I got done working tonight."

"She's got good instincts choosing you as a safe male companion." Surprisingly tired from the day, Eli is ready to wrap up the conversation when he hears the knock on the door.

"Hold on a second, I'll be right back." He goes to the door and opens it in time to see Nora walking away. There is a big plate full of a couple of homemade burgers and a heap of fries dropped on his doorstep. He didn't know who the cook was, but he appreciates their work. He picks up the plate and sets it on the small table on his way back to the bed.

"The food delivery fairy just struck again."

"I'll let you go while it's hot. Are you going to call back or go to bed early again?"

"Unless there is something else you want to talk about, I think I will go to bed early again. They weren't kidding about sunup. Like I said, it's not hard work, but after a whole day of it, I'm so much more tired than it feels like I should be."

"It's okay, honey, you don't have to explain. I know you're working hard. Plus, you're doing something new and that's more tiresome than you might realize. You get some sleep. Just know that we love you and miss you so much. I can't wait till you're back home."

"Me too. See-no is a good cuddler, but she can't hold a candle to you. Tomorrow night you go first. I want to hear how work and school are going for you. Good night, I love you."

"I love you too," she echoes.

Eli disconnects the phone and drops it on the bed to keep charging. He turns his attention to See-no, "Did you see what we got for dinner?" he asks. The little dog wags her tail in excitement to show she had in fact noticed the plate. He pulls the chair to the table and sits down, as he takes a big bite of the burger. A muffled "mmm" escapes his lips. He pinches a piece of meat off the remaining burger and hands it to a grateful See-no, before taking another massive bite. He quickly polishes off both burgers, sparing a couple bites of each for See-no before turning his attention to the fries.

There are some ketchup packets under the foil on the plate; he opens them and empties them out onto the plate. He dips his first fry with low expectations, not usually a fan of homemade fries. These, however, came from a fryer, whether it was an oil fryer or an air fryer he didn't know or care. They taste heavenly. He reluctantly shares a few of them with See-no. Finally, he has to stop, even though there are a couple left on the plate his stomach is at capacity and then some. He thinks to himself, "I'm going to gain back the weight I lost working with Terrance sitting on my butt all day and eating like this," but he shoves in one more fry to punctuate the thought. After he finishes eating, he lies down on the bed not expecting to fall asleep, but he does as soon as See-no curls up next to him.

CHAPTER 17

The next morning, Eli sleeps through the knock on the door and wakes instead to the little dog licking his face, trying to get his attention. He rubs his eyes with his knuckles and slowly gets to his feet. His body is stiff from the firm bed and his injured shoulder is especially stiff from lack of use the day before.

He slowly makes his way to the door and opens it, bleary-eyed. Nora is standing there with a smile. She goes around him to find the little dog. She pets the dog but doesn't take her this time. She graces him with a bigger smile and says, "Breakfast is ready. Come on in when you are." She walks away briskly.

He makes his way to the bathroom, splashes some water on his face, uses the facilities quickly, changes his clothes, sits on the bed beside the dog, petting her briefly before pulling on his socks and shoes. He sets her gently on the floor, and together they walk out of the little cabin and make their way into the house.

When they get there, Nora and Harper are halfway finished with the food on their plates. There is a full plate sitting in front of the empty chair for him. He sits down, and See-no wanders off to attend to her own breakfast. There is very little discussion at the table as the women finish their breakfast and put their plates in the sink. As she walks out the door, Harper says, "Come on out to the field when you're ready."

Caught with a mouthful of food, Eli simply nods in agreement that she can't see and isn't looking for. He is feeling bad about moving slowly this morning. He quickly finishes the meal and follows after her.

Once he has returned to his station in the combine, she sets off to do he doesn't know what. As he drives long rows at slow speeds, he makes sure to move his arm and do as close to the stretches his aftercare instructions gave him as the size of the cab allows. Like the day before, Harper shows up with beverages and lunches, and both take turns emptying the combine into the grain cart as he continues to drive along. Unlike the day before, he enjoys the time to think, but still finds himself more relaxed than usual. He thinks of Terrance and their time together and what an unexpected pleasure their friendship turned out to be.

He thinks of his wife and son and hopes in the near future they'll be able to get his son the dog he's wanted almost since he could talk. He thinks of poor little See-no and the suffering she experienced before finding Nora and Harper. Thinking of the two women, he admits to himself he likes them both, even though he's holding them at arm's-length, not ready for another goodbye as difficult as the one with Terrance was.

That evening passes much the same as the one before. But he ties a knot into a dirty sock and plays a little bit of tug-of-war with the little dog in between some stretches to loosen up his body that is even more sore from another day of sitting for long hours. He hopes it will help in preparation for another night on the extra firm bed. Rachel catches him up on what he has missed in her routine. Mason, tired from the night before, barely says hello before he is gone and wanting his mom's help with bath time.

Eli again falls asleep much more quickly than usual for him. But he does hear the knock on the door in the morning. This time, he picks up See-no and hands her gently over to Nora. She gives the dog a kiss before setting her down on the ground.

"Breakfast is ready when you are."

She walks away, happy to find the little dog following after her. Eli gets dressed in the clothes he had set out the night before and makes his way to the kitchen before either of the women have taken their first bite. The two women exchange looks.

Harper says, "We were going to knock off an hour early today so that we could share supper with you, seeing how this is your last day here. If you want to, of course," she hesitates. "If you choose not to, we understand. We're trying to make it so that you can if you want to, but we certainly don't want you to feel like you have to."

Eli is more stuck on it being his last night there than anything about supper, or dinner as he still thinks of it.

"What do you mean it's my last night here?"

Harper says, "I'm sorry, I thought you knew. We have students coming in tomorrow. We just needed a few days' help to get the soybeans harvested before they arrived. I'm not sure where you're off to next. I know someone's going to pick you up tomorrow morning right after breakfast."

Eli contemplates the news while he slowly finishes his breakfast. He finally realizes that Harper is waiting for something, but he doesn't know what. He looks at her, "I'm ready when you are."

She gets up and takes her plate to the sink. He follows and does the same thing.

"What about supper?" she asks again.

"Of course, I would love to join you for dinner. Sorry about that. I was distracted, wondering what is coming next."

Nora pulls a five-dollar bill out of her purse and hands it to Harper. Eli watches the exchange with a questioning look. Nora explains, "I bet her five dollars that you wouldn't want to come to supper. I figured out how you got See-no's guard down so quickly, you're as skittish as she is. I didn't figure you would want to sit still for supper."

Eli isn't sure how to respond. He knows he has been standoffish towards the women and feels bad they noticed. It has nothing to do with them. Now that he is leaving soon, he regrets not taking more time to get to know them.

He graces her with a broad smile and says, "I'm sorry I cost you five dollars. To make it up to you, I'll do the dishes after dinner." She reaches out a hand to him, and he takes it and shakes it.

"Deal," she said.

Harper, impatient to get the day started, interjects, "All right, let's get after it."

The trio makes their way out the front door. Nora heads to the large barn, Harper and Eli heading to the combine at the end of the field. When they reach it, Harper realizes she didn't need to walk out there with him.

"I guess you know what you're doing by now." She hands him the key, "I'll be out after a while with snacks and beverages. You can finish that field, and I'll be out to move you to the next. If you get done before I make it back, stretch your legs and relax."

He gives her a little salute as he climbs the steps into the cab and starts another day at the rip-roaring pace of three to four miles an hour. The day goes by faster than the previous two, he assumes it's from the greater comfort with the activity that had seemed so foreign initially, and the knowledge that it is his last day. It changes the feeling from tedium to enjoying the peace while it lasts. He is a little sorry when he sees Harper signaling the end of the day from the edge of the new field he is working. It is much smaller than the previous, and he finished most of it. He would have liked to complete the job before he left.

Harper is in a little ATV; he climbs in next to her, and she has a little fun zipping back to the farmhouse at a much higher speed than he had been driving all day. They come to a stop rather suddenly and somewhat sideways, stirring up dust. She shoots him a devil-may-care grin, "Come in whenever you're ready. I imagine you want to clean up. We'll be there whenever you turn up."

As is her habit, she is off without waiting for a response. He gets some fresh clothes and heads to the outdoor shower. He enjoys the feel of the sun on his skin as the water washes away all the dirt and grime from the day. He quickly gets dressed, deposits his dirty clothes, and grabs his previous night's dinner plate from the table on his way to the house.

Eli finds Nora and Harper in the dining room instead of at the normal table in the kitchen. Half of the table is covered with a sewing machine and fabric. There is a pattern pinned to different fabric. The women sit at the other end of the table, a bountiful meal spread before them in an empty place waiting for him. He studies the sewing project, suddenly feeling a little shy.

"That's just my hobby," Nora dismisses her work in progress.

"It's more than that. She brings in some good money selling her projects," Harper corrects.

He feels more comfortable and joins them at the table, feeling silly for his moment of reluctance.

Nora says, "We say grace at supper. You're welcome to join us if you care to, no mind if you don't." He watches them clasp hands and close their eyes. He bows his head and closes his eyes as well.

Harper starts, "I'm grateful for another beautiful day." Nora adds, "I'm grateful for the abundance we have on this table and in our lives." Harper says, "I am grateful my father took off ten years ago."

"I am grateful he never returned," Nora adds.

"I am grateful for our new interns arriving tomorrow," and adds, "I'm grateful for the great help Eli has been to us these past few days."

"I'm grateful for the healing See-no has experienced in Eli's presence," Nora chimes.

"I am grateful for the many opportunities small farmers have today," Harper says.

"I'll second that," Nora adds, "and grateful we are healthy and well, and so is every living thing that resides here."

They raise their heads to look at Eli, see his head is bowed and his eyes are closed. Harper asks, "Is there anything you'd like to add?"

Eli nods, "I am grateful for my family, for their love and for their continued good health. I am grateful for the opportunity to be here and for the work that I am able to do right now to help my family. I'm grateful for new friends, two-legged and four-legged."

They give approving smiles and pause a minute, making sure he's done. When he doesn't continue, Nora finishes with, "In Jesus' name we pray." No one says much of anything for the next minute or two. While food is dished up and plates are passed if things are out of reach.

Eli thinks about their prayer. He'd been to a number of churches as a young adult and had never heard one quite like that. He really likes it. He thinks he might try it with Rachel and Mason after he gets home. He is a little surprised not to see meat of some sort on the table, instead there is a casserole-type thing which he is suspicious of until he takes his first bite.

"I don't know what this is," he says, pointing to his plate with his fork, "but it's amazing."

Harper smiles, Nora looks at her, bursting with pride. "We go vegan about once a week, which is about as often as I cook incidentally. This is my vegan surprise casserole."

He doesn't ask what the surprise is because he doesn't want to ruin his enjoyment just in case there is something too weird on the ingredients list. In between bites, he asks, "Where is the rest of your farm help?"

Harper looks at him like he's a little slow and says, "We have new interns coming in tomorrow."

"I know," he acknowledges. "But surely you must have someone else here on a regular basis," they both shake their head no. "How many acres do you have?" he asks.

"We have a hundred and fifty of our own," Harper says. "We lease another three hundred currently for the soybeans. We are phasing them out and we've been dropping about a hundred acres a year for the last few years."

He has tried to think about other things, but Eli's mind just can't ignore the gratitude for Harper's father walking out on them. He truly wants to know how they could possibly keep afloat with such a small farm, or how they could manage it by themselves. First, he has to know about the father issue.

He starts unsure, not wanting to offend, yet unable to ignore the topic. "I hope you don't mind my asking, but I noticed you were grateful that Harper's father walked out on you guys when she was ten."

"Ten years ago," Harper corrects.

"Okay," he doesn't see how that would make a difference. "I guess I was just wondering how you can be grateful about him leaving, or if you really are?"

"Heck yeah, we're grateful," Harper says passionately. Nora nods vigorously.

Eli feels he should share a little if he is going to be probing them and offers, "My dad walked out on me when I was a kid, and it never once occurred to me in all these years to be grateful about it, so that's why I'm asking."

"He was a mess," Nora says. "A hot mess."

Harper adds, "He was headed for trouble. He was running this place into the ground. He got hurt, he got hooked on pills, he was in a foul mood all the time. He wasn't the person Momma met and fell in love with. He wasn't the man that I had known and loved when I was little. By the time he left, we were just thrilled. The farm had been in his family for generations, and he eventually let us buy out his half. Before that, I couldn't wait to get out of here. Once he left, I could actually explore whether or not this life was for me. The nicest thing he could have done was leave."

Eli hears what they're saying and says emphatically, "Wouldn't it have been better for both of you, for all of you if he had stayed and gotten help and turned himself around?"

"Nope," Nora said, and this time Harper nodded in agreement. "He was cut from a different cloth. He wasn't one to listen to either of us. By the time he was ready to go, we were happy to be rid of him, as bad as that might sound. He wasn't open to either of our ideas about farming, and people that cling to the ways that he liked to farm tend to go under. Whereas people that are as creative and ambitious as Harper here do really well, even with very small farms. Which we are not," Nora adds.

That makes some sense to Eli, but he has to poke it a bit more. "But don't you feel like you missed out on something not having him here the whole time you were growing up?" He directs this at Harper.

"No. I think that I, like most kids, are better off having one happy, loving parent than two miserable parents. Momma and I were walking around on eggshells, frustrated because we weren't being heard and didn't have any say in what was happening around us."

Eli can sort of see that, although he doesn't like the idea that being without a dad can be a good thing. "How about you, Nora. You guys made a commitment to spend your life together, to be partners until the end, didn't it bother you to have him not keep his word?"

"Not in the least," Nora says. "I know a lot of folks from the previous generation around here, and some of them have a good thing, and I envy them, but there are also a mighty awful lot of people who stayed together because they said they would. It's a lofty goal, but forever can be a long time. People grow and change, and the man he was by the time he left is not someone I would've said yes to a single date with, let alone an eternity.

When I was young, all his bossiness was attractive because he was so confident when I wasn't. As I grew into myself and became a mother and had such a wonderful, strong-willed daughter, and saw that the roles that women had been adhering to for so long weren't the only possibility, I didn't like that about him anymore. He wasn't someone who was willing to grow and change with me. Bottom line, he left, and we're thankful, and we've been thankful every evening for thirteen years now. We'll continue to express our gratitude for his leaving, but we wish good things for him."

Eli still can't imagine feeling that way. Seeing the doubt on his face, Harper adds, "It's the kindest thing that you can do if you're not happy and you're not contributing positive things, and you're not interested or willing to make changes so that you can be. Leaving is a gift, and that's what we're grateful for. He gave us the gift of taking his miserableness elsewhere and letting us be free to live our lives and run our farm the way we want, and to be joyful, which we are every day."

He thinks about it for a minute and slowly, painfully comes to the realization that their perspective has valid points. He never considered it anything but wrong and outright cowardly for his dad to walk out on him and his mom. She had never really presented it any other way either. Honestly, she hadn't said too much about it, period.

Eli says, "I'm glad that it was good for you two. It wasn't good for us. I saw how hard my mom worked, and I knew that if he was there, she wouldn't have had to work so hard."

"So, if he had stayed, but drank or did drugs or gambled away every penny they both earned, would you have been better off?" Nora asked.

"No."

"How about if he made a lot of money and wouldn't let your mom work at all, but treated either or both of you like punching bags? Better off?" she fires off.

"No."

"How about if he left your mom and was one of those weekend dads that break your heart every time you believe he'll show up. Would that be better?" Harper takes a swing.

"No. There are other options, though," he protests.

"You mean if he was a loving father and husband and a hard worker?"

"Yes!" They are finally understanding what he is saying.

"Sorry, buddy. Healthy, well-adjusted guys that are ready and stable enough to be a husband or father don't leave for the fun of it. Guys that aren't can be kind enough to leave or stay and cause a lot of pain all the time or over time. Feel however you want about it, we are grateful."

He nods, assimilating the new perspective. In his mind, he moves on to his next set of questions.

"How can you make a go of it with such a small farm, and why are you turning away from soybeans?"

Nora looks to Harper, who proceeds, "We're turning away from soybeans because it's the biggest crop in the state. There's the most competition for it, and I think the soil is tired. Plus, I don't like having all our eggs in one basket. I'm just interested in a lot of new things, and we're actually making more money than we ever have with less acreage than we've ever had."

"That doesn't seem possible."

"You're right, he's a ghoster," Nora says.

Eli waits for them to elaborate, but assumes that it's in reference to him not joining them for dinner the other nights.

Harper finishes her bite and then explains, "That's our term for people that have ghost rules," she pauses, searching for an example. "Like you assuming that because the combine is big, it would take a long time to learn how to drive it or it would take more physical effort than it does. You're assuming that it would be a bad decision to turn away from the number one crop in the state. You're assuming that you can't make a go of it unless you're a huge commercial farm.

There are probably things in your life that you assume that you can't do, just like you couldn't imagine someone leaving being a positive thing. We call it being a ghoster because ghost rules aren't real unless you believe them. Daddy was a big ghoster. It was weird for us because we didn't know what were real limits and what were his assumptions. We tested things one at a time and found he was wrong most of the time. We started with trial and error and figured out if it was a real rule, law, or limit we could find documentation of some sort."

He and Rachel had a couple of those situations. He was usually the one to assume the limitation, and when she was tired of living with whatever it was, Rachel was usually the one to find the truth. This wasn't something he wanted to bring to the table.

"So, how do you stop being ghoster?"

"The first thing is any time you catch yourself thinking 'I can't,' 'they won't let me,' or 'it's not allowed,' any of those limiting sentence starters, pay attention. 'In order to' is a big one, like 'in order to find a girlfriend, you have to move to a big city.'"

He didn't see that one coming and looks at her quizzically to make sure he understands.

Harper gives him a little shoulder shimmy and a wink that tells him there is much more to her than he thought.

"Yes, you can be gay in the Midwest. We even have pride events here. Well, not here exactly, but in St. Louis and Kansas City."

He smiles, "I like the Midwest more now. If you could get rid of the humidity, I'd even consider living here. Tell me more about defeating the ghost rules, please."

"To start, just get in the habit of hearing it. Once you start hearing it, start asking questions. Is it true? How do I know it's true? Can I prove it? If it is true and you can prove it, then there is nothing for it. But if you can't prove it or if you don't know why you think that it's true, do a little investigating. It's been our experience, nine times out of ten you discover you can, and the limits are your imagination and nothing more."

He sits back, blown away. "This is a conversation I wish I'd had ten years ago. I don't want to admit or even think about how much 'can't' shows up in my head. I see now I really did myself a disservice not joining you two for dinner every chance I had."

"No need for regret," Harper says, letting him off the hook. "That's our best tidbit for sure, so far anyway. That's where our life changed, and that's where we started phasing out soybeans and got involved in gourmet mushrooms and medicinal herbs and flowers and when we became an organic teaching farm and started doing CSA's for the produce and," she pauses.

Eli jumps in, asking, "What's a CSA?"

"CSA is community supported agriculture for people who want to have a more direct relationship with their food and the farmers that grow it. They share the risk and reward. They pay a fixed amount up front, and they get a box or bag every week, most of the year here. Some have shorter seasons depending on what they grow and where they are. If it's a great crop, then they get a heck of a good deal for their investment. If it's a bad crop, then they don't get as great a deal for their investment. Farmers know they have someplace to sell their produce before they even plant the seeds.

We do CSA's for about half of our produce yield each year. The other half we take to the farmers markets because of the apprenticeships that we do. Folks pay to come out and learn. They do everything except for anything to do with soybeans and do the farmers' market. We do it more for them because it gives them a chance to network with other farmers and have experience selling directly to the public. That way, if they decide to have a garden or start a small farm of their own and want to do the same thing, they already know what it's like."

"That CSA thing," Eli asks hopefully, "do you think they have that in Oregon?"

Nora smiles. "It's pretty much nationwide. It depends on the community. Communities that are more enthusiastic about organic farms and sustainable practices are more likely to have more of it than communities that aren't. As far as I know, there's some sort of CSA offering in every state that has farming and agriculture in it." Harper nods, agreeing.

Eli looks down at his phone and realizes he needs to call home to say good night to Mason. Hesitant, he says, "I need to call home so I can say good night to my son. Is it okay if I come back in a few minutes? I swear I am not trying to get out of our agreement about the dishes," he says, referring to the deal he struck with Nora this morning.

"You're welcome to come back in if you'd like," Harper says, "if we're still in here. You just may find us out on the front porch eating pie. If you're going to want some, I'll bring along a piece for you. Don't feel obligated, and don't worry about the dishes. I took care of most of them as I was cooking. There are only these couple of plates, and I'll knock them out before we cut into that pie."

"I will definitely be back and wanting some of that pie. Thank you."

He is feeling such gratitude for these two amazing women, and half he wishes he was staying longer.

CHAPTER 18

Once outside on his way to the cabin, See-no, who had been napping on the porch, wakes up and follows him to his cabin. They settle on the bed, and he calls Rachel. She answers on the first ring.

"Hi, I'm so glad you called. I was just getting ready to put him to bed. Let me put him on, okay?"

"Okay," Eli agrees.

A moment later, he hears the tell-tale breathing.

"Hi, Dad. How do you like farming today? Did you drive the combine?"

"I liked it just fine, and I did drive the combine." Eli stops himself from telling the boy about CSAs. He wants to see what is available first.

"How do you like whatever you and your mom got up to today?" he asks instead.

"We went to the park. I got to play with some dogs. I liked it just fine, and I did all my schoolwork. Mom says I have to go to bed."

"I guess you better listen to her," Eli says. "I love you, Mason. Have sweet dreams."

"Love you too."

When Rachel gets the phone back, Eli says, "I guess this is my last night here, so I joined them for dinner tonight. They're waiting for me to have pie. Can I call you back in a little while?"

"It's been a long day, and I didn't get much studying done. Why don't you enjoy your last night, and I'll hit the books? We can talk tomorrow when you are... where will you be?"

"I don't know. Someone is picking me up, and I'm going somewhere in the morning. That's all I know now."

"Text me when you find out where you are going. Are you okay with waiting until tomorrow night to talk?"

"Yes, that's fine. Happy studying, and sweet dreams when you get around to it."

"You're the best. I love you."

"I love you too."

He puts his phone away and gently picks up See-no. He carries her back to the front porch and deposits her where she had been napping prior to his interruption.

Eli sits by himself on one of the porch swings next to a large piece of cherry pie waiting for him. He picks it up and takes a bite. "This is so good."

That is enough to have See-no at his feet. When he doesn't pick her up fast enough, she tries to jump onto his lap but doesn't make it without help and falls back to the porch. He immediately sets the pie down, unsure if he should pick her up or wait for her to come to him. She stands back up, shakes herself off, and goes straight back to him.

He is relieved that she understands he didn't try to hurt her. He picks her up and sets her on the opposite side of him and digs a piece of cherry out from the pie, which he offers as a consolation. The two women watch in silence, smiling, content with the outcome.

"So, what do you think of your time as a farmer?" Harper asks, smiling.

Eli considers his words for a moment before he answers, "I don't think I get to call myself a farmer for what I did for the last few days, but I enjoyed my time here. It was a nice reset. And honestly, your whole idea about the ghost rules certainly made it worth my time. I want you both to know I will be looking at that in my life going forward."

"That's good," Nora says. "If you find something works for you, it's good to use it and even better to share it." With that, she and Harper touch forks in a cheers-like fashion. As much as Eli likes both women, he would really like the opportunity to speak to Harper alone so that he can ask her some questions about the group. They sit in a comfortable silence for a few minutes, and then Nora gets up and collects everyone's pie plates.

"I hope you two will excuse me, I have an earlier morning than usual, and I need to get to bed." She sets the plates down on a chair and walks over to the swing Eli's sitting on. She pets See-no on top of the head and turns her attention to Eli after a moment.

"Are you a hugger?"

He would've said no a few weeks ago, but he finds himself saying, "Yes, I am."

He stands, and the older woman gives him a hug. "Thank you."

"No, thank you," he returns.

Once she is gone, Eli pauses for a moment, not wanting to pepper Harper with questions the second Nora leaves. When he can't bear to wait any longer, he begins, "Do you mind if I ask you a few questions?"

"You can ask," she agrees, "I don't know if I'll have an answer, but ask away."

"Thanks. Do you really give ten percent of everything you make to the group?" he asks, nodding towards the ring on her hand.

"Yep, absolutely. And I'm happy to do it."

"So, it's worth it?"

"For me, without a doubt, it is. It changed my life and definitely changed the way we look at farming and the future here."

Her response gives him more questions. "Can you tell me what the rite of passage is like, the initiation or whatever?"

"Nope. I couldn't if I wanted to, and I don't want to. It's a pretty special experience, and I wouldn't want to take anything away from you. I will say this, it's different for everyone, and I've never met anyone who didn't say theirs was perfect for them."

"I don't know if everyone I meet who has anything to do with this group is just extraordinary, or if I just haven't been willing to see things in other people for a while? I've learned a lot of things in the short time I've been away from home."

"That makes sense, we used to have the interns just come out for a couple of afternoons, but we spent a lot more time arguing than teaching. When we brought them out and had them stay full-time, even a short stint, everything changed. People are a lot more receptive to new ideas and growth when they're outside of their comfort zone. Since I learned that, I try to do things on a regular basis that put me out of my comfort zone. Not anything too crazy, but just enough to stretch so I don't get stuck in a rut like I see a lot of people doing."

"I can see the value there. I think I was pretty comfortable before the coronavirus happened. I got pretty lucky when it comes to my wife and son. I've got a great family, and I had a good job, and financially we were comfortable. I know I'm using 'comfortable' excessively, but we were. I have certainly been uncomfortable since I left. My wife said the other night that it must be hard for me not knowing where I'm going or for how long, or what I'll be doing because I like to have a plan."

"Nothing wrong with having a plan," Harper says amiably. "As long as you're flexible. And that is it right there, staying flexible. Do it as often as you can, to take you far enough out of your comfort zone for new and exciting things to happen."

"Good advice. Thank you and your mother both for your hospitality and for the opportunity to come here. I've enjoyed my time here. I missed out not spending more time with you two the first couple evenings."

"I wouldn't worry so much about it," Harper says. "Odds are pretty high, you got exactly what you needed to. Life has a funny way of making sure you do. I appreciate your help, and I know Momma is over the moon for the healing that we've seen in See-no while you've been here."

"Honestly, I don't know why she likes me so much," he says, petting the little dog. "I like her too."

"Well," Harper says, "I know you didn't care for the way she phrased it, but I think Momma was on to something when she said that you are as skittish as See-no is. You didn't push yourself on her at any point. You always wait and let her come to you, or at least let her tell you it's okay, and I think in our rush to heal her and love her and give her a different experience, maybe we didn't give her the same space that you do. I appreciate getting the chance to see you with her because I know Momma and I both learned something from it."

"Can I ask you one more thing?"

"You just did," Harper teases. "Go ahead."

"Do you know what's happening in the morning?"

"Somebody is coming here, we have a little runway over there between those two fields, a remnant from the old days when Daddy used to crop dust, before we went organic. They are coming to collect you in a little Cessna." She holds up her hand before he can say anything else, "I know nothing else. I'm supposed to have you ready after breakfast, and they'll get up here as soon as they can in the morning. We'll have breakfast, and if you're willing, you can help me set up a couple things to get ready for the interns to arrive, and when we hear the plane, we'll hop on the ATV and head on over to the runway."

"Okay," he agrees. "Thank you. I'm going to call it a night. Good night." He stands up, sets the little dog gently on the ground, and walks down the stairs. She follows after him, and they disappear into the cabin.

"Good night," Harper echoes, watching them with a serene smile on her face.

The next morning, Eli arrives at the table after Nora has left, and Harper is halfway through.

"Boy," said Eli, "I thought I got over here pretty quick after you knocked. It looks like it took longer than I thought," he says, gesturing to her plate.

"No, it was Momma who knocked on your door this morning after she got finished with breakfast. I thought we should let you sleep a little extra. Not knowing what the rest of your day is going to look like. I'm going outside to spruce up the other cabins. Take your time, come find me when you're done." She sticks her plate in the sink and leaves.

He had collected his belongings and packed them back in his bag the night before. He got his things out of the cabin and set it outside. All the dogs come and sniff him as they had when he arrived. They quickly lose interest in him and go to find something more exciting.

See-no keeps looking at the bag and Eli. He assumes he is imagining things, but he thinks she looks sad. And he feels a pang at the thought of leaving her behind. He helps Harper clean the cabins until they hear and then see a small plane heading their way. He picks up his bag and clothing and tosses them into the open back of the ATV. Without asking, he scoops See-no onto his lap in the passenger seat. Harper climbs in, and they race over to the small dirt landing strip.

The plane comes down for a near-perfect landing just as they arrive. Eli lingers in the ATV, not wanting to put the little dog down yet. He reluctantly sets her on the ground and grabs his bag and clothes from the back of the cart and stops to give Harper a one-armed hug.

"You take care now," she says.

"Thanks, you too." He walks towards the plane as the second most beautiful woman he's ever seen gets out. She is tall and tan with dark hair and dark eyes, very much like Rachel.

At that point, See-no gives him a "yip" of dismay. He hasn't heard the dog make a sound other than scratching since he's arrived. The look of surprise on Harper's face confirms she doesn't make noise often. He sets his bag down and walks away from the woman waiting for him and goes to the dog. He lays down in the dirt, and she cuddles up against his chest like she has each night since his arrival. He hugs her tight in his arms for a moment, loosens his hold, stroking her scruffy fur gently.

"It was sure nice getting to spend time with you. You're a special little girl. If there was any way that I could take you with me, I would. But I can't, and you've got people here that really love you. I think you'd be better off here, even if I could take you."

She gives his face a couple of licks and, seemingly content, walks back to Harper, who happily picks her up. Eli resumes his walk towards the plane, collecting his stuff on the way. When he reaches the woman, he reaches out his hand and somewhat loudly to be heard over the engine of the plane says, "Hi, I'm Eli Asher."

"Isabella Perez Garcia," she responds, shaking his hand. She follows him around to the passenger side and pushes the seat forward so he can stow his gear in the small space behind the seats. They both climb in. She points to a headset that matches the one she just put on. He puts it on, and he can now hear her clearly.

"I'm going to take off now. Once we get in the air and are heading home, we can talk more."

He nods. She starts to taxi forward, and when she reaches the end of the dirt runway, she makes a tight turn and quickly gains speed, heading back in the opposite direction.

Moments later, they are in the air. The woman holding the dog, the massive barn on the tidy little farm getting smaller and smaller. If he had tried to guess the next thing that Isabella would say to him, he would have been off by a mile. He never could have anticipated what came out of her mouth.

"Do you have any trapeze experience?" she asks.

"What? No!" he exclaims, alarmed.

"That's alright, I assumed as much. How is your shoulder doing?"

He moves it a little before responding, "Good, a little stiff, but good." It suddenly dawns on him to ask, "How did you know about my shoulder?"

"You were originally going to come down here from Mississippi, but after you hurt your shoulder, it seemed a good idea to give you a few days to heal up. I had to reschedule things, and we still don't have much time. Your job is fairly simple, I think we'll be okay."

He notices the ring, and because it's a more comfortable topic than trapeze is, he asks about it, "So you're in the group also?"

"Group?" she asks. He points at the ring.

"Oh, yes."

"I assume since you're wearing the ring that you are happy about it?"

She beams. "Yes, it was the best decision of my life."

He settles back a little bit. No one he has met is anything but thrilled with their decision to be part of the group, and he is feeling better about the decision with every passing day. He relaxes, enjoying the unique experience of flying in a small aircraft, being able to make out much more of the world below than you can see in a commercial plane, except for take-offs and landings, of course. Isabella doesn't seem too interested in talking, but he isn't completely comfortable with the silence.

"When I heard someone was coming to pick me up by plane, I thought it might be Zeke."

She immediately smiles and turns to him, "You've flown with Zeke?"

"Yes, I did. He flew me to Mississippi from Portland."

"That's great," she says. "Zeke is amazing. He's actually the one who inspired me to start flying. I met him at an air show and was flabbergasted he could fly like that at his age, and it seems like a lifetime ago. I got my pilot's license after speaking with him that day and eventually started flying cargo for a while. Flying is fun as a hobby, I didn't want it to quit being fun, so I quit.

Then I didn't know how to get back in the air because I couldn't afford to rent all the time, and I couldn't buy a plane outright. Zeke put me in touch with some folks who helped me buy a share of this plane, so there are four of us that own it, share use and costs like maintenance and hangar fees. It all worked out perfectly, and if it hadn't been for Zeke, I probably would never have had the guts to get my license in the first place."

Eli is not surprised. Everywhere he went with Zeke, people treated him like a rock star, and everything that Terrance had told him helped him understand why. Zeke is a remarkable guy and clearly makes a difference in a lot of people's lives. Eli hopes he will get a chance to see him again. He regrets how he left things when they parted company in Mississippi. He is lost in his own thoughts.

When Isabella asked, "Have you ever been to Sarasota?"

"No, I've never been to Florida at all. My wife and I had planned on taking a vacation a few years ago, then we spent a bunch of money fixing her car, and I got sick and missed a week of work, so that used up my vacation time. I've always wanted to; we just haven't gotten around to it."

"Do you know anything about Florida's circus history?"

"No? About all I know about Florida is there are beautiful beaches, NASA launches, and alligators. Oh, and oranges."

"The Ringling Brothers circus started wintering in Sarasota more than a hundred years ago. More circus performers, working and retired, live here than any other town in the world. John Ringling's house is a circus museum, it has amazing circus art and great history."

"Is that where we're going?"

"To the museum? No. I just like to share the history."

"Thanks, I appreciate it. My son will love it, when I tell him."

"In that case, if you head north towards Tampa, there is a place called Gibsonton or Gibtown. That's where a famous sideshow couple started a fish camp that grew into a town for sideshow folks so they could live in peace. They have an International Independent Showmen's Museum and a huge carnival trade show there."

"Is the circus still running?"

"No, they shut it down after one hundred and forty-six years in 2017. Animal rights were the last blow. I can't say they were wrong, but it's still sad to me."

"I'm sorry, I didn't know."

"The elephants were supposed to get a happy ending at the Center for Elephant Conservation in Polk City. I can't say for sure, but I hear things that make me fear they haven't found their happy retirement yet. It's better that things change. We need to evolve and get better over time, or at least try to. Anyway, now we have the Cirque du Soleil type thing. The circus was affordable for most everyone, and even if you couldn't afford it, you could at least catch a glimpse of the animals and performers if you hung out a while. It brought the world and wonders to people that would have never seen it otherwise. Now the next version is pretty darn expensive, I hope something else will come along that is more accessible to everyone."

"Thank you for sharing that. When I do get a chance to bring my family here, we will get much more out of the trip than we would have before I met you." He doesn't know what to say about the circus shutting down or the uncertain fate of the elephants or her sadness, instead, he changes the subject, "You were asking about trapeze earlier?"

"Yes. I run a trapeze school, and my training partner is in New York at the hospital."

That gets Eli's heart rate up. Not wanting to replace someone that is in the hospital. Then it dawns on him, "New York's a long way to go for a hospital."

She looks at him like he is an idiot and says, "No, he's there for his father, who is recovering from heart surgery. He's been up there a couple of weeks now, and I don't know when he'll get back. I need to fill up another class to keep the school going while he's gone. I need you to be able to perform with me so that we can show folks the high-flying fun and build some interest and get some students for the next session."

"I've already been away from home for just about three weeks now. I was only supposed to be gone four to six. I don't know that I'm the right one to help you," he says with a mix of relief and regret.

"No, this isn't going to take three weeks. This is going to be four days."

"What?" he asks, completely astonished. "How are we supposed to do this in four days?"

"Trust me when it comes to aerial trapeze, I know what I'm doing. You don't need to do a whole lot, just catch me," she says nonchalantly, as though it's no big deal to catch another human being, hurtling through space. He is about to protest until he thinks of his conversation with Harper last night about comfort zones and what they both taught him about ghost rules. He has a lot of ghost rules ready to form in his head. Most of the thoughts racing through his mind began with "I can't," followed by a sundry of reasons.

Seeing his apprehension, "I have been teaching this for a long time. I know what I'm doing. Trust me, trust the process, and I promise we'll get through this. You'll be amazed at what you can do in a few days with some hard work."

He has no choice but to agree. She waves him off. After flying with Zeke, he recognizes the sudden intense focus and the extra chatter in the headset. They are either passing through airspace, and she needs to communicate with the tower to avoid running into someone, or they are getting ready to land. It turns out to be the latter, and he experiences her smooth landing from inside the plane this time.

A few minutes later, she has taxied the plane to a hangar, conducted her post-flight checklist, and powered everything down. They get out of the plane and climb into a little Prius parked in the corner of the hangar. He quickly transfers his gear from the plane to the car, and they are off.

CHAPTER 19

Isabella takes the scenic route along the ocean since it is his first time in Florida. The beaches took his breath away. Oregon also has coastline, but the beaches are a different kind of beautiful and don't look anything like this.

"I'll try to make sure you get a chance to get out there once or twice while you are here," she says. "Just not right now, we're here." She pulls into a driveway and there is a sign on the fence saying "aerial trapeze training this way" with an arrow. Up ahead, he can see some sort of structure high in the air and is relieved as they go further up the drive to see a much lower one. This one has a net.

"Come on over here," Isabella walks towards the high rig. Eli leaves his gear in the car and follows along. "You climb up on this side," she says, "and I'll climb up on the other side. Once you're on the platform, I'll explain how to get onto the bar."

He pauses, thinks about the lessons of the last few days and slowly reaches for the ladder. She smacks him on the hand and pushes him away.

"What are you, stupid?" she hisses.

Bewildered, he asks, "What do you want?"

"I want to know how safe you are. I'm not happy with my answer." The more emotional she gets, the more her accent comes out. He has to muster his focus to hear what she is saying and keep the dumb grin off his face.

"I don't know what I'm doing here, you're the expert and the teacher. I trust you to know what's right and what's not because I don't know the difference yet," he responds in his defense.

"I appreciate it. I did just tell you to trust me, and there's an important distinction everyone needs to make. So, let's do that."

She looks to him for agreement. He nods. "Many people avoid fear anytime they feel it. For them, fear means they can't do something; they let fear stop them everywhere in life, until they are practically living in a cave. That you don't want to do. Fear actually lights the way; it says come this way. This is where you can grow. This is where you can learn. This is where you can expand."

He nods in agreement. "On the other hand, you want to pay attention to danger. Danger is something you should avoid. Going up that high with no instructions, no experience and no safety lines is dangerous. Whatever had you hesitating before you reached for the ladder, you want to pay attention to, because it was telling you there is something dangerous."

He thinks about it and admits, "It makes sense. I haven't looked at it that way, but I can't argue with any of it, and trust me, I want to. Especially the fear part, but when I think about the things people are afraid of, there's something they can learn, gain or there is more freedom they could get from facing the fear or however you want to phrase it." Suddenly feeling self-conscious, he stops.

She graces him with a big smile. "Exactly. Before we start, how's your shoulder?"

He holds his arm up, getting ready to move it around. She grabs his wrist and gives it a yank. He pulls back and scowls.

"That's good," she says, "that's honest. How did it hurt? Is it a sharp stabbing pain like when you get injured and it causes damage, or is it more like the kind of pain at the gym?"

"Neither," he says, "it's more like it hasn't been moved enough the way it's supposed to be for the last few days."

She smiles again. "That's good. This is what I need from you. I need you to be honest because you are going to be my catcher and my safety is going to be in your hands to some extent. We will have a net for your safety, of course, and mine, because I'm going to be teaching this to you and I want both of us to get through this in one piece. The thing about trapeze is you need to have good communication and trust with the person you're working with. My partner and I have been working together for years. You and I will have days."

He steps back and sizes her up more closely. She's lovely, she's smart, and has a much sharper edge than his wife. It makes sense for the circumstance they are in, and he can't find fault with it, but he does find her more challenging to deal with than the others he's met so far.

"In a minute, I'm going to show you where you're going to be staying, and if you have comfortable sweats, you can change into them. Sweats and a T-shirt will be fine; you'll want to tuck it in. Don't forget socks, the thicker the better. Our main goal today is to get you up and down the ladder safely and show you how to fall and how to get down from the net. When we get started, I will demonstrate everything. First, I'll talk you through it. I'll get a verbal confirmation from you that you understand, and I'll trust that you will ask any questions you might have before you make the attempt. If we get far enough today, I will teach you the catcher's lock. If not, we'll start with it tomorrow morning. Do you have any questions now?"

"How about shorts?" he asks hopefully, "it's hot and humid."

"Tights work, shorts are a bad idea unless you want net rash."

"Net rash? Is it contagious? My wife will kill me."

She starts laughing, and it softens her intensity and makes her more attractive.

"No, it's not contagious. It's when you scrape off skin, kind of like road rash for bike accidents."

"Sweats sound great." She has succeeded in changing his mind.

She smiles approvingly.

"Am I going to be doing any high-flying stuff?"

"No," she says. "I could catch for you if you had experience. I do for my partner occasionally. You'll just be a catcher for this. I will use a static trapeze for part of the demonstration, and then I will do some aerial trapeze with you catching, and that's going to be most everything that you do. Getting up safely and catching me multiple times safely."

"Thank you for taking the time to explain, I am more at ease now that I know how focused you are on safety."

"Killing new fliers is bad for business. Just add the distinction between fear and danger, and you should live a long, happy, healthy, amazing life."

"Sounds like a plan."

"Let's go get your bag."

He follows her to the car, then follows her through the gate. She leads him to the entrance of the garage, which has been converted. It is a studio-style space with a small kitchen and what looks to be a bathroom in the corner. The bed looks like it could fold back up into a couch. Kind of on par with his other accommodations, which is to say sparse, but reasonable enough for the short term.

"I'm going to go ahead and let you settle in and change. I'll go outside and get a couple things set up. Come on out when you're ready, we'll get you harnessed up and start."

"Okay," he agrees. "I'll see you in a minute."

He goes to the dresser and opens a couple of drawers, finding that they're empty. He unloads some of his clothes, pulling out a pair of sweats and a fresh T-shirt since he's already sweaty from the increased humidity, in spite of the nice breeze from the gulf. He doesn't see a place to hang the clothes, but there is an open cabinet in the kitchen, and he hooks the hangers around the side so they hang awkwardly down from the side of the cabinet to the side of the counter. He takes his toiletries to the bathroom to see what kind of situation he has and is happy to find a full-size tub shower combo and a fairly generously sized sink and vanity.

He puts out all his toiletries, adds an extra application of deodorant, changes his clothes, and goes back outside for his next adventure. When he gets there, Isabella is waiting for him by the other, shorter rig.

"I'm going to harness up and put a rope on you, and just have you climb up the ladder, fall down, come off the net, and climb up the ladder. We're going to do that a few times, but before you touch the ladder, I'm going to show you how I want you to fall and how I want you to come off the net, okay?"

He nods in agreement; very clear she is not someone he wants to get on the wrong side of. She flies up the ladder like a spider monkey. When she gets to the platform, she dives off like she's going into a pool, not a net, halfway down she does a flip and hits the net on her back with her arms crossed over her chest.

"This is the ideal position to fall," she says, "you don't want to be flailing your arms. You don't want them to bounce and smack you in the face. You don't want a finger to get caught in the net or get scraped by the net. It will scratch you up good if you don't treat it with respect. The main thing is you don't want to do a swan dive. You don't want to land on your head. You absolutely can injure or break your neck. The net will keep you from hitting the ground. It does not keep you from getting injured. You have to treat it with respect and use good sense. Okay?"

She looks him squarely in the eyes, and he nods along with her. She continues nodding. He says, "Okay," which is apparently what she's waiting for. She crawls to the edge of the net.

"This is how I want you to get off of the net," she says.

She grabs the outer edge of the net with her hands and, headfirst, slowly lowers her body until her torso is hanging down, and it's just her legs up on the net. Slowly, in a very controlled way, she flips her legs over and lowers them down, letting go of the net and dropping the last couple of inches to the ground. "You don't want to roll off the net, you don't want to jump down from the net. It's a good enough drop you can hurt yourself; you want to come off just like I did. Nice and slow. Make sure you've got a good grip on it, the outer edge only - no chance of getting a digit or limb stuck in the net in any way - then come down nicely. Do you have any questions?"

"No, thank you, that's clear, and I feel comfortable trying it. Do you want me to try now?"

"Yes, once we get you harnessed up and get a rope on you." She steps into the harness and shows him how to fasten it, then hands it to him. "Repeat what you just saw."

He does, except the connection is a little more complicated than he thought. He can't figure out how to loop the webbing back over itself.

"Why do you think that's not right?" she asks.

"When you did it, I couldn't see that red tape," he says and points to it. "Also, there was less left over, and I think it should be the other way around."

"Great, Eli. Very good work. I need to get back in teaching mode and not in training mode yet. That tape is there for that exact reason, to warn you your harness isn't ready to do its job. The short hand is red means you're dead. Probably not in these circumstances, but you get the idea."

He does, and he likes the teaching Isabella much better than the training version. She assists him with the webbing, showing him again more slowly how it is threaded through and how it crosses back over itself and back under the metal bar. She ties a rope to him and pulls a harness on to herself. She connects the rope to some metal thing attached to the front loop of her harness.

He looks down to see if he has one, he doesn't, just a big knot that looks like a figure eight lying on top of a figure eight. He notices and likes that all the things meant to keep him safe are tied or threaded twice.

"I'm going to belay you up to the platform. I'll climb up and attach you to the safety line so we can get through this today. I think I will be able to have a biscuit here tomorrow, and we'll have some student helpers for the demonstration." She stops and turns to him. "How are you with heights?"

"I don't love them. I like the ground, but I don't have a paralyzing fear."

"Do you think you'll have any problems holding the pole and standing on the platform for a minute while I climb up to you?"

"No, I'm sure I'll be fine."

"Ready?"

He nods.

"You need to say it, and up there, be loud enough so someone twenty feet away can hear you."

"Ready," he says, loud and clear.

"Hup!"

He surmises correctly it means "go" and does.

"If you get too far ahead of me, I'll have you slow down so that I can catch up. I don't want to have too much slack until you're comfortable with the ladder."

He starts up the ladder, the beginning of it is easy for both of them, but by the time he reaches the height of the net, he's already slowing. She had gone up so quickly. He assumed it was easy. Now he can see and feel he was wrong. He continues along, but she doesn't have to worry about him getting ahead of her. By the time he reaches the top, he's anxious to get onto the platform. He's also happy to fall down instead of exerting the effort climbing requires. He barely has a moment to catch his breath before she joins him on the platform.

"I'm going to try to put a safety belt on over your climbing harness, because we're going to do this several times, and if we have to swap gear every time, it's really going to slow us down. Are you okay with that?"

"If you think it's okay. I'm okay with it."

"Let's try it," she says, slipping a belt around his midsection that has ropes attached. "Okay," seeming satisfied, she turns to him, "I'm going to jump down again, and I want you to wait until I get to the ground. When I am attached to your safety line, you'll be able to feel some resistance. When you're ready, tell me, and then I'll say 'hup' before you go. Tomorrow, when we work with a biscuit, the first thing I'll say is 'listo,' that's what instructors use to make sure that we are ready, then the student will say 'ready.' No one does anything until you hear 'hup'. We'll start with that for today, don't go until you hear 'hup'. When you do, jump or fall down.

I have the line, so if you're going to make a mistake, I'll be able to minimize it. Still, it's really important you try to land on your back. If you're going to miss it, go ahead and do a face plant. You won't like it, but you'll be happier than you'll be landing on your head. The closer to the center of the net, the better off you'll be. Those sweatpants and T-shirt will protect you from the worst of it, if you should have rougher early attempts. Any questions?"

He thinks to himself, "Yes, what the heck am I doing here?" To her, he says, "No." She flips off the platform again, lands close to the center on her back and bounces high enough that she lands the second time on her feet. She pushes off and does a small flip before she lands on her back and comes to a stop after a couple of small bounces. Again, she crawls slowly towards the edge of the net, grips the side, lowers her top half down towards the ground, flips her legs up and over. When she is upright and dangling from the net, she drops the last couple inches to the ground.

She walks over to a rope and attaches it to her harness, after making some adjustments he can feel the slack leaving the line. The resistance that she mentioned kicks in. He waits for an extra beat, unable to remember if he's supposed to say "ready" or wait for her to say "hup." When she looks at him expectantly and says nothing, he assumes that she must be waiting for him.

He says, "Ready."

She immediately says, "hup."

He jumps off, feeling like he can fly before he falls. He intends to do a flip like her and land on his back, and is afraid he might not make it all the way over. His mind goes into overdrive, before his body catches up. He feels the rope pull him. With her help, he makes it the rest of the way over. He lands squarely on the net, arms partially tucked in.

He is a little surprised by how hard it feels when he lands, after he's seen how much give the net has. It looks like a trampoline the way she bounces on it. But it does not feel like landing on a trampoline. Although from that height, a trampoline might feel the same way. He rolls over and slowly makes his way to the edge of the net and does a perfect imitation of the technique she had shown. When he gets to the ground, she disconnects the safety line and gestures for him to take off the belt.

While he does, she asks, "How did that feel?"

"It was good," he says, "it was different than I expected, it was a challenge being the first time, and it was a blast. I can see why people want to do this for fun and not just for work."

She snickers, "Be careful, you'll get bit by the flying bug. It feels good to fly. You're right, more people learn for fun these days than anything to do with professional goals. There are certainly a lot of trapeze schools across the country that give people the chance. We do some of that. I prefer to focus more on students with professional aspirations. Are you ready to go again?"

"Yes, I think I am."

"Great, let's do one more and then we'll break for some lunch." She pulls on the ropes the leather belt is attached to, and it floats in the air near the platform. He looks at her standing at the base of the ladder, wondering if it's okay for him to go.

Finally, she asks, "Are you ready?"

"Yes," he says.

"Then tell me," she says.

"Ready," he says, embarrassed he forgot the order again.

"Hup!" she says, and he starts climbing immediately. He starts out a little slower. The ladder is still narrow, and it still feels high, but it's a little easier to reach the platform. While waiting for her, he thinks about grabbing the belt out of the air. "Maybe next time?" he muses.

"Ready?" she yells.

He yells, "Ready," back, not quite sure what he's ready for. As soon as she starts climbing the ladder, he realizes she was asking if he was ready to be off the rope. Once she is on the platform, she hooks him into the safety belt, goes to the end of the platform and turns around so that her back is facing the net. She falls backwards this time, but still manages a flip before she lands in the center of the net below. This time she rolls close to the end of the net and only crawls a couple feet to the edge before she flips down to the ground. She connects to the rope on the safety harness and waits for him to call down.

He does, loud and clear, "Ready," he both states and asks, while waiting to hear her release.

"Hup," and with that, he dives like last time, minus the hesitation. He makes it all the way over without any help from her and lands squarely in the center of the net. He bounces almost high enough to get his feet under him like she had, but not quite. He's content to ride out a couple smaller bounces before he starts crawling to the edge of the net. He flips down and joins her on the ground. She steps out of her harness, and nods at him, telling him to do the same.

"Leave the rope," she says, so he works on releasing the webbing from the metal buckle. When they're both unencumbered, she walks toward the gate they had gone through earlier. This time, she walks further and turns at a footpath that takes her to the sliding door at the back of the house. She waves for him to join her.

He sits at the peninsula in the kitchen. From what he can see of the house, she likes open space. Like her interactions with him thus far, it seems like efficiency is number one, with style and comfort coming after. Not that they are ignored, they just aren't the focus. The ceilings are high, but not Terrance high. There are a couple of large fans that hang down from the tall ceilings with blades that look like palm fronds. The kitchen is compact for the size of the house.

"Do you like ropa vieja?" she asks him.

He shrugs, confused. He doesn't remember much from high school Spanish, but he thinks "ropa" means "clothes."

"I don't know."

She takes the lid off the crockpot and gives it a stir. The smell is heavenly.

"I don't know what that is, but it smells very good."

"That is the ropa vieja. It's shredded beef with tomatoes, peppers and onions. Any issues there?"

He notices that most of her questions sound more like a challenge. He's happy to say, "No. That all sounds good."

She pulls out two dishes and a bowl from the fridge, which she dumps contents into a saucepan on the stove top. When it's warm, she scoops rice and black beans from the pan on the stove onto both of their plates and tops them both with a generous serving of the ropa vieja.

They both dig in and don't talk much until the food is gone.

He says, "That was delicious. I've never heard of or had it before."

"Where are you from?" her voice disbelieving.

"I was born in Washington state," he says, "but my family and I live in Portland."

"That explains it. If you lived in Florida, you would know about this."

"Is it a Florida thing?" he asked.

She shakes her head no, "it's a Cuban thing." Which she pronounces very differently than he would.

"You guys are a little closer to Cuba here then we are in Oregon," he agrees.

Not offering more invitation to chat, she looks at the clock and says, "Why don't you go rest and take thirty to give yourself time to digest before we have you swinging upside down, and then we'll get back to it."

He's uncertain if it's a question or statement, so he just agrees, "Okay." He leaves, feeling dismissed. So much so that he doesn't even ask about putting up his dish. Once he's in the converted garage apartment, he thinks about calling Rachel, but decides not to. Instead, he takes a quick nap on the soft bed. Soon it is time to get back to work, and he rushes to get out the door before she has to come get him.

As soon as he joins her outside, she takes him to a stationary bar. It's like the bars they swing on in the circus, but it's lower and doesn't move. It looks like an upside down version of the bars the girls used to play on at recess when he was a kid. Most of the guys quickly lost interest in them, once they'd hit them in the wrong spot. He was hoping this wouldn't have any of those unpleasant moments in store for him.

She shows him how to get up onto the bar and then how to maneuver into the catcher's lock.

"This will be the majority of what you do for the demonstration. You will swing from the catcher's bar. I will do a number of tricks, and you will catch me, and you may learn a net trick for your dismount, but primarily you're just going to be catching. We'll see how you do in the next couple days to decide for certain what we can and can't include."

He agrees with her as a matter of course. He is enjoying the trapeze. He is beginning to understand why this experience ends up on some bucket lists. This is a double or triple win. He is getting paid instead of paying, and still getting the experience. Seeing the discipline and focus that Isabella brings puts him at ease. By the end of the day, she is quite happy with him.

CHAPTER 20

That night, he has a long video chat with Mason and Rachel. It is great to see their faces, and they love hearing about the circus history of Florida. They both plead for a video of him on the trapeze. After Mason grudgingly goes to bed, Rachel eventually agrees they can look for a half-day trapeze school they can go to as a family. They also talk about getting down to Florida in the next two or three years so they can take Mason to Disney World and see the new sites Eli has learned about, and spend some time in the warm white sand. Rachel is also keen to find out the fate of the retired elephants.

By the end of the second day, he remembers and understands the lingo that relates to his job. It is very helpful having a "biscuit," which is the person on the platform that serves the bar and is there to help. The biscuits are on the flyer's side, not the catcher's, usually, but having her there to help while he gets the basics makes it so Isabella doesn't have to climb up behind him every time. Plus, he gets to hear them interact, which helps with the lingo.

Most importantly, he is very clear about his job as a catcher. It boils down to catching Isabella by the wrist when she flies his way, except for the last trick when he catches her by the ankles. He understands the difference between the "fly bar" and "catch bar" and has a little first-hand experience with "net rash." Thanks to Isabella's insistence, he covers as much skin as possible, so it's minimal. It is all coming together. He is enjoying everything but the thought of performing in front of a crowd. Isabella assures him that it will be a small crowd, no more than thirty or forty people. She also assures him that everyone will wear masks and have their temperature checked at the gate. He appreciates that, but is more concerned about there being at least twenty-eight more people than he was comfortable performing for.

The next night, when Eli calls home, Mason gives him a brief hello and goes back to watching his movie, "The Greatest Showman," which Eli can hear in the background.

Rachel says, "Hold on a second, I'll go sit on the porch. It's a nice evening, and I'll be able to hear you better."

He waits for her to relocate.

"Okay, how's that?" she asks.

"Much better. I wish I was there with you."

"Me too," she agrees. "Last night was great. I don't know why we didn't think of video before?"

"When I'm with you, I don't have any reason to video with anyone, so I get why we didn't think of it right away. It is esteem-crushing that it took almost a month to come up with it." They both chuckle.

"How is it going?"

"It's going really well. This whole experience is bringing up a lot of stuff for me. I'm just looking at things differently and questioning things."

"Like what?" she asks.

"Everyone that I've met so far has something mind-blowing to share. I already told you about Terrance and his 'challenge by choice.' And then I met a lady as I was leaving Mississippi who says that you have to be one hundred percent responsible for your life if you want to be the hero of your story, and if you make excuses about why things aren't your fault, you wind up being the victim or the villain.

I know the coronavirus and losing my job was not my fault. But that doesn't excuse me from being responsible for my life. Before all this started, I was starting to feel like a victim, now I don't. The circumstances were unfortunate and unforeseen, but they're not the end of the world. In fact, we're really lucky. I've got a beautiful, healthy wife and a beautiful, healthy son, and happy relationships. You and I both have skills, and we have a nice house. I'd like to own it, but we have a nice house to live in and food on the table. We are fortunate, and I was feeling anything but that when I left for this trip.

Then those ladies in Missouri with the 'ghost rules.' It's working. Every time I start a sentence in my head with 'I can't' or any limiting phrase, I hear it and I question it. It is a whole different way of looking at things. I know I can have a tendency to avoid new people. Now I wonder if I've been missing out on stuff like this all the time. Or is it that everyone associated with this group, directly or indirectly, is pretty incredible?"

"No, honey, I'm glad you're having such an enriching experience. You sound different now. I know Terrance was really good for you. It was hard for you to leave him, but you are more open to hear what people have to say and more willing to see if it works or not."

"Yeah, you're right, it's me. The change in perspective on many levels has me paying more attention to the things I wouldn't have listened to before. I know what Isabella said to me yesterday is going to be a big one, and I want you and I to figure out how we can help Mason with it."

"Okay, we can do that. I want that little dare devil to know to avoid danger, and I don't like seeing him so fearful any more than you do. I feel like you understand him more now, which means he'll be more likely to listen to you. Maybe we can teach him when we go trapeze?"

"That sounds great. I'm glad he is watching a movie, and we get a little extra time tonight."

"Me too. Have you gone to the beach yet?"

"No. I'm tired. She's quite the taskmaster, it's a great workout, but it's like working out for eight hours a day. Fortunately, I got in a little better shape with Terrance, but after sitting home all those months during lockdown and then spending those days driving the combine and not doing anything real physical, it's kicking my butt. Hard."

She giggles a little, "It sounds like it's well worth it, you're having fun and learning so much everywhere you go. I was concerned when this first came about, but it's turning out well."

"I agree. So far, so great. The only downside is being away from you and Mason this long. I think it'll be worth it, though, because I think you'll like the guy you get back better than the one who left."

"I don't know," she says, "we liked the guy that left an awful lot."

He smiles and yawns.

"Do you want me to let you go?" she asks.

"I kind of do. I feel bad, because as much as I want to talk to you, I'm tired and want to go to bed soon."

"Don't worry, I understand, and I don't want to leave Mason vegging out in front of the TV for too long anyway. Did you guys already say goodbye for the night, or do you want to talk to him again?"

"I think he's done with me. I'll talk to him tomorrow."

"Okay, I'll let you go then with one condition."

"What's that?" he asked.

"You have to get to the beach and take pictures for me. Not tonight, but before you leave. Will you do that?"

"I promise, I will take a picture of the beach for you before I move on. Do you want me to bring you some sand or a shell?"

"No, don't take anything but pictures, unless you want to pick up some trash. I love you."

"I love you too, good night." He hangs up, smiling. He gets a text and assumes it's from Rachel. Instead, it's from Terrance, it's a really bad selfie of Terrance and Pearl. Mostly Pearl, with a little of Terrance's chin and chest. Another comes in a second later, it just says "Thank You."

Now he's feeling very confident and happy, which is weird to him when he thinks about it, but he's been in different environments with different people doing different work than he's ever considered in his life, and been successful at everything he's tried so far. After not working for all those months, not being able to take care of his family, he is starting to feel good again. He takes a hot shower and crawls into bed, still smiling, feeling content.

The next morning, Eli opens the door as Isabella has her fist posed to knock.

"Good morning," he says with a smile.

"Good morning," she says back, giving him a quick smile before she turns towards the rigs. "I hope you're well-rested and ready for an exciting day."

"Exciting?"

"Yes, today we're on the high rig. That's where we will be performing tomorrow, so we need to get you up there and used to it today. Yesterday went very well. Today, we are going to start by getting you up and letting you get comfortable. Once you're more comfortable with the height, we'll start running through the routine just like we did yesterday until it's perfect every time."

"Great," he says sheepishly, suddenly less confident. The first time he climbs the ladder on the high rig, he is shaking by the time he reaches the top. It is much narrower and taller than the other rig. He's glad that they have a full crew, so there's two people on his safety lines and a biscuit on top to give him instructions. Right before he prepares to swing out on the bar, he wonders again, "What am I doing here?"

He slowly sits down on the bar and slides his rear, then the back of his legs down the bar until he is hanging from his knees. He quickly loops an ankle around each side and forces himself to let go with his hands. He is in position and should be ready to catch, but isn't. He sees the distance from the net and the ground further below, and adrenaline races through his body. He takes a couple of deep breaths to stave off panic.

"Think," he commands his mind, "I can do this, I did it yesterday. I am not in danger and have safety lines and a net. This is fear, I can grow."

He feels better. As horrid as the moments before were, he is sure they weren't an actual panic attack. He remembers a story Rachel had shared about a patient who had high blood pressure and was really stressed about it. They tried not to show him his numbers when they took his blood pressure because he would have a full-blown, "put your head between your knees, breathe in a paper bag" panic attack, which of course spiked his blood pressure. He smiles and begins to swing.

Isabella gets to her feet on the platform and looks at him, "Ready?" this time it is a question.

He is perplexed, she is supposed to say "Listo" first, oh well, "Ready."

"Listo?" She shouts. "Listo!" The line pullers respond.

"Ready?" she shouts to him. "Ready," he responds again.

The biscuit serves her the bar. "Hup!"

Isabella takes off, does a simple flip, and magically their wrists find each other mid-air. Seconds later, she does what looks like a simple half-turn to catch the return bar and go back to her board. At that moment, he feels taller than Terrance. She repeats the same trick three times before moving on to the next. He takes short breaks to sit upright on the bar and allow the blood to flow to the lower half of his body, then back to hanging upside down. He is ready to come down when she calls lunch, but not because he is uncomfortable with the height anymore.

Clearly pleased with him, her face is all sunshine when he meets her on the ground.

"Great job, Eli, you should be proud of yourself. You are doing wonderful work."

"Thanks. It's fun and challenging. I'm glad to be here and able to help. I was wondering why you need me, to be honest."

"I wanted to do a demonstration with someone who had zero background with trapeze and only three days to learn a routine. Then I found out that you were available, and I took that as a good sign that my plan was on the right track. And here we are."

He always says his wife is a force of nature, but Isabella makes her seem tame. Her being happy doesn't mellow that. He is quite relieved that he has impressed her. His phone starts ringing. Isabella is distracted, so he takes the opportunity to look at the screen. It's Rachel, and he sees she has tried to call several times. He holds his phone up, waving it to get Isabella's attention. "I need to take this. I think something may be wrong."

She looks at her watch and yells, "Lunch! I'll see everyone in one hour."

Eli gets out of the safety harness and goes into the converted garage to return the call in privacy.

Rachel answers on the first ring. "Hello," she sounds very sharp, and Eli's taken aback.

"What's wrong, sweetheart?"

"I just got an eviction notice. That's what's wrong." Eli can't remember ever hearing her sound this angry.

"Don't worry, honey, I'll take care of it. I'll call Joe."

"No! I will call Joe. You need to tell me what you think he needs to know. You need to tell me what's going on."

"Okay, well, just let him know that I am going to be gone between 4 to 6 weeks and I'm three and a half weeks in now. I will be getting ten to fifteen thousand dollars, depending on if it's four or six weeks. As soon as I get back, I will get everything squared with him. He knows I'm good for it. I'm pretty surprised he sent an eviction notice, that's why I'd like to call him."

"No, I will call him. You told me everything was fine, and I trusted you. Everything is not fine when we're getting an eviction notice. I can't believe that you didn't tell me this was even a possibility."

"I didn't want to tell you. You knew I was worried, but I didn't want you to know how much because I knew you would drop out of school and go back to work full time."

"So, you thought it would be better for us to get put out in the street. You thought that would be healthier for our son than for me to hit the pause button on school."

"No, we're not going to get evicted. I will take care of it, but you say 'hit the pause button on school' like it's no big deal. Remember when I left school? We hit pause, I'm still not back, and I've been thinking about it. I want to go back, but I don't even know when that's going to be possible. I don't want both of us deferring our education and our dreams. It's tight right now because of all the things that have happened, but we will get through it. I just didn't want you to quit school, and I didn't want you to worry because I knew I would figure something out, and I did."

She's calming down some, but her voice still has a sharp edge.

"You should've told me. We tell each other everything. We're partners, you know that. I don't understand this."

He counts to three in his head before he answers so that he can keep the irritation out of his voice. "Listen, sweetheart. I was trying to do what's best for all of us. It's not like I was running around on you or doing anything that should make you so mad."

"You not telling me the truth is enough. Bottom line, we're in this together. You could've told me it's bad, but I still don't want you to leave school because I'm figuring it out, and we could've talked about it. I don't know what I would've said or done, but I would have had a choice. I would've known what was going on so I wasn't blindsided by this. That's what married people do. They talk to each other."

"That's what you grew up with," he says defensively. "Your parents may have talked things out together and made every decision together. That's not what I grew up with. My mom made all decisions and all the sacrifices for both of us because she was doing it on her own. That's what I saw, someone taking care of her family, making all the choices and bearing all the consequences on her own. You can't expect me to know how to do it perfectly when I didn't have twenty years of perfect role modeling like you did." He feels bad about raising his voice, but also feels justified.

She confirms it by coming at him with a much softer tone.

"You're right, I've never thought of that. You make a good point. We did have different experiences growing up. Also, I was the one that handled the money for most of our relationship, before I went back to school. I always talked to you when there was anything unusual or any decision to make or any possible change we wanted to look at. It never occurred to me that it wouldn't be natural for you to do the same thing. I still love you very much. I'm going to go because I want to get a hold of Joe and get this squared away right now. I will talk to you tonight at the normal time, and we can talk about this more."

"Okay," he agrees. "I love you too, talk to you later."

He's disappointed that he missed out on lunch with Isabella. He enjoys her cooking, but would feel uncomfortable walking in and expecting lunch now. Instead, he makes a sandwich for himself with the few groceries he bought when she took him to the store after yesterday's workouts.

The rest of the day continues to go downhill for Eli. When they resume after lunch, he is unfocused, and Isabella goes from irritated, to livid, to concerned and questioning whether she should cancel. His timing is off, he doesn't have a fully clean catch, and there are some close calls. He just can't focus, and when timing is everything, focus isn't optional.

"That's it!" yells Isabella, "Listo?" The echoing "Listo" is almost instant.

She doesn't even yell "net clear," knowing it is. She dives, bringing to mind a Valkyrie, and if she did have the power to cause death, he would be a goner. He lingers on the bar, deciding if he wants to fall with the assistance of the safety lines or make the long slow climb down. As loath he is to face her, making her wait will not help.

"Ready?" he calls. "Ready" comes the response. "Net clear?" He knows it is, but doesn't want to add ignoring procedures to his list of sins.

"Net clear!" she shouts, increasing his reluctance to come down.

When he reaches the ground, she pins him with her piercing gaze. "Do I need to cancel the show tomorrow?"

He wants to say yes and run home, both to avoid her anger and make things right with his wife. Knowing what the delay could mean for her business, instead, he says, "No, I'm sorry. I know I haven't been focused. I got bad news from home. Give me one more chance. I'll get it right this time."

Her expression softens, "Bad news at home as in that's where you need to be right now? Or bad news that is a distraction?"

"It was a distraction. I'm not distracted now. Let's do this," he says with more confidence than he feels.

She gives a small nod, and everyone gets back in position. They run through the entire performance start to finish. It is their best run-through of the day. Eli suspects Isabella would like to get ten more like that out of him before calling it quits. Instead, she amazes them all.

"That's it for the day. Thank you for your hard work, everyone. I'll see you in the morning."

She looks his way, "Come ready to work." The six former students don't linger.

Eli starts for the converted garage, feeling bad. He knows Isabella is frustrated and is worried he will let her down. He is worried about it too now. The confidence that he'd been building over the last few weeks has been knocked out of him. He is still more confident with the height, but more nervous about letting Isabella down and performing in front of others, especially considering all the mistakes of the afternoon. And this is one of the very rare times that he can recall that he isn't looking forward to talking to his wife.

"Hey," Isabella's voice catches him before he opens the door.

He turns to face her, ready for a dressing-down now that they are alone.

She is holding car keys in front of her. "This is probably a good time to go to the beach. It usually soothes whatever ails me. Siesta Key has a nice public beach less than five miles from here. If you don't like it, you can look up others on your phone and figure out if you want something more secluded or more active."

"That's so kind. Thank you."

"Are you sure you don't need to go home?"

"Yes."

"Please work out whatever you need to, so I can get the best out of you tomorrow. I respect you staying, and you did a better job on the last go-around. Better isn't good enough for tomorrow night. I need your best."

"I understand," he agrees.

She goes toward the house, and he goes into the garage. He checks his phone once inside and sees he has barely missed a call from Rachel. After a quick debate, he decides if he is going to be miserable, he might as well do it on the beach. After a quick change into some shorts and a fresh t-shirt, he picks up a towel on his way out.

CHAPTER 21

After a short drive, he parks and walks toward the beach. He is greeted with a sign declaring Siesta Key the number one beach in the country. He takes a couple of pictures of the white sand, impossibly turquoise water, blue skies and a couple of palm trees waving in the breeze. He finishes up with some shots of sandcastles, a couple of paddle boarders and one behind the yellow lifeguard station showing the different colors of beach umbrellas scattered around it.

He debates sending the pictures now or saving them until after he finds out what kind of mood she is in. He sends the best two and calls her back.

"Hello," she says. No my love. No other endearment.

"Hi." He doesn't embellish his greeting either. Instead, he waits for her to share her news.

"Well, I talked to Joe," she said. "It's good news, bad news. He said he'll forget the late fees and count our deposit as this month's rent as long as we pay what we still owe from last month and we move out in thirty days without issue. I swore to him that we would do it, that we would be out at the end of next month with the house clean."

"Why? Why are we moving? Why can't we just pay him up and stay? We'll have the money."

"He doesn't want to be a landlord anymore. He's pretty freaked out because of the moratorium on evicting people during the pandemic. He's had people that didn't pay for a couple months in a row and then instead of paying just move out on him. He said he can try to collect, but even if he takes them to court there is no guarantee that he will ever see any of it. Then with this new thing that they passed that if somebody is evicted or rents are raised beyond what they can afford the landlord has to pay them three thousand dollars for relocation.

He said he thought real estate was a good investment for his retirement. Now he says you have to be a millionaire to be a landlord in Portland. He is afraid he is going to lose everything. He said if he kept his properties, he would have to raise rents 9.9% a year for the next couple years to be clearing enough to cover the risk of having to pay relocation assistance. And you know as high as our rent is, it's a couple hundred less than it probably ought to be."

"That's terrible. I didn't realize it was so bad for him. It's going to be tough to get a new place if other landlords are feeling the same way and have to raise rents to protect themselves. Does that sound right to you? Did you check into that?"

"No, there was something about it on the news. It doesn't matter, he wants us to move and I said we would. He did say that as long as we were out at the end of next month, he will give us a good reference for all the years that we've been here. He was understanding and sympathetic. I tried to convince him to let us stay and it's clear he's going to sell everything he has and move someplace else that's less expensive."

"I wish we could afford to buy it from him and if we had more time, maybe we could. Right now, it's just not a possibility."

"I know." she agrees. "I love the neighborhood and Joe was a great landlord. And I do like the house, even if it is small."

"You know we're going to have to get a place where we can have a dog, right?" he asks.

"I don't know that we'll be able to be picky about that. We might not even be able to get a house at all. We might have to look for an apartment at this point," she says trying to be the voice of reason.

"No we're not living in an apartment. We will get a house and if we want any peace it needs to be a house that will let us have a dog. I don't know how yet but we will figure it out."

"We'll see." She isn't convinced. "How did this afternoon go?" She changes the subject.

"Not very good to be honest. I was distracted and didn't do a very good job. I think Isabella's pretty frustrated with me. I have to do better tomorrow. I know I'm done here after the demo, but I don't want to let her down. She hasn't fully spelled it out, but I think her business is hurting and she needs to get students from the show. I want to help."

"Of course, you do. Your intentions are never the problem."

"What did you think of the pictures?"

"It's gorgeous. I'm excited for our trip, eventually. I don't want to hurt your pride, but I don't really understand why you are there. Isn't there someone else with experience that could help her get students?"

"I know right? I guess that was part of the draw, to show how much she can help someone improve. She wants to work with people that are looking to do this professionally and especially someone that wants to rent the converted garage that I've been staying in and train full-time. You know, like somebody that wants to get on with Cirque du Soleil or do that kind of performance type stuff, it's a good skill set for that."

"Okay now I really don't understand how you fit into that."

"That's the hook, that's what I was saying, I barely even heard of a trapeze before I came here. I'd never been on one or even thought about being on one and here we are three days later and I can catch. I guess that's a big deal, those intro classes teach you to fly not catch. Plus, I even know a couple of net tricks. She's going to show what she has been able to do in three days. If she can take somebody that's never set foot on a board or been on a bar and teach them to fly and catch, imagine what she can for someone with basic or intermediate skills."

"Some of that is Greek to me, but I think I understand the gist of it. I hope tomorrow goes better for you."

"Thanks, I do too. Listen Rachel, I'm sorry. I know moving is stressful, but I think we will come out better on the other side. In fact, I'm sure it will wind up being a good thing. I know we've been happy there, but it's not everything we want. Joe's a nice guy and we're pretty good at having kind people in our lives. There is nothing that says we won't find another place we love with another great landlord."

She doesn't respond, instead, she says, "Is there anything else I need to know? Is the power going to go off tomorrow?"

"No, nothing like that, we're a little behind in some things but nothing is going to get shut off or repossessed or anything else. It's just been a little bit of a juggling act. Once I get paid for these jobs we'll have enough for first, last and deposit and be able to catch up on anything we're behind on. Between that and what you bring in we'll have a small buffer for me to get another job and I'm sure it will happen fast."

"I hope you're right, for all of our sakes. Hold on. I think Mason's coming in. Let me put him on the phone so he can say good night."

He hears her phone land on a hard surface so he doesn't bother with a reply.

"Hey Buddy, how are you?"

"I'm okay dad, how are you?"

"I'm good. I miss you."

"I miss you too," the boy's voice drops to a whisper "Mom's been real mad all day. I don't know how come. But she's not fun today."

"I'm sorry, it was probably my fault, I think she's mad at me. I know it doesn't have anything to do with you. Just be a little patient with her. I'm sure tomorrow will be a better day. Okay?"

"Okay. When are you coming home? You've been gone a long time."

"Soon, I don't know exactly when. A couple more weeks at the most. I promise when I get home, I'm going to spend a bunch of time with you to make up for this."

"Okay, I'm going now."

"I love you. Be good."

"I love you too, bye."

A moment later Rachel gets back on the phone, "I need to make dinner so I can get him to bed on time, our day got side tracked by this stuff. I'll talk to you later or tomorrow, okay?"

"Sure, whatever you want."

"We'll talk tomorrow. I love you."

"I love you too," he gets out before she hangs up.

He watches the waves for another twenty minutes. By then he suspects he feels as good as he can while his family is miserable. He returns Isabella's car and goes to bed.

The next morning is a blur for Eli. They start first thing in the morning and practice is much better than the day before. His catches are clean, his timing is impeccable and he is focused. He can see Isabella's concern melt after each successful trick. By the time she calls lunch. She is all smiles again when he meets her on the ground. She comes over and hugs him.

"You're doing great today. Looks like that time on the beach was helpful. Thank you, for whatever it was, I see the difference and I appreciate it."

"Thanks for your patience. I know yesterday was rough."

"How are you feeling about the performance?"

"I'm not going to lie, I'm not wild about performing in front of people, but I'll get through it. I promise you."

"I have a lot of faith in you. I'm sure you will. We're going to have a long break today, so you can rest up for the show. We're going to do one more run through about half an hour before people are due to arrive and then just one more time after that. Like I told you before, it won't be a big crowd. I did hear this morning that you are headed out tonight. I guess you're off to Vegas next."

He groans, "Vegas. I hope it's not more performing."

She smiles, "I think you'll be safe, either way I'm sure you'll do a great job. Enjoy your rest. I like some time to mentally prepare, so I'm not having anyone to the house for lunch but if you're interested, I'd be happy to have some food dropped off for you."

"Please do, that would be amazing. I've enjoyed my short time here, but I think my favorite thing has to be your cooking."

"My grandmother would be happy to hear you say that. Okay, I'll see you this afternoon."

He goes to the converted garage, takes a cool shower and tries to relax. He doesn't know why performing in front of others is such a big deal. He's been doing the same tricks for a few days now. Except for the first day there's been a biscuit and line pullers around, so people have seen it. He shakes his head trying to think of something else.

The next topic that comes up is getting back to Portland just in time to move his family when he doesn't have a job and his credit scores have taken some hits, in a city that doesn't have a lot of affordable housing and might soon have even less. That is not helpful.

Fortunately, a soft knock on the door distracts him. He opens it and one of the line pullers is handing him a plate of food from Isabella's kitchen.

"Thanks," he says, taking the plate from her hand. She gives him a weak smile and walks away with a second plate in her hand. He sits down and eats, he is not sure what, but very much enjoys every bite.

"I'm going to have to find a good Cuban restaurant to take Rachel and Mason to after I get back and we are resettled," he thinks to himself. He wonders again about Vegas and what he'll be doing there and, finally, to take his mind off all the uncertainty he streams a movie on his phone. He finds himself a little sleepy between the meal and the movie and takes a nap.

The final run through also goes well, but Eli's jitters are impossible to miss. It is finally decided that Isabella will also be on safety lines for the performance. His relief over that decision was tangible. People were starting to arrive and he is thankful that there is only a short amount of time to kill before the show. He goes back to the garage to pack knowing that he is going to be leaving shortly after the show is over. About the time he finishes there is a knock on the door, letting him know it is time.

When he returns, everything looks pretty much the same except there are a number of people sitting on the four tier bleachers beside the rig. When he approaches the ladder, he freezes for a moment and then has the idea of leaving everything on the ground. With every step up, he decides he will be further away from the panic that keeps tapping on his shoulder about his family's housing situation and from the discomfort and shyness he feels at the idea of performing in front of others. He is further away from any insecurity he feels about being good enough or worthy enough or even capable enough to help Isabella sell her school to this audience so her business can persevere.

By the time he reaches the top. He is as confident as he's ever been in Florida, possibly in life. Once he gets on the catcher's bar, he flashes a big smile at the audience below and gives them a wave before dipping down quickly into the catcher's lock.

And then, they disappear. The only things that exist are him, Isabella and the rhythm and timing of the trapeze. He knows even with the safety lines she is putting her trust in him on many levels. He will not let her down.

Before he knows it, the routine is done and the cheers from the audience are enthusiastic. By the time they both reach the net and then the ground, they are surrounded by admirers. A number of people approach him asking, "Is it true that you've only been doing this for three days?"

"Yeah," he confirms.

"Incredible." As one masked face turns away, the next one arrives with a similar version of the same question. He looks over at Isabella, who is surrounded by people. He's never seen her so happy.

Twenty minutes later, people are drifting away and she looks at her watch. She excuses herself from the couple she is talking to and approaches Eli. She hugs him again.

"You did amazing. Thank you so much, we filled the class and the waitlist which is much more than I had hoped for, and I think I have a renter for the studio."

"That's great news, I'm thrilled to hear it," he says sincerely.

"I'm sorry to say, it is time to get you to the airport."

He follows her and they make a quick detour by the studio. She waits outside while he changes and then they get in the car.

He fidgets, wanting to say something, suddenly feeling shy. He takes the leap, "I know working with inexperienced people isn't your thing. But I thought I'd throw this out there for you since your partner does more of it. I was kind of intrigued at how much focus I can give to someone if I have to, and how it felt having someone's safety in my hands."

She nods along waiting for the punchline.

"I was thinking you should do classes for couples on the trapeze. It's pretty clear if people are present and listening to each other when they're on the trapeze. I know newbies don't usually catch, so I don't know how you would make it work. I could be crazy, but it seems to me like there's potential of some sort there."

"I think that's pretty smart. There's a high degree of trust required, many performers are family members or couples. I don't know how we would incorporate it, but I will certainly consider it. I think it's a great idea."

Feeling proud, Eli continues. "I've talked to my wife about us doing a basic trapeze school, once I get back home, together with our son to help him with some of the things he's working through right now. That's what got me thinking about how I wished I could've had the experience that I've had with you with my wife as well."

"Thank you for sharing. I like anything that can help more people discover trapeze and keep it alive as long as possible."

They arrive at the same airport they had come in to. He's not sure how he's traveling this time, but guesses it won't be commercial. It turns out he is right.

There is a mid-sized jet on the runway near what he thinks is Isabella's hangar. She carries his hanging clothes, while he carries his bag and walks him to the plane. He doesn't know what type of jet it is, only that it isn't Zeke's. Still, he hopes that somehow Zeke might be the pilot. The flight attendant meets him at the stairs and takes his luggage such as it is and goes ahead of him to stow it for the flight.

Eli turns to Isabella. "Thank you, I know things about myself that I didn't know before I came here. I love Cuban food and trapeze. It was a rewarding experience."

"I'm glad. I'm very grateful for what you've done for the school. When you get back this way with your family, be sure and look us up. I'll be happy to give your wife and son a chance to fly for an afternoon if you want."

"Count on it. Thank you."

The flight attendant is standing at the top of the stairs again and clears his throat.

"Goodbye," Isabella says.

"Goodbye," he says and turns and walks up the stairs ready for his next adventure.

CHAPTER 22

As soon as he pulls the door closed behind him, the young man that Eli thought was the flight attendant says, "I'm sorry to rush you. The owner of the jet is asleep in the back, please do not disturb her. There is food available for you in the galley if you'd like a sandwich or a beverage. Please help yourself, there are some additional items in the refrigerator, I was asked to convey the request for you to leave those alone. I need to go to the cockpit as I'm the co-pilot. Once we get airborne, I can come back and check on you."

"Great, a sandwich sounds good right now. Thank you."

The co-pilot returns to the cockpit. Eli gets a sandwich and soda from the galley and goes to sit down. He's glad he did because shortly after, the plane takes off. After eating, he reclines. The seat goes back much more than the stingy inch the commercial flights recline and he quickly falls asleep. At some point during the flight, the co-pilot must have come out because when Eli wakes up, he can feel the plane descending, but the plate that his sandwich was on, and his soda can, are gone.

A few minutes later they're on the ground and the co-pilot reappears with Eli's bag and clothing. He walks to the door and when the plane has come to a complete stop, he lowers the stairs.

"This way, Sir."

Eli gets up and accepts his bag and clothing on his way out. "Thank you."

"You're welcome. I hope you enjoyed your flight and had a good rest."

"Thank you, I did."

"I believe the gentleman you're meeting is over there." He points to a middle-aged Asian man, possibly Chinese, standing by a Nissan thirty feet away.

As soon as Eli's feet hit the tarmac, the stairs retract behind him and the jet begins to taxi away. He realizes, belatedly, he did not even find out whose jet he had the privilege of traveling on. "Oh well," he thinks. He's never been starstruck. He may envy the wealth, but not the fame. He approaches the man by the car who pops his trunk and quickly takes the bag and clothing from Eli and puts them in.

He closes the trunk and tentatively offers his hand. "Randy Yang," he pronounces very clearly.

Eli takes and shakes his hand, "Eli Asher. Nice to meet you."

Randy has his hand sanitizer out first and Eli gratefully accepts some and pulls his mask on since Randy is already wearing his.

"Yes," the man agrees, motioning towards the car. Eli climbs into the passenger seat and they drive away from the airport.

"Randy, do you mind if I ask what I'll be doing here in Vegas?"

"We will be clearing out the back half of the warehouse. It's not hard, just takes time. There are many things in there that must be sorted and cleared out. I need the space."

Eli notices that he clearly enunciates each word and speaks slowly doing so. He doesn't know if it is because the man is self-conscious about his English, or if that is his normal speech pattern.

"Your English is very good. I always admire people that can speak two or more languages. I have tried to learn Spanish a few different times and that is supposed to be an easier language to learn, but I've never made much progress."

Randy smiles at the compliment.

Fifteen minutes later they are in a residential neighborhood that could be anywhere in the Southwest. They come to a stop in the driveway of a stucco style house with a tile roof. The men get out and Randy retrieves Eli's luggage which Eli accepts and follows him inside.

"I hope you don't mind staying in the guest room. It will only be for two or three nights."

"Sure, that will be fine. Thank you." Eli feels a little uncomfortable staying with a stranger, but like Randy said, it's only for a few nights.

Randy shows him the guest room at the end of the hall and the bathroom across from it, they will not be sharing. Eli feels better about staying here, he doesn't like running into anyone but his wife in the bathroom in the middle of the night.

"Help yourself to anything in the kitchen. Make yourself at home. I will make breakfast at seven. If you want to join me at seven thirty, you are welcome. I would like to leave here at eight or eight-thirty."

"Thanks, I'll see you in the morning."

Randy gives a little bow and heads off down the hall. Eli returns it too late and walks into the bedroom exasperated with himself.

He sends a text to Rachel.

I think we're in the same time zone, if not for sure closer. Just got to Nevada. I will call you tomorrow night, love you. Good night.

She responds almost instantly. *Glad you're safe. How did the show go?*

Stupendous. Can't wait to tell you about it.

I'm looking forward to it.

Eli hangs his shirts and slacks in the closet and puts the folded clothes from his bag in a couple of the empty dresser drawers and unpacks his toiletries in the bathroom so he will be ready for a shower in the morning. He would like to shower now, but he doesn't want to disturb Randy and is exhausted. He assumes it is the nerves he experienced before performing and then the performance itself, which was an intense workout on top of the stress.

He falls into the bed, appreciating the soft sheets and thinks of Goldilocks when he lies down and feels the more agreeable firmness of the mattress. The next morning, he wakes up, showers and makes his way down the hall to the kitchen where true to his word Randy has just finished preparing breakfast. Randy is just putting some plates on the table.

"Good timing," Randy says.

Eli walks to the table a little slow, not quite sure what breakfast is going to consist of. He sees some weird round light-colored balls. He sits down at the table hoping that he's able to eat them. Not wanting to offend his host.

"This is bao, this plate is salty," Randy points, "eggs, pork. This plate is sweet, berries and custard." He scoops up a few.

Eli's not sure if it's pork or pork and egg bun on his plates. Eli selects one that he's hoping is pork and egg, and a custard one. He waits until Randy takes a bite, so he can see how to eat them. Randy, understanding his hesitation, "You're welcome to eat them with your hands if you'd like, I prefer to use a fork and knife. Do whatever you're most comfortable with."

"Thanks." Eli follows his example and uses his fork and knife, he cuts into the first one which is filled with what appears to be ground pork and takes a tentative bite. He's not sure what the outer part is made of and is not his favorite experience. The texture and taste of whatever the contents are wrapped in is strange, but the ground pork is very good, once he gets to it. He smiles, "This is very good."

He now tries a bite of the custard one. He likes the custard too. He's still a little unsure about the outer wrap of both. His hunger is greater than his uncertainty about the wrapping and he quickly finishes the two buns and reaches for a third.

Randy also reaches for a third. "It's good you have a healthy appetite. We have much work to do today. I am most thankful that you're here."

"I'm glad to be here, I need the work and I'm happy to help."

When they've finished, Randy takes their plates. He stacks one of the bun plates on top and carries the other bun plate in his other hand getting everything to the kitchen in one trip. Once he has dispensed with dishes, he returns with his car keys and motions towards the door. Eli follows him and then goes through the door first so that Randy can lock it behind him. They get in the car and a few minutes later they are in a small warehouse in an industrial part of town. Still no indication that they're in Vegas.

Randy unlocks the building. They go inside before they're even settled, the door opens and a group of people join them. Mainly women, mostly middle-aged, there's one that stands out as being much older and a younger man and one younger woman also. They walk past the office. Eli waits for Randy to finish with whatever he is attending to on his desk.

"This way, please." Randy walks in the same direction the group of people have gone. Eli sees them settling at what looks like industrial sewing machines. Now the machines are six feet apart and there are plexiglass shields creating almost a cubicle for each machine. Eli can see marks on the floor from where the machines used to be much closer to each other and there are unused machines lining the back and one side of the room. Randy continues through the room, returning smiles and waves and opens the door at the opposite end. He turns on the lights.

Moments later the fluorescents blink on and Eli lets out a low whistle. The room is massive. There are large boxes stacked well over head height in much of the room. There is a forklift and a small amount of open space for it to maneuver, but not much. Randy walks past all of that and, grabbing a chain, goes hand over hand as he rolls up the big loading dock door at the back end of the room.

"This is what I told you about last night. We must make this space a workspace. So, we must clear out as much as possible."

Eli feels instantly overwhelmed and can see why Randy would want help with this. He hopes there will be further instruction, because he has no idea where to begin. Randy gets on the forklift and brings down a large cardboard box. Eli doesn't want to say box because it's really big and has no lid, but it fits almost perfectly on the pallet. He lowers it to the ground and both men approach, looking to see what's inside. Randy pulls out the first box from inside the massive box and opens it.

"This, when you find this, it can go in the truck for donation." He opens another box. This one has what looks to be magazines, but nothing Eli's ever heard of. "This goes to recycle."

Eli hopes that Randy does not intend to leave him on his own yet. He's not sure yet what he's doing, and he is still very overwhelmed by the massive quantity of stuff in the room. To his relief, Randy continues to open boxes and say the destination for the things within it. By the time they've gone through all contents of that box. There is a nice pile for recycling and a fair amount that's supposed to go on the truck to be donated. Finally, the smallest stack is the little bit that Randy says needs to be saved.

Eli's getting a little more of an idea of what goes where. It seems like most of the paper products are bound for recycling and may have been left over from the space's previous tenant. Any fabric they come across is to be saved and for the most part the clothing they come across is supposed to be donated. That is confusing to Eli at first because of the industrial sewing machines he assumed that was the product they were making. After he sees the fabrics being saved, he realizes they are much heavier fabrics so he wonders if the clothing is also a remnant of a previous tenant.

Randy brings another box down to the ground so they can start sorting it. He starts and Eli comes to help.

"Please put the donation stack in the empty gaylord."

Eli has no idea what he is asking. It sounds like playground taunts from less politically correct times.

Randy points to the pallet size box with no lid, "There, please put donations there."

He dives into the next box, by the time Eli is caught up the second gaylord is almost done. Instead of diving in to help, he stands there waiting for instructions.

Randy looks up, "As soon as I'm done with this, we'll put everything saved in this box. Do you mind taking recycling out to the bin?"

"Not at all," Eli says, wondering if he's supposed to take it one box at a time. Randy points. Eli looks behind him and sees a handcart. He quickly stacks up several boxes and takes it out the small door, once down the ramp he sees the blue dumpster for recycling.

After he dumps the boxes, he can't resist taking a quick look at his phone. First, he puts in "gaylord" and gets a bunch of stuff about a hotel and a few other businesses. Next, he tries "what do you call a pallet sized box" and, sure enough, gaylord comes up. He would have bet big Randy was using the wrong word. He promises himself to never assume he knows more as a native speaker than someone who isn't. He jogs back up the ramp with the hand truck.

"Do you want me to keep doing this, or come help you with that?"

"Keep doing that, please."

Eli loads another stack of recyclables and takes the boxes out. When he comes in for the third load, Randy is putting donations in the original gaylord and fabric in the second one. He has also created a new stack of recyclables, so Eli continues what he's doing.

As Eli is coming up the ramp with the empty hand truck, Randy takes one of the pallets to the end of the loading dock and drops it on the ground. He goes back for another gaylord, bringing it down so they can sort it.

They continue steadily for about two hours. Both men are sweating and Eli now understands why Randy opened the loading bay door, the breeze coming through is helping the warehouse be more bearable than it would be with the door shut. Randy puts a hand on his shoulder to stop him from leaving with his next stack of recyclables.

"Come on, let's take a break." They walk through the main room that they had originally come in through.

His presence draws looks from the people working at the sewing machines. He notices a few people are missing and finds them when he passes the break room. Randy doesn't stop so Eli follows him to the office. Randy opens a small fridge and pulls out two waters, handing one to Eli and opening the other.

"I leave the breakroom for them. My door is open most of the time, if they want to see me, they come in, if they don't, they have the break room," he explains.

Eli wonders if it's more about keeping him away from the workers, most were old enough to be at higher risk. They wear masks when they aren't at their sewing machines. He and Randy had abandoned theirs in the heat, but it is an open space and they are rarely less than six feet away from each other. He is still lost in thought when Randy signals it's time to go back to work.

They dive right back in and work through the rest of the morning until Randy says, "It will be lunch in a few minutes. I have to take care of something in the office. Come and find me in ten or twenty minutes?"

"Will do." Eli stacks another set of boxes on the hand truck for recycling. He continues the hard but simple work of separating and dispatching the items Randy has sorted. When twenty minutes have gone by, his alarm dings and he walks towards the office.

The smell hits him before he makes it to the door of the breakroom. He doesn't know what he's smelling. He does not want to disrespect anyone and he's praying to a God they won't offer to share any of whatever they're eating with him. He keeps walking, eyes straight ahead not risking eye contact as he makes a bee line for Randy's office. With great relief Eli makes it inside.

"I eat traditional dishes, but I don't go in that room, at lunchtime," Randy shakes his head. He steps back, showing a pepperoni pizza sitting on the desk with a plate on either side, "Help yourself. I hope you like pepperoni."

"Thanks, this is perfect." Eli is full of enthusiasm. "What is that smell?" he can't help asking.

Randy shudders again, "Stinky tofu," he opens the small dorm fridge and offers Eli a drink. "They make it a competition who can make it stinkiest."

Happy to see both water and Gatorade, which is becoming his magic combination when he's sweating so much, he takes one of each. "Does it taste like it smells?" With drinks in hand, he sits down and dishes up some pizza.

Randy sits on the other side of the box further down the bench-like desk.

"Does it matter?"

"Good point."

"You're a hard worker."

"Thank you. I've been in three different places recently that had a lot of humidity. It's nice to be someplace drier."

Randy laughs a little. "People talk about humidity and dry. I think hot is hot. It's very hot here. But this is where my business is so this is where I will be."

"Where would you be if your business wasn't here?"

Randy waves that off as though it's a silly question and Eli doesn't expect an answer. "Hawaii," Randy states, matter-of-factly, "If I didn't have a business and I had more money. It's very expensive."

The two men talk casually as they share their lunch.

"Do you mind if I ask why you need my help? Can't you have your employees help with this?"

Randy shakes his head, "No, we were lucky to be essential. Many of our customers were not essential, so business is much less, but I kept everyone working full time. To accommodate distance, I had to have two shifts which meant double electricity for lights and air conditioning. Now the demand is more, and I need more help, but I can't afford it. I have to clear that room and be able to get all the machines back in operation on one shift to cut expenses and eliminate shift differential so I can afford extra help."

"Why didn't you cut back hours or lay somebody off temporarily?"

"When I started a business, I told myself that every employee that I hire who works hard and does a good job will have a job for as long as I have my business. I will keep them working in the best conditions for the best wages that I can possibly offer through whatever life throws my way. Things are a little tough right now, but it's a small price to pay to have kept my word."

"That's great that you kept your word to them."

"No, you are mistaken, you do not understand. I kept my word to myself. Keeping your word is something some people think you do for other people. I know keeping your word is something you do for yourself." Eli finishes chewing his last bite. Randy stands up and stretches. "Are you ready to go back to work?"

"Sure."

Back in the warehouse Randy brings down the next gaylord.

As they start to sort, Eli asks, "I understand the value of keeping your word. Where I just came from, I had to perform in front of people and I was really uncomfortable about it. I was there to help the woman who owned the trapeze school and I was committed to doing it so I overcame my fear and nervousness. I did it by just focusing on keeping my commitment to helping her. I don't understand what you mean by keeping your word is something you do for yourself. Are you willing to explain?"

Randy looks at him, sizing him up, "Are you familiar with the religious persecution in my country?"

"No," Eli admits, shaking his head.

"Since the last political change some religions have become persecuted by the Chinese government. Tibetan Buddhist, Muslims, Protestants, Catholics and Falun Gong. I practice Falun Gong and people are being abducted, tortured, harvested for organ transplants and sentenced to what are essentially re-education labor camps. If you practice this religion in my country, you know this could happen to you. Even if you don't practice my religion in my country, this could happen to you if you are accused or believed to practice."

"I've never heard of Falun Gong. What can you tell me about it?" Eli is a little uncomfortable with the topic of religion and certainly uncomfortable with the idea of religious persecution existing today.

"It's a moral teaching. We have a meditation, four gentle exercises that help to improve our health and energy. The core values of Falun Dafa are the most fundamental qualities of the universe - truthfulness, compassion and tolerance. Much of this is about self-cultivation to have greater insight and purity. Our founder Mr. Li Hongzhi is a five-time Nobel Peace Prize nominee. In the nineties, before the government changed its views, he received much positive recognition. In a short time, he had a hundred million followers and by the end of the nineties, we were being persecuted. Mr. Hongzhi has always insisted that the practice be taught for free. People can get all of the books and videos about it for free on the website. It's insane how it can go from getting praise to its followers being arrested, tortured or worse."

"I am so sorry to hear that. I had no idea."

"Many don't. There is a group of dancers that some Americans have heard of called Shen Yun who are trying to bring awareness, so that American people will encourage their government to bring pressure to our government to stop this treatment of our followers. Many outside of mainland China seek to do this. This has made things worse. In the last few years, persecution has gotten worse and our followers have been accused of conspiring with the West to destroy our country."

"With compassion, truth and tolerance? How do you try to destroy a nation with truthfulness, compassion and tolerance? That doesn't even make sense." Eli doesn't think Randy is lying, but can't understand how this could be true. He tries to get back to things he can grasp. "Where does keeping your word for yourself come in?"

"When I was still in China and continued to practice Falun Gong, I knew that I could be taken, and I would not give a name to spare myself pain and I would not deny my beliefs to spare myself suffering. That is who I wished to be. But we do not know who we are until we find ourselves in the situations we imagine. When I realized this, I made a practice every time I gave my word to anyone, to know I was also giving it to myself. I started keeping my word, no matter what. No matter if it was inconvenient, or if I didn't feel good, I kept my word. Over time, fortunately I did not experience what I was concerned with. I did learn by cultivating the habit of keeping my word I could say I would do something I didn't know how to do, but because I know myself as a man who keeps my word. I know I will find a way. This is how we got through this crisis and how we are still moving today."

"Wow, thank you so much for letting me come here and help you with this small thing and sharing with me this big thing that you're doing."

Sensing that he has an ally, or at least a sympathetic ear, Randy continues, "Your president does not like immigrants. Except those he marries," he smiles for a moment pleased with himself for the joke. "And then the pandemic started and he accused China of many things. The people that work for me, the people in my community are very afraid of what will happen. They cannot go back home because they don't know what is happening. It was important to me that they keep having work and money to feed themselves and keep a roof over their head. They would not seek help from your government right now, no matter what, out of fear of what might happen."

"He's not my president, but my wife would love you."

He notices the puzzled look on Randy's face.

"I just meant; I didn't vote for him. I don't usually vote unless my wife makes me."

Now Randy was looking at him as if he were crazy. He wonders if there is a language issue.

"Why do you not vote?"

"I just don't think it makes much of a difference. Twice in my lifetime already we've had presidents that weren't elected by the popular vote. I see more and more homeless people in my city no matter who is in the White House. I'm just trying to keep that from happening to us right now. I know that sounds bad, with everything else that is happening in the world."

"No, caring for your family is a good thing. When you are stable again just remember it's not the only thing. Do you want to add to your education?" Randy asks, gesturing towards the forklift.

"Sure." After the trapeze and the combine, a forklift doesn't warrant a second thought.

Five minutes later he gently lowers the next gaylord to the ground.

"What is all this from anyway?" Eli asks, as he opens a box of clothes that looks like they were made and left untouched since the sixties.

"All businesses that have been here before. The landlord lives out of state. Finally, the back got so full he doesn't even rent it, just gives easement from the front to the loading dock. When I asked him about the space he said if I cleaned it out I could have it for ninety days no raise. If I keep it, I have to pay a little more. If I do not, I will lose my easement but not have to pay more. We will see."

A woman sticks her head in and says something in a language Eli doesn't understand.

"Excuse me. Please keep going." Randy walks over to talk to her and Eli sees what looks like a shift change. He pulls his phone out and sees that it's five.

When Randy returns, he starts with, "I'm sorry it is later than I realized. I can take you home and come back."

"You're going to keep working?" The man nods.

"I'm all in. I want to help, let me call home at seven and I'll stay as long as you stay."

Randy is thrilled and readily agrees, "I will go and get us dinner."

CHAPTER 23

While Randy is gone, Eli dives into sorting the rest of the gaylord that he brought down. Randy returns about fifteen minutes later with burgers, fries, and chocolate shakes for both of them. They eat at opposite ends of the loading dock, legs hanging down.

After talking as they work most of the day, they eat in silence. When they are finished, Eli collects the garbage, hops down off the edge of the loading dock, and shoots it into the dumpster from about ten feet away. Randy applauds.

"Thank you." Eli bows.

They fall back into their previous rhythm and work until Eli calls home at seven. Rachel is over the moon that they are in the same time zone again. Mason is his normal heavy-breathing self with his machine-gun quick hi and bye. After relenting to Rachel's insistence that he reach out to Isabella as soon as possible to see if anyone recorded the performance, they say good night.

A few minutes later, Randy and Eli are back to work and push through until ten, only taking bathroom breaks and pausing while they talk for a few here and there. By the end of the night, they have made good progress. There are two tall stacks of pallets in front of the loading dock door, and the box truck they put the sixties-style clothes for donation in is three-quarters full.

"How do you say, 'poke me with a fork? I'm done?'"

"Close, 'stick a fork in me, I'm done.'"

Randy repeats the phrase multiple times under his breath.

"Can I ask you something?"

"Yes, ask."

"Has someone ever given you a hard time about your English?"

"Yes, when I first came. I was trying to buy things at a convenient store. I did not know the correct words, and the men there laughed and told me to go back to China."

Eli is angry. "How many languages do you speak?"

"Three: English, Mandarin, and Cantonese."

"How many do you think those men spoke?"

"I don't know?"

"I'd bet you a hundred dollars that they speak one and probably not well. People that speak more than one language successfully are smart enough to know it isn't easy and wouldn't be making fun of someone like you."

Randy stands a little taller. "Let's be done."

"Agreed. Hey, if you say something that is a little off, do you want me to tell you? You do great, your English is almost better than mine, it's just little conversational things."

"No, you tell me. My English was better before; since the pandemic, I speak much more Mandarin than English."

"The one little thing I noticed is we call them convenience stores, not convenient stores, though technically you would hope that convenience stores would be convenient. Sorry, I get goofy when I'm really tired."

Randy is repeating the whole phrase, nodding to himself when he says both words under his breath. When he is finished, he is ready. "Let's go."

When they pull up in front of the garage, Eli asks, "Will it bother you if I take a shower?"

"Nothing will bother me. There is a washer and dryer in the closet at the end of the hall if you need to wash clothes as well."

"Great, thanks."

Once inside, they part ways. Eli tries to hunt up clothes for the morning and comes up nearly empty. He takes a quick shower and dumps his dirty clothes into the washer in one big load. He starts it and lies down, setting an alarm for sixty minutes so he can transfer them into the dryer before morning.

In the morning, Eli comes down the hall freshly shaved and with his clean clothes washed and packed. He joins Randy at the table for leftover bao. After they finish eating, they go to the warehouse and dive back into work. A little bit of small talk passes between them, but they both seem content to remain in their own worlds for the most part. It doesn't take them long to finish filling the truck with items to be donated. Eli stands at the loading dock and watches the recycling company empty the dumpster while Randy goes to his office. He returns just as a recycling truck is pulling away.

"Good timing, now we have more room."

"Yes," Randy hands Eli keys. "I should ask, can you drive the truck?" He nods at the box van.

"Sure," Eli is happy at the prospect of getting out of the warehouse. He is more than willing to help Randy, and he has a lot of respect for what he's doing for his employees. Still, being stuck inside the dusty warehouse is tedious after his last few experiences. Randy hands him a clipboard with a carefully printed list of names and addresses and hands him a stack of envelopes that are tucked in, but not sealed. "You start at the top and go there. They take what they want, then you go to the next place, they take what they want, when the truck is empty come back."

"Okay, so it's a free-for-all? They just take whatever they want to use. There's no set amount for anybody?"

"Correct," Randy agrees.

"Okay, will do." He fishes out his phone and puts the first address into maps. Randy turns back to his sorting work and continues on the last gaylord they brought down.

Eli hops down from the loading dock onto the back bumper of the truck, then onto the ground. He climbs in the cab. Moments later, he's driving along the street looking for his first stop. It's amazing to him how when you get a little way away from the strip, Vegas looks like any other town, but the closer you get to the strip, the more unique the town is. He makes his first stop and is greeted by a grateful pair of volunteers. It appears to be a shelter of some type; Eli doesn't know if it's homeless or domestic violence, but they only take a couple boxes of clothing for their residents. He hands them one of the envelopes and accepts a donation receipt, not sure if Randy wants them or not, and heads off to his next stop.

When lunchtime rolls around, the truck is close to empty. Eli's feeling like Santa Claus. He wishes he could get a job doing this every day. It's much better than the sorting work in the warehouse. He appreciates Randy even more for giving up such a rewarding job. His stomach reminds him loudly, it's time to eat.

He pulls through a drive-through. Normally, at home if he goes to a drive-through without his wife or son, he would have burgers and fries, maybe even a shake. Now, after eating a lot more foods prepared at home and healthier food, he is feeling the effects of the pizza and the burger and fries last night. He orders grilled chicken salad and a water. He is glad no one he knows is there to witness this and tease him for ordering like his wife. He eats the salad and drinks the water, feeling guilty about the plastic as he drives.

When he gets to the next stop, he climbs out and helps unload. They take everything left in the truck. He hands over a letter and accepts a receipt.

He wishes he had thought to get Randy's number so he could call him and offer to bring him back some lunch. He pulls over again to see if he can find it somewhere in the truck. He opens one of the letters that simply states, "If you have people who have work and need work clothes, but can't afford any, have them call me. Thank you, Randy Yang."

Eli tries the number but gets voicemail. He drives back to the warehouse feeling revived by the food and the good feelings making all those donations gave him. Also from knowing he is helping such a good guy. When he gets back, Randy has another pepperoni pizza waiting for them in the office.

He takes a single slice and tells Randy about all the gratitude that the different charities expressed for his donations. He shows him how far down the list he got and tells him there's a stack of donation receipts in the truck he forgot to bring in. He excuses himself to go get the receipts, and when he returns, Randy's finishing his lunch.

They dig into work again and make great strides. There's one corner left where the gaylords are stacked three and four high; ninety percent of the space has been cleared, save for some single-layered ones along one wall. Surely there's enough room to move the sewing machines in and start creating Plexiglas cubicles for their inhabitants.

Randy looks at Eli. "Do you want to sort or do you want to move machines and make work stations?"

Feeling the Vegas vibe and also feeling both happy to be helping and happy to be almost done helping, Eli smiles and says, "Dealer's choice." Randy understands the gambling reference and smiles his approval.

"You sort."

"Sounds good." Eli hops on the forklift as Randy goes off to the other room and starts pushing the big sewing machines in. Again, it is dinnertime before they notice. It's only as other people are leaving that they notice the time. There are about ten gaylords left to sort, and most of the machines still need Plexiglas cubicles constructed for them, although Randy has marked off the 6-feet spacing with tape on the floor.

He looks at him. "Dinner? Or home?"

"Both, of course."

"Do you want to be done and go home to have dinner, or do you want to get dinner and keep working?" Randy clarifies.

"Let's finish it. We can keep working until we're done. I just need to stop at seven for the call."

"Okay," Randy agrees happily.

This time he surprises Eli by asking him what he wants for dinner. Eli has no idea at this point. He's now used to others making those decisions. Falling back on his previous answer, he says, "Dealer's choice."

Randy nods and leaves, coming back a short time later with two large sub sandwiches. Again, the two men sit at the loading dock with their legs hanging down, eating dinner from their laps. When they finish eating, they go back to work, not worrying about how long a dinner break they take. Knowing that the longer they take now, the later they will work tonight.

Eli stops at seven to call home. Mason answers the phone instead of Rachel.

"Hi, Dad."

Eli breathes heavily into the phone, hoping Mason will remember what he's been told about holding the phone too close.

"Hi Mason, how are you?"

"Good. How are you?"

"I'm good, I'm tired, I've been working really hard the last few days."

Mason ignores the response and instead says, "Mom is mad, sorry Dad. Good night."

"Good night. I love you," he hopes his son heard before he passed off the phone.

With some trepidation he says, "Hello honey, I'm sorry I haven't been able to talk much the last couple days. It's been crazy between the performance and the travel and the work here. I'm here for such a short time and it was a huge project. Hopefully, we're almost done with this." He stops talking, hoping he has headed some of Rachel's anger off at the pass and wishing Mason would've stayed on the phone long enough to tell him what she was upset about.

"How could you?"

"How could I what?" unsure what could possibly have her so mad after they just got through the eviction crisis.

"How could you drop our insurance and not tell me?"

"Oh, sorry, it all ties back to losing my job and not wanting you to drop out of school. The COBRA was high, and between COBRA and rent, it was almost more than unemployment. There just wasn't enough to keep it going, and I didn't want to spend all of our savings trying to do that."

"Savings, that's another thing. Where did it all go?"

"It went to try to pay off Mason's hospital bill."

"That's a much better thing to spend it on than insurance premiums."

"Hindsight's twenty-twenty," Eli shoots back.

"No! Having insurance when you have a kid is absolutely essential. Kids do things, kids get hurt, kids get sick. It doesn't make sense not to have insurance. We are so lucky it was a concussion and not cancer. What would we be doing if he had broken an arm and we found out he had bone cancer or something and we couldn't get treatment for him because we had no insurance and didn't have the money to pay for it?"

Just the thought of it drives Eli to his knees. "I never thought of that. I never expected it to go this far, last this long. I was just trying to get us through the rocky patch we were having. I thought I would have a new job with insurance long before now. I never considered the chance of Mason or any of us getting seriously ill. You do a pretty good job of keeping us on the health bandwagon. I'm sorry, Rachel."

"I am too, Eli. I am too. I love you, but I don't know how to do this right now. I have to talk to you later."

"Wait, honey, please don't go."

"I'm sorry, I'll talk to you tomorrow. I should be more calmed down by then. Unless you have some other fun facts you forgot to tell me, and then maybe not."

"No, I really think you've got the whole story now."

"I'll talk to you tomorrow. I do love you, and I am furious with you."

"I love you too. I'm sorry." Eli hangs up the phone and works his way back to his feet.

He honestly had not considered the possibility of his son being seriously sick or what would happen if he were to get sick while they didn't have insurance. The thought of not being able to get his son actual lifesaving treatment because of money just about made him lose his mind. He had never felt like such a failure as a father or husband. He looks at Randy in the warehouse busy constructing Plexiglas cubes and thinks of what he'd shared about your word being something you give to yourself. He looked towards the sky, towards a benevolent source that he hopes is there and vows, "I will be better. I will find a way to provide for my family. I will find a nice house for us to live where my son can have a dog, and I will find a job that has insurance." He nods to the sky, "If you're listening and you can help in any way, now would be a great time."

He lopes up the ramp into the warehouse and finishes distributing the material that he sorted from the last few gaylords. Once he is done with that, he goes to help Randy construct the last few Plexiglas cubicles.

They quickly finish the last of the cubicles. Eli goes to move the forklift to the corner by the loading dock so there is room for the last station. Once he parks, he stands up to get off of the machine and his phone drops to the cement floor, hits hard, and bounces out of the loading dock, shoots through the pallets stacked next to the door like a ball in a pinball machine, finally landing on the pavement. He is impressed to see that it didn't shatter into several pieces but not happy when he sees the screen looking more like an incomplete puzzle or funhouse mirror than a cohesive picture of his family. Not wanting to make a big deal of it in front of Randy, he shoves it back into his pocket, irritated at the extra obstacle to deal with and an inevitable extra expense in the near future.

He's halfway up the ramp to go back inside when a man in an old eighties Datsun pickup pulls into the parking lot with a few pallets in the back. In broken English, and with hand gestures, he asks if he can take the pallets stacked below the door. Eli holds up a finger, telling him to hold on.

He trots inside to ask Randy, "What are you going to do with the pallets?"

"Someone will come to get them. I will let them have them."

"Someone's here now. Should I let him have them?"

"Yes, go ahead."

Eli goes back and gives the man a thumbs up. He starts stacking pallets above the bed and eventually above the cab of the little truck. When he's about halfway through, Randy comes out and sees who is taking the pallets and has a fit. The two men start yelling at each other. Eli doesn't know either language but can tell that much of what they're saying is in different languages with some very clear insults in English being volleyed back and forth. He goes down the ramp just as the shoving match begins and quickly inserts himself between the two men.

He looks at Randy completely dumbfounded, "What's wrong? I told him he could have them, you said I should give them to him, right?"

"No wrong. He is Japanese. I thought you gave them to the Mexican, not the Japanese. He cannot have my pallets."

Still holding the men apart, Eli looks at the other man, "I'm sorry, I misunderstood. No more." He waves his hand while saying it. The man shoots him a dirty look but walks towards the cab of his little truck. Randy approaches the truck ready to start unloading pallets when the man jumps back out and the shoving match resumes. Eli gets between them again.

"Randy, please, this one time, I promise I won't let him take anymore, but can't he have the ones he has already loaded?"

Randy looks at Eli's earnest expression and understands that he will lose face if he does not agree. He consents and walks back into the warehouse, looking over his shoulder occasionally to glare at the Japanese man who is now tying down his treasure of pallets.

Eli helps him thread the rope back and forth, throwing it over the top around the tie-down and then back over the top. He doesn't want to appear as though he's taking sides. He just wants the man to leave as soon as possible so that they don't get into it again. The man gives him an short wave before he pulls out onto the street.

Eli walks inside still not understanding the hubbub. As usual, Eli goes with sometimes the best defense is a good offense, "I'm so sorry about that. I thought it was okay to give them to him. I told him it was okay because I thought that's what you said. I didn't mean to cause any problems."

Randy shakes it off with both hands emphatically, "No, not you. You're not trouble. It's him. Japanese are the worst."

"He's the worst or all Japanese are the worst?" Eli asks.

"Both," says Randy emphatically.

"Okay." Eli understands he has stepped in the middle of something that is much bigger than what happened at the loading dock.

"What do you want me to do now?" Eli asks.

"Come with me," he says, waving to him, beckoning to him with his hand. He follows him into the warehouse where the original sewing machines are. Randy walks up to a sewing machine where an older Chinese woman is carefully sewing a made in the USA label to the waist of the work pants she has just finished. As soon as she's done, Randy takes them from her and offers them to Eli.

He holds them up, "They're very nice, thank you. Very good quality."

They are thick and have a gusseted crotch and knees for easy movement and are heavy enough to not be worn out easily and to protect you from minor scrapes and pokes depending on what work you're doing and the environment you're doing it in. Plus, they're quite warm, too warm for Vegas, but he won't be there much longer.

Randy and the woman smile broadly, looking very proud of their work, and Eli smiles with them, thinking to himself the people that are most concerned with buying made in

America might not be happy to see what he just witnessed. He himself loves it. He wishes his phone wasn't broken; he would take a photo of the moment, but too late for that.

One of the women in the back of the room gets Randy's attention and points to the loading dock. Randy does a slow jog in that direction. Eli follows, gaining ground with long quick strides, concerned that the man in the Datsun has come back. When he reaches the loading dock, he sees there is a semi with a trailer trying to back up to the dock but can't because of the remaining pallets.

He hops down to join Randy in moving them. Once they are clear, Randy guides the driver all the way back. The driver joins them on the dock to unlock the door. Once the door is opened, the forklift races by with a pallet of medium-sized boxes shrink-wrapped together. Eli wonders who is driving as they maneuver the forklift so quickly and efficiently it somehow looks graceful. When it passes by again, he sees the driver is the eldest of the day shift women. He stares in awe and she gives him a wink. He can hear her cackling with laughter as she whips around the corner.

"I'm going to have to pay more attention to these wily seniors," he thinks to himself; he had underestimated Zeke and this woman whose command of the forklift is equal to Zeke's with a plane. She makes two more trips. The driver closes the door.

"I'm ready when you are. I need to call dispatch, so you've got a few minutes. Don't take too long."

"We'll get his belongings and be right back," Randy reassures him.

They walk through the building together and retrieve Eli's stuff from Randy's trunk. When they get back to the sewing room, Randy gives a signal and they all clap and say,

"Thank you, Mister Eli," almost in unison.

Eli makes a few shallow bows, hoping to convey respect, but gets concerned that maybe Chinese don't bow and he is conveying the opposite. He sees nothing but smiling faces, so he makes a few more and smiles at every person he passes, until he reaches the forklift driver. She gets a wink and her cackling laughter tells him he made the right call.

When they are back at the dock, the two men face each other.

"Thank you again for your help."

"It was a pleasure to meet and work with you. Thanks for the work jeans too."

There is an awkward moment where Eli isn't sure if he should offer a hug. Randy sticks out his hand and Eli shakes it, content with that, even though he is open to hugging outside of his family now.

The driver honks and Eli walks down the ramp one last time to climb up into the cab.

"Hi, I'm Eli," he says as he struggles to get in with his cumbersome luggage.

"Gene," is the only response.

Eli barely sits down when the truck lurches forward. He gets settled and sits quietly until they reach I-15.

"Where are we headed?"

Gene spares him a look, "You don't know where you're going?"

"Not yet."

With disdain he says, "You are headed for Fresno, Courtyard by Marriott Fresno to be exact."

Eli starts to ask something else.

"You're not one of those talkers, are you?"

Amused, Eli can't help but have a little fun, "I don't know, what kind of talkers are you referring to?"

"The ones that do too much of it."

"Probably not, unless you have some brilliant insight you want to share."

"Sure," the man agrees, "some people get really lonely driving trucks, some don't. I'm the latter."

"I was starting to ask if you would mind if I lie down in your sleeper. I've worked a couple long days and am really tired. I can stay up here and keep you company if you prefer."

Gene finally smiles, "Make yourself comfortable. You've got just shy of six hours."

"Thanks."

The sleeper cab isn't as tidy as Blaine's, so he uses one of his clean t-shirts as an impromptu pillowcase and lies down on top of the patchwork quilt. He is out seconds after his head hits the pillow.

CHAPTER 24

He wakes when Gene taps the wooden base of the bed with the toe of his boot and says, "You can sleep all you want, but you can't do it in here."

Eli slowly gets up and makes his way to the front; sure enough, they are at a Marriott.

"Do you know who I am supposed to ask for? Will they be here this early?"

"All I know is you are supposed to give your name at the desk."

"Okay. Thanks for the ride." Eli fumbles and stumbles out of the truck and makes his way into the hotel.

The desk clerk greets him, "Good morning, sir. How can I help you?"

"I'm Eli Asher."

"Yes, Mr. Asher. I just need you to sign our non-smoking facility notification and I'll give you your keys." She consults a handwritten note. "Your seminar is providing lunch. Your breakfast and dinner will be taken care of for you in our bistro."

"Seminar?" he asks.

"Best Life Blueprint. You'll be meeting just down the hall there. They ask that you be in the room at eleven for prep. I guess the attendees are due at one."

His head is swimming. He hopes he isn't supposed to be giving a seminar. He is very tired and doesn't understand why she keeps calling it his seminar. He signs the form and accepts the key card.

"Enjoy your stay."

"Thanks, have a good day or I guess night." He doesn't bother settling in. He just kicks off his shoes and crawls into bed, pretending like the middle of the night interruption never happened.

Eli wakes himself up with his own snore; startled, he wipes the drool from his face. He rolls over and sees the time on the clock next to him. He jumps out of bed, showers, does a quick shave and pulls the least crumpled pair of slacks and button-up shirt he can from the closet. He notices that they fit more loosely and comfortably and that he looks like he slept in the outfit.

No time to do anything else, he goes directly to the bistro where he orders breakfast. While he waits for his meal to arrive, he tries to send a text to his wife. He has no idea if she'll get it, or if she responded to the one he sent the night before. His phone is a puzzle, more so than a screen at this point in time. The food arrives quickly and he eats it even faster. He arrives at the room the desk clerk pointed out the night before at one minute before eleven.

"You must be Eli." A young-looking Hispanic man approaches him, his hand outstretched to shake. Eli takes his hand, appreciating the firm shake.

"I am."

"I am Alejandro. Great to have you here. Do you have everything you need?"

"I don't know, what do I need?"

Alejandro laughs, "Your room and meals. Everything is working out. Right?"

"So far so good."

"Okay, let's go ahead and get started. This is Eli, everybody. He is going to be my right-hand guy for this. If you have questions and you can't get to me for whatever reason, go ahead and ask him. Eli, I'll make sure you get a chance to meet everybody before our participants arrive. For now, let me just say that this is my small team of very dedicated volunteers whom I love and appreciate so much." The volunteers smile and give a light smattering of applause.

"Eli is going to take care of the registration desk here, and Kathy, you help him out until we hit seventy percent, and once we hit that number, go ahead and shift into the room. The room team will let you know what's needed at the time. So, the table should be pretty simple. Participants will give you their name. If for some reason you can't find it, I know it sounds silly to have to ask, but just double-check that it's the name they registered under. Sometimes, people get married or divorced or whatever else and their name changes or they decide to start using a different name. We only want to be able to find people. They can use whatever name they want here, but we need them to check in with the same name they registered under, then make sure they are wearing a mask and do a temp check before letting them in the room. I believe everyone is paid up, so there's no need to collect any funds.

People pay good money to attend this event, so we want to make sure that they get the absolute most out of it that they can. This half day is generally about people showing up. They come and gradually disconnect from whatever's distracting them in their normal lives, and it takes a while before they are fully present. So tonight, we will introduce some of the ideas of the seminar.

We will start with some very basic activities, but just know that tonight is about showing up physically and mentally and emotionally and giving people the space to arrive. Part of that is the example we set, so no cell phones in the room. Eli, no cell phone at the welcome table. I will need to have someone at this table on the breaks in case people have questions and for whatever reason they don't want to approach me. Also, I try to be available to them most breaks, but sometimes I need a rest too.

Eli, that person will often be you, and depending on the demand, we can partner you up with somebody to help you. When you are in the room, all of you please do your best to be here or at least look like you're here. We want to encourage people to be fully present and our example will help with that. Obviously, if someone has an emergency, we don't want to keep them from that, but we would like them to take it outside of the room to deal with. They can call home, they can leave early, go home, whatever they have to do to take care of themselves or their families, that's great and we would like to help them do that with the least amount of distraction to the rest of the room. Are there any questions so far?"

Most are shaking their heads no. Eli understands the whole idea of giving people the first evening just to show up. He's feeling that himself at the moment, not really understanding what he's doing or knowing anything about what the seminar is about.

"All right, great. The first day is kind of the bad news day and the activities we do on that day tend to be a bummer. The change you see between that day and the next day is where the magic happens. So, we need to try to keep people in the room physically and mentally and emotionally as much as possible that first day. We want them to do the activities, we don't want them to quit and go home, and if someone's in distress then we want to get them the support that they need. If someone's just quitting because they don't like the answers that they're getting, we want to be able to help them get to the gold on the other side. I warn you now about the challenge of tomorrow. That's why we are just getting present today. All of you having been through this understand what that day is like."

There are some groans and nods and smiles from the five volunteers.

"Since you're here, I'm assuming that you've decided the work of the day is well worth the payoff."

The smiles get bigger, nods are emphatic. Eli doesn't know what he's in for, but he can tell that Alejandro has made a difference in the lives of the people that chose to volunteer for him. He sees the glint of light on the Phoenix ring and is further reassured that whatever the downside of the first full day is, it must be a bridge to something better like Alejandro is saying.

They go into the room and Alejandro breaks volunteers into teams of two. He covers who will be overseeing the beverages, lunches and communicating with the hotel staff to make sure these things arrive on time, but doesn't interrupt the momentum of what's happening in the room. He assigns someone to make sure that he always has water since apparently talking constantly dries you out more than you would imagine.

All the volunteers are asked to take their phones to their car. Eli will take his to his hotel room. Attendees are supposed to leave their phones in their cars or in their rooms. If someone is particularly resistant to that because of an ongoing medical condition with a family member, they can leave their phone outside the room at the registration desk and check it hourly, knowing that they will miss some things. He gathers everyone back together.

"Ideally people want to be in the room at all times during the seminar and if life happens, support people in showing up as best they can. We have not lived a day in their life, so please be respectful of everyone, even if their issues seem trivial or if it seems like they're full of it. It's always better to err on the side of caution when it comes to other people and their right to think what they think, feel what they feel and express their needs, however they do it. Sometimes people will react in a big way over a small thing because it symbolizes something else for them. So, if the water pitcher at the back of the room being empty is enough to make somebody cry, we'll find out in the next day or two what the upset is really about.

People are resilient, people try to heal, and we are here to help them in any way that we can, even if we don't understand what they are healing from or how this process can be part of it. I give you that example not so you'll expect it. Only so you will be aware that people might behave in ways that don't make sense to you and it does not mean that their experiences are any less real. Everyone understand?"

He scans every face, making eye contact with everyone getting nods, then looks at his watch.

"Okay, if you guys don't mind, let's keep getting the tables set up along the sides for our small group breakout sessions and Eli, if you could be responsible for getting a workbook and pen onto every seat and into the hand of every volunteer and yourself as well. I am grateful for you all and I definitely need your help. But that does not mean that I don't want you all to get everything you possibly can out of the experience as well. One last time, does anyone have any questions for me?"

The youngest one of the bunch, a girl who looks like she's possibly a college student, raises a hand. He smiles and walks over to her and asks in a quiet voice what the question is, somehow understanding it's not meant for the whole room. He puts a hand on her shoulder and they walk a few feet away and have a brief conversation and she comes back smiling, happy with whatever the exchange was.

Eli goes to the boxes behind the table at the back of the room and picks up one box of the workbooks, drops two boxes of pens on it and takes it to the front of the room in the middle and starts going up and down the rows. He is impressed by the efficiency and diligence of the volunteers. At twelve fifteen the room looks perfect, exactly as Alejandro had asked for it to look. Eli goes to the back of the room and out the door looking for Alejandro who is coming back.

"Hey Eli, how are you?"

"I'm good, thanks. I think we're good in there."

"Perfect, we have some people checking in right now that are in our program, so we'll need to get you to the table soon. We are providing lunch but it's going to be late, about two thirty. If you need to get a snack, now would be a great time."

"No, I had a late breakfast. Thank you."

"Listen, I know you got in very early this morning and it sounds like you had a couple long days before that. Please know that this is not knocking you in any way. Just trying to support you and," he shrugs, "you are the first impression people are going to have when they show up for the seminar so I spoke to the manager and they had your room cleaned first thing and it's not something they normally do, but I was able to get them to iron a couple shirts for you. If you haven't already taken your phone to your room, please do that before people show up to register and go ahead and change into one of those fresh shirts."

Eli is embarrassed. He knew he looked bad when he came down in the morning. He just didn't have time to do anything else.

Alejandro puts his reassuring hand on his shoulder, "I travel a lot doing this. This is my home base, so it's easier for me when I'm here, but I really do know what it's like when you're on the road and away from home for weeks at a time. Please don't feel bad, I was glad we were able to get you what you need, and I appreciate you showing up and your willingness to jump right in."

"Thank you again. I'll go take care of that right now. I'll be back in five minutes."

"You don't have to break any speed records, but sooner is better."

Eli goes towards the elevator. Alejandro goes into the seminar room. A few minutes later, Eli is back at the table outside the door where he is joined by the woman Alejandro called Kathy—a short, thin middle-aged brunette with some salt in her pepper hair and pleasant smile lines around her eyes. The sparkle in her light-colored eyes implies she is friendly and likely a great co-conspirator.

"So, you haven't been to Alejandro's workshops before?"

"No, this is my first time. I am very excited."

"Remember what he said about the participants tomorrow and what it will be like the day after. The first day of this is rough stuff, but it definitely is worth it. He's a pretty amazing guy, especially for someone so young."

A couple of women approach the table and say their names. Kathy finds one and crosses the name off the list while the woman finds her name tag on the table. Eli crosses the other off, while she also looks through the nametags until she finds her own. Kathy takes their temperatures with the touchless thermometer and they proceed into the room.

Kathy and Eli get into a steady rhythm. For the next twenty minutes they are swamped and there's always a line. At about five after one, it goes down to a trickle.

Kathy checks the counts. "We're at sixty-eight percent. Would it bother you if I go in now?"

"No, not at all. Will you do me one favor?"

"Sure, what is it?"

"If I'm not in the room with you by the time they do lunch, will you bring me some? Please?"

"Sure thing." Her chipper attitude is somewhat contagious.

She enters the room and Eli looks up to face the next participant ready to check in. He notes the group is predominantly female, so far, with only a dozen or so men. Beyond that, it's very diverse both in age and ethnicity and, if clothes are any indication, also economic backgrounds. People continue to trickle in.

Eli is still at the table when she brings him lunch, which is a salad and a sub sandwich.

"Here you go. I didn't know which one you would want so I brought you both. If that's not enough I'll bring you some more."

"No, this will be great. Thank you. I appreciate it so much."

"My pleasure." Her mask has a painted smile, but he can tell when she smiles by the lines around her eyes.

He throws the bun from the sub away, tears the meat into smaller bites and sprinkles it on his salad and is pretty darn happy with his lunch. He easily eats it in between new arrivals. He sits outside the door until ten after four, waiting for one final participant to arrive. The gentleman at the front desk walks over and hands him a note. He's not sure if it's for him, but it's not in an envelope so he reads it. He is glad he did; apparently his wayward participant will not be attending. He gathers the check-in papers and picks up the final name tag and joins everyone in the room.

Kathy and the other volunteers are at one of the tables in the back. The participants are just coming back from some sort of partner exercise and a young woman is sharing about the woman that was her partner for the exercise. What she hopes to get out of the seminar that is worth going through the challenges and uncomfortable moments of the next day.

Eli has no idea what the next day will bring, but he isn't looking forward to it. The discord in his marriage is enough to make him uncomfortable; he isn't in the market for a seminar to add to his discomfort. He sits up straight and has his eyes pointed towards Alejandro, trying to appear present as the man had requested, but his attention is definitely elsewhere. He is startled when all the participants get up and make their way out the doors.

Alejandro gives the volunteers and Eli instructions by way of thanks. "Thank you so much for straightening the chairs and tidying the room before you leave. I look forward to seeing you all at 8:40 tomorrow morning. Have a great night." With that he leaves looking as fresh as he did when Eli first met him in the morning.

The volunteers and Eli make quick work of the straightening and tidying chores. When they are done, Eli stops by the bistro and orders something to go. When he attempts to tip, he is told they are also included. He thanks the waitress and takes his dinner up to his hotel room. He isn't sure what else is in Fresno, California; he isn't interested at the moment. He wants to eat some dinner and try to think of something to say to his wife if she will talk to him.

His phone is fully charged by the time he gets back. He dials Rachel's number at 7:15 so he can say good night to Mason. If the call goes through, he can't hear it. He dials Rachel's number from the hotel phone with a twinge of guilt and a bit of apprehension about how much a long-distance call will cost. He'll mention it to Alejandro in the morning and make good on it. The phone rings and he gets Rachel's voicemail. He had gotten rid of the landline a few months ago when he was trying to cut costs, even though he was the one who initially insisted they have it in case of winter power outages, which were not unheard of in the Northwest. Frustrated, not knowing what to do, he calls Rachel's phone again and leaves her a message.

"Hi Rachel, I know you're upset and I don't blame you. I just called to say good night to Mason and see if you felt like talking. I'm sorry about last night. I don't know if my text went through. I finished with Randy and am now in Fresno, California for my next project which is a two-and-a-half-day seminar. I hope I'll be coming home after this, but I don't know yet. I'm at the Fresno Marriott, please call me. I'm registered under my own name. If you don't reach me, please do leave a message so I know you guys are okay."

He pauses and the voicemail cuts off. He dials again and continues, "My phone is on its last leg and I don't know if my texts are going through and you're not responding or if they're not going through. It's probably best if you call me at the hotel while I'm here. If I do go someplace else after this, I'll make sure I know how to get into my voicemail and if I can't get messages directly on this phone, I should be able to check voicemail. I hope I get a chance to talk to you soon. I miss you so much. It's been hard being apart from you and it's been so much harder feeling apart from you the last few days. Please tell Mason good night for me. I love you both. Bye."

After that, he goes to the hotel gym and vents all his frustrations with a vigorous workout. When he's exhausted himself, he returns to the room for a nice long shower before he lies down and falls asleep watching a rerun of *The Big Bang Theory*.

CHAPTER 25

He opens his eyes, looking for the source of the sound. It turns out to be the alarm clock, which he doesn't remember setting. Alejandro was quite good at taking care of details; perhaps he had housekeeping set the alarm when they were cleaning and ironing. It's 8 a.m., he has forty minutes to get to the seminar.

He takes a trip to the bathroom to take care of his most pressing business and then splashes some water on his face before a quick shave. He plugs in his razor and gets dressed. He makes it to the bistro with a full thirty minutes available to get his breakfast ordered, delivered, and eaten. He arrives a couple of minutes early, which does not go unnoticed by Alejandro.

"Good morning," he looks at Eli and each of the volunteers, including everyone in his greeting. "Yesterday went really well, just top-notch work in the room and obviously out at the registration desk. I understand we only had one no-show; that's fantastic. I'd like to start today the same way if you can just stay at the desk until most everyone's in, just in case someone arrives with a question or issue you can address for them without distracting from what's happening in the room. Do you feel like you can handle that by yourself, Eli?"

"I think so, sure. If for some reason I can't, I'm sure I could get Kathy to come out and help me."

"That's a great plan. We'll make sure Kathy's at the back of the room in case you need backup; otherwise, we will let you handle this, and we will get onto the business of changing lives today. I'll remind you again, this is a tough day for people, and if they are not present, if they don't participate, if they don't stay in the room, they're not going to get the gold. So please really be intentional in supporting people. Any questions?"

Everyone shakes their head no.

"Great, I'm excited and I'm glad you're all here." With that, Alejandro enters the room, followed by his small flock of volunteers. Eli settles himself at the table as their early birds show up ready to face whatever ominous materials will be covered that day. There's a pretty steady flow of people until about five after, and a trickle after that. Eli stays outside maybe a little longer than he needs to.

Finally, at ten, he enters the room. Same as yesterday, he finds a spot in the back and does his best to look present. All his curiosity about what the bad news is quickly goes away. He doesn't understand why people would pay to come to the seminar, and he wants nothing to do with it. Alejandro is talking about embracing your dark side and owning your crap.

Minutes slowly go by, feeling more like hours. The energy in the room seems to match his mood. Eli can't wait for the day to be over. He does his best to appear present and, at the same time, tries his best to be anywhere but here. Each time there's an exercise that involves writing things down, he diligently pulls out paper and pen and starts writing. However, his list has nothing to do with the instructions and contains statements like "I don't want to be here. Will this day ever end, and I want to go home." There is a collective sigh of relief when they finally reach lunchtime and there's a break.

Some attendees lunch in pairs or small groups, many choosing to stay solo. There's not a lot of conversation, and it is low-voiced, low-energy. Once the seminar resumes, Eli is amazed to see that everyone has returned. If he had signed up for this, he would have been out the door at lunch and never come back.

About twenty minutes later, it looks as though a young woman has that exact idea. She gets up and bolts out the door. Alejandro meets Eli's eyes, and Eli nods, getting up to go after her. He catches her in the hall where she is losing her battle with tears.

Before he can say anything, she says, "Don't even try. I'm not going back in there. This is ridiculous." She starts crying harder. Eli holds his hands up in front of him to show he means her no harm.

"Hey, I'm with you. It's rough in there. Everybody that signed up for this knowing what they were coming to is tough stuff in my book. I don't know that I would ever intentionally sign up for something like that."

She stops crying a little and looks at him, waiting for a but, or some sort of punchline. He doesn't disappoint.

"I'm guessing whatever it was that you were hoping to get out of this must've been pretty big for you to have taken the time and the money to come to this, right?"

Slowly she nods, "But I didn't know it was going to be this bad."

"I bet." Eli shudders. "I am just blown away by everybody's commitment to put themselves through this, and if you want to leave, I totally understand. I just want to share something with you my really good friend Terrance told me. Who knows, maybe that'll be the best thing you get out of the seminar? He's a pretty smart guy; if it helps you, great. If it doesn't, that's okay."

Interested, she nods for him to go ahead.

"He says that life is challenge by choice. You can consciously choose your challenge, or you can choose the challenges of your life by what you avoid. I'm summarizing, he says it better. So, you made the conscious choice to challenge yourself and show up for this because you wanted whatever you hoped to get out of it. Whatever you're facing right now is challenging you, and I'm not trying to take anything away from that. I don't know you or anything about your life, but something about your life must be challenging you enough for you to be willing to try something like this. It really comes down to the question: is the challenge of facing whatever's coming up for you right now to get what you hope to get on the other side worth it, or is it a better choice for you to choose the challenges that are waiting for you through those doors?" he says, pointing towards the double doors.

She thinks for a minute and startles him with a rib-crushing hug before going back into the room with the same intensity she came out of it with. Eli turns to go back in and sees Alejandro standing behind him just outside the door. They look at each other for a moment. Eli is hoping the other man will approve of what he said.

"Nice job. I couldn't have done it better myself. You've got some skills," he puts his hand on Eli's shoulder, and together they walk back into the room.

Eli goes back to his spot at the table, and Alejandro goes back to his stool on the stage, waiting for whatever activity the participants are in the middle of to finish. Finally, shortly after four when the exercise is finished, Alejandro says, "I know that today is tough. Today is all the bad news. The final activity of the day is going to be making a list of everything that you think about yourself, that you've ever been told about yourself, or that you've ever been afraid might be true. Everything, write it all down." There's a collective groan. "It's not fun to start the process, but you'll be happy that you've done it."

Eli can't believe people pay for this stuff. It sounds like the worst advice he has ever heard.

Alejandro is still talking. "Have you ever made a to-do list in your mind or a grocery list? A list of any kind, things that you need to keep track of and don't want to forget?"

He looks at the audience, and most hands go up. "Have you ever noticed that when you finally get around to writing it down or put a note in your phone, it's a relief?"

There are many nods around the room.

"That's what your crap list will do for you. Once you get it all out and written down, you don't have to keep track of it anymore. It's not your brain's responsibility to hold onto it anymore. By owning it in a sense, you become free of it."

He clicks a button on the small remote he is holding. There's a picture of a big scary shadow on the screen, some sort of monstrous shape, the stuff nightmares are made from.

"These might be a fear of things, a fear of doing something, or a fear we might be perceived as being all those things we have to prove that we're not. Whatever type, they can all feel overwhelming. When we bring them to the light of day, oftentimes our work is done. Once we have found the courage to name and claim them, we discover their power is gone."

He clicks the next button, and there is a chihuahua puppy with a large bone in its mouth, casting the ominous shadow from the slide before. People laugh, finally enjoying a little levity in the room.

"There are occasionally folks that have something heavier, and simply owning and listing it doesn't resolve it for them. I'm not asking anyone to raise your hand, but if there's anyone here in this room who's ever done a twelve-step program of any type or who is familiar with it because of family or friends that have, you'll know that one of the steps is to take an inventory of yourself. Many self-help folks talk about the dark side and say that in order to heal that part of yourself, you must embrace it in the light. Again, usually that's enough. If there's something that owning it and listing it does not resolve for you, then you can figure out a way to make amends. But for today, for this week, for the next couple of weeks, simply make your list. Be with it."

He clicks the button again, and an extensive list flashes on the screen. It says things like "I am a thief, I'm selfish, I'm sexist, I am impatient, I am rude, I am arrogant, I am..." and the list goes on and on. Eli can only imagine what kind of jerk that list belongs to.

"This is the list that I made while I was still in prison."

Eli is stunned by the bombshell; the overall reaction in the room is small to nothing. He must be very upfront about that because no one besides Eli seems the least bit surprised to know Alejandro's history. Eli can't imagine a list even a third the length of what's up there being things that apply to the man that he has spent the last day listening to and getting to know a little bit.

The room goes into their list-making with much more enthusiasm after that last tidbit. It almost seems like there's a contest to have the longest, worst list possible. As much as Eli likes Alejandro, and even respects his willingness to show up warts and all, he has no interest in making such a list. He is much more concerned with getting a hold of his wife, who is probably making a list like that for him right now. The exercise ends, and Alejandro calls it a day, encouraging people to read their list over a few times and, if they are feeling exceptionally brave, share with friends or family to see if there's anything they left out.

"Please, please, if you have a rough time tonight facing your list, come back tomorrow. I promise you that the challenges of today will be rewarded tomorrow."

People get their belongings and race out through the door. Alejandro gathers volunteers together. "Thank you all so much for today; it was such a success. And thanks in advance for tidying the room before you go."

He makes his way to the door, but from the back of the room, he calls Eli over. Eli joins him, and they go to the welcome table.

"That was fantastic work this afternoon. You have a real knack for this. If you're interested at all, I'd love to have you come aboard full-time. It wouldn't pay much right now, but as it grows, and it is growing pretty fast, I would, of course, increase your salary. It does involve frequent travel, so if it doesn't work for you, I understand. Please think about it though, and we can talk more tomorrow if you're interested."

Out of respect for the man, Eli doesn't shut him down immediately, but he has no intention of taking a job that involves travel. Being away from his family has been one of the hardest things he's done in his life, even though the experiences he's had so far have been some of his best. Eli goes to the desk at the hotel to see if there are any messages waiting for him. There aren't. He goes upstairs and checks his phone, and as best as he can tell, there are no texts or messages on the phone. He finally goes down to the lobby to use the computer in the business center to look up a toll-free number for his cell phone provider to find out how to remotely check his voicemail. He does have a message from Rachel.

"I am sorry I was so upset I couldn't talk the other day. If I had any idea how challenging communication was going to become, I wouldn't have done that. I am very mad at you, don't get me wrong. You did make a good point about the way that we both grew up, and I've had time to calm down. It was not your finest hour for sure. I'm really disappointed that you made the choices you did. We will work it out, and we both miss you very much. I told Mason that your phone is broken and that you'll do your best to call, but he knows that it might not be every night between now and when you get home, which will hopefully be soon. Call me when you can. I tried to call you at the hotel, but they said that they didn't have an Eli Asher there, so I couldn't get a room number for you. Hopefully, you will figure out your voicemail and broken phone and be able to get this message."

Eli calls down to the desk. "Hi, I guess my wife called earlier trying to find me and was told that you didn't have me registered here. I'm just curious what's going on. I was able to register the other night with no issues just by giving my name."

"Let's see here, you are in 203?"

"Yes, that's correct," he confirms.

"Mr. Archer?"

"No, Asher, A-S-H-E-R."

"Mr. Asher, hold on a second, please," she comes back. "I'm sorry, there was a mistake made in the entry. The original reservation was entered as Asher; when you checked in, it was entered as Archer. I do apologize for the inconvenience. If you'd like to have your wife call back, I'll gladly connect her to the room."

"Thanks."

"Is there anything else I can help you with?"

"No, that's it. Thanks." Eli calls home again and gets Rachel's voicemail again. Frustrated, he leaves a brief message.

"Hi, I miss you guys like crazy. I can't wait to talk to you and better yet, see you soon. I'm going to try again about seven fifteen. Hopefully I'll be able to catch you then. I got the name confusion fixed with the front desk and I'm in room 203 in case they mess up the name again. I love you. Talk to you soon, bye."

He decides to go to the gym. He works out hard, trying to shake off the funk of the day. When he finishes his workout, he stops by the bistro to order dinner. As soon as it's ready, he takes it back to his room. He eats dinner with an episode of *The Simpsons* in the background. He takes a quick shower and calls home again. Mason answers, "Hi Dad, are you good?" He is slow, hesitant, his voice saturated with guilt.

"Hi Mason, I was. Is that going to change?"

"Probably," Mason admits, "Mom is really mad. She wants the phone. Bye, I love you."

"I love you too," Eli blurts out before Rachel comes on the line. He can hear her say "Go to your room" in the background.

"For the first time since you left, I am really glad for your sake that you're far away right now."

That's not a good indicator or a good opening line for a positive conversation.

"I just got a message from you saying you understand that the insurance thing was stupid, but we will work it out. What now?" he asks, disheartened to be having the next argument before they have reconnected after the last.

"You told our son to not tell me you guys went to Jen instead of the doctor and you bribed him with a candy topping and an extra big yogurt and you told him he could get an extra big one the next time too?" All fury and disbelief.

"Oh." He couldn't catch a break to save his life.

"That's all you have to say for yourself? Oh? You tell your son that men don't answer women honestly because you don't want to make them feel bad! Are we so fragile we can't handle the opinion of a mighty man?"

"No, of course not, Rachel. You know I'm not like that. I just didn't want you to quit school, so I didn't want you to find out about the insurance and I didn't want to tell him it was okay to lie. I know it sounds lame, but I was honestly trying for the lesser evil in the whole situation."

"Here's a big hint for you going forward. Any time not telling your wife something is the lesser evil in your plan, your plan stinks!"

"Okay, I get it. I agree. I've had stinky plans."

"I hope this is the end of it. I thought I knew you and this is really shaking me to the core. Not telling me about some financial challenges is one thing, letting me think that we have insurance when we don't and making the choice to not have insurance for our son is another thing of epic proportion. To bring him in on your scheme and have him lie by omission makes me think I don't even know this guy you are now."

"I know. I don't know what to say. I wish I had an answer that made sense. I was doing the best I could at the time, and I can tell you that my best is so much better now. I know I made a mess. I understand that with your help I'll be able to get through it so much better than I was on my own, keeping it from you."

"Well, that's a step in the right direction, I guess," she concedes. "Anything else I need to know? And keep in mind you are on thin, thin, thin ice."

Eli takes a deep breath, "The collection company that's after us for the rest of Mason's medical bills threatened to put a mark on his credit so that we couldn't just abandon our bad credit and rack up debt in his name."

"They did what?" He is glad to be far away from home now too.

"They threatened Mason's credit, which is why I took this temp job so I could make money and get us out of the situation. If it hadn't been for that, I would've stayed home and kept trying to find a job that could have solved our issues without having to leave you guys."

She has no interest in what he just said, "What is the company's name and what's the name of the person you spoke to?"

Eli tells her, hoping he won't be testifying about this moment at a trial in the future.

"Okay, thank you. What else?"

He has been dreading this moment. "You know how I didn't get that job that I really wanted and I told you it was because the guy that did get the job was in the same organization as the hiring manager."

"That secret society thing?" she asked.

"Yeah, that."

"Okay, what about it?"

"Well, I said I wanted to join it, because it opens doors. In fact, it opened this door. I don't know if they're actually paying the bills or if it's just from their network of people, but this temp work that I'm doing is definitely linked to this group."

"Okay, where's the bad news?"

"Well, it's not bad news necessarily, but one of the conditions of joining the group is that they get ten percent of your income."

"I'd say that's bad news. How long is that for?"

"Forever."

"I see. And that is another decision you thought you should make without talking to the person who is supposed to spend the rest of her life with you?"

"Well."

"Well nothing. What do you get for ten percent of your income for the rest of your life?"

"To be honest, I'm not a hundred percent sure."

"Why on earth would you agree to something like that without knowing what you're getting?"

"Well, I know it opens doors. That job I didn't get was amazing. It could have been a complete game changer for us and if those are the kind of doors these people can open, it's worth ten percent and I figured ten percent of something was a whole lot better than one hundred percent of the nothing I was making then. I know it's a big leap of faith and honestly, it was a really uncomfortable one to make so I can understand if you're not instantly on board.

I have to tell you everyone that I've met on this journey so far has been extraordinary and they are all happy. They really, really love what they're doing. Terrance and Isabella and the farmers, Harper and Nora, even Randy Yang, he doesn't have the most exciting work, but he's making a difference in the lives of his employees and feels very good about what he's doing. I don't know what door exactly will open for me, but if I can be as happy at work as I am at home, and maybe somehow have some reason to believe I'm making a difference, it's worth ten percent."

"Darn it!" she says exasperated. "Why do you always make it so hard to stay mad at you?"

He smiles, relieved, "Well it's either my charming disposition, my hot bod or my animal magnetism. I can't narrow it down more than that for you."

She rewards the response with a small chuckle. "Come on, I just had dinner, don't make me sick."

"Besides being extremely upset with yourself for your poor choices in life, how are you doing?" he asks.

"My poor choices?" she responds.

"Well, you did marry me."

"Don't remind me," she says, and they share a tentative laugh again.

"We're doing well. I think Mason's missing you more than he wants to admit and we're both feeling pretty stressed about moving, otherwise we're fine. I've got him sorting through his toys, deciding what has to make the move and what could maybe be donated, and I'm doing the same thing. So that's a heads up for you when you get here, you'll be doing the same thing too."

"Okay, that sounds reasonable."

"So, do you know when you're coming home?"

"No, I don't. It's got to be getting close. I don't have a specific person that I talk to that tells me here's A and here is Z and here is everything in between. Each stop I make, they know when it gets towards the end that the end is coming and where I'm going next. Usually, they don't even know that, they just know someone is picking me up at a certain time and place. So, I know tomorrow night is the end of this seminar I've been helping out with. I imagine I'll be leaving Fresno. But I don't know if it will be to come home or to go someplace else."

"Okay, let me know as soon as you find out. I've been picking up a few extra shifts in the evening so if you try to call and I'm not here, it's because I'm working. Jen has been watching Mason in the evenings and you know he's always happy to be over there with the dogs."

"I understand that I'm possibly risking my life saying this, but please don't work so much that you can't study."

"Yes, that is a bold and daring statement," she jokes, "but no, I'm still good with my studies. I'm not working a ton, just a couple extra shifts."

"All right, I will talk to you tomorrow night when I know where I'm going if I can, if I can't then I'll contact you as soon as possible. Did you get my text?"

"No, I haven't gotten a text from you since you broke your phone. I don't suppose we have insurance on that?"

"No."

"I do love you."

"Who are you reminding? Me or you?"

"Both. Why don't you get a new phone? You have to have one."

"I don't know if I will have a chance before I get back. I will if I can."

"Eli, I know you want to get a great paying job and find a house where we can have dogs, but you might need to think about accepting a job that isn't perfect for the short term, or we may need to get an apartment until we save up for a house. I know it's not what you want and it's not what I want either, but please be open minded just in case."

"I know you are worried and I understand. Something will work out. I already got offered a job tonight from this seminar guy."

"What's his name again?"

"Alejandro Santiago."

"Yikes, is he as sexy as that sounds?"

"I will not justify that with an answer."

"So that's a yes. What's the job?"

"We didn't get into a lot of detail. I'm not interested."

"Why not?" she demands.

"I would have to travel to wherever he is offering the seminar. This has been a rewarding experience, but I am ready to be home with you guys. Next time I travel I want you two to be with me."

"So, what you are really saying is you don't want me to fall for and run off with the sexy seminar guy?"

"No, how does it have anything to do with you? I don't want to fall for and run off with the sexy Alejandro."

"From the sounds of his name, he probably is your type."

"Hey, don't limit me, I can fall for whoever I want."

"Sure, as long as they have dark hair, dark eyes and tan skin. I would be less surprised if you ran off with him than I would be if you ran off with a blonde and I know you have a deep and abiding appreciation for the female form." Her voice drops to a husky whisper.

"I have a deep, abiding appreciation for your form."

"Mom, are you still mad?" Mason yells from the other room.

"I better go. He was pretty upset when I was done waterboarding him for the dirt on you."

"Poor guy. I'll have to make it up to him."

"Don't you dare, the little extortionist got the large yogurt with one candy topping today and the promise of one more next time."

It feels so good to laugh together they are both reluctant to say goodbye.

"Mom!" Mason yells again from his room.

"Bye, I love you."

"I love you too. If he tells you I owe him ten dollars from the last treasure hunt it's true. Bye."

He hangs up before she can respond, confident that good humor will win out over any annoyance she might have. He feels much better now that he has reestablished contact with his family and knows that he and Rachel will work through their challenge. He is relieved to have his secrets brought to light, which makes him think of the seminar activities of the day.

He pulls out a sheet of paper and does what he was unwilling to do earlier in the day. Making his list to own his crap, he puts things on it such as overspending, being judgmental, being aggressive, holding a grudge, being a failure, being aloof, being stubborn and sometimes righteous. He fills most of a piece of paper with everything that he felt was negative about himself at any point in time and anything anyone had ever said about him. When he finishes, he reviews it, putting a single line through anything he doesn't consider true now or ever. When he is done, the list feels more manageable, but there are still more negative traits than he cares for.

CHAPTER 26

The next morning, he goes downstairs to get breakfast and go to the seminar with his list in his pocket and a lightness in his step. Alejandro sees him in the bistro and joins him.

"Do you mind if I eat with you?"

"No, that would be great."

Alejandro sits down and the waitress comes over. Once his order is in, he turns his attention back to Eli.

"Have you given any thought to the job?"

"I am so flattered that you would even consider offering it to me after so little time, but it's just not a fit for me right now."

"I'm so sorry to hear that. Would you mind sharing what part in particular isn't a fit?"

"I have been traveling for more than a month now away from my family in Portland and am just very ready to get back home to them. I would've loved a job that involves traveling before I got married, at this point in my life it's just not something I'm open to."

"If you've got any sales and marketing experience, which I'm assuming you do just from seeing you the last couple days, I can offer you the opportunity to market the seminars and split the fee for every attendee that you send 50-50."

"Yeah, that sounds like something I could do on the side. Right now, my family is going through a transition. We have to move out of the house we've lived in for the last several years and I have to have a base salary and benefits, and commission, all that good stuff. But I like what you're doing here, at least what I've seen so far. I would be more than happy to try to fill some seats for you, but I can't commit to doing anything more than on the side."

"I understand. Eventually maybe I'll grow this thing enough that we could offer what you need. In the meantime, I'd be thrilled to have you refer anyone you'd like, and I'll pay you for anyone that you do. I always ask people where they heard of me, so anyone that you send, just tell them to put your name down and I'll make sure you're taken care of."

The waitress returns to the table and sets a plate down in front of Eli, "Yours will be right up, hon." She flashes Alejandro an inviting look.

"Thank you," Alejandro says. "I'd love to hear more about you and your family, but I realize it's impolite to ask someone whose meal was just set before them a bunch of questions. Hopefully we'll get some more time to chat when the seminar is over this evening."

Eli finishes chewing the bite in his mouth and says, "Do you know where I'm going next?"

"I believe you're going to Seattle for a few days. Does that make sense?"

Eli shrugs, "It could, I live in Portland so it's closer to home and I could be working for another week or so. Do you know how I'm getting there?"

"No, someone is supposed to contact me this evening and give me those details. Speaking of which, if you don't mind, could you check out of the hotel at lunchtime and bring your bags into the room? Just put them under the table that you're at, I'd appreciate it."

"No problem. I'll take care of it," Eli agrees.

Alejandro's food arrives, and both men focus on their breakfast.

When they finish eating, they go to the meeting room. Everyone falls easily into the rhythm of the last two days. Eli takes his post at the door. By the time the strays have arrived and are in the door and Eli's in the back of the room, they are just wrapping up people sharing their experiences of making the list the night before.

"Now, time for some of the good news. I want you to make a new list today. This one is of your strengths. No playing small, be as rigorous and fearless as you were yesterday."

He doesn't say much more, realizing that he has lost the attention of most of the group who are busy starting their list.

Eli follows suit, both to respect Alejandro's request that he and the volunteers appear present and a readiness to see something to balance out the negativity. He makes his list with loyal being number one — thinking of his family, and confident being number two. Thinking of his experiences in the many different jobs and situations recently, he adds competent and continues with the list. When he's finished, it's almost as long as the negative list.

He muses to himself, maybe that's the best any of us can hope for. Certainly, all the protesting and all the statues that were brought down remind us that nobody is everything. Ordinary people can do amazing things and awful things. Nobody is all one thing, we are a mix of traits and potentials from moment to moment. He hopes people will judge him for the best of him, not that he thinks there will ever be statues of him.

In a light and playful voice Alejandro says, "We're done with lists for the day." That evokes a cheer from the room. "Now when I first started doing this, we would burn the bad list. We don't do that anymore." There's a collective groan.

"I know, I know. But I came across some information from a Dr. Mark Wahlberg who says that as soon as you destroy the list, your mind is busy keeping track of it again. As long as you have it with you it is pretty much off your plate, so the advice instead is if you have a vision board somewhere to keep your list with it. If you don't have one, make one."

Hands immediately shoot up.

"Hold on now. I know most people are outraged at the thought of keeping something perceived as negative near the vision board when it's not something you want to create. The fact is, it's something that you believe is already here. And it's being unwilling to embrace it that increases your resistance to it. Is there anyone in this room who hasn't heard 'what you resist persists?'"

He looks around. Not a single hand goes up.

"Excellent, and you understand the meaning here. Hopefully having written it down, bringing it into the light of day takes a lot of the emotion out of it and it's the things that we focus on with emotion that we create in our lives. It doesn't matter if we say we do or don't want it. If we focus our attention on it with emotion it will show up. So, I want you to be very comfortable with this list and I highly recommend, I won't be there to babysit, but I highly recommend that you keep it. I hated the advice and didn't think much of the man who gave it to me.

However, after I destroyed the list, I found that a lot of the negative self-talk that hadn't been present since I'd made the list slowly started coming back. I was frequently thinking of past mistakes or when someone had told me something that was on the list. Once I made the list and kept it that stopped. I feel that if I hadn't made this list and kept it, I wouldn't be where I am today."

He clicks the button and puts his list back up on the screen.

"I wouldn't be in front of you. There were plenty of people that told me when I was in jail, and when I was first getting out of jail, that I would never amount to anything. My father, who would just as soon hit me as look at me, told me almost every day growing up that I would amount to nothing and I believed him. When I continued to hear those voices throughout my life, I believed them."

Eli notices some misty eyes in the room, Kathy is up passing out tissues before he finishes the thought.

"If you had told me at any of those points in my life that people would ever pay to hear what I have to say I would've said you were crazy. Embracing the dark side helped me find the light. Because whatever's on that list is not all of who you are and when you're not worried about other people knowing that you're not perfect, by the way is anybody in here perfect?"

He looks around the room again, no hands go up.

"Great, neither am I and when you're done worrying about it you can give all your attention and energy to what you do want to, what you do deserve. So, what will make your life beautiful and what are the ways that you can contribute and help make other people's lives beautiful. That's what we're going to do this afternoon. Forgive ourselves and others for being human and give you a head start on creating amazing possibilities for the present and future of your whole integrated self. As soon as we get back from morning break," he adds.

This gets some laughter and chuckles from the crowd, who slowly stand and stretch and meander to the bathrooms or cars to check phones, or outside to smoke or wherever else they want to go. Eli adds the list of strengths to the list of negative traits in his pocket. He will share them with Rachel and see if he's missed anything on either list after he gets home.

The day flies along quickly. Time is moving as fast today as it had dragged along the day before. The mood in the room is much lighter. There are a lot of people volunteering to share every time Alejandro gives them the opportunity. Eli is moved by some of the things people are doing. There had been a couple of people that mended relationships with parents or siblings that they hadn't spoken to in years. There were people committing to starting nonprofits and businesses and families that they had wanted for a long time but fear had held them back. It all seemed very odd and counterintuitive to him, but he could not deny that there was a power available in owning your crap as Alejandro had put it.

By the time Alejandro wraps it up that evening, the audience seems to feel invincible. Now thoroughly convinced that the worst of them was not a weakness but an asset. A small number of people bounded out the door ready to take on the world. Some lingered, not wanting to leave the feeling of this space. A good size crowd gathered around the stage to ask Alejandro questions or thank him for the event.

Eli looks up, surprised to notice someone waiting to talk to him as well.

It was the woman he'd followed into the hallway.

"You remember me?" she asked.

"Of course, what can I do for you?"

"Nothing. I just wanted to thank you for yesterday. If you hadn't come after me and I had gone home, I would've missed out on something wonderful. It really made a difference in my life, probably more than you know."

Eli is very uncomfortable with her compliments and feels she is a bit dramatic, still he does not want to offend or diminish her. He gives her a bright smile with some crimson in his cheeks.

"Thank you. You're too kind."

She continues waiting until he asks again, "What can I do for you?"

She holds out her arms for a hug, which he gives her. Afterwards she turns and leaves the seminar room. The crowd around Alejandro is shrinking. He's down to just a couple more people.

He catches Eli's look and holds up his index finger to say one more minute. Finally, the last few attendees leave. He gathers all the volunteers around at the back table.

"I know that you guys didn't come to do this for me, you came to do this for them and for what you knew this evening would look like after they went through the process. I don't mind that one bit. I thank you for your generosity, for your time and your presence, for your compassion and caring for these people. Some you may have known; many were strangers to you. I know that you've made a positive difference in their lives and mine," with that he starts clapping until everyone else joins in. After a minute the applause dies down and he says, "I hope to see you guys next time, take care."

They grab their stuff from various points in the room and congregate in the lobby, ten or fifteen feet away, not ready to say goodbye yet. Alejandro turns to Eli, "Hold on one more second, I need to check in with the front desk. I'll be right back, okay?"

Eli agrees, having no other choice. Alejandro goes over to the desk, a moment later he's on the phone. After that, he returns with a file. "I need to get some paperwork from you so you can get paid."

Eli squirms a little. "I'm not sure that I'm your guy to help you fill your seminars. I have no problem telling people what I know about it and recommending you, but I don't know if it will be enough to make a difference. I think we probably better wait and see what happens."

Alejandro laughs. "I appreciate your honesty, but I'm not asking for myself. I was asked to get the paperwork for you so you can get paid for this temp work you've been doing."

"I've been wondering how that was going to work."

"And now you know." Alejandro opens a folder and it has all the typical information for a W-2 employee. He is both happy and distressed to see the W-2 instead of a 1099. He won't have to double pay on certain things like you do with a 1099, but they will take taxes out upfront. That might leave them short in their housing search. He keeps his face passive, not wanting to go into his difficulties with Alejandro.

While Eli fills out the forms, Alejandro takes his driver's license and social security card and makes a photocopy in the business center, returning a minute or two later, he gives the items to Eli who in turn gives him the papers.

"Well, sadly, you don't want to come work for me. Yet!" Alejandro adds with a devilish grin and "I understand that. This," he taps the ring, "opens things up in ways that you probably can't imagine until it happens. But if for some reason your feelings about travel change down the road, let me know."

"I have to ask, why are you so into the idea of hiring me? I'm sure there's plenty of great people that you could have in an instant."

Alejandro starts talking, "So some of the big guys don't do anything but steal material from the little guys. I know of a guru who used to be my hero. He's got this coaching course that I spent thousands on; he barely had anything to do with it, and most of his involvement was old videos of him ripping off other people's work and not even citing them as the source. The HeartMath stuff he used was verbatim, but if I hadn't known it was their information, I would have thought he was making it up on the spot. He talked about brain science and brain scans and heart math and coherence between heart and brain and a number of other things.

"Somebody like me, they don't want to hear that stuff. They don't know that the things I say have science behind them. Somebody like me, that's not what they're looking for. If I was a PhD or one of the big self-help gurus, maybe they would be interested in the science but me, a young guy who, until fairly recently was a poor guy with a prison history, they want to hear stories, and that's fine. There's a certain audience that will be drawn to me because of my style that wouldn't be drawn to some of these other folks and vice versa."

Eli is not sure if he's actually answering his question or evading it.

"That's part of what I loved about you when I heard you in the hall with that woman. You just used a story from your own experience, but you were smart enough to recognize the information as profound, and it is, plus you had the integrity to cite the source. I actually want to find out more about your friend because if I can, I would like to use the material and, of course, cite him as the source."

Eli figures Terrance will act like he expects the world to knock down his door to hear his wisdom, but really, he will be shy and touched to know people think it is meaningful.

"I will certainly ask my friend if he's open to that; if he is, I will give you his information."

"You have my card, right?" Alejandro asks.

Eli holds it up.

"I guess there's nothing for me to do but take you to the airport. Unless of course you want to call your wife and see if she likes the idea of traveling more than you think she would?"

Eli laughs, admiring the man's doggedness. "No, we talked last night and after hearing your name, her first question was about your looks. I don't think we'll be coming on the road with you."

Alejandro laughs. "Is she a looker?"

"Oh yeah," Eli says, nodding his head, "I still don't know what she's doing with me."

"Listen. If that doesn't work out for you, be sure to give her my card, okay?" Again, with the devilish grin.

"Yeah, I will absolutely be sure to never do that," Eli agrees wholeheartedly.

"Good man," Alejandro says, laughing. He reaches out his arms to hug Eli.

"It was good to meet you, I wish you and your family all the best. Keep my offer in mind; it's not going anywhere. Let's get your gear and get you to the airport." He gives him a final slap on the back and ends the embrace.

Alejandro drives him to the airport where he squeezes in the back of a Piper Cub four-seater. At least that's what Alejandro told him it was as he was climbing out of the

SUV. No jet tonight. The couple in the front seats keep each other company and Eli falls asleep leaning against his bag.

A short, uneventful flight later they touched down at Boeing Field, in South Seattle. The plane comes to a stop and taxis near a building. Still half asleep, he mutters, "Thank you" as he extricates himself and his stuff from the small plane.

CHAPTER 27

He stands on the tarmac for a moment, smelling the air. It's sweet and fresh; it smells like the Northwest and home. He even enjoys feeling the chill of the night. He looks around and notices an Asian woman waiting next to a box truck.

She approaches him, "Are you Mr. Eli Asher?" she asks.

"Yes, please call me Eli."

"Eli, I am Suki Lee. I understand you're here to help us for a few days."

"Yes, I am not sure what I'm helping with, Suki, but I'm happy to help anyway I can."

"It's too late tonight to worry about that. Have you had dinner?"

"Yes. I had something on the way to the airport."

"Very well, let's go." She motions towards the box truck and he climbs up into the cab while she walks around to the driver's side. A few minutes later they are in Seattle's International District. Eli knows from a past faux pas as a tourist not to call it Chinatown. It is the International District, with many languages spoken and many people represented. Chinese, Japanese, Vietnamese, Filipino and Korean being the main ones that he remembers, but he has no idea of the specific demographics. He is curious how people that lived and worked in the area get along after his recent experience with Randy and the Japanese man in Vegas.

She parks at the curb and gets out; he follows, gear in tow.

"You will be in this apartment." She opens the door between two street-level storefronts and he follows her up a flight of stairs. She is holding a door open when he arrives. It is a small but adequate space. The studio-style apartment has a tiny kitchen and bath. There's a bed made up and an open bar above a dresser for clothing. He puts his bag beside the dresser and hangs his clothes on the bar.

"What time do you want me to be ready in the morning? Where do you want me to be?"

She pulls a card from her back pocket and gives it to him. "Call me when you are rested."

He looks around the apartment to see if there's a phone available. "I'm sorry, I don't have a working phone right now. It got damaged last week. If you just tell me what time, I'll be there."

"I hear you had a very busy schedule. It is late. You sleep until you are rested," she insists. She goes across the hall and knocks on the door there. After a brief conversation in another language, there's some sort of mutual agreement and the door closes. She comes back and says, "When you're ready, knock on the door and they will let you use the phone to call me."

It's clear to Eli he is not going to win this argument about being ready at a certain time versus waiting till he's rested, so he agrees with her instructions.

"I don't suppose you have a phone I can use for just a second?"

She pulls her phone from her pocket, unlocks the screen and hands it to him.

"Thank you, I really appreciate it." He taps out a quick text to Rachel letting her know that he is in Seattle and asking her to tell Mason good night for him. He hands the phone back feeling relieved to have his own space, to be so close to home and to be communicating with Rachel, at least in some way.

"I will see you tomorrow," She pauses at the door, "Is there anything else you need?"

"No, this is great. Thank you."

She closes the door and Eli pulls a few things from his bag. He assumes he won't be here long enough to fully unpack. He wishes he'd asked how he needed to dress. With a shrug, he decides he'll figure it out in the morning and takes a quick shower before laying down. It takes him a while to fall asleep, partly because the bed is very firm and partly because his mind won't stop racing. Being so close to home and being closer to his family being evicted. He's discovering it's hard to shut it off. When he finally does fall asleep, he sleeps long and hard.

When he wakes up, he can't believe it when he sees it's ten thirty. He bolts out of bed, uses the bathroom, gets dressed as fast as he can and knocks on the door across the hall as instructed. The woman calls Suki and hands him her flip phone wordlessly.

Suki answers on the third ring. "Hello, how do you feel, Eli?"

"I feel great. I'm sorry I'm getting such a late start. Obviously, you were right. I needed to sleep."

"That is good, come downstairs and I will pick you up."

"Okay, I'll be right down."

He hands the phone back to the elderly Asian woman and smiles. She smiles back for a moment and shuts the door again. He goes down the stairs and waits on the curb for maybe two minutes before the box truck pulls up next to him. He climbs in and she drives a couple of blocks before she turns a corner. They get out and go into a small mom-and-pop restaurant.

"We will have breakfast here and then we will work."

"We don't have to do this on my account. I can wait until lunch. I hate to get such a late start on the day."

"We're not here solely on your account. These people have had this restaurant for many generations and they are struggling now. This pandemic has been very hard on our people. Many have faced harassment and assaults; business, like all business, is down. Ours maybe more? Before the pandemic I rarely ate out, since the pandemic I rarely cook. We have to support our community."

"When I was in Vegas, I worked with a very nice Chinese man and then all of a sudden he had this altercation with a Japanese guy over some pallets that he was getting rid of anyway and I was pretty surprised by that. Do you have much of that here?"

She shakes her head, instantly weary.

"There are some people that hold onto the past. We need to come together as a community and let go of the hurt so we can get through this. The seniors in my community have much fear after the internment camps. The Chinese have much fear after the Chinese Exclusion Act and many other acts of aggression against our people through the years. This is nothing new for us. The fear is very high."

A young girl approaches the table and in a language that did not sound like what she used last night, Suki orders breakfast, apparently for both of them.

It was a weird feeling for him having someone else order for him while he was sitting at the table without asking. He realizes women have been dealing with that sort of thing for a long time.

An ancient couple slowly makes their way from unseen parts of the kitchen out into the dining area. They move slowly but with dignity and somehow grace. Eli can't help but think of the rings in a tree and how they can tell scientists about the environment year after year. He feels like their faces could tell many things. If only he could decipher the code to be able to read them. Suki stands and instead of going towards the couple, she goes towards the door. He braces himself, hoping this will not be another encounter like the one he experienced with Randy. Suki stops at the window and taps the coronavirus poster that says "Viruses don't discriminate, neither should we."

The woman's face lights up and the man says slowly in clear English, "If you see something, say something." Suki returns the effort with a brilliant smile and a small clap.

"Very good!" She goes to give them both a hug. They talk rapidly, having complete privacy with him in the room, language keeping him out better than any wall could. A few moments later the food comes.

She joins him at the table. "I'm sorry. I have been rude. These are the four things that Westerners usually order here. You can have all of one thing or some of everything. It was just faster to order those four things than to try to explain each item on the menu to you. They don't have an English version. Some places here are more tourist-friendly, but many are focused on serving this community."

She points to each dish, "This is Korean egg roll, similar content to an omelet. This is egg fried rice." She looks at him to see if he needs more explanation. He nods for her to continue, "These are Jeon vegetable pancakes; they have meat and vegetable, the sauce is spicy. These are Enoki mushroom pancakes. You should try them; they are very popular."

She waits for him while he cuts a small piece off each item and puts it on his plate to try. He likes everything but the weird pancakes with the spicy sauce. He cuts a bigger piece off the egg roll, scoops up more egg fried rice and takes a whole Enoki mushroom pancake and the one he had cut a bite from previously.

She finishes off the Jeon pancakes, and in between bites pulls some empty glass containers out of her bag. She puts the leftovers in the containers and waits patiently for him to finish what's on his plate. She goes to the counter to pay and then they are back in the van. Again, she only drives a few blocks up, pulls over at the corner near a line of people.

"Okay, it's time to get started."

She jumps down and first goes to a few people sitting on the sidewalk along the wall; she quickly disperses the leftovers. She motions for Eli to follow her around the back of the box truck. She flips it open and rolls the door to the top. She climbs on, moving a few things out of her way. There are numerous boxes and bags sitting in the back that were prepared ahead of time. She motions for the first person in line to come up and she gives them a box, a bag and a smaller version of the poster he'd seen in the restaurant. With smiles and waves they take the items and move on, allowing the next person in line to come forward.

Eli stands there feeling extraneous; she pauses for a moment. "This will go very fast. As soon as there's room on the end, please start bringing things forward, always moving things forward."

He nods in agreement. She turns her attention back to handing out the items. She is correct. It does not take long for the back third of the truck to be depleted and he works hard to keep up, moving the prepared boxes and bags to her. Soon they have run out of supplies and Eli is distressed to see that the line is not finished. Suki jumps down and gathers the remaining people around her. After a brief conversation she gets several nods. She hands them all big red cards. She motions for Eli to come with her and points up to the door. He grabs the strap and pulls the door down with him as he jumps from the truck. She heads towards the front, so he follows and meets her in the cab.

She starts the truck and immediately pulls away from the curb. Five blocks later she turns down an alley and backs the truck up to a loading dock door.

"We will reload the truck and go to the next location."

By the time the truck door and loading dock doors are open, a number of people are there working to load the truck rapidly. In the back of the truck there are shelves that can stack the goods higher. In the front it's all one level.

Fifteen minutes later with the truck loaded, they are off again. They go to a different spot this time, but follow the same procedure. There's already a line again and Eli recognizes a few people at the front of the line with the red cards as the ones who were at the back of the line at the first stop.

Eli asks, "Can I help pass things out?"

Suki shrugs, "You can try".

She says something in a few languages and motions to Eli with each iteration. When the first person comes forward, they go to Suki. Eli motions for the next person in line to come to him, but they don't. After four people have gone to Suki to get supplies and no one has approached him, he understands why she said you can try.

A young woman with a young boy wrapped around her leg slowly makes her way to him and accepts the bag, the box and the flyer from him with a reticent smile. She moves away and someone else steps up to him as well. He is still averaging about one for every four or five that go to Suki, but feels satisfied somehow that at least a few people thought coming to him was better than waiting in line.

It is time for him to jump back up into the back of the truck and start moving supplies forward so they can be distributed more quickly and it seems to be a relief to everyone, himself included. He doesn't blame this community for not embracing him and it isn't the first time that he has been a minority in a particular instance. He can't imagine feeling like that all the time or feeling unsafe and threatened, unwanted and especially trying to raise a child feeling like that.

He is more determined to do everything he can, to give it everything he has and help as much as he possibly can in the short amount of time that he is there. They empty out this truck even faster than the last and he has worked up a serious sweat by the time they finish. When they get back to the warehouse, she tells him, "Go get water and take a rest."

He ignores her and joins in with her small army restocking the truck. He is lapping almost everyone else, making at least two, and in some cases three trips to their one. The harder he works the more she scowls. He is totally confused.

They get back in the truck and this time before she starts it she looks at him, "What do they tell you on the airplane?" Baffled, he gives her a blank stare. "When the flight attendants talk about safety. What do they tell you to do if the oxygen masks come down?" she asks her question more explicitly so that he can understand.

He has to think for a minute because until recently he hadn't done much traveling and his recent travel hadn't been commercial.

"They tell you to put your own mask on first, right?"

"Exactly. If you want to help other people, you have to take care of yourself first. If you don't, you don't help anyone for very long and then you are a burden instead." She looks him in the eye. "Go get water."

He scrambles out of the truck, appropriately chastised, and tracks down the water where she had said it would be earlier. He grabs a few bottles, not wanting to waste the steps to go back later. As soon as he is in the truck, he shows her the bottles and offers one to her. She shakes her head no, showing her glass container filled with water. He cracks one open and drinks half of it in one gulp, trying to placate her. It's then she starts the engine of the truck and heads off to the next location.

"I'm confused," he says. "Why don't people just come here?"

"They used to before the accusations against China for starting coronavirus and lying about it and wild rumors and speculations about it being manufactured and intentional. Then there were retaliations against this community. You asked earlier about Chinese and

Japanese not getting along. We do better here because to the rest of the world we're all the same, and that helps us be close even if some wouldn't be in other places.

"After some graffiti, bullying and violence, people did not want to come here because they were afraid they could be a target here. The community is in more need than ever, but we have to go to them instead of having them come to us. Where we will be is only released a day or two ahead of time and only in this community. We never stay in any particular spot very long and there are multiple places throughout the day so that lines don't get too long, so too many people don't congregate anywhere."

"That's terrible," Eli doesn't attempt to be more eloquent than that. "Is it that bad? Is it necessary to go that far?"

She shrugs. "I cannot say. What's happened so far is not, but if you are a student of history, you see that when a government starts to blame a certain section of their population for their challenges or to make them less than the rest of the population or less than human, that group is wise to be afraid."

Hitler's treatment of the Jews immediately springs to mind. That one is impossible to argue with. She pulls over to the curb next to a line of folks waiting again. He jumps out and sprints to the back of the truck, opening the door before she gets to it. The people at the front of the line move back, intimidated by his fast approach. She shoots him a dour look and though he stands there with a bag, a box and a flyer, no one will take them from him. Once he understands, he gets in the back of the truck and begins moving stuff up so that it's readily available for her reach. This time he moves everything multiple times so that she barely has to move at all. Everything's under her hand ready to go. He's breathing a little heavier by the time they finish and drenched in sweat.

Back in the cab, she gestures to the water which he drinks without protest. He waits for the scolding he is sure he will get for his excess enthusiasm at their arrival, but she doesn't bring it up.

He does. "I'm sorry, I didn't think how it would feel to them if I ran around to get the door for you."

She just shakes her head, not wanting to talk about it and they pull into the alley. She turns her attention to backing up again. As before, he is lapping the other folks helping reload the truck when he accidentally bumps into a teenage boy who falls down.

"I'm so sorry," Eli offers a hand to help him up. Tentatively, the boy takes his hand. Eli pulls him up and bends down to pick up what the boy had been carrying. The boy brushes himself off before accepting the load again and moving away from Eli quickly.

Suki comes over to him. "You have to go."

"Sorry, what?"

"Go get in the truck," she says and waves him away.

Since the truck is almost loaded and he can see she's very frustrated, he complies. He would much prefer to continue to help load it. Once they are back on the road, she drives down a street that looks familiar to him. He again notices how foreign this neighborhood feels to him and can only imagine what a comfort it must be to its residents and shoppers, who find a piece of home in a place that is foreign to them. She stops in front of the door. She leaves the truck running, but gets out and motions for him to follow. She opens the door and he follows her up the stairway and into the apartment he slept in last night.

"You have to go," she repeats.

"I don't understand. What do you mean?"

"You have a good heart," she says but points to his head and shakes, no. "I tell you, you have to take care of yourself first. You are a bad volunteer."

Confused and more than a little hurt, he holds up his hands like what.

"You're here for a day or two. My regular volunteers need to come back every week. We always need more help, all the time. Especially at this time. Some of them work one job or two jobs and still come and volunteer; they have to take care of themselves first. They have to rest, they have to drink water, they have to eat food, they have to use sense." She smacks her head with the palm of her hand.

"If you make it a race and they start to run, they wear out and they will not come back. That's bad!" She emphasizes the word. "You go." He takes a couple steps into the apartment.

"You stay. I will come later for what's next."

"Are you firing me?" he asks.

"Yes," she agrees, smiling. With that she closes the door behind her.

He fights the urge to chase after her and ask for another chance; he doesn't think she is likely to give him one and he doesn't want to add to his embarrassment. He's never been fired in his life, laid off a couple times but never fired. He has to admit it stings. He paces around the apartment burning off his excess energy.

Finally, he figures he should be as productive as possible, so he takes a shower, shaves and readjusts his bag with the dirty clothes on the bottom, clean on top, fortunately a garbage bag he had found was now separating the two. He's just finishing when there's a knock on the door.

He opens it to find Suki standing there. "Are you ready?"

"Ready for what?"

"To go somewhere else."

"Home."

She shakes her head. "No, North Dakota."

Ah that's just craptastic, he thinks to himself. "This day just gets worse. I go from getting fired to trying to figure out how I'm going to get myself home tonight to getting further away, going to North Dakota."

The one potential silver lining is that he's guessing the distance from North Dakota would get him on a plane instead of a truck and that might give him another chance to see Zeke.

She motions to his bag. He picks it up ready to leave. She shakes her head, he's utterly hopeless, and she points to his clothes still hanging on the bar. He goes back to get them, very glad to be leaving, wishing he could be anywhere else right now.

They get in the truck and on the short drive to Boeing Field he says, "I'm really sorry. I had no idea what your community was experiencing and I just wanted to help. I wanted to help as much as I could for the short time I was here."

"I can tell you have a good heart, but you are a bad apple in my volunteer basket. I have to preserve the health and wellness of all my volunteers so they can help preserve the health and wellness of our community. You come visit here anytime, just no volunteering."

"Well technically I wasn't a volunteer, so that's another reason I felt like I should be working harder than them."

"The volunteers don't know this. I'm not telling this to them. You are a volunteer to me, you're a bad apple in my volunteer basket," she reiterates, putting an end to the subject.

"I didn't think of that."

She waves him off. "Just remember to put your own mask on first."

He smiles. It sounds silly, but he knows there is wisdom to it. Rachel had gone through some rough times after she became an RN. It took her a while to learn to say no when she needed to so she could take care of herself and save some of herself for her family. If he had put his own mask on first, he would've finished his degree instead of dropping out so that Rachel could first get her RN and now her nurse practitioner license. If he had gotten his degree first, he couldn't help but assume that his family circumstances would've been better through all this.

In that way, what she said, even though it sounds like promoting selfishness, is actually a much smarter way to be able to contribute to a family or a community. He would have to think about that more. He feels worse because he likes Suki quite a bit and certainly admires her and the impact she has on her community with her dedication and leadership.

Eli gets out of the box truck slowly, still regretting the circumstances that cut his time in Seattle short.

He looks up at her. "You're doing great work. I wish I could have helped."

"I know," she smiles. He is not sure which of his statements she is saying "I know" to. He can tell she's ready to leave.

"Do you have any extras of those flyers?"

She hands him a couple, her smile broadening. "There is the website address," she points. "You can get more, posters or fliers."

"Thanks," he obliges her and closes the door. She has the truck in motion seconds after. He watches until she is out of sight.

CHAPTER 28

There is a light jet on the tarmac in front of him; he approaches hoping it will lead to a better outcome than the last trip did.

Eli makes his way up the steps; a woman is waiting for him at the top. She quickly takes his bags and stores them in the closet just inside the entry.

"I guess I should have asked this before stowing your bags, but I trust you're Eli?"

"Yes," he smiles.

"I am your captain. We are going to take off in just a minute; is there anything you need help with prior to take off?"

"No, I don't think so. Is this somebody else's jet? I mean, of course it's someone else's jet, I definitely couldn't afford it. I mean, is there someone else on board in the bedroom or something?" he stumbles, obviously uncomfortable.

"Sounds like you've had some interesting travel."

Eli nods, "Yeah, lately."

"You are the only passenger today. This was recently sold and my co-pilot and I are flying it to its new owner on the East Coast. We were just asked this morning to drop you off on the way, so that's what we're going to do."

"That's good. Where are you going to drop me off?"

She shakes her head, looking at him like she has a crazy person on her flight. "We're going to Rapid City Regional Airport." In spite of the forced enthusiasm in her voice, he cannot muster excitement about the destination.

He knows nothing about Rapid City or South Dakota, but with everything going on, he wants to be moving closer to Portland, not farther away. She's still staring at him like he might need to be ejected from the plane before it takes off, so he says, "Great! Rapid City sounds exciting," with the same forced enthusiasm she had used and, still smiling, goes and sits down. She gives him one last look before pulling the door closed and going to the cockpit.

His mind is racing over the events of the last few days and with the last few weeks. He is a little relieved that Seattle won't be his last stop since it was his first epic fail of the whole trip. It would be nice to end on a high note rather than a failure. He didn't like getting kicked off a job or shuttled off to a different location.

He can't argue that Suki's intentions are good or that her fierce protection of her loyal volunteers is not justified, especially with her community facing the crisis they are at this time. He wonders where he is off to next and hopes that he can do a better job. He will definitely keep Suki and "put your own oxygen mask on first" in mind.

He hates feeling disconnected from his wife and son; he wishes he had a chance to get a new cell phone. He couldn't find the will to ask Suki to use her phone again and hadn't thought to ask the pilot. He is uncomfortable with approaching the cockpit, so he is waiting until someone comes out of it. The stress, boredom, and the large amount of energy he expended in the morning catches up to him and he falls asleep.

He wakes when he feels the change in altitude. They are on the ground at Rapid City Regional Airport shortly thereafter. The cockpit door opens and this time a slightly younger woman comes out; Eli assumes she is the co-pilot. She lowers the steps to the ground and opens the closet, handing Eli his bag and clothes. She gives him a nice smile, "I hope you enjoy your stay here in Rapid City."

"Thanks, I'm sure I will. I appreciate the ride." He walks down the stairs, which close immediately behind him. Ahead of him by the hangars is a Forest Service green truck and a young woman standing beside it looking at him expectantly. He guesses this is his next stop.

He walks over to her. "Hi, I'm Eli Asher. Are you waiting for me by any chance?"

"I am. Nice to meet you, I'm Jo Thunderchild."

"You too."

"You want your stuff in the cab or in the back?"

"Whatever is okay with you is fine; it looks like there's plenty of room up front," he says, motioning towards the quad cab truck.

"Actually, someone's in the backseat, but you can lay your clothes over the back of the bench seat and put your bag at your feet or in the bed; it's up to you."

"Okay," he drops the bag in the bed and carries his hanging clothes around the side.

Once he is in, she starts the truck and slowly guides them through the airport, picking up speed once they are on the highway and a few minutes later Rapid City is getting smaller in the rearview.

After a few minutes of awkward silence, Eli asks, "Where are we going?"

"Custer National Forest."

"Great. What are we doing there?"

"Are you familiar with the Junior Ranger program?"

"A little bit? I think my son has gotten a couple of those badges where they do the activities in the booklet and review it with a Ranger. Is that what you're talking about?"

She nods. "Are you familiar with the Youth Conservation Corps?"

He shakes his head. "No, I don't think I've ever heard of it."

"It's a summer youth employment program that gives them meaningful work and hopefully teaches conservation and stewardship."

"That sounds great. I'm happy to know something like that exists."

"It is great. What we're doing isn't that. It's supposedly a bridge between Junior Rangers and Youth Conservation Corps, kind of an outdoor education priming the kids for the Youth Conservation Corps."

"Okay, what is it really?"

She looks over her shoulder to make sure the passenger in the back seat is still asleep.

"It's my plan to get rich white kids to care about national forests so we still have them in the future. I do as much teaching as I can before they check out and they help a little with things like clearing trails, picking up trash, and other maintenance within the park."

He looks at her to see if she is serious. Feeling his gaze on her, she adds, "No offense."

"Why would I be offended? Because I'm white?" He smiles, thinking of Terrance.

"White and, you know, the jet."

"I wish. That wasn't mine, not by a long shot. I was more of a hitchhiker. I drive a Honda that I'm still making payments on. My family rents a house in Portland that we're getting evicted from at the end of the month."

Her demeanor changes and she is more relaxed.

"That's a neat trick; you'll have to teach me."

"What's that?"

"How do you hitchhike with the jet set? Hitching is not safe to do around here, especially for native women."

"To tell you the truth, I don't know. I was strapped for cash, couldn't get a job, stumbled across an offer for some temp work. I've been all over the country for the last month or so. The work has been great, all stuff I would gladly do as a volunteer in different circumstances. I never know where I'm going until I'm climbing into the cab of a semi or a small personal aircraft or the occasional jet."

She shoots him a dirty look. "I said no offense. You could have just said you were offended. You didn't need to feed me all that bull."

"I wasn't offended; I can understand it being hard to believe. I still have moments and I've been living it."

She studies his face in short glances between him and the road in front of them.

He continues, "If I had a jet, I'd admit it. I mean, I wouldn't try to brag, but I wouldn't exactly hide it. And no offense," he says pointedly, "I wouldn't be here, I'd be flying home to my family in Portland."

Now willing to believe him, she asks him to tell her about his temp work.

He tells her about where he's been, the work he's done, the people he's met and the things he's learned. He leaves out his conversation with Abed and anything to do with a secret society. They talk comfortably and continually for more than two hours. He really admires her sharp wit, thoughtful intelligence and fierce sense of self.

Even though the landscape isn't the most exciting, he is glad for the drive. It forces him to get to know her more than he would have if he were able to retreat like he had done at other times in his travels. Like those times, it would certainly have been his loss.

They passed another billboard that said "Invisible No More" with a Native American woman with a red handprint over her mouth. It was talking about the number of Native American women reported murdered or missing in 2016.

"What is MMIW?" he asks, not fully understanding the meaning.

"Missing and murdered indigenous women," comes the sharp-tongued answer from the back seat.

Apparently, the sleeper in the back is awake and spoiling for a fight.

"There are so many of us missing that they can't keep track. Actually, it's that they don't care enough to keep track. We don't matter enough to keep track of or to investigate our murders and assaults. We were the first people on this land and invading colonizers came in and built a country on top of us and we've been last ever since. We were the last to get citizenship and we've been the last in everything else except poverty."

"Sarah Sparrowhawk," Jo's tone is a warning, which Sarah readily ignores.

"Unless you're lucky enough that whatever crappy land they forced your tribe on for a reservation is close enough to civilization that people might go that far to visit your casino. In that case you might get a little money and, if you're super lucky, you get a lot of money. But if your tribe hits the jackpot, you better watch out because then they start acting like white people and get greedy. Then they start kicking people out of the tribe and increase the amount of tribal blood you have to have for rights. They don't do anything to help out tribes that aren't as lucky and thanks to the few that did hit the casino lotto, most of the country thinks we all live in mansions instead of trailers with rotted out floors and black mold. Native lives matter!" she declares, her pain and frustration impossible to miss.

"Like Black Lives Matter." Eli looks in the back seat; his eyes are drawn to a thick, ropy, angry pink scar that goes across her throat.

He feels Jo take a sharp breath; Sarah pulls her shirt collar up high enough to cover the scar. He looks at Jo, her eyes the size of saucers, shaking her head.

"Of course black lives matter," Sarah spits with contempt, "black men only got the vote fifty years before women did and ninety-two years before First Nations people did. They have so much funding for police they want to defund them, but we haven't been able to get funds for our police, no matter how many times we've been promised. For years we didn't even have the authority to investigate and prosecute non-natives on tribal land. Now that some tribes have the right to help with this quote-unquote hidden epidemic of missing and murdered indigenous women, they can't afford to hire prosecutors and build jails and do all the stuff that the feds want done in order to have that privilege. When we leave it to states or feds to prosecute, they don't because they don't care.

When they want, they just run another pipeline across our land, and bring in a bunch of drunk fools making money hand over fist with nothing to do. That's a big part of why Native women are victims of violence far more than any other population in the country."

The emotion leaves her voice and she sounds like an infomercial announcer.

"More than half of us experience sexual violence and we are ten times more likely to be murdered. All of that? All those numbers, all that violence against us, mostly by non-native white and black men."

He thinks she is done, but she sucks in a big breath and continues.

"The government killed enough of us with their genocides while stealing our land; they have been killing our people since they set foot on our land. We are now the smallest minority and they suppress our votes by not accepting reservation addresses for voter registration, or making it so grandmothers have to make a four-hour round trip to get to the closest ballot box. That's why they don't have to care enough about us to prosecute our murders. They have taken our voice.

How many Native Americans do you see in movies or in TV shows or hell even commercials compared to how many African-Americans? Then do the math on the percentages of the population and you'll see who is really underrepresented. We still haven't had a woman president or Native American president, so when can we start talking about black privilege, you tell me that."

Eli hesitates, expecting her to continue her rampage. When she doesn't, he finally speaks.

"Probably not while the image of that cop kneeling on George Floyd's neck for eight minutes is still fresh in people's minds, I'm sorry." Eli says, wishing he had anything to offer her.

"What are you sorry for?"

"That this is your experience, that you're obviously hurting, and that I don't know how to change any of it." She sits back quiet long enough that Eli starts to think she has gone back to sleep. Suddenly she kicks the back of Jo's seat violently.

"Let me out."

"To get in the bed?"

"No."

"Then I'm not letting you out until we get to Ashland."

"Let me out."

"To get in the bed?"

"Yes."

"If you make me regret this, I won't let you ride with me anymore."

"Okay, let me out." Jo stops, Sarah jumps out and climbs into the back of the truck, banging on the window to signal to Jo that she's ready. Jo pulls back out on the highway.

"Is she okay?"

"No."

"I'm sorry."

"I think she will be."

"Was her attacker black?"

"Some."

The one-word answer paints a much fuller picture for him; he shakes his head wordlessly, trying to get rid of the image.

"What is your take on all that?"

"She isn't wrong, but she doesn't really have a problem with black people. She cried when she saw the video of him dying. She didn't even cry when..." she trails off. "She just hoped it would bring some attention to our struggles as well. It takes time for these things to trickle down to us, if they ever do."

"How do you deal with all that?"

"I just focus on what I can do. We are both from Pine Ridge Reservation. I make more in two months with the forest service than most people on the res make in a year. It's got the highest poverty in the country, high nineties, I think."

"I didn't think the forest service paid that well."

"They don't, but when most people you know are living on three thousand a year, it looks pretty good. There are so many things I hope will change. It seems like people will always fight; if we don't take care of the Earth, it will be too late and won't matter anymore. I just do what I can."

Jo stops in front of a small single-wide trailer. Sarah's head pops up, she jumps out and walks inside without looking back.

"She doesn't really sleep anymore unless she is in a moving vehicle," Jo explains Sarah's presence as she turns the truck around. A few minutes later they pull into the parking lot of a grocery store. "You'll be staying in a cabin at the park. There isn't really anything there other than a few snacks in the info center." She pulls forty dollars out of her front pocket and tries to hand it to him.

"I can't take your money; I can buy my own groceries," he protests.

"It's not mine. I was told to give it to you."

"Keep it for gas."

"I was given that too, and something for my time." He really doesn't want to accept it, but doesn't want to offend her.

"Thanks." He isn't sure what he will have in the cabin, so he buys cereal, almond milk, and sandwich supplies. He notices a barrel for a local food bank at the front of the store. He makes another run around the store. He fills the cart with peanut butter, canned fruits and vegetables, soup, and rice. At the checkout he puts the seventy-some dollars on his credit card and keeps the cash. He deposits all the extra non-perishable items in the barrel on his way out, wishing he could do more.

Jo hops out and opens the back door for him to put his groceries in. Fifteen minutes later, they are driving into Custer National Forest. It seems highly inappropriate to Eli, but he doesn't see what can be gained by him commenting on it. Instead he says, "Can I use your phone? I hate to ask. Mine was pretty much destroyed a while ago and I haven't been able to talk to my wife for a little bit."

They pull up in front of a small cabin similar to cabins that Eli and his family have paid to stay at in parks in his area. "You're going to be here for the next couple nights. It's not fancy but you'll survive."

"It will be great."

"Go ahead and use my phone if you want. I'll just let you keep it tonight."

"That's not necessary," he objects, uncomfortable with having her phone and more uncomfortable with her not having it.

"I live close, don't worry about it. Get it back to me in the morning." She leaves and he calls home. He tells Rachel about getting kicked out of the food bank in Seattle and how bad he feels about it. She comforts him as best she can before handing him off to Mason.

"When are you coming home?" replaces hello.

"Soon."

"That's what you always say and you keep saying it and you're not home." He gives the phone back to Rachel, who needs to go so she can console him. Eli makes a sandwich and paces around while he eats it. Afterwards, he takes a short walk around the cabin. Back inside he lies down and tries to go to sleep. The bed is just as bad as he remembers in the other cabins, about as comfortable as sleeping on a bag of rocks. He doesn't understand how a normal, flat mattress with a plastic cover can actually be a torture device, but somehow it is.

CHAPTER 29

He wakes up miserable, stretching, trying to work out the kinks. After a bowl of cereal, he gathers his toiletries and clothes for the day and makes the trek over to the bathroom. He takes a long, hot shower so he can be a little more presentable and hopefully capable of moving normally. Jo knocks on the door about a half an hour later and hands him something that looks like a cherry Danish. He takes a bite.

"Oh my god, that is so good. What is it?"

She smiles at the compliment. "Frybread." He finishes it off, wishing there were more.

"Ready?"

"Sure," he hands back her phone.

"Thanks." She takes it without breaking her stride. A group of kids matching the description Jo had painted to a T arrives shortly after. By midday, Eli is astonished that she would choose to seek out a group like this and create programs for them.

The kids are less than enthusiastic for the program in general and outrageously disrespectful to her, both to her face and especially behind her back, remarking on her looks and her attractive build. When they break for lunch, Eli pulls her aside and tells her some of the things he's seeing and she looks at him with sympathy.

"I know. There's at least a few in every group, every single time I do this. Sometimes it's most of the group, sometimes only a couple. But it's always there. I'm a woman and I'm Indigenous and in a lot of these households, that means I'm nothing. I wish I knew how to change that, but smarter people than me have been trying for a few hundred years now. They can think whatever they want about me, but if I can get them to care about the national forest and parks, and care about the wildlife and protecting and conserving all of it, I'll be happy."

In the afternoon they do some work to repair a trail that is starting to become overgrown and it's readily apparent that Jo was not exaggerating when she said the boys do a little work. They take a lot of bathroom breaks and a lot of water breaks and run their mouths a lot and do very little. Eli is very relieved when the day is over. Jo gathers the group,

"You all did great work today. I look forward to seeing you all tomorrow."

The only responses are whispered comments followed by laughter. Eli is in absolute awe of her dedication to conservation. Nothing but an amazing level of dedication would have someone tolerate what she had that day, let alone create the program and perpetuate it. The boys drift off towards the parking lot.

Jo hands Eli a small handful of pages, "Here's what we're going to cover tomorrow. If you're comfortable, I'd love for you to cover the material. It would give me a break, which I guess you understand now, I'm always ready for, and maybe they'll hear you differently than they hear me. I don't care how they get the message, just that they get it, so I'm up for trying anything."

"I'll be happy to do it, simply because they don't deserve you."

She smiles, "You're all right. I appreciate your help. Are you all set for the night?"

"Could I use your phone to send a text home?"

"Just keep it," she hands it to him.

"No. I just want to send a quick text if you're willing to let me, but I refuse to keep your phone again." She shrugs whatever.

"Go ahead, do whatever you want. I need to go to the office to take care of a couple things. I'll be back in ten or fifteen minutes on my way out."

"Thank you." He sends a text to Rachel. "I love you both like crazy. I miss you. I know Mason's mad. I will be home in less than a week I'm sure, but hopefully even sooner."

He leaves the door of the cabin open so that he'll know when Jo approaches. It lasts for a couple minutes, then the flies and mosquitoes change his mind. He closes it and is rummaging around for a flyswatter or something he can use as one when she knocks on the door.

He answers the door with the phone in his outstretched hand, "Thank you very much. I will look over those papers this evening and I'll be ready for our lovely group," his voice dripping with sarcasm, "tomorrow morning."

"See you tomorrow," she accepts the phone, sliding it in her pocket without another thought. The next day when they gather again, he holds up the sheets of paper that Jo had given him the night before.

"I've got some interesting things to cover today but before that, I want to talk to you guys, to get to know you a little bit. I want you to get a chance to know me a little bit. I'm especially interested in the things that maybe you guys don't like, things in your world, things that you see or hear, or things about yourself. I know it's hard sometimes to go first, so I'm going to get that out of the way by going first myself. I am married to a wonderful, strong, opinionated woman and we have a beautiful son. I honestly do not care what color someone's skin is, how much education they have, what their beliefs about God are or who they sleep with. I have never intentionally caused harm to anyone, and even spiders are on the catch and release program at my house. For a long time, I thought that was enough. I thought that made me a good man. I thought that no one had the right to find fault with me living my life that way. I tried hard to be kind even to people who made it challenging. I really believed until recently it was enough. I've had the opportunity to travel around this spectacular country of ours and meet some incredible people. Some of whom are up to awesome things, all of whom are amazing in their own way. As the days went by, I liked who I saw in the mirror a little more in some ways and a lot less in others. There are so many deserving causes in this country. This is a wealthy nation, people should not be going to bed hungry, should not be homeless, we should not be destroying the planet that we all live on and I've always known all those things and I did volunteer here and there when I had free time. Until now, I never realized what a privilege it is to be part of making the world a better place on a consistent basis just because it's the right thing to do." He is pleased to see the boys looking at him, listening. "Not doing harm, not being mean, is not enough of a legacy to leave. You guys are the first ones to hear my commitment; to find a way to do more, to give more, to be more." He feels awkward and is ready to put someone else in the hot seat.

"Okay, who's next?" he asks, making direct eye contact with each of the boys. They squirm under his gaze. One boy Travis slowly raises his hand. "Go ahead, you don't have to raise your hand, just don't talk over each other."

"I don't like when my dad's boss comes over for dinner and he says stuff that I know my parents don't agree with and they would freak out on me if I said but they don't say anything. They don't stand up for what they believe even in their own house."

"That's because you're poor," the alpha male of the group says.

"Let's hear from you, Levi."

"I don't know, I don't pay attention to stuff like that."

"I think it's pretty clear it's not what I'm asking. But that might be all the depth you have to give so I guess we'll have to settle for it." If Eli has to let him off the hook, he's taking a big verbal swing at him while doing it. Another kid Rudy starts,

"I don't," he changes course. "Sometimes when my friends are picking on somebody, I don't like it. I don't join in, but I don't stop them. I don't like that about me."

Slowly each of the boys talks. Everyone says something and finally it comes back to Levi, the original alpha boy. His voice so low Eli can barely hear the boy, "I don't like it when my dad hits my mom."

"Thank you, all of you." Eli again looks at each of the boys, "I appreciate your courage today, sharing about yourself or things that you see. It's important to recognize these things and to find ways to stand up in those situations. To say something, to become an ally, to be part of making a difference. It's not always safe for us to do it directly. But if any of you want help finding resources that might help with some of these things, please come and talk to me at lunch or at the end of the day. I'll make sure that we get you what you need. Now for an exciting change of topic, who is ready to learn about invasive species?"

The boys listen a little better and for longer than they had the day before. They also interact with Jo much more respectfully over lunch. Levi catches Eli alone by the garbage. "I want to know what to do."

"You're in a tough situation. I can't tell you what to do. Have you talked to your mom?"

"She wants to get me off to college before she leaves him. I don't want her to wait. I don't care what happens or if we're poor, I don't want her to stay."

"Have you told her that?" He shrugs in answer. Eli pulls out his wallet, and looks through it. He retrieves a card.

"This is for the national domestic violence hotline. If you call them, they might be able to help you talk to your mom more, let her know how you feel and that you don't want him to hurt her anymore."

The boy accepts the card and stuffs it in his pocket. He starts to walk away, "Thanks."

For the first time Eli can see the scared little boy in the awkward teenage body and he is glad that he hadn't torn into them the day before when he had wanted to. For the rest of the day, anytime anyone asks a question or Eli comes to something he isn't certain about, he makes a big point of deferring to Jo and her extensive knowledge and experience.

While they are working on the trail restoration in the afternoon, Eli overhears pieces of a conversation. "My parents are freaking out because my sister has racked up like fifty thou in student loans. They're paying her tuition. She is supposed to have a job and be paying some of her expenses. She isn't working and has been living large running up all that debt. They yelled at me last night like I did it, not her," the boy complains.

Eli didn't hear the response or care what it was. His mind is racing. He has been so stupid in his avoidance of credit and debt. He can't wait for the day to be over. When it finally is, they gather again. "I want to thank you all for today. You did great work. I also want to acknowledge Jo for being such a great resource and for her powerful commitment to conservation as well as education." They give her some applause.

Once the boys leave, Jo comes over to Eli. "That was unbelievable. Thank you so much. I could've talked to them for six months straight and not made the impact that you did today. I never thought to be that open with them and I would never have dreamt that they would open up too. I don't know if it will work the same way for me but after witnessing what you did today, I'm going to try."

Eli is thrilled that she's happy with what he did and is feeling very good about the day as well. He's excited to call home, but wants to check into a few things first. "I'm happy to help. I'm so sorry to even ask and wouldn't if I didn't have to."

She pulls her phone from her pocket. She hands it to him but doesn't let go. "You can use it if you just keep it. I'll get it back from you in the morning."

"Thank you and thanks for yesterday and today. I didn't think I'd enjoy working with them so much, but today was really great and if it wasn't for you, I would never have had the opportunity."

"Then we both got something and so did they, it's a good day for everyone. I'll see you tomorrow."

"Sounds great, have a good night," he says, wanting to hug her, but unsure if it would be welcome. She starts out for her truck.

He goes inside to start looking at tuition rates for online colleges that he could finish his teaching degree through. He looks up the blue book value of Rachel's car and starts a for sale post for Craigslist. It's ready to list except for the photos. He'll get her to add those to the post and then she can publish it. He is so excited to share his new plan with her, his hands shake with excitement as he dials.

"Hi Love." Rachel answers casually.

"Honey, guess what? I figured it all out."

"Figured all what out?"

"Everything! It was crazy, it was the strangest source, but I overheard a couple kids in the program talking about one of their sisters racking up a whole bunch of student loan debt that the parents aren't too happy about because they're paying for her to go to school mainly which obviously is not the point. The point is both of us will make more money when we have our degrees and trying to do it one at a time and not incur debt has been stupid. It's been slowing us down. If I had been willing to go into debt, I would have had my degree years ago and you would already have yours and we would have never had to go through all this. But I found a place where I can enroll and do everything online like you are, everything but my student teaching anyway. By the time I get to student teaching stuff, the world will be more normal and I'll be able to get that part done and get a job." He sucks in a big breath to keep going. "I wasn't sure for a while there if teaching is right for me, but I just had this amazing experience with these kids and I'm sure that I could really make a difference. So instead of trying to get a job I'll enroll in school and we're going to run up a ton of debt in student loans. It will be fine, because eventually we'll both be working at great jobs. We'll pay it off fast and we can sell your car. I got the Craigslist post ready. I wish we could sell mine. but we owe more on it right now than what it's worth, not by a lot. Actually, that's not a bad idea, if we could come up with a little money to pay my car down, we could sell it and share your car and then we wouldn't have a car payment. I think that might be a really good plan."

Unable to listen to anymore Rachel interjects, "At what point were you going to discuss this with me?"

"At this point. I'm telling you I figured it all out."

"I swear to God, for a smart man you can get really stuck on stupid sometimes."

"I don't understand, what's stupid about moving ahead? Both of us getting our degrees and jobs that we want for the long term. Getting rid of one car makes sense when we'll both be in school and mainly online, one car should be plenty. I don't understand what the issue is."

"I can see that and I can tell you that's the problem. I don't know what the future's going to look like for us, but it's going to be different I guarantee you that."

"What do you mean?" he asks horrified. He gets no response. He looks at the phone and sees it's dead. He resists the urge to hurl the phone at the wall. "That's great, perfect timing," he rants while pacing back and forth.

He hadn't even thought to ask for the charger when he borrowed the phone. He hunts through his bag for his phone charger knowing that it doesn't fit, but pulling it out anyway just to make sure. It does not fit. He doesn't have any change, the offices are closed and it's too far to walk into town. He might try it if it wasn't getting dark or if he had a flashlight or if he even knew for sure what direction to go. He knows from riding out here with Jo there's not a lot of traffic on the road and he assumes there are bears and other creatures in the forest that he wouldn't want to bump into by himself at night.

He flops down on the bag of rocks they call a mattress, only to jump up and resume pacing. He had been so excited to share his plan with her, he has no idea what she is mad about. They'd gotten through everything, she found out all the things he wanted to keep from her about the realities of their current situation. She had been wonderful through it all and now that he finally figures out the next step that will put them better off in the future she freaks out on him.

What she said about the future definitely being different kept running through his mind. Of course, the future's going to be different. That's why it's the future and not now, but the way she said it sounded so ominous. He doesn't like being apart from her for so long and feels more physically and emotionally disconnected from her than he ever has since the day they met. He finally lies back down and nods off early but wakes an hour or two later and tosses and turns the rest of the night, not able to shut off his mind or silence his worries about his relationship.

Jo knocks on the door. He opens it and she's holding a charger for the phone. "I noticed this when I got home, and I thought you might need it." He takes it out of her hand like it's a winning lotto ticket.

"Thank God," he plugs in the charger and connects the phone immediately.

"Seems kind of urgent?"

"My wife and I were having a disagreement, we got cut off in the middle because the phone died. I couldn't figure out any other way to reach her."

"Sorry, I thought about bringing it last night and I didn't. I should've driven back over here I guess I just don't get that worked up about having my phone so I didn't think it would be that important."

"Don't be sorry, you've been great letting me use it so much I really do appreciate it but do you mind if I?"

She interrupts, "Take all the time you need. I'll be here around the office until the kids arrive and then I'll be out in the field with them." "Thanks, I won't be long." "Either way," she says, walking off her peace clearly not shaken by his drama.

He calls his wife's number and a man answers. He hangs up dials again this time paying more attention to each number he enters. The same man answers, "Hello."

"Hello, who is this?" he demands.

"Who is this?" the man rejoins, not giving any information.

"This is Eli, why are you answering my wife's phone?" He hears a small snort before the call disconnects. He sits there boiling, unsure what to do. Under any other circumstance, he would be unfazed by a strange man answering his wife's phone but after the absence of the last month and half, all of the challenges they are working through he feels a little fear creeping in. He tries to think of a plausible explanation, they were going to be moving. He still assumes it will be together so there would be no reason for her to have a mover there before he gets back. There are a couple guys that she studies with and works with, but he knows them and none of them would talk to him like that.

His mind goes round and round trying to come up with any explanation why a strange man would be answering his wife's phone. Unable to do so, a very dejected Eli trudges over to the field just as the kids are arriving. Seeing his body language and the look on his face Jo takes the lead for the morning and he is grateful. Even the kids can tell something is off with him and give him a wide berth this morning.

He calls home in the afternoon, gets no answer and leaves no message. If he's too late he doesn't want to look like an idiot because he still believes in them. He doesn't want to be what her and some new guy laugh about lying in bed together at night. Even as he has the thoughts his mind tells him he is being ridiculous, but again when he tries to come up with any other explanation he fails.

He sleepwalks through the rest of the day with the kids, until Jo gathers them at the end of the day. He forces himself to be present for the goodbyes and assures them his distance was due to a personal issue and had nothing to do with them. After they leave Jo comes over, "No news or bad news?"

"No news." She pats his shoulder sympathetically.

"I'm supposed to take you to the airport in Billings tomorrow."

"Montana?" He thinks he recognizes the name.

"Yes."

"How far is that?"

"A couple hours give or take." He gives her a quizzical look. "We're in Montana now. When I was asked to pick you up, I asked if it could be Rapid City so Sarah and I could visit family on the res. It only takes thirty or forty minutes longer. Would you like to get dinner somewhere or something since it's your last night?"

He would love to say no, much preferring to try to reach Rachel or even stew in his own misery. Jo certainly deserves better than his company. Still, he won't risk offending her. "Sure. That will be nice." She motions for him to follow her to the truck.

"Do you like Chinese food?"

"American Chinese food or Chinese, Chinese food?"

"Probably American, half the menu is fried."

He nods, "I like it."

"What's the deal with the other kind?" He tells her about Vegas and the employees contest to have the stinkiest version of stinky tofu.

She wrinkles her nose. "That makes it worth the clarification."

"They made these work pants," he pulls the seam out so she can feel it without touching his leg. "Nice." She pulls into a little Mom and Pop Chinese restaurant. They didn't put much effort into ambiance, Eli hopes it's because they put it into the food instead. They pick a table and place their orders a couple minutes later.

"Do you think the company you are working for is hiring?"

"I'm not sure, give me your phone."

She hands it to him yet again. He calls himself and hands it back to her.

"That's my number, call me in about a week. I'll check with them when I get back and I'll have a new phone." She nods.

"I'm surprised you are looking for work? I thought you love what you do."

"I do and if I was just thinking about myself, that's all I would do. I know that I can only do so much, even if I work my whole life at it. If I can help more people, maybe more people would want the same things I want."

He cocks his head, "Tell me more."

"So many people do jobs they don't like, don't care about or even outright hate. If you ask them what they want to do instead, they have no idea. I think it's pretty simple."

"Don't keep me in suspense."

"If you have a roof over your head, food on the table and aren't too broken from life so far, most people want to contribute to others in some way."

Eli nods, "Very astute."

"Follow your bliss is good advice, but people make it so impossible, like once I have twelve degrees and a million dollars I can do, fill in the blank with whatever it is they want to do."

"What would you do differently?" he asks.

"Keep it simple, it's usually best. Who do you want to help, how do you want to help and what do you need to get there?"

"My god where were you ten years ago?" The waitress sets dinner down in front of them.

"So, do you think that would help?" she asks, unsure for the first time.

"I just figured out most of that in the last month, probably the last two weeks. I think I could have gotten there faster if I had the right questions to start with. Those are good questions. I think most people start with the survival stuff and never get beyond that."

She finishes her bite. "Right! I think if most people were happy and doing something meaningful to them the world would be unrecognizable."

"I've probably met more people doing what they love on this trip than I did in the ten years prior. I don't know how it is for everyone, but they all had a very generous spirit."

"Like speaks to like, when people are miserable, they want everyone else to be miserable. When they are happy, they want to spread that too. Please be honest, where do you think I can make the most impact? Doing what I'm doing and trying to expand the program or finding a way to help other people find their path?"

"Honestly, I don't know. I don't think I'm who you want advice from." She looks a little disappointed, at what seems like a cop-out. He continues, "I have a feeling that you will make a difference no matter what you do. I suspect you are already making much more of one than you realize." Once they finish eating, they squabble about the bill. They finally agree to treat each other.

They chat amicably on the way back to the park. When Eli sees the sign he asks, "Does that bother you?"

"I'd rather have a Custer National Forest here than no national forest at all. It would be nice if the renaming of things makes its way up here eventually. There are a lot of things people find offense with, and for good reason. It's just not what I want to spend my energy on."

"If you could rename it, what would you name it?"

"Keep in mind I'm speaking for myself only. I would name it Chief Joseph National Forest. I'm named after him; my mom is Nez Perce. She moved here after she married my dad, his mom was sick, after she passed, they stayed."

"I love that guy. "From where the sun now stands, I will fight no more forever." He was awesome," Eli remembers the quote from Pacific Northwest history in school. She looks at him, curious. "I'm a student of history and I've always been sympathetic to Native Americans. I didn't have any idea how rough things still are. Until now, I doubt it would have made a difference if I had. I feel ashamed to admit it."

"You meant what you said to the boys yesterday don't you?"

"Yes totally." She pulls up by the cabin and looks at him like he's a curious zoo animal or alien species, "It's been interesting to meet you."

He laughs. "That's pretty open to interpretation. It's been an absolute pleasure meeting you."

"I'll be back at seven to take you to Billings. Do you want my phone?"

"Do you know where I'm going after Billings?"

"I was told to take you there so you could catch a flight to Portland."

He smiles, home finally, now that it might be too late. "Keep it. I'll deal with it tomorrow." He climbs out, they wave to each other before he goes inside and she drives away.

CHAPTER 30

The next morning Eli can't stop yawning and is struggling to keep his eyes open.

"I have that effect on my passengers. Go ahead," Jo nods to the backseat.

"Maybe we can get coffee? I don't want to sleep through my last couple of hours with you."

"This is a see you later not goodbye, right?"

"Absolutely."

"Then go to sleep. Your yawning is making me tired. This is going to be a big day for you and you look like crap." She nods to the backseat again.

"Ever thought of moving to Portland?"

"Never. Parts of Montana are too crowded for me now."

"Fine, be that way," he teases. "Are you going to pull over?"

"Just climb over. Try not to kick me in the head while I'm driving."

His departure into the back seat is anything but graceful; he does manage to get there without kicking her. He sees why Sarah likes to sleep in Jo's backseat, and he drops off in a couple of minutes. Jo wakes him up as she pulls into the airport. He wakes up slowly, rubbing the sleep from his eyes.

He is excited to see the jet on the side of the runway. It looks familiar, and he hopes he will finally see Zeke again. The doors open an instant later, Zeke emerges, looking around, he sees him and waves at him to get on the plane. "Do you want to come meet my friend?"

"Another time? I have to get back."

"Okay." He would like to hug her, but she doesn't seem to be a hugger. He pats her on the shoulder. "Thanks for everything. I'll talk to you soon."

He gathers his stuff and climbs out. Jo pulls away while he is still walking to Zeke.

As he gets closer, "Come on, I've got things to do."

With a big smile, Eli jogs the remaining distance and follows Zeke up the stairs. He looks to the right and sees the co-pilot napping and assumes that he will be up front.

Zeke calls, "Come sit down." Eli does, and a couple minutes later they are in the air.

"You're looking a little different since I saw you last."

"Yeah," he agrees, rubbing his arms. "I got some good exercise and a tan."

"You on top of the world yet?"

"Ah, Zeke, I messed up so bad I can't believe it."

"What's going on?"

"Well, every bad decision I made and tried to hide from my wife before I left came out while I was gone. She forgave me over and over again, as unbelievable as it is. Then, after I thought we were out of the woods and after she thought I'd heard her, I came up with this stupid plan. I was going to save my family by going back to school while Rachel was still in school and running up a bunch of student loan debt and selling her car and had everything planned out without talking to her. Which was the one thing that she had been telling me that she wanted and needed, that we talk about things and make decisions together.

I broke my phone in Vegas, and it's been hard for us to communicate since then and we hadn't been able to talk much for days, and when I finally got through to someone on her phone, a guy answered. I think, well I don't know what to think. Part of me is afraid it's over, part of me thinks I'm being stupid. She's not really that kind of person but I don't know the guy that answered, and he apparently had no idea who I was, and I've been gone a while, and I've been messing up pretty bad. Part of me doesn't even want to go home."

Eli can't believe he is pouring his heart out to Zeke and finds it even more implausible that the man is listening to him.

"You're smarter than that," Zeke replies.

"Your compassion is overwhelming."

Zeke seems to like that. "Take it from me, running away isn't the answer. You need to go home and face your wife and tell her whatever you got to say and listen to whatever she's got to say and then figure out what the future looks like because you're going to be involved with each other one way or another the rest of your life."

"You're right. I do have to face her. It's like that thing with the cat in the box and it's alive or dead until you open the box and then you see, then it's one or the other so if you open the box and look and it's alive it's great, but if you open it and it's dead," he shakes his head, "I don't want my marriage to be over."

"Schrödinger."

"What?" Eli is completely at sea.

"Erwin Schrödinger, the one with the paradox about the cat in the box."

Eli realizes he might be bringing up painful things for Zeke. Maybe he is trying to change the subject, or maybe he is simply rubbing it in more about how much Eli had underestimated him. He changes the subject too.

"Whatever happens with my family, I'd love for you to join me for Christmas."

"Well, I don't know where I'll be and I like to get together with the boys from the VA. Lots of them don't have family or don't have family that welcomes them."

"Well, there's this neat thing about being a pilot with a jet. I bet you could be just about anywhere you want to and not take too long to get there. Don't feel like you have to, but please do know that you're welcome."

"I appreciate that."

"So what about that father of yours?"

"What do you mean?"

"Is he still responsible for everything wrong in your universe?"

He considers for a moment. "I have a different perspective on that now. It was hard with him gone but it might've been harder if he stayed. I'll tell you another thing, very few, if any people are all one thing. We're all a mix of good and bad and everything in between. The exact amounts might differ but nobody's perfect."

"It almost sounds like you have forgiven him." Zeke says it like a statement, but Eli can hear the question in his voice.

"Yes. If he ever shows up, I would hear anything he has to say and take it from there."

"I guess you had a pretty eventful trip."

"I did. Terrance was so great. I think we will be friends for life. I'll always be grateful to you for taking me to him."

Zeke grins. "I had a funny feeling you two might hit it off. How about Abed? That boy is going to help save the planet."

"Really?"

"He's got some contraption that can be deployed in a hurricane or tornado that sends some types of seeds or something way up in the atmosphere to fix the ozone, and he's got some other process that gives companies another way to offset their carbon footprint, like some sort of big vacuum. That's why he hired on with Phil, so he can learn how to sell high ticket items to corporate types, do some networking and learn how to hire and train a sales force of his own. Those two get on like a house on fire."

"I'm glad to hear that." It's crazy to Eli to think he ever begrudged Abed the job.

Once they land in Portland, Eli gives Zeke a brief hug, torn between wanting to continue the conversation and his anxiousness to get home. The pull of home wins, "Promise not to be a stranger."

"I promise, as long as you don't get too sappy." He claps him on the shoulder.

"Do you want me to wake up your co-pilot?"

"What for?"

He leaves the cockpit laughing, grabs his gear and goes down the stairs Zeke lowers. In a couple minutes, he's in his car and crosses his fingers that it will start after sitting for so long. It turns over on the first try and he drives home. He gulps at the thought that home will be someplace different no matter what in a couple weeks, and he desperately hopes home will be the same place for all three of them.

He pulls up in front of the house and a car pulls to the curb right behind him. At first, he is afraid he's getting pulled over but then he recognizes the sports car. A moment later Abed gets out with a manila envelope and a small box in his hand.

"Welcome home," Abed says with a smile, holding out his hand.

"Thanks," Eli says. "I'm kind of a hugger now if you don't mind?" Abed gives him a hug with a hearty pat on the back.

"You look great. I trust your travels were agreeable for you."

"It was phenomenal. I don't know how you feel after the rite of passage, whatever that is, but so far, you're right, I'm so glad I took the leap."

"The thing is," Abed says, tucking the manila folder under his armpit, freeing both his hands to open the ring box which he presents with a flourish, "you just completed your rite of passage. Congratulations."

Speechless, Eli takes the phoenix ring out of the box and holds it up so the sunlight, which gives it the fire appearance. He slides it on his finger and is pleasantly surprised to find it's a perfect fit. He is thrilled to know that he is accepted into this group and honored by the company in it. He really wants to talk to Abed, but being home and not going inside is killing him. Abed catches his look and understands.

"So here are some doors that you might find open for you quite easily, if you're interested."

Eli takes them without opening the envelope. "Thank you, if I still have a wife, I will discuss it with her and get back to you. If that's okay?"

"Of course, if you don't object, I'll stop by in a couple days."

"Great, I look forward to it."

Just then the front door opens and Mason runs out yelling, "Dad, Dad."

Abed steps back towards his car ready to leave, Eli catches him by the arm and pulls him over to the gate where Mason's waiting. He picks the boy up into a big bear hug and when he releases him, he says, "Mason, this is my friend Abed. Abed, this is my son." Mason shakes hands with him. "Hi, Abed."

"Hello Mason."

"I'll see you in a couple of days, Eli."

"Okay."

This time when Abed attempts to leave, Eli doesn't stop him. He swoops his son up onto his shoulder in a fireman's carry, making the trip extra bouncy to increase his reward of giggles from the boy.

When they reach the door, Rachel opens it.

"Mason, why don't you go play," they say in unison.

He snorts a laugh at them and runs off.

"I don't know who that guy was that answered the phone. I don't care, it doesn't matter. The only thing that matters to me is you and Mason. I know we can get through all of this if you'll give me a chance. I know I might not deserve it; I've been an idiot and I wouldn't—"

"Shut up!" Rachel interrupts.

Crestfallen, Eli complies.

"You had me at 'I've been an idiot.'" She kisses him tentatively at first, quickly building steam. She breaks the embrace and steps back to compose herself.

"That's a little much for the front porch," she says.

"Yes, but we're moving anyway," he steps towards her again.

She puts a hand on his chest. "Hold on. This is going to happen, trust and believe me. I missed you and this bunches. Let's go inside. We can catch up, I can call Jen, we can have some time with Mason and dinner and hopefully he can go stay with her tonight."

"You should always be in charge," he acquiesces.

"I know, but you are way too much of a handful. Don't let that go to your head, I'm talking about what a pain in my butt you can be."

"It's a free country, you say what you want and I hear what I want." He catches her wrist, spins her to him and dips her for another deep kiss. She swats his shoulder, "That's the problem, bucko."

His response is another kiss.

Once he releases her she says, "So you don't care who that guy was?" She steps out of his reach with a teasing grin.

"Okay, maybe I care a little."

She steps closer, the kiss he is hoping for turns out to be a much harder swat on the shoulder.

"You really are an idiot. It would take a minimum of a week and a half, maybe even two weeks to get over you and be ready to move on. He was here to buy some of my nursing books. I thought it was a good idea to sell some of my old ones in case we need the money and if we don't, it can go towards buying new ones next quarter."

He moves towards her again. She puts a hand on his chest, holding him at arm's length she gets up on her tippy toes and leans in to give him the softest of kisses on his lips. She reaches her free arm behind her and picks up her phone. She is ready to hit the green dial button before she removes her hand from his chest.

"Go get your stuff out of the yard."

He had completely forgotten about everything else once he laid eyes on her. He hurries outside to find the manila envelope Abed dropped off and get the bag and clothes he'd lugged across the country.

He hears, "Hi Jen," as he pulls the door shut behind him. He crosses his fingers, hoping Jen will say yes. He missed his son like crazy, but he really wants some alone time with Rachel. He picks up the envelope and flings the bag over his shoulder. Mason comes out as he is reaching for the clothes.

"Let me help Dad." The boy gives him a quick squeeze around his midsection before picking up the hangers. He leads the way inside, proud to be helping. Eli doesn't say anything about his shirt tails dragging on the ground. They need a date with the dry cleaners anyway.

"Can I get some toys and play out here with you guys?" His hopeful expression was too much for either to resist.

"Go ahead, can you put those in the laundry room first?" Rachel asks.

"Okay."

"If they ever need a new Flash Gordon, they should give him a shot," Eli remarks.

"I know, he is picking up speed for sure. Not quite the daredevil he was before the accident, not quite as anxious as he was after."

"That's good."

She nods in agreement. "What's that?"

"Oh this?" he asks casually, even though as soon as he was reminded of the envelope, he's been dying to open it.

Rachel gives him a look, not the look, but one of its lesser cousins. He stops playing and hands her the envelope.

"Abed said these are some doors that should open easily. I told him if I still had a wife, I would talk it over with her. He is going to check back in a couple of days."

Rachel has her thumb just under the flap poised and ready to open it. She looks at Eli who nods. She rips it open and dumps the contents on the table. He joins her, eyeing the check first.

He picks it up, just as she sees it. It's for seventeen thousand dollars.

"That's more, right?"

"Way more."

"What happened?"

"I don't know." He quickly scans the half page folded behind the check.

"Oh my god. They took out taxes, this is the after-tax amount!"

"That's wonderful. It's still more than you expected if you were gone for six weeks and you were gone five and a half."

Instead of responding he hands her the check stub that shows the original amount and the taxes withheld. There is a handwritten note explaining that the extra was a hazard pay bonus that Terrance insisted he receive.

"Why would you need hazard pay for working with Terrance? What else haven't you told me?" Her tone is amused and annoyed, so he decides it's safe to put her off a little longer.

"I'll tell you tonight. Let's look at these doors before Mason comes back with his toys."

"He must be bringing every single one he has left in his room." Rachel nods towards the papers.

They each pick one up and study it for a moment, before passing it on or setting it down. They both look at all three offers, one draws a whistle from Eli and a gasp from Rachel.

Mason arrives with a heaping box, toys falling out leaving a trail behind him. He dumps the entire box in the middle of the floor with a deafening crash.

"Oh boy, you are really ready to play with your dad."

Mason gives a nod so big the entire top half of his body moves up and down.

"Can you do one more thing first?"

He gives an exaggerated sigh, his whole body slumping. "What?"

"We are going to play for a while and then we are going to have pizza for dinner and frozen yogurt for dessert to celebrate your dad being home. Then you are going to go and stay the night with Jen and the dogs while your dad and I catch up and maybe do some packing. Can you go pack a bag to take to Jen's?"

His departure is his answer.

"Packing?" He cocks an eyebrow at her.

"Isn't that what you had in mind?"

He shakes his head no slowly, giving her a sexy smile while undressing her with his eyes.

"What did you have in mind?"

"Come here and I'll show you."

"Tonight," she says and points at the potential jobs on the table.

"What do you think?"

He picks up the one with the biggest number. "Once you finish school and get a job, I think we would be one percenters if I had this job. I mean, I don't know for sure, but this is a lot of money."

"Yes," she agrees, not wanting to influence him yet.

He picks up the next one. "This one doesn't pay as much but would be a big step up into a management position that could pay much more than this in a few years."

She nods.

"This one," he says, picking up the last one, "this one doesn't pay as well, but it has some really great benefits."

"Tell me more about that one."

He isn't sure exactly what she is asking. "The ropes course? It is basically teaching, but outside in the woods. Experiential education..." he trails off, unsure if he answered her.

"And it's in Washington, only about two hours from here and closer to your mom."

"Yes," he agrees.

She is trying to control her impatience, "What do you think?"

He hesitates. "I'll go for whichever one you want me to."

She shakes her head, "Like I'll ever make it that easy for you. Tell me which one you want to try for first."

"I like the assistant director of the ropes course. I know it pays a quarter of this one," He picks up the highest paying offer, looking at each number again. "Still, it comes with a house and I could finish my degree for next to nothing with this exchange they have with the college that teaches some of its outdoor ed curriculum on their course. I just don't know how it would work for you with school, or if you would be okay passing on that much money," he sets the paper down in front of her.

"I can get a job pretty much any time, anywhere, that's the nice thing about being a nurse."

"What about as a nurse practitioner? I don't want you to drop out or not be able to get a job after you worked so hard."

"With Covid school is predominantly online. When I have practicums or anything I can't do from there, I can stay with Jen. I'm sure she'll be okay with that."

"You'd really be okay with me taking this job?"

"It's the one I was hoping you would pick."

"Really?" he says in utter disbelief.

"I didn't marry you for your money, you didn't have any remember?"

"I know, it was for my body heat."

"No, it was for your hot bod, spider relocation and barf removal."

"That's more like it." He stands a little taller and assumes a bodybuilder pose to show off his bicep flex.

"Save that for tonight."

"Okay," he agrees. "You're really okay with me taking this one?"

"I'm okay with you applying for it. I'd be thrilled if you got it."

"I'll get it. Don't worry about that."

"You think this means that much?" she asks, touching the phoenix ring.

"I think it means quite a bit and I would feel good about this job anyway. I've got some great ideas and I know I have a lot to offer."

The true gifts of his recent experiences become evident to Rachel. She has a feeling that he will get the job, will be more than capable of getting himself up for the interview and won't need any esteem boosting to get him out the door.

Mason comes back and drops his backpack by the front door.

"Come on, Dad." He uses his foot to clear a spot to sit amid the cars, action figures and Legos he scattered everywhere.

"Go ahead, but sign this first. I'm going to deposit it."

He signs the check and hands it back as she logs into the bank app on her phone.

He joins Mason on the floor. They start on a Lego creation, but he quickly abandons it to turn the couch into a fort. "You can do Legos every day, couch forts are special," Mason decrees.

Rachel joins in, bringing most of the pillows in the house with her as well as a couple of flat sheets. By the time they are done, the living room is transformed into a three-walled tent with stacked chairs holding the front up and the slanted back end of the roof resting on the couch. The floor is sectioned off with couch cushions creating separate toy zones and kingdoms.

Finally, stomachs start to growl.

"What do you say we go get some pizza?" Rachel asks.

"I'm in," says Eli.

"Yeah," agrees Mason. "We don't have to take the fort down, do we?"

"I think we can leave it up until we have a chance to play in it again tomorrow. What do you think?"

"For sure," Eli agrees.

After pizza and yogurt, they drop Mason off with Jen who gives them a knowing smile and says, "There is no rush to pick him up, the afternoon will be fine." Eli can't get home fast enough.

CHAPTER 31

They burst through the door and Rachel leans against it once she closes it. They start making out like teenagers. Unable to wait any longer, Eli picks her up; she in turn grabs up a pillow on the way by.

A few short minutes later, they lay side by side catching their breath.

"That was pretty fast," Eli pants. "For you too, right?"

"Oh yeah," Rachel agrees.

"Still pretty good for a couple of minutes?"

"A couple of minutes and a few weeks," she corrects.

"Ah, that must be it. Let's not make a habit of that."

"I agree."

He rolls to his side facing her and starts kissing her lightly.

"Hold on. The first one was a freebie; the rest are going to cost you."

"The rest?" he asks, excited and somewhat concerned about what her expectations for the evening might be.

"Yes, the rest. We have all night and up until lunch tomorrow, so you better stay hydrated."

He knows from past experience she isn't kidding when she says that. He drags himself out of bed.

"Bring me some water too, please," she asks while openly ogling him.

"Hey, I'm not a piece of meat," he protests, enjoying every second of it. He gives her another bodybuilder pose and flex as he leaves the room.

"That's too bad; you look pretty tasty," she calls out after him.

He stops. "At least Terrance treated me with respect." He poorly pretends outrage.

"Yes, about that!" she yells. "I want to hear about the hazard pay."

He returns with a towel around his waist, a full glass of water, and a second turned upside down over the gallon of water he has in his hand.

"We should have closed the curtains," the tone of his voice matching the blush in his cheeks.

"No," she says, shaking her head.

"Oh yeah," he nods.

"Well, we're moving soon."

"Thank God," he agrees. "Don't be surprised if I don't leave the house during daylight before then," he gripes, slipping into bed next to her.

She sits up to take a drink from the glass he handed her. "Spill it, why did you need hazard pay?"

"Oh," he grumbles, "you're going to be mad. Do you really want to do this now?"

She pulls the sheet up over her; the only skin exposed now is her arms and shoulders.

"Okay, okay." He surrenders.

"I really don't need hazard pay, and I do want to make sure Terrance isn't the one who provided it before we spend any of it, because it wasn't his fault at all."

She hits him with the pillow.

"I got bit by a rattlesnake."

She drops the sheet and sits up, searching for where. He holds up his hand and shows her.

"That's it? I thought it would be twice its normal size, black and bruised."

"It's been almost a month, and I got really lucky because of how Terrance responded and it was a shallow bite."

He takes a big swig of water straight from the gallon and lies down to tell her the whole story. He shares Terrance's theory that the snake tried to bite the glass bottle first and that's why Eli got so lucky.

"That's a good theory," she straddles him. "Now explain to me the shoulder part of a snake bite on your hand."

He tells her the story about his mishaps on the way out of the emergency room. She collapses on him laughing so hard. It feels so good to be laughing together again, to feel her warmth against him, to feel the trembles of laughter moving through her body. She bolts up and races off to the bathroom.

"Don't go," he protests.

"I can go or I can pee on you."

"Don't be too long," he changes his position on the matter. This makes her laugh harder.

"So help me, if you make me wet my..." She interrupts herself with a sigh of relief having reached the toilet.

She comes back and gives him a look that takes his breath away. Being loved and wanted by someone like her is the best feeling.

"Tell me what you wanted me to know about the check," she says. "If you don't get yourself into horrible trouble on that one, I'll be ready for the next round."

"It's so romantic when you make it sound like a prize fight."

"What can I say?" she asks, rolling her shoulders. "I want a TKO."

"Don't you mean a KO?"

"No, a TKO: long, drawn out over multiple rounds, down, not out until the decision comes in, TKO. Now stop changing the subject and spill it."

"Sheesh, you say something like that and expect me to think. There is no blood flow," He points to his head. The look she shoots him helps restore it.

"First, the bonus part: I don't want to keep it if Terrance paid it. Second, I don't know if the ten percent has been taken out or not, so I'll have to find out. Either way, there are some things I want to do with it."

"Keep talking." The tension of waiting for him to get to the bad part getting to her.

"I want to donate ten percent if the ten percent I've already committed to hasn't been taken out and twenty percent if it has. I know that probably sounds like a lot, and I know I've made some bad decisions about money before. There is still enough to pay almost everything we owe and put some back in savings. I know it doesn't make sense, but if we wait until we're debt-free and have a pile of savings and never have to give money a second thought, we won't be helping anyone any time soon. No matter how rough it's ever been for us, we have been much better off than so many; I just don't want to keep ignoring that." He winds his sales pitch down and gives her his best, trust-and-buy-from-me smile.

"Okay," she instantly agrees.

"Really?"

"Of course. I always wanted to do more than you were up for. I knew you didn't have much growing up, so I understood and didn't push you, but I've always given more than you knew about. Not that much, but I'm all for it."

"Have I mentioned how much I love you?"

"Not nearly enough. But hold that thought for a second. What do we owe that we can't pay out of that?"

"The rest of the collections for Mason's medical bills and my car."

Her face is split in two with the biggest smile he has ever seen on her.

"We can pay the rest of Mason's collections, everything we owe except your car, and if we get to keep the bonus, put some in savings."

"They say women aren't good at math; I guess they are right." He covers his face to protect from the barrage he knows is coming. Instead, she plucks a hair from his happy trail on his lower abdomen.

"The face would have been better," he grumbles.

"You had it coming and you know it, so no sympathy. You know I'm good at math, so stretch your man brain and try to figure out how what I'm telling you could be true."

He thinks for a minute and can't come up with a realistic explanation.

"A giant meteor landed in their office and took out all the computers, so they have no idea what we owe."

"Close," she says. "I called and got a hold of the manager, who I threatened to sue within an inch of his life. Then I told him I'd call every news station in town and tell them that we are getting evicted because one of their agents used vile, if not illegal, practices to force you to give them rent money to protect our grade school-aged son's credit, and then I got mad and really let him have it."

"I almost feel a little bad for him. Almost."

"I did too, but they brought it on themselves. I know some of the protections that were given at the beginning of the pandemic are wearing off, but there are plenty of people still struggling, and there is no excuse to be pulling that heavy handed garbage. It's unacceptable!"

He sees the fire blazing in her eyes and holds up his hands. "I agree, I'm on your side one hundred percent."

"Good thing too; they settled for ten percent of the remaining balance. We can pay it off or make monthly payments of a hundred dollars. We owe about seven-fifty."

"Pay it off!" Eli is emphatic. "You really dropped the ball letting me handle this stuff when you are so much better at it than I am. I really don't know what you were thinking," he teases to hide his awe of her.

"Oh, that's it," she mimics hitting a bell with a little hammer. "Ding, ding." She signals the start of the next round, straddling him and holding his hands over his head while she kisses him.

"Wait, one more thing."

"Hurry," she urges.

"I want to buy some collectibles to add to the box my mom gave me from my dad so Mason will have it for a rainy day."

"Done. You can tell me the rest of the story after."

During the next rest period, he says, "I want to start eating different foods too."

He can see she is ready to argue.

"Healthy, mostly, but different. I was with different people who were all Americans, so it seems like everything they eat should be considered American food; most of it is called ethnic food and relegated to its own aisle or even its own market. I liked almost everything I tried, and I wouldn't have tried any of it without this trip."

She puts a hand on his forehead to check his temp.

"Ha ha," he says, understanding she is implying he must be unwell.

"I had to check, what with Mr. Meat and Potatoes talking about eating ethnic food."

"You don't know what I eat anymore."

"Really?" she dares.

"I loved the vegan casserole that Harper made."

"Now I know you're lying."

In one quick move, he flips her off and pins her under him, making eye contact. "Never again. I learned my lesson."

She stretches up to kiss him, beginning the next round.

The night continues like that, cuddling, talking, and teasing in between rounds. Reconnecting at every level. By mid-morning, Eli has told her almost everything, expanding on Pearl's ideas about what it takes to be the hero of your own story and adding that it depends on who is telling the story. Using the example of Terrance being a hero in Eli's eyes, but a villain in the eyes of some of the members of the congregation of his former church, and added Randy Yang as hero to his employees, but villain to the Japanese man that wanted the pallets, because the Japanese were China's enemy in the war. Rachel is crying softly against his shoulder by the time he finishes telling her about Sarah Sparrowhawk.

"It's so complex and so simple. Simple in the way all the jobs I did were, simple but not easy. Nobody is all victim or villain or hero, and it depends on what lens you are looking through, who is looking. No more lumping people together by groups or living in the past. It's about what we do today, as people, as a nation and a world really."

He tapers off. When she doesn't say anything, he continues, "Am I making any sense? I feel like I'm rambling. It's been a long and wonderful night."

"Yes. I think so. Unless you think you have the answer. I missed that part."

"No, I don't think I have the answer. I think people are the answer. Remember that movie *The Best of Enemies*? When you get people together and get them talking, things change. When you tell people they are wrong and try to make them change, nothing really does. When you only hang out with people that look like you and say you're not racist, you probably are, no matter what color you may be. When you wait for the government to fix it, nothing gets fixed. I don't know what the final outcome will be for me; I do know that I am changed and changing because of the people I met and the conversations I had. When I'm doing my best Tarzan swinging from the trees on the ropes course, I'm going to share with them, the kids especially, the things I learned."

"Two questions."

"Shoot."

"First, are you thinking about going into politics?"

"No!"

"Glad to hear it, but it's too bad. I think you'd be better at it than much of our current leadership."

"That's a low bar. Next question."

"Was Alejandro as hot as he sounded?"

With a deep sigh, he admits it, "Sure, if you're into that whole handsome, smoldering good looks kind of thing. I mean, he is awfully pretty."

She laughs at him. "I just like to watch you squirm. I told you when we started dating, I like white guys. You make me look so good on the dance floor."

"Those are just the kind of racist, insensitive remarks that will not be tolerated in the new world order, missy; you better get yourself up to speed." He tickles her. "White people have feelings too."

Her expression changes, and he holds up his hands in a T, making the time out gesture before she can ring the bell again.

"No, you don't. If you want to keep using me like a piece of meat, you have to feed me first."

"Because I'm a woman?" She asks in mock dismay.

"No, because you have worn me out thoroughly. I think I may have lost the use of my legs."

"Reasonable," she agrees. She pushes off against his chest and gets up. He starts to say something before she walks down the hall but stops himself.

She returns a moment later and pulls on his t-shirt.

"Curtains?" he asks, smirking.

"Curtains," she agrees. "Not smart to do to someone who is about to prepare a meal for you."

"I just want to share life with you. All of life, my love."

"I love you; it's axiomatic."

He grabs his phone and looks up the word. Self-evident and obvious are all he needs to see. "That's my new favorite word, and the same is true for you."

CHAPTER 32

A couple mornings later, Abed knocks on the door. Rachel answers and gives him a hug before he can introduce himself.

"Come in. Eli, Mason, Abed is here," she shouts over her shoulder. "Would you like some coffee?"

"Sure," he says, not understanding the reception. Eli enters and walks over to give him a hug too. They've barely finished when Mason gives him one of his side squeezes.

"Mom, I'm going to take down the fort so Abed has somewhere to sit."

"That's a good plan," she agrees. "Until then, why don't you two sit on the porch so you can have some quiet and privacy. I'll bring the coffee out in a minute."

A wide-eyed Abed follows Eli back outside. They sit in the Adirondack chairs on the porch. "I'm sorry I was so side-tracked the other day. I appreciate you coming back by."

"It was no problem. I knew you were just getting home; I only wished to give you the envelope. I see you have a new phone." He nods toward the phone in Eli's hand.

"Yes, it was like Christmas. I had some texts from Terrance about his dates with Pearl. A video of my trapeze performance, a picture of a little dog I love cuddled in bed with Nora, and texts from Alejandro reminding me that his job offer is still on the table."

Abed smiles. "Very good. I also understand you already have an interview scheduled for tomorrow."

"Yes, I'm very excited."

"It doesn't pay as much as the others."

"Nope, it sure doesn't, but I'm excited about it. I'll be excited about going to work. A good friend told me that was important before I even knew he was a friend."

Abed is pleased. "I am glad to hear that. I just wanted to see if you have any questions and tell you a little more about sharing with non-members."

"What is it called? That would be a good place to start."

"Ah, Fraternal Order of the Phoenix Fire. A bit of a mouthful, we usually just call it Phoenix Fire or PF around others."

"The rings make perfect sense then," he holds his hand up, the ring catching the sunlight giving it the glowing fire appearance. Rachel comes out and sets the coffees down.

"The fort is now a couch if you want to come in. If not, don't be a stranger, Abed. I know you're up to big exciting stuff, but come visit once in a while."

"Thank you," he watches her retreat, baffled.

"I told her about the people I met through PF," Eli says, trying it out for the first time. "She said my family grew. For her, it's as simple as that. You are all family and will be treated like that around here."

"I like her," he declares.

"Do you want to go inside?"

"Yes, in a few minutes. If you come across someone who inquires about the order, you must act as I did when we first met. Try to dissuade them. If they persist, give them the commitments. If they continue, contact anyone on this list," he hands a laminated card over. Eli takes it, squinting to see the names. "Here, you need this to read it." Abed hands him an opaque piece of plastic with a purple tinge about the size of a credit card.

"Spy stuff, huh?"

"When you read the list, you will understand why some of our members are so particular about privacy." Unable to resist, Eli puts the plastic key over the laminated card. It takes him a minute to line everything up just so; once he does, his jaw drops open.

"Melinda, is that the same one that's married to Bi--" he sputters, "the same one from around here?" he asks in disbelief.

"Keep reading," Abed encourages.

"Holy cow!" He lets it sink in for a moment. "There is a lot of money, power, talent, and fame on that list."

"Indeed," Abed agrees. "Mind you, that is not the full list, just who you should contact if the need arises."

"It already has. Jo Thunderchild. I don't know if she wants to join, but someone should talk to her. She is impressive and committed to making the world better." Abed notes the name in his phone.

"I will address this. Normally, if someone wants to join, they have to ask at least three times. You need to ask a question or two in order to assess their character, and you cannot talk them into it. They have to decide to take the leap of faith. Then, and only then, do you contact someone on the list on their behalf."

"You didn't ask me questions to assess my character," he objects, not feeling comfortable with that part.

"Ah, but I did," Abed reminds him. "I asked you about hoarding toilet paper and why you wanted the job I got."

"That told you my character?"

"When you approached me, your distress was apparent, yet you didn't insult me or use racial slurs. You were angry, but didn't direct it at me. You were courteous at all times. When I questioned you, you didn't ask how dare I. You were thoughtful and gave honest answers with good humor. When you left, I regretted there weren't two positions available as it seemed we could easily be friends."

"I know, right? I thought the same thing. Still, not using racial slurs seems like a pretty low standard."

"Look at the world right now."

Changing the subject, "I have to ask, what keeps someone from selling this list to some journalist or something?"

"You yourself can see how being a member could open doors?"

"Yes."

"Can you not see how betrayal could close doors?" Eli shudders at the thought.

"Good point. Is there any other time I should contact someone on the list?"

"If you need resources, if you have an idea that would serve the betterment of humankind, or encounter someone who does. If you find people of high integrity doing good works, even if they aren't interested in being a member, the group is often able to be of help. For now, if in doubt, you can call me if you would like."

"Thank you. I would much rather call you. I feel underwhelming compared to these people, you too for that matter, but I am more comfortable talking to you."

"Those people on that list are well aware of you, Eli Asher, and all consider you a worthy addition. I wonder, how much longer will you hold yourself back from the true vision of yourself?" Eli stares at him, slack-jawed again. "If it is my honesty you doubt, please turn that over. I'm sure that everyone else on the list would give a similar verdict."

Eli turns it over and sees the name and number of everyone that he met, separated by members and non-members. "This is great." He studies the list.

"There is at least one woman on here that would disagree."

"Ms. Suki?" Abed asks.

"Yes, how did you know?"

"Everyone fails at some point. The greats fail many times. It is not that you fail, but how you respond that defines you, and so everyone must fail at some point on their rite of passage. You did very well with a broad range of tasks and environments. Ms. Suki would have whipped you into shape had you not needed to fail, as she was the last chance. She sends her regards."

Eli lets that sink in for a moment. "Last two questions."

"Please proceed."

"How do they decide what doors to open?"

"They don't; the initiate does. There are ten basic ways that you can serve others: transport them, house them, protect them, feed them, entertain them, employ them, be a voice for them, inspire them, educate them." Eli thinks he's lined each up with one of his experiences and counts them out on his fingers just to be sure.

"That's only nine."

"Technically, there are eleven. The first being to love and nurture them. We hope that occurs long before people are seeking their vocation. If it doesn't, it moves to number ten, which is heal them. After your experience in the hospital, things were adjusted somewhat."

"There are other ways to heal people," Eli objects.

"Indeed. Before a different opportunity in that area was arranged, your unique talents were becoming apparent."

"I should have said a hundred more questions, but we better get inside soon. I just need to know if the ten percent was already taken out of my check and if the bonus was paid by Terrance."

"You needn't worry about the ten percent this time. It will start with your new job, and no, your friend did not pay the bonus. When his money was refused, he insisted it be paid by the order."

Eli smiles about Terrance and the family call they had enjoyed with him and Pearl the night before. "Come on," Eli stands and motions to Abed to follow him, one more question burning on his mind.

Abed rises and correctly guesses what's on his mind. "Your choice has pleased everyone. If later you should want to open your own facility or branch out in some other way, you should find it easy to do so."

Unable to resist, "If I had chosen something else?"

"Other doors would have been available to you." They enter the house together, and most of the day slips away before Abed leaves.

Late the next afternoon, Eli calls his wife.

"Well?" she says by way of greeting.

"I got it," he states. "They were really enthusiastic about all of my ideas for the kids' groups. I told them what I had shared with Isabella about couple's trapeze, and they loved the idea of doing some couples programs to round out the schedule. I'll have a whole month off every year. We can take a cross-country trip so I can show you and Mason all the things I want to and introduce you both to some very important people."

"And?" she asks, waiting for her final question to be answered.

"We can have whatever pets we want, even a Rottweiler. It just has to stay in the yard or be on a leash."

"He's here. Do you want me to put you on speaker?"

"Yes."

"Guess what, Mason?"

"What?"

"We have triple good news for you, and your mom is being really nice and letting me tell you all of it."

"Is he there?"

"He's listening," Rachel assures.

"I got the job." No response, so he ups the ante.

"We are moving to a really cool house in the forest, and when it's time to go back to regular school, it will be a brand-new school."

Sounding like his mother moments before, the boy finally breaks and says, "And?"

"And you and your mom better start looking for a Rottweiler rescue, because you are getting a dog."

"And you're getting a dog," the boy fires back, sounding like Oprah talking about cars.

"Yes, but they can't come home with us until we move. Joe has been very good to us, and we need to respect his rule about not having pets just a little bit longer."

No response.

"Did he hear me?"

"I don't know. He isn't here now; he flashed off to his room about the time you said yes. You can take care of it when you get home."

"Sounds good."

"Yes, it does, and honey, congratulations. I've never been happier about being married to you."

"When I've finally conned you into moving to an isolated place in the middle of the woods away from friends and family? You're sick."

"Probably, but you love it."

"I do." He hits the disconnect button.

Before leaving yesterday, Abed had shared the whispered phrase that, along with the ring, helps members identify each other. "Isn't it wonderful when life is so grand it feels like you're dreaming when you're awake?" He feels it deeply in that moment; he rolls down his window.

"Yes, it is," he shouts, thrilled to be alive.

CHAPTER 33

Oone Year Later

Eli stands on the back porch with Mason. A large fenced-in yard spreads before them, giving way to ferns and brush, pine trees and then mountains. Eli never tires of the view or his time in the yard with his son, the black and tan miniature wiener dog and the boy's rottweiler.

"Don't let Daisy pick on Sampson too much. I'll be back in a few minutes."

"Dad, why does he let her boss him around? He has squeaky toys bigger than her."

Eli considers for a moment before answering. "First, things tend to work better when women are in charge and second, if he used her as a squeaky toy, he'd have to live without her and he'd be miserable."

Mason nods, something in the answer resonating for him. Eli reaches the kitchen just as the coffee maker finishes. He pours two cups and doctors them up. He carries them down the hall and sets them on the nightstand.

"Good morning, my love. You have gross medical stuff to heal today, people need you."

She yawns and rubs the sleep from her eyes. After a drink of coffee, she responds.

"You have trees to hang from and young minds and hearts to mold and my degree costs more. Go figure."

"Mason's outside with the dogs."

"He won't let your little brute pick on his big baby." She takes another swig of coffee and adds, "Too much."

He laughs, "She is terrible. If it was the other way around, I'd be afraid." Even as he complains about the ornery little dog, his love for her is clear.

"Remember when you used to ask me how I could wake up in such a good mood all the time?"

"Yeah."

"Now it's your turn to answer."

"Easy, marry way, way out of your league, find work that you love and spend the rest of your life living up to your good fortune."

"That's what worked for me," she agrees, leaving a trail of clothing behind her as she gets in the shower and turns the water on.

She peeks out, "Too bad you have to get back outside."

The End.

AFTERWORD

I hope that you enjoyed A Simple Job. If you did, please take a minute to leave a review or suggest it to someone you think might enjoy it.

If you are interested in the next book in the A Simple Job series please go to Kellyke nyon.com to join our list for updates.

I fully support Black Lives Matter, Native Lives Matter, peaceful protesters, good police officers, essential workers and each and every one of us trying to live our lives with all the integrity, courage and compassion that can be mustered in these unprecedented times.

It is not my intention to take attention away from any group or movement or to create any discord between any peoples. It is my desire to broaden the conversation and offer as many perspectives as possible in the pages I had, in my attempt to remind my readers that race is not a black-and-white issue; it is a people issue and therefore people are the solution. You are an integral part of the solution. This was an educational journey for me, one that I hope helps me become part of the solution as well.

I also want to note the right to vote has been, and continues to be, a complex issue both in our country and in much of the world today. Just because a group of people has the right to vote does not mean that they're able to do so or able to do so without massive amounts of interference. Cowardly men did things to prevent black men from being able to vote for decades after they had won the right, and in some cases that continues today, as it does for Native American communities and as it does for women in many parts of the world.

Having the right to exercise your voice and cast a vote for who will govern us is a cornerstone of democracy. The right to vote is only the first step, a significant one, but a meaningless one if the right is in name only and not in practice. Please do all that you can to make your voice heard and support politicians locally, nationally, and globally who truly support their citizens' right to vote and don't attempt to hamper or restrict it.

RESOURCES

National Domestic Violence Hotline 1 800-799-7233

National Suicide Prevention Hotline 1 800-273-8255

Concerned about the epidemic of murdered and missing indigenous women learn more

Coalition to End Violence Against Native Women - https://csvanw.org/

In 2021 President Biden issued a proclamation designating May 5th became Missing and Murdered Indigenous Persons (MMIP) awareness day.

Please help spread awareness and become an ally anyway that you can.

Native lives matter - https://lakotalaw.org/resources/native-lives-matter

NAACP - https://naacp.org/

The American Civil Liberties Union -https://www.aclu.org/

Voter Registration – https://www.usa.gov/voter-registration